"You're pulling my leg, right?"

"No," Decker said solemnly. "Does the age difference bother you?"

She gave a disbelieving laugh. "Decker, you've told me about life mates, and I know you think I'm yours, but—"

"I don't think, I know."

She started to slide off the bale of hay, but he caught her arm.

She wanted him to kiss her. She wanted to kiss him back. She wanted— Giving her head a shake, she pulled her arm free and started walking toward the door.

He caught her arm and spun her around. "Don't run from me, Dani. I'll just follow."

"I'm not running," she whispered, her eyes on his mouth.

"Yes," he growled, "you are." And then he did exactly what she wanted and kissed her.

By Lynsay Sands

THE IMMORTAL HUNTER
DEVIL OF THE HIGHLANDS
THE ROGUE HUNTER
VAMPIRE, INTERRUPTED
VAMPIRES ARE FOREVER
THE ACCIDENTAL VAMPIRE
BITE ME IF YOU CAN
A BITE TO REMEMBER
A QUICK BITE

Coming Soon

THE RENEGADE HUNTER

LYNSAY SANDS

THE IMMORTAL HUNTER

A Rogue Hunter Novel

AVON

An Imprint of HarperCollinsPublishers

AVON BOOKS
An Imprint of HarperCollins*Publishers*
10 East 53rd Street
New York, New York 10022-5299

First Avon Books paperback printing: April 2009

Prologue

hat's taking so long?"

Decker Argeneau Pimms glanced up from a very bored contemplation of his twiddling thumbs at that question from Garrett Mortimer. He watched the fair-haired enforcer pace back and forth in front of him twice before saying, "I'm sure they'll be done soon."

When Mortimer merely grunted and continued to pace, Decker leaned his head back on the dark leather couch and closed his eyes. The energy in the room was heavy with anxiety, and he would have liked to leave. Unfortunately, this was his cottage. It was also supposed to be his vacation, but that had fallen by the wayside with one call. The third day of his vacation Lucian, his uncle, but more importantly the head of the immortal enforcers and his boss, had called with the news that there had been multiple reports of mortals with bite marks in the area. Two Council enforcers were on their way north to find the culprit. Could they stay with him? Would he help out with the search? Like an idiot, he'd said yes.

Decker grimaced at his own stupidity, but knew he hadn't had much choice. He too was a Council enforcer, the equivalent of a vampire cop. His job was to hunt down rogue immortals who threatened the well-being of his people or mortals. While the mortals would not be damaged by a bite so long as too much blood wasn't taken, it did threaten the well-being of their people by increasing the chances of their existence being discovered. That was why with the advent of blood banks, biting mortals had been outlawed in North America. It was no longer allowed except in cases of an emergency. Unfortunately, some preferred the old ways, and risked exposing them all by feeding "off the hoof," as they called it. Those who did had to be caught and stopped for the safety of the rest, and it was enforcers like Decker and Garrett Mortimer who took on that job.

Most of the time, Decker got a certain amount of satisfaction from protecting his people, as well as mortals, from rogue vampires. However, this wasn't one of those times. His vacation had been ruined for nothing. They'd spent the last two weeks searching for a rogue immortal who had turned out not to be a rogue at all.

He opened his eyes and swiveled his head to peer at the supposed rogue sitting on the opposite end of the couch. A slender, dark-haired man named Grant. Decker hadn't bothered to find out if that was a first or last name. He'd been too annoyed once he'd realized that his vacation had been trashed not to capture a rogue vampire, but because some paper pusher at the

Argeneau Blood Bank had a quarrel with the man and had been deliberately losing and delaying his shipments of blood. It had forced Grant to feed off mortals between shipments.

Decker suspected the man wouldn't be in trouble for his actions, since feeding on mortals in such emergencies was allowed. However, Grant was chewing viciously at his nails and looked as anxious as Mortimer. Decker couldn't blame him. Having to face Lucian Argeneau could be a pretty intimidating event. The head of the Immortal Council, as well as leader of the Council enforcers, was also one of the oldest living immortals around and, consequently, could be hard as stone.

"Maybe I should go up and see if everything is all right," Mortimer muttered.

Decker shifted his attention back to the blond-haired man as he came to a halt in front of him. He shook his head. "Not a good idea, my friend."

Mortimer frowned, grunted, and then continued his pacing, but his eyes kept shifting to the stairs at the end of the room. Decker knew it wouldn't be long before Mortimer couldn't restrain himself anymore and went charging upstairs to be with Samantha. Decker understood that completely. He'd probably feel the same way if the woman were his life mate.

He leaned his head back and closed his eyes again, thinking that Mortimer's finding Samantha was the only good thing that had come out of this hunt. One of their kind finding a life mate was always a happy event. It was just a shame that the woman came from a family in which the parents had died and the three daughters left behind weren't close to the few relatives left. It meant they were one another's only family . . . and that Sam was reluctant to be turned and have to disappear from their lives in ten years to prevent their catching on to the fact that she wasn't aging. That decision was the reason she was presently upstairs being grilled by Lucian while Mortimer went slowly crazy, waiting to find out what his future held.

If Lucian decided that her not becoming one of them was fine and she posed no threat to their people, the two could be together. However, if he decided otherwise, Sam would either have to agree to the turn, or her memory would be wiped and she would not remember ever meeting the man presently pacing a hole into Decker's basement carpet. Mortimer, however, would be left remembering everything, a love found and lost . . . and he would never again be able to go near her for fear of bringing back memories of their time together. It was a hell of a thing to have to go through, and Decker sincerely hoped he was never faced with such a situation.

A low sound of frustration brought his eyes open again. Mortimer had stopped pacing and was now eyeing the stairs grimly. Afraid the man had reached the end of his tether and was about to do something he would later regret, Decker tried to distract him by asking, "What's this I hear about a new enforcer headquarters and you possibly running it?"

Mortimer tore his eyes from the ceiling and shrugged. "Now that Lucian has met his life mate, he's finding it inconvenient to have us using his house as a home base when we're working in the area. He decided a proper headquarters was the solution and has arranged for the purchase of a house not far from his place on the out-skirts of Toronto. He offered the job of running it to me when he got here."

Decker nodded, pretending he hadn't overheard the entire conversation earlier. He then commented, "It will allow you to stay close to Sam."

"Yes." Mortimer sighed, and then frowned and added bitterly, "If we're allowed to be together."

Decker grunted, mentally kicking himself for not re-alizing this conversation would lead right back to Sam and what was going on upstairs. He was trying to come up with something else to talk about when he heard the sound of a chair scraping across the hardwood floor overhead. It was followed by the soft pad of footsteps. "It sounds like they're done talking."

"Thank God," Mortimer muttered, but Decker couldn't help but note that he didn't appear relieved. If anything, the man was growing even tenser as he waited to hear his future.

Decker looked toward the stairs, watching as first Sam and then Lucian came into view. He didn't bother looking to his uncle, who was always stone-faced and hard to read. Instead he focused on Sam, but she was as expressionless as the man behind her, a result of being a lawyer, he supposed. A poker face probably came in handy there, he thought, and read her mind. What he found was a muddle of both anger and relief. It seemed Lucian had been his usual heavy-handed self, telling Sam point-blank the punishment would be death should she ever betray their people and give their presence away. But he'd agreed to allow her to be Mor-timer's life mate without turning.

Decker also found that Lucian had managed to convince her to give notice at her law firm and come to work for the enforcers. Decker found that surprising because he knew that until meeting Mortimer, her career at the prestigious law firm had been the focal point of her life. It seemed, however, she'd realized these last two weeks that she didn't care for the fact that it had almost taken over her whole life, and while she wasn't ready to give up her sisters, she was willing to give up her present position to find the time to make a life with Mortimer. It had helped that Lucian had told her there were a lot of legal issues that needed tending when they hunted down and exterminated rogues. People could not just disappear in today's paper-plagued world. Not even immortals.

"Sam's agreed to work for us," Lucian announced as he stepped off the stairs. "She'll do what she can to help you organize the enforcer headquarters, and handle any legal matters that come up on the job."

Decker didn't miss the relief that flashed across Mortimer's face as he hurried to Sam and slipped his arm around her waist to draw her to his side. Engrossed in each other, neither paid attention when Lucian moved to stand in front of Grant and glared grimly down at the dark-haired immortal.

"I understand you've been having trouble getting your blood supply and have been forced to feed off of mortals?" he asked.

Grant nodded, fear plain on his face. When Lucian simply stared at the man, his gaze fixed, Decker was positive he was reading the immortal's thoughts. Apparently he was satisfied by what he found there, because he nodded and said, "Someone is already looking into the situation with the employee who was holding up your orders. I've also arranged for a generator to be delivered and installed so that your blood supply isn't ruined every time the power goes out up here. That should keep you from having to feed off the locals in future. But," he added sharply, "if you have any further problems, you're to call Mortimer at once. I won't forgive another incident like this."

Grant cringed back into the cold leather cushion at the warning. "It wasn't my fault. I——"

"You forget I can read your mind," Lucian interrupted grimly. "Pride is the reason you didn't contact someone about the problems you were having getting blood. That and the fact that you really prefer your meals warm, and the situation gave you the perfect excuse to feed off the hoof. If you really want to feed that way, you'd best move to Europe. It isn't allowed here. The next time a situation like this comes up involving you, you'll find yourself staked and baked. Got it?"

"Y-yes sir," Grant stammered.

Apparently satisfied that he'd made his point, Lucian glanced to Mortimer and then to Decker as he commented, "Fortunately, there doesn't appear to be any cleanup to do here. Grant, at least, had the good sense to take his meals in a wide area, feeding as far north as Parry Sound and all the way down to Minden. It means he's managed to avoid raising suspicion among the mortals, so you boys can gather your stuff and head——"

"Excuse me," Grant said timidly from the couch.

Lucian frowned and turned on the man. "What?"

The immortal shrank under his glare and then stammered nervously, "I never fed in P-Parry Sound . . . or M-Minden."

Lucian stared at him for a moment. "We had reports from other immortals who had spotted bite marks in Parry Sound, Burk's Falls, Nobel, Huntsville, Bracebridge, Gravenhurst, Minden, and Haliburton."

Grant shook his head. "I never went further south than Bracebridge. Gravenhurst, Minden, and Haliburton weren't me. Neither is Parry Sound to the north." He licked his lips and then suggested, "Perhaps I am not the only one who has been having trouble getting supplies."

Another moment of silence passed as Lucian apparently read Grant again. Lucian cursed and turned to Decker, saying, "It seems your work here *isn't* done. You'll have to split up and check both the north and the south, but first contact Bastien to see who else gets supplies from the Argeneau Blood Bank and might be having similar problems to Grant. We'll check with them first."

Decker raised an eyebrow at the mention of his cousin, Bastien Argeneau, the head of Argeneau Enterprises. His gaze slid toward the window, where sunlight was visible on the horizon. "The sun's rising, Bastien will have left the office and gone home by now."

Lucian grimaced. "Yes, and since meeting his life mate he's started shutting off the ringer on the phone while they're sleeping unless there's an emergency call he's waiting for." He thought for a minute and then glanced to Grant. "Do you know any of the other immortals up here?"

"Not many. I tend to keep to myself," Grant said apologetically.

"Well, you can stop that," Lucian growled. "An immortal without family and friends is more likely to go rogue."

"I have friends," Grant said quickly, and then added reluctantly, "Well . . . one. He lives just north of Minden and I visit him every couple of weeks." Apparently afraid Lucian wouldn't believe him, he added, "You can ask Nicholas. He'll vouch for me."

"Nicholas?" Lucian asked sharply as Decker stiffened at the name. "Nicholas who?"

"Nicholas Argeneau," Grant said, sounding bewildered that he would even need to ask. "I saw him on my way out there the last time I went. I told him I was headed to a friend's. He'll remember. He can tell you."

Lucian had gone stock-still and Mortimer muttered a curse. Decker himself felt as if the blood in his veins had turned to mud and stopped moving. Everything in him had come to a screeching halt—his blood, his heart, even his thoughts as those words echoed in his head.

It was Sam who asked in a whisper, "What's wrong? Who is this Nicholas Argeneau?"

"He's a rogue who's been evading us for nearly fifty years," Mortimer growled.

"What?" Grant paled and shrank back into the cushions again as if afraid Lucian would reach out and throttle him. He started to babble, "I didn't know Nicholas was rogue. I moved up this way fifty years ago to escape the city and hadn't heard. I would have called

Argeneau Enterprises at once if I'd known Nicholas was rogue."

"Go home," Lucian ordered grimly. When the man breathed out his relief and rushed eagerly for the stairs, he added, "And no more biting or I'll come deal with you personally."

A handful of breathless assurances of future good behavior drifted back to them as the man hurried up the steps. They ended on the clack of the screen door slamming upstairs.

"So," Mortimer said quietly into the silence that had fallen over the room. "What are we going to do about Nicholas?"

Decker's gaze slid back to his uncle to find Lucian staring straight at him. His face was its usual expressionless mask as he answered, "We hunt him."

Chapter One

W here the hell is he going?" Decker muttered under his breath as he steered the SUV down the rutted dirt road to follow the white van ahead.

"Hell if I know," Justin Bricker answered.

Decker glanced briefly to the younger immortal, his temporary partner for this hunt, but didn't bother explaining that he'd been talking to himself. He returned his concentration to the road, squinting in an effort to see where he was going. While their kind could see in the dark better than mortals, even he was straining in the almost complete absence of light out here. It was a starless night, and Decker had turned off the headlights several miles back to prevent being spotted by Nicholas. The enforcer SUVs had several modifications; an absence of driving lights that came on every time the vehicle was started was just one of them.

"I didn't expect it to be this easy to track him down," Justin said suddenly.

Decker grunted, surprised by it himself. Nicholas

Argeneau had been rogue for a good fifty years, during
which time no one had even caught sight of the man.
For it to have taken a mere day of showing his picture around to pick up his trail seemed too easy. Way
too easy. It made Decker suspicious and wary. Why
hadn't Nicholas erased the memories of the mortals
he'd encountered? He must have done that in the past
to have remained off the radar, and yet suddenly he
wasn't doing so. Instead he appeared to have left a trail
as clear as radioactive green cookie crumbs.

Justin cursed beside him and grabbed for the dash-
board as the dirt lane came to an end and they followed
the van off-road, bouncing over tall grass and bushes.

"Maybe he's tired of running," Justin suggested suddenly through gritted teeth, no doubt to keep from
biting off his tongue as they jolted over the uneven
trail. "Maybe he wants to be caught."

Decker didn't respond. He didn't for a minute think
Nicholas was giving up, and he didn't know what was
going on, but Justin Bricker's constant need to talk
was beginning to drive him crazy. He had no idea how
Mortimer, Justin's usual partner, had taken it all these
years.

"He's stopping."

"I can see that," Decker muttered between his teeth,
steering the SUV to the side of the road. He parked
as far into the woods as he dared without risking getting stuck. Hoping it was far enough that their prey
wouldn't notice them, he then turned off the engine and
ordered, "Watch him."

Leaving the keys in the ignition to save time should
Nicholas notice them and try to get away in the van,

Decker crawled over the seat and all the way to the back of the SUV where the blood and weapons were. He moved to the cooler first, retrieving a couple of bags of blood and tossing one over the seats into Justin's lap. "Drink up. You'll need your strength."

"I gather you don't think he's going to give up when he sees us, then?" Justin asked dryly and then slapped the bag to his mouth.

Decker snorted at the very suggestion. He waited for his own canine teeth to drop down, and slapped a bag of blood to the fangs with one hand as he reached with the other to unlock and flip open the nearest weapons case. His eyes slid over the guns inside. While you weren't likely to kill an immortal with a gun, you *could* slow him down and even temporarily incapacitate him . . . especially using bullets that were coated with the tranquilizer Bastien's techie boys had developed.

"He's getting out of the van," Justin announced.

Decker glanced forward to see that Justin had already drained his bag and was shoving it in the small bag at his feet, one filled with fast-food wrappers. The man liked to eat as much as he liked to talk, Decker had noticed. Shaking his head, he glanced past him to peer out the front windshield, but couldn't see much over the seats. Pulling his own now-empty bag from his teeth, he asked, "What's he doing?"

"Walking around to the back of the van . . . opening the door . . . he's digging around inside, getting something—I think he's getting out weapons." Justin glanced back, worry on his face as he asked, "Do you think he spotted us?"

Decker's mouth tightened. He set aside the empty bag and turned back to the case before him. "Come pick your weapons."

"Should we call Lucian or Mortimer?" Justin asked as he headed back to join him.

Decker considered the question as he chose two guns and a box of coated bullets. Lucian had sent them north as a mere precaution. He'd also sent Mortimer and Sam west for the same reason, but he and his life mate, Leigh, were searching the Haliburton area where Nicholas had actually been seen by Grant. Decker suspected his uncle had expected to find him there, and hoped to be the one to get to him first. It meant both couples were far enough away that they weren't going to be of any use at this point. He shook his head. "It would take at least an hour, possibly two for either of them to get here. We're on our own."

Justin nodded slowly, and then transformed from the good-natured, slightly mischievous sidekick he usually acted, to the hunter he was. His shoulders straightened and his expression became grim as he began to select weapons from the case.

Unwilling to risk Nicholas creeping up on them while they were distracted, Decker took his weapons and the box of bullets and made his way up front to the driver's seat. A glance showed that Nicholas now had a quiver full of arrows and a crossbow slung over his back, but was still digging around in the back of the van. Looking for more weapons, Decker supposed, and kept an eye on him as he loaded his guns. Nicholas was still busy in the back of the van when Justin rejoined him in the front of the SUV.

"Now what?" Justin asked, eyeing the rogue. "Try to creep up on him and get the drop?"

"Sounds good to me," Decker muttered. He reached for the keys in the ignition and then thought better of it. If Nicholas became aware of their presence before they reached him, he might hop in the van and try to take off. If that happened, Decker didn't want to be fumbling to get the keys in the ignition to give chase. Leaving them in the ignition, he reached up and shut off the SUV's interior light so it wouldn't come on when the door opened. Fortunately, another modification performed on all their vehicles ensured there was no beeping to warn that the keys were still in the ignition, and he was able to slip silently out of the vehicle even as Justin did.

Afraid even a quiet click would give away their presence, Decker didn't close the door all the way, but left it cracked open. Justin did the same, and the two men moved cautiously forward, easing through the grass as silently as possible. Neither man spoke, but halfway there, Justin moved to the other side of the trail so that they were approaching from opposite sides. It was the kind of thing Decker's usual partner, Anders, would have done automatically, but he and Anders had worked together for decades. Decker supposed he shouldn't be surprised by Justin's actions. This might be the first time he'd worked with him, but Justin had done this with Mortimer for years and knew what he was about. Dropping his worry about the kid being able to handle himself, Decker turned his full attention to their quarry as they moved up silently on him.

They were both perhaps six feet away when Nicholas

straightened and said, "It took you long enough to find your balls and approach. I was starting to think I'd be standing here until dawn."

Decker stilled, aware that Justin had as well. All three were silent, and then Nicholas raised his hands and slowly turned. As expected, time had little changed him, his dark hair was a little longer than Decker remembered, but his eyes were still silver-blue and he was still handsome, with chiseled features that would make most women's hearts flutter. The only change was that the easy smile and charm he used to exude had been replaced by a cold, grim expression Decker was more used to seeing on Lucian's face. He also had a gun in each hand, both presently pointed skyward.

"We were choosing and loading weapons," Justin explained, apparently stung by the comment.

Nicholas nodded solemnly, but his gaze was on Decker as he said, "Must be hard to choose what to shoot your own blood with."

Decker merely shrugged, but acknowledged to himself that this wasn't easy for him. Nicholas was family . . . but he was also a rogue. "How long have you known we were following you?"

"Since the restaurant. I waited a long time there for you," he informed them, and then added grimly, "I hope not too long."

"What do you mean you *waited* a long time?" Decker asked suspiciously. "How did you even know we were around?"

"Because I arranged it," Nicholas said as if that should be obvious. "Why do you think I let Grant see me when we both happened to stop at the same gas station?"

"Are you saying you *wanted* us to come find you?" Decker asked.

"Yes." His mouth twisted down when Decker didn't hide his disbelief, and he added, "When I saw Grant I realized that his seeing me might not be a bad thing, so I walked over to say hello. I knew that when he reported the sighting Lucian would send a couple teams up to hunt me." Nicholas paused and then continued with displeasure, "I just didn't realize you guys had gotten so lax in your job. You should have been able to track me down by the day before yesterday. I left a clear enough trail. And still I had to wait for two days for you to show up."

"Grant didn't report the sighting. He didn't know you were rogue. It was only blind luck that he mentioned you this morning," Justin explained, the defensive note to his words making Decker scowl. They had nothing to prove to the man.

Nicholas narrowed his eyes at this news, and then sighed and nodded.

"Then I can't blame you if these girls die," he muttered unhappily, and shook his head. "It will be my own fault for waiting."

"What girls?" Decker asked. "And why would you want to be found?"

"Because I got on to—and have been following—a nest of nasty rogues. By the time I spotted Grant I'd realized I was going to need help bringing them down. Running into him at the gas station seemed almost fortuitous. At least, it did when I thought he'd turn my ass in," he added bitterly, and then berated himself. "I shouldn't have counted on his reporting me, I should have called it in. Those girls would still be happy and oblivious otherwise." Nicholas paused and then said solemnly, "These are some really bad ones, Decker."

"Aren't all rogues bad?" Justin asked dubiously.

"I guess they are," Nicholas said, a weary note to his voice, and then he continued, "But there's bad, and then there's real demon seed—slaughter the innocent, roll around in their blood for the hell of it, and laugh while you're doing it sickos."

"Jesus," Justin breathed.

Decker eyed Nicholas narrowly. "Are you trying to tell me that you're still hunting rogues even though you're rogue now yourself? Why would you do that?"

"It's hard to kick old habits," Nicholas said bitterly. He shifted impatiently. "Now, I've explained enough. We have to get moving before they start in on these two."

"Just a minute," Decker snapped as Nicholas lowered his hands and turned away to start up the side of the van. "We're not going anywhere, and who are these two girls you keep talking about?"

Nicholas glanced back over his shoulder to say, "They're the two girls these rogues took from the grocery store parking lot before you guys showed up at the restaurant. Once they grabbed the girls, I couldn't wait anymore for backup. Fortunately, you showed up just as I was heading out and followed. Now we can—"

"How do you know they took two girls at the grocery store?" Decker interrupted. "The restaurant where we caught up to you is well away from—"

"Jesus," Nicholas interrupted impatiently. "We don't have time for this now. Can't you hear them screaming?"

Decker opened his mouth to insist that Nicholas explain, but paused as he became aware of the panicked shrieks coming from ahead. Either it had just started or he'd been concentrating so hard on what Nicholas was saying, he'd blocked it out. He was hearing it now, though, and once heard, those desperate, bloodcurdling screams couldn't be ignored . . . nor could the cruel male laughter that nearly drowned it out.

"Shoot me in the back if you want to," Nicholas snapped. "But I've seen what those bastards do, and I can't just stand here explaining while they cut up those women." He then whirled and charged ahead, crashing into the trees.

"Do I shoot him?" Justin asked, his gun aimed at Nicholas's quickly disappearing back.

Decker ground his teeth together and then shook his head as another scream resounded. "Not yet," he snapped, and broke into a run after his cousin, aware that Justin was hard on his heels.

Dani peered over Stephanie's shoulder at the "no signal" message on her phone, snapped it shut, slid it back into her pocket, and hugged the young girl close, whispering, "It's going to be okay, Stephi."

It was a lie, one to make them both feel better, but Stephanie wouldn't let the lie stand. Arms tightening around her waist, the teenager sobbed, "No, it's not."

Heart clenching at the despair in her voice, Dani twisted her head around to glance at the man who stood behind her. Tall and skinny, with long, lank blond hair, he'd been left to stand guard over them while the others had gathered wood, built a fire, and attended other unknown duties. He watched them with a concentration that gave her the creeps, and most of his attention, she noted worriedly, was on Stephanie.

Dani tightened her arms protectively around her sister and then glanced warily toward the others as they returned one after another. Appearing out of the darkness like pale specters, they stepped into the circle of light cast by the fire, five men all so similar in looks to the first that they must be related. Some were empty-handed and simply took seats on the logs placed in a square around the fire pit. The others dropped what wood they had found next to the fire and joined them so that two sat on each of the three logs facing Dani and Stephanie. Firelight flickered over their faces, the shadows and light licking at them like the flames of hell as they watched Dani and Stephanie, cats eyeing a pair of juicy mice. Dani managed to withstand their silent inspection for a moment, but then blurted, "What are you going to do with us?"

The moment the words left her lips, she wished she could take them back. The question brought cruelly amused smiles and low chuckles from the men as they exchanged glances. Even worse, one of them then stood and started across the clearing. Dani watched warily as he paused beside the fire and bent to grab one of the logs. He lifted the burning wood into the air, holding it aloft as he continued toward them, and for one terrified moment she feared he would swing it at them. It was almost a relief when, instead, he reached out with his free hand and caught her by the upper arm.

Dani immediately released Stephanie so that she could try to pry the hand off her, but before she could he was pulling her to her feet.

"No! Leave her alone!" Stephanie shrieked and clawed at Dani's other hand, trying to keep her from being taken away, but neither her efforts nor Dani's own prevented the man from dragging her away. She continued to struggle to no avail as he tugged her across the clearing, but paused to glance around when he stopped. At first she couldn't see anything but darkness before her, and then her captor held out the makeshift torch, and she saw that they stood on the edge of a shallow ravine.

Dani instinctively struggled to back away, afraid he intended to throw her off, but it was the log he threw, tossing it out so that it tumbled through the darkness, rotating end over end before coming to a landing with a soft thud of sound. She saw then that while the drop-off was steep, it wasn't very deep. No more than ten feet, Dani guessed, and then gave up that worry as she realized that there was something lying in the bottom of the ravine amid the grass and trees.

Unable to help herself, she stopped struggling and even leaned forward, pulling against the hand holding her to try to make sense of what her eyes were seeing. Dani was immediately sorry she had. In her capacity as a doctor, she'd seen a lot of horrible things, but never in her life had she even imagined seeing anything as gruesome as the twisted and bloody bodies in the bottom of that natural ditch. The sight itself was terrible, but not half as terrifying as her sudden realization that she and Stephanie were doomed. There was no hope for them at all. They were meant to join the two women who lay rotting in that ravine . . . and judging by the state of the bodies below, it would be a long and painful journey getting there.

This isn't happening, Dani thought faintly, her mind

unable to accept the turn her life had taken. She was a doctor who spent most of her time working. This weekend had been an uncommon bright spot in her life, a rare bit of time off filled with sun and sand in the bosom of her family. The McGill family reunion had been four days and three nights of laughing, swimming, fishing, and just enjoying one another's company. Dani had soaked it all in and had been happy and relaxed for the first time in years as they'd started the long drive home. Then they'd stopped for snacks for the eight-hour journey and . . .

It wasn't supposed to end like this, her mind howled. This was Canada, for God's sake; boring, safe Canada where nothing as monstrous as this happened. But it *was* happening, she acknowledged as Stephanie began to shriek hysterically, interrupting her dazed thoughts. She turned her head to see that the younger girl had been dragged over by one of the other men to bear witness to the contents of the ravine. Now she too knew how hopeless their situation was, Dani thought unhappily.

As Stephanie's screams rose in pitch and hysteria, Dani began to struggle again, frantic to get to her, but the hand holding her was hard and strong, and all her kicks, hits, and attempts to bite her captor merely made him laugh harder . . . much as the man holding her sister was doing. These animals seemed to find their horror and panic amusing. That brought fury bubbling up inside Dani, and she redoubled her frenzied attempt to break free and get to the girl.

"She's a screamer," the one holding Stephi proclaimed with a laugh, shaking her so that her shrieks vibrated somewhat. It only made him laugh even harder.

Dani was just wishing she had a gun and could shoot the bastard when he suddenly stiffened, surprise crossing his face. He released his hold on Stephanie, letting her collapse to the ground as he reached toward his back where an arrow now protruded from between his shoulder blades. The sight so surprised Dani that she briefly stopped fighting her own captor and simply watched the man turn in a slow circle, like a dog chasing its tail, as he tried to reach the arrow. Everyone else had frozen too, except for Stephanie. Sobbing and whimpering, her sister was crawling away across the dirt. The sight drew Dani out of her shocked stillness and she was about to kick back at her captor and try to break free when a hissing sound made her freeze. Suddenly an arrow was protruding from her captor's arm, the fletching quivering next to her cheek.

Dani found herself not only released, but flung away as the man roared in pain. She careened toward the edge overlooking the ravine, but—recalling what lay below—wasn't eager to land there. Dani grabbed frantically for something to save herself. Her fingers closed over what felt to be several thin branches of a bush. However, the hold swung her around so that she slid over the edge feetfirst and began to slide down the sharp incline. Dani ignored the sting as the branches ran through her fingers, stripping the leaves along the way. Desperate to stop herself, she tightened her grasp, but the branches immediately snapped under the full brunt of her weight. She released them, reaching for something else to save her, but there was nothing, and Dani was left clawing at the dirt she was now sliding down.

Fortunately, the combination of that and her brief hold on the bush slowed her enough that Dani came to a halt halfway down the small ravine. She closed her eyes and sent up a silent prayer of thanks before peering up toward the ledge.

The sounds now coming from the clearing were chaotic and loud. Her sister was screaming again, but the sound had been joined by men's shouts and several sharp cracking noises. Apparently arrows were no longer the only weapons being shot up there. Her thoughts on Stephanie, Dani began to climb back up to the ledge, her heart seeming to echo the cracks of gunfire from above. She reached the ledge, managed to get one arm over the top to hold her weight, and pulled herself up far enough to take in the scene in the clearing. Three of their six captors were down, two others had taken cover behind a large log and were being fired on by at least two, possibly three or more men crouching behind trees in the woods surrounding them. But Dani couldn't see the sixth kidnapper . . . or her sister.

"Dani!"

The scream drew her gaze to the right to see Stephanie being dragged off, used as a shield by the sixth man as he slid away into the woods. Cursing, Dani ignored the gunshots going off around her and began to struggle to pull herself out of the ravine.

"One of them is getting away!"

Justin's shout dragged Decker's attention from the two rogues shooting at them, and to the one slipping away through the woods. He was dragging the younger female with him.

"I've got it," Nicholas barked, and was off, leaping from his cover behind a neighboring tree and moving through the woods around the clearing, ducking and weaving as he went.

"No! Wait, Nicholas!" Decker roared, and instinctively lunged after him to give chase, but another shout from Justin brought him to a halt. Turning back, he followed the younger immortal's gesture to the woman presently trying to drag herself up onto the ledge on the far side of the clearing. Decker had seen her go flying off the cliff after Nicholas shot an arrow into the arm of the rogue holding her. He'd feared she would either be dead or seriously injured from the fall, but it appeared she'd managed to save herself and was now struggling to pull herself back to safety.

Even as Decker noted this, the woman slipped and began to sink from view. The desperation on her face and the way her fingers clawed frantically at the ground to stop her slide suggested to him that it would indeed prove deadly should she not be able to save herself.

Cursing, he immediately changed direction, charging straight through the clearing toward the cliff. Decker moved as quickly as he was capable, gritting his teeth as bullets whizzed past. While the rogues' bullets wouldn't be coated with tranquilizer like their own, they could still cause pain and a good deal of damage . . . and if they were lucky and shot him in the heart, he'd be down and helpless to prevent them from finishing him off.

Decker was surprised, and not a little relieved, when he made it to the ledge without taking a bullet. He managed to catch the woman's hand just as her fingers slipped from the edge . . . and that's when he finally caught one of the bullets being shot his way. It slammed into his back with enough impact that he nearly released the woman and tumbled forward off the cliff himself, but then managed to brace himself with his other hand. Pushing at the ground to keep from rolling forward, Decker jerked the woman upward with the hand grasping hers, turning back toward the clearing at the same time. The combination put more force behind the action than he'd intended and didn't just bring her back up to the safety of the ledge, but pretty much tossed her several feet away from it.

That's when the second bullet hit him, puncturing his chest below the shoulder and knocking the wind out of him. It felt like a serrated metal band was being cinched around his chest. Forcing himself to ignore the pain, Decker raised his gun hand. Pushing himself to his feet, he began firing in the general direction of the two men pressed up against the log, quickly moving sideways away from the mortal woman as he did. It was an effort to draw the gunfire away from her as he took in the situation. Both rogues had given up their cover and were now standing, one shooting at him and the other aiming for Justin, who was charging from the other side of the clearing.

Seeing that, Decker stopped moving, took aim at the one shooting his way, and hit him point-blank in the chest. He waited long enough to see the rogue clutch at the wound with surprise and start to fall back, but then immediately turned to aim at the second man. However, that one was already falling, shot by Justin.

Decker glanced toward the woman then, only to see

her disappearing into the woods in the direction Nicholas had taken. Leaving Justin to handle the men in the clearing, he chased after her, intent on catching up to Nicholas. He followed the sound of the woman thrashing her way through the underbrush ahead and soon found himself back out on the wider path where they'd parked the SUV . . . only it was no longer there, nor was Nicholas's van.

Decker closed his eyes on a curse. He'd left the keys in the SUV, and apparently the rogue had taken advantage and stolen the vehicle.

Cursing again, Decker turned his attention to the figure standing where his vehicle should have been. Her back had been to him since he'd stepped out of the woods, but she turned now, a woman of medium height, with a curvaceous figure and mid-length blond hair that fell around her face in loose curls. It was all he really noticed just then—that and the fact that she came to an abrupt halt as she spotted him, her eyes shifting toward the road and back to him with a combination of worry and uncertainty. It seemed obvious the worry was for the girl who had been taken. The uncertainty was no doubt because she was unsure if he was friend or foe.

Decker hesitated, briefly considering taking the time to reassure her she was safe, but his back and chest were aching from the bullets he'd taken, and he wasn't in the mood to deal with an undoubtedly emotionally distraught woman. Besides, they didn't have the time for it; he and Justin had to do what they could to clean up the mess here and then head out after Nicholas . . . again, he thought irritably, and simply slipped into her thoughts to take control of her . . . or tried to. Much to Decker's amazement, he couldn't seem to pierce her mind.

That fact made him give her a second look. This time he took notice of her blue eyes, her almost too-wide mouth, and her straight little nose. While she wasn't classically beautiful, somehow those individual features—when put together—made up an attractive face. But it was the face of a woman he couldn't read. The question was whether it was because she was upset at the moment, her thoughts possibly in enough chaos after recent events that no immortal could have read her? Or was there another reason he couldn't penetrate her mind?

Decker hesitated, and then concentrated once more on trying to pierce her thoughts, but met a wall of blackness that was hard and impenetrable.

"Who are you?"

He glowered at her for interrupting his concentration, but she merely glowered back. It surprised him into answering.

"Decker Argeneau," he said, and then frowned at the slip and said, "I mean Pimms." He hadn't used the Argeneau name for over a century now. He refused to. The name carried a certain cachet with it, elicited a certain respect from his kind, but he didn't want respect just because of his last name. Decker would rather earn it based on his own merits.

"All right, you're Decker-Maybe-Argeneau-Maybe-Pimms." The woman sounded grim. "But telling me your name doesn't really tell me who you are and why I shouldn't be running in the opposite direction right now, does it?"

"You're safe," he said, and when she didn't respond or relax, added, "We just saved your life, lady. You're safe."

She hesitated and then asked a touch sharply, "And my sister, Stephanie? Your friend went after them. Will he be able to get her back?"

"I don't know," Decker admitted, "And he's not my friend."

She frowned. "You were together."

"No. Justin and I just followed him here," Decker announced, digging his phone out of his pocket and peering down to find "no signal" flashing on the screen.

"Your phone won't work out here," she announced, and then added, "At least mine didn't. Where's your vehicle? We have to go after my sister."

"I don't have one," Decker muttered, not bothering to explain that it had been stolen. He ignored her then and raised his phone skyward, turning in a circle in hopes of catching a signal. When that didn't work, he snapped it closed with a sigh and slid the useless item back in his pocket. Decker turned his attention back to the blond then, only to find that she'd started off up the trail toward the road.

Rubbing absently at his chest, he instinctively tried to take control of her once more, but this time was no more successful than the last two attempts. Cursing, he gave it up and hurried forward to grab her arm and draw her to a halt, "Wait."

The blond turned on him sharply and glared at the hand he had on her arm.

Decker ignored that and asked, "Where do you think you're going?"

"After my sister," she answered succinctly, and, tugging her arm loose, turned to start walking again.

"On foot?" he asked with exasperation, trailing her.

"Yes, at least until I reach an inhabited house or cottage where I can borrow a car or something."

"No one's going to just give you their car," Decker pointed out grimly. "And you can't go after these guys alone. They aren't your average bad guys. Let us handle this. It's what we do."

She paused and turned to peer at him uncertainly. "Are you a cop or something?"

"Or something," he said vaguely, and took her arm to urge her back the way they'd come. He ignored the way her eyes had narrowed and that she was dragging her feet.

"Are you with the OPP?"

"No. We're not with the Ontario Provincial Police."

"RCMP?"

"No. We're not with the Royal Canadian Mounted Police either."

The blond dug in her heels, refusing to move further. Rather than force her, Decker sighed and turned to say, "Look, we *are* in law enforcement. We go after bad guys, but there's no sense my telling you the name of the organization I work for. You wouldn't recognize it. We aren't well known by the average citizen. But you *are* safe."

Her eyes widened at his claim and she asked eagerly, "You mean like CSIS? You're like a secret agent?"

Decker hesitated; he had no desire to claim he was a member of the Canadian Security and Intelligence Service, Canada's version of the FBI, but he'd already said no to all the usual law enforcement organizations and he couldn't tell her the truth, so merely muttered, "Something like that."

When she opened her mouth to ask another question, he forestalled her by quickly asking, "What's your name?"

"Danielle McGill."

"And the other girl is your sister, Stephanie?"

"Younger sister, she's just fifteen," Danielle said. Worry overtook her expression once more, and her gaze again slid up toward the road.

Before Decker could ask anything else, a low whistle drew his attention to Justin's arrival.

The younger immortal peered to where their vehicle had been and said, "You left the keys in the SUV."

It wasn't an accusation, just an observation. Justin knew exactly why he'd left the keys in the ignition and hadn't protested it at the time. Neither of them had known about the nest of rogues or expected it to lead to the vehicle being stolen.

A choked sound from Danielle drew Decker's attention just in time to see her spin away with disgust and start up the road again. Irritation beginning to get the better of him, he set out after her once more, catching at her arm. "Hang on. I thought we agreed you'd let us handle this?"

"I didn't agree to anything," she snapped, shaking off his hold. "And, frankly, I'd rather not trust my sister's life to some Austin Powers version of a government spy who can't even remember which name he's using as his cover, *and* who leaves his keys in the car to make it easier for the bad guys to get away."

Danielle McGill spun away to start out up the trail again.

Mouth tightening, Decker barked, "Justin, take control of that woman and bring her back here."

Justin nodded and started to turn toward Danielle, but then paused, eyes snapping back. "Why haven't you taken control?"

Decker ground his teeth together. "I can't."

The younger immortal's eyes widened. "You *can't*?"

"She's upset," Decker muttered. "Just see if you can, all right?"

"Man," Justin breathed, shaking his head, "first Mortimer and now you. You guys are dropping like flies."

"Just stop Danielle, will you," Decker said tiredly.

"She prefers Dani," he announced.

"Bricker," he snarled.

"All right, all right. Keep your pants on." Justin moved past him, adding, "I'm just saying . . ."

Decker ground his teeth together and then realized exactly what the man *was* saying. To know she preferred being called Dani meant Justin was able to read her thoughts. It wasn't just that she was too upset to be read. She was his . . .

Life mate.

Decker lifted his eyes skyward, expecting something to happen. He didn't know what, perhaps for the stars overhead to explode into shimmery fireworks, or for the sky to crack open and pour down rain and thunder to mark the moment. But nothing happened. The most important moment of his life arrived not with a bang as he'd always expected, but with the quiet rustle of wind through the trees and a serene breeze brushing his cheeks.

Shaking his head, Decker forced himself to turn his attention back to the business at hand. They were stuck in the woods in the middle of nowhere with a clearing full of bad rogues who were down but not dead. They needed backup to clean up this mess before some unsuspecting mortal came across the scene. And they needed to start hunting for Nicholas again . . . as well as the other rogue and the girl he'd taken.

Decker wasn't at all sure that both targets would lead in the same direction. It was entirely possible either that Nicholas had been riding with the nest they'd just decimated, or that he'd known about them and led Decker and Justin here when he'd realized they were on his tail because he'd hoped to make his escape while they were busy with the other men. Nicholas certainly had hightailed it out of there pretty quickly the moment the opportunity arose.

But even if he really had deliberately drawn them there with the express purpose of taking down this nest, it didn't mean Nicholas would still be on the rogue's tail now. He was a wanted man. It would be smarter for him to leave it to Decker and the other enforcers to chase after the girl and her kidnapper and take this opportunity to disappear into the ether as he had done fifty years ago.

If that was the case, they had probably lost him again. Their only hope of catching him was if Nicholas Argeneau had somehow seen the error of his ways and was indeed chasing after the girl and the other rogue. Then, at least, they had a chance of catching him . . . but Decker wasn't holding his breath on that count.

He rubbed at his chest again, recalling that—on top

of everything else—he presently had two bullet wounds his body was trying to repair . . . and their blood was in the SUV along with their weapons. Perfect, Decker thought with weary frustration. This was a hell of a time for him to finally meet his life mate. His gaze slid to the woman in question. Dani.

Justin had managed to stop her and turn her around. She was now walking back toward them, her body relaxed and expression blank.

"I think you have something you want to say to me," Justin said, tongue in cheek as they watched her return.

"You want a thank-you for bringing her back?" Decker asked dryly.

"No, not that."

"What then?"

The younger immortal rolled his eyes. "Oh, I don't know. I thought you might just want to apologize for all that grief you guys gave me for using the cover that we were in a band on our last case. I mean . . . a government spy?"

"I never—" Decker stopped when he saw the teasing grin on Justin's face. Cursing at himself for allowing the kid to get a rise out of him, he barked, "Just bring her and come on."

"Yes, sir, Mr. Bond, sir," Justin said cheerfully.

"Smart ass," Decker muttered under his breath as he turned away.

Chapter Two

T he two girls are sisters," Justin announced, catching up to Decker as he reached the kidnappers' van. It was parked on the edge of the clearing, and while he hadn't taken much notice of it when they'd rushed by it earlier, Decker found himself considering it now as a possible way out of there. He paused to glance back at Justin, scowling when he saw that the kid was dragging a blank-faced Dani along by the hand like they were boyfriend and girlfriend.

Justin rolled his eyes at his expression and dropped her hand to take her arm instead.

"I know they're sisters," Decker said, relaxing a little. "She told me that."

Justin nodded, but continued recounting what he'd learned from reading Dani's mind. "Their family was up here for a long weekend. The two of them were kidnapped from the grocery store parking lot like Nicholas said. Their captors were a bit rough, but other than a bruise or two she seems all right."

Decker grunted, his attention on negotiating the uneven ground as he led the way around the van and into the clearing.

"I gather from her memories, though, that there are more than the immortals to deal with," Justin warned, following him.

That made Decker pause and glance back in question.

"It would seem Dani and Stephanie weren't the first victims," Justin explained. "There are a couple of women in the ravine she fell into. Pretty messed up from what I saw in her memory. Oh, and it turns out the ravine wasn't very deep. The reason she was so desperate to get out was because of the bodies."

Decker frowned and glanced toward the blond again. She appeared calm, her eyes blank. The sight rather bothered him. He didn't like the fact that Justin had taken control of her like this. Unfortunately, it was necessary. He didn't have time to try to talk her out of running off after her sister alone, and they had things to do before they could leave the clearing. Things she wouldn't understand, and that he didn't want her to be a witness to.

"Have you tried your phone?" Justin asked suddenly. "I tried mine before I followed you out of the clearing earlier. I was going to call in a cleanup team to pick up the rogues, but couldn't get a signal."

"Neither could I," Decker admitted, continuing on into the clearing.

"I guess we're on our own," Justin said, not sounding terribly pleased at the prospect. "What are we going to do?" Before Decker could answer, he added hopefully,

"I don't suppose we could just behead the bastards and be done with it?"

"You know better than that," Decker said dryly. It was all he had to say. Enforcers weren't like the mortal, and fictional, James Bond with a license to kill anyone they deemed it necessary. If they had a kill order on a rogue, that was one thing, but like mortals, immortals believed in due process. These men had to be taken in to be judged by the Council. Decker understood that it was necessary to ensure innocents weren't killed in error, but sometimes it was a terrible pain in the butt . . . as now, he thought as he contemplated how they could possibly incapacitate the men so that they didn't recover and escape before a cleanup crew could get here to collect them.

"So? What are we going to do?" Justin repeated, interrupting his thoughts.

Shifting, Decker shrugged and said, "Find something to tie up the men, search them for the keys to their van, take that to get out of here and, as soon as we can get a signal, call Lucian. The SUV has a GPS tracking system. Someone at Argeneau Enterprises will be able to track where it is so we can give chase. Lucian can also arrange for a cleanup crew to come in and take care of these guys."

As he talked, Decker had knelt to empty the pockets of the nearest prone rogue in search of the keys to the van, but paused and glanced up when Justin gasped, "One of them is missing."

"One of what is missing?" he asked.

"One of the rogues. There were six of them," he pointed out. "The one Nicholas is chasing and five others, but there are only four here now."

Decker straightened and quickly counted the men in the clearing. He cursed when he saw there *were* only four remaining. One of them either had faked being hit or had recovered much more quickly from the tranquilizer in the bullets than he should have. The thought made him peer warily over the others. They'd have to tie them up quickly . . . and didn't have the proper tools to do it. Those were in the SUV.

"Why didn't he take the van?" Justin asked, distracting him from this worry.

Decker glanced sharply to the dark van parked on the edge of the clearing, grimacing when he saw the problem. "It's got a flat."

"A stray bullet must have hit it," the kid pointed out, and then eyed Decker. "Speaking of bullets, how are you feeling?"

Decker grimaced. He was feeling a little queasy, a little weak, and both wounds were hurting like a son of a bitch, but all he said was, "I'll live."

Justin stared at him worriedly for a moment, and then released Dani's arm and turned away, saying, "I'll see if there's a spare tire in the van."

"No," Decker said quickly. "If the fifth man was hit and somehow recovered from the tranquilizer this quickly, he might not be fully recovered. He may have simply regained consciousness and enough strength to drag himself into the woods. But there's also a possibility that he faked being shot."

"Either way he's probably out there, watching us," Justin realized unhappily. They were both silent for a moment, eyes scanning the woods, and then Justin glanced to the unconscious man Decker had been searching and said, "What if the tranquilizer that coated the bullets was from a bad or weak batch? They might all be recovering."

Decker turned his gaze to run it over each rogue, looking for signs of recovery. The one Nicholas had shot with the crossbow had taken the arrow through the heart. He wouldn't recover without someone first removing the projectile. Decker was pretty sure the man he'd shot at the end of the skirmish had taken the bullet in the heart too. If the slug had lodged there and not traveled through, then it would at least keep him down a little while. However, Decker hadn't been concerned with making a heart-shot with the first man he'd hit, and doubted Justin had with the one he'd taken out either. They would have to tend to the men in the clearing before they could search the woods.

"Check the van and see if there's anything useful in there," Decker ordered, moving to examine the two men he was most concerned with. "And check for a spare while you're at it."

"Will do," Justin said, and turned away.

"Justin?" Decker called. When the kid paused and turned back in question, he added grimly, "Keep your eyes and ears open."

Justin's gaze slid to the four rogues in the clearing, and then over the woods surrounding them. He nodded solemnly, and then moved more cautiously toward the van.

Decker stepped out of the trees and crossed to the fire to drop the burning log he'd been using as a torch to search the woods while Justin changed the tire on the van. He hadn't found a thing. It seemed the fifth rogue from the clearing had gotten away too.

He glanced over the remaining rogues. They lay where they'd fallen, trussed up with some rope Justin had found in the van. Decker had insisted on it before going to search for the missing one. While the rope wasn't likely to hold any of them long if they woke up, he'd hoped it would slow them down enough that he or Justin could shoot them again before they got completely free. He might have been fooling himself, it might have been as useful as wrapping limp, overcooked noodles around their ankles and wrists, but it had made him feel better about leaving Justin and Dani alone in the clearing with the rogues while he'd searched the woods.

Decker's gaze now slid to the woman. His woman. His life mate, he thought with not a little wonder. She lay curled up and sleeping peacefully by the fire compliments of Justin. While he didn't like to keep her under the other immortal's control like this, it did seem for the best at the moment.

"Did you find anything?"

Decker glanced to Justin as the younger immortal crossed the clearing to his side. He shook his head. "Not a thing."

Justin nodded, but smiled with satisfaction and announced, "I did when I took the flat tire off the van."

When Decker raised an inquiring eyebrow, Justin held out his hand and opened it to reveal two small electronic gizmos on his palm. "These were stuck to the wheel well with some kind of Silly Putty."

"What are they?" Decker took the offered items and knelt next to the fire to examine them.

"They're how Nicholas knew the rogues had grabbed the girls and brought them here. I'm pretty sure one is a listening device and the other some sort of tracking device."

"Hmm." Decker turned first one device over and then the other. "It figures. Nicholas always was a techie at heart. If Annie hadn't died, I think he would have given up being an enforcer to work in Bastien's tech lab."

"Annie was his life mate?" Justin asked.

Decker nodded.

"What happened to her?"

"She died." Decker closed his hand on the electronic gizmos and straightened. "Her death is what drove him over the edge."

Justin was silent for a minute and then said, "I've been thinking."

"Always a dangerous pastime," Decker murmured almost absently, his gaze shifting to the van to see that while he'd been searching the woods, Justin hadn't just removed the flat tire, he'd finished putting the spare on too. They could head out after Nicholas.

"Ha ha," Justin muttered, and then said, "I'm wondering if it's such a good idea to leave the rogues here for the cleanup crew to deal with. If they—"

"We're taking them with us," Decker interrupted. The problems with leaving the immortal rogues behind had struck him as he'd searched the woods. The downed men might wake before the cleanup crew could get there, or someone might have heard the gunshots earlier and there might—that moment—be an OPP car cruising around trying to find where the shots had originated. If a mortal cop stumbled on the clearing

and found the bodies before the immortals did wake. . .
Decker didn't even want to think about the trouble that
could ensue.

When Justin relaxed beside him, obviously relieved
at this news, he added, "But we aren't taking them until
we're damned sure they aren't going to wake up in the
back of the van and attack us."

"What are we going to do?" Justin asked.

Decker's answer was to lift the long branch he'd
found in the woods. The action sent pain shooting
through his chest and back, but he ignored it. It wasn't
as bad as it had been and the queasiness had passed.

His gaze slid to Justin to see that the younger immortal was eyeing the stick dubiously.

"You're going to beat them?" he asked uncertainly.

"No," Decker growled, just managing not to grind
his teeth together. He began snapping the branch into
three pieces. "We're going to stake the three who were
shot with bullets. The one with the arrow doesn't need
it, but the others are a risk if there isn't something to
ensure their heart can't pump."

"It could kill them if we leave the stakes in too long,"
Justin pointed out quietly.

"We won't. We're only leaving them staked until we
can meet up with a cleanup crew," Decker assured him,
and then asked, "You said you found a tarp in the back
of the van?"

"Yeah," Justin said, and raised an eyebrow in question.

"After we load them in the van we'll cover them with
that so that Dani doesn't see them and get upset."

"I could just keep her asleep," Justin pointed out.
"There's no need to wake her up."

Decker glanced to Dani. It would probably be less upsetting for her to continue sleeping, but he didn't want that. He wanted her awake so that he could talk to her, and hopefully redeem himself in her eyes. Right now the woman thought he was an inept oaf, and he'd dearly like to rectify that impression. But he also just wanted to get to know her better. She was his life mate, or could be if she agreed. After two hundred and fifty-nine years alone, he was ready for her. He just had to change her opinion of him and woo her into seeing him as something other than the Austin Powers she'd accused him of being.

Decker shook his head. He was usually the epitome of intelligence and competency, but he'd been set aback by realizing he couldn't read her and what that might mean.

"She might be able to tell us something about the man who took her sister that could help us catch him," Decker said finally, but knew it was a lame excuse. Justin had already read her mind and probably got any and everything from her that they could use. When the younger immortal didn't call him on it, though, he handed him one of the sticks and said, "Come on. Let's get this over with and get going."

"Shouldn't we sharpen them or something?" Justin asked, accepting the makeshift stake.

"No time," Decker said. "Just put some muscle into it."

Justin moved toward one of the men, then glanced back to ask, "What about the bodies in the ravine?"

Decker glanced toward the edge of the clearing overlooking the shallow ditch. He considered the matter and then shook his head. "We leave them. Lucian will arrange for someone to find them so their families can give them a proper burial."

Dani woke up abruptly, almost unnaturally so, she thought with confusion as she sat up on the hard, vibrating bed and glanced around. It took her a moment to sort out that she wasn't on a bed at all, but lying on the hard metal floor of a van. Memory rushed in then, and for one moment she feared she'd dreamed the rescue in the clearing and was still being held by the men who had kidnapped her and her sister, but then Dani glanced to the seats she lay behind and saw the man presently smiling at her from the front passenger seat. Not Decker-Maybe-Argeneau-Maybe-Pimms, but another man she didn't recognize.

"The name's Justin," he introduced himself cheerfully, and then pointed to their driver and added, "I'm with Decker-Maybe-Argeneau-Maybe-Pimms."

Dani let her breath out slowly, but didn't relax. Worry for her sister was now crowding her brain.

"How are you feeling?"

The question made Dani glare at the man with disbelief. How was she feeling? She'd been kidnapped, knocked about by a bunch of brutes, caught in the middle of a shootout, and—worst of all—her sister was missing, still in the clutches of one of those brutes. How did he think she felt? Shaking her head with disgust, she muttered, "This is the best CSIS could come up with? This is the Few and the Proud?"

"The Few and the Proud are the U.S. Marines," Justin informed her, seeming rather amused. "We CSIS men—" For some reason, he paused to cast a taunting glance toward Decker, and then continued, "We CSIS guys are the Cute, Strong, Intelligent, and Sexy."

"I'm sure," Dani said dryly, and then ignored him as she tried to sort out how she'd ended up in the van again. The last thing she recalled was hurrying toward the road, determined to find a house with a phone and a car so that she could call her family and do what she could to help find her sister. Dani had no idea at all how she might have ended up back in the van and sleeping.

"It's nothing to concern yourself with," Justin said, as if she'd spoken the worries aloud. "Everything's fine. We're on the road and, hopefully, soon we'll be able to get a cell signal to call in backup."

Dani found herself caught by the intensity of his eyes and, oddly enough, how she had gotten where she was suddenly didn't seem that important anymore. As the worry slipped away, she pulled herself to her knees between the seats and peered curiously out the window to see that they were just coming to the end of the grassy trail and bumping onto the gravel lane. She hadn't slept long then, Dani thought, and turned to peer at Decker. For some reason they were driving with the interior lights on. She had no idea why, but it allowed her to get a better look at the man who had so annoyed her earlier. He appeared to be extremely good-looking, with dark hair, fine features, and eyes that appeared an arresting silver-blue in this light. As she recalled, he'd been tall and well built too. In the looks department the man fit the James Bond image of a spy, she thought. It was just a shame that he was missing the "intelligent" from the Cute, Strong, Intelligent, and Sexy quota.

"Don't be too hard on Decker," Justin said suddenly, obviously reading her expression and guessing where her thoughts had led her. "After all, the man was in shock."

"Shut up, Justin," Decker snapped.

Dani ignored the driver and glanced to the other man in question. "Why would he have been in shock?"

Justin hesitated, and when he spoke she suspected it wasn't what he'd intended to say. "He was shot when he ran out into the line of fire to pull you back onto the cliff."

"Ah hell," Decker muttered as Dani's head swiveled sharply back to him. She noted absently that he sounded annoyed and embarrassed, but ignored that as she leaned farther forward to peer at his chest. Her eyes widened when she saw that there was, indeed, a bullet hole in the shoulder of his shirt.

"You *are* shot," she said with dismay. "Why are you driving? You should— Have you bound the wound or anything?"

It didn't look to her as if he had. His short-sleeved buttoned shirt was black so she couldn't tell if there was blood on it, but the cloth lay flat on his upper chest without any bulk to suggest a bandage beneath. Dani reached out to pull the shirt away from his skin to check. What she found was a hole in his shoulder with dried blood crusted around it . . . and a whole lot of naked male chest. Forcing herself to ignore the naked male bit, Dani concentrated on the wound. It looked like the bullet had gone through the muscle below his shoulder blade, missing any bones. That was good news at least. There should have been more blood from the wound, though, and Dani could only think that he'd done at least something to stop the bleeding. But it really needed to be cleaned, the bullet removed, and bandaging applied.

"Stop that," Decker muttered, knocking her hand away so that the shirt fell back into place. "I'm driving here."

"Yes, well, you shouldn't be," she said firmly. "Stop the vehicle so I can have a look at it. Your friend here can drive."

"Justin," the friend said, reminding her of his name.

Dani ignored him and tugged on Decker's shirt. "Pull over."

"No. I'm fine. The bullet just grazed me."

Dani snorted. "It didn't just graze you, it went through your subscapularis."

"His sub what?" Justin asked with amazement.

"His subscapularis," Dani repeated, and when he looked blank, explained, "It's a muscle that starts under the shoulder blade and runs to the front of the upper arm. It rotates the arm inward."

Justin's eyebrows had risen up his forehead in amazement, and he now asked, "What are you, a doctor or something?"

"Yes." She turned back to Decker. "Pull over so I can tend your shoulder."

He merely shook his head. "We need to get to where we can get cell reception. We need backup and we need to track the SUV. Remember your sister?"

Dani bit her lip, torn between insisting he stop and keeping her mouth shut. On one side of the argument, he was injured. Gunshot wounds were nothing to mess with, and untreated could result in infection and even septic shock, which had a fifty percent chance of killing the victim. On the other side of the argument was her sister, who was still in the clutches of one of the men who had kidnapped them and who might even now be suffering hellish abuse.

"I've got a signal," Justin said suddenly, saving her from having to make a decision.

"Good," Dani said with relief as Justin held the phone up, his gaze concentrated on the screen. She turned to Decker and pointed out, "Now you can stop and let me look at your shoulder while he makes the call to track your vehicle and tell us where it is."

"How strong is the signal?" Decker asked, ignoring her.

"One bar," Justin answered. "But we're getting there." Decker nodded.

"You might want to speed up," Justin suggested. "You're not going to get away without her tending to the gunshot. She's a doctor. That being the case, it may be better to let her see it sooner rather than later."

Dani frowned at the meaningful way he said the words. It felt like there was a silent message in there. If so, she didn't understand it. Decker seemed to, however, since he put his foot down and urged the van to a swifter speed. It made the ride much bumpier, and Dani found herself bouncing backward on the metal floor. When her foot knocked into something, she caught at both men's seats to steady herself, and glanced over her shoulder to see what she'd bumped into. Her eyes slid over lumpy shapes covered with some sort of tarp.

"What—?" she began, and then snapped her mouth closed after nearly biting off her own tongue as they hit a rut in the road. Rather than risk losing her tongue, Dani decided to find out for herself what lay beneath the tarp, and reached back to lift the closest edge. The old van's small overhead light cast shadows across the small pile of bodies revealed, but she had no problem recognizing the men who had kidnapped her and Stephanie. She was slower to understand what was sticking out of the chests of the ones that she could see and presumably the others too. It looked like lengths of a thick branch had been punched through their chests where their hearts would be.

"Two bars," Justin announced, and Dani glanced to the front to see that his head was still bent over the phone, watching the screen. He hadn't noticed her checking out the bodies in the back. She let the tarp drop back into place and shifted back to where she'd originally been, her mind in chaos as she tried to sort out the meaning behind what lay under the tarp.

The sight of the bodies didn't upset her; Dani had seen a lot of dead bodies while in medical school and she knew they'd been shot and most likely killed in the shootout in the clearing. It was the branches through their chests that had her mind running around inside her head like a small dog chasing its tail. What had been done to those bodies was not standard police procedure. Dani doubted defiling a corpse was standard procedure for an organization like CSIS either, and it suddenly occurred to her that she really had no idea who these men were except for what Decker had told her. She'd seen no badges or identification of any kind.

For all she knew, they could be a couple of nutcases as dangerous as the first six men.

"What's under the tarp?" she asked suddenly, and didn't miss the way the two men glanced to each other, exchanging a silent message before Decker cleared his throat and admitted, "The men from the clearing."

Dani was silent for a minute and then asked, "And what about the women in the ravine?"

Another silent exchange occurred, and then Decker said, "We had to leave them behind for now. Lucian, our boss, will arrange for the local authorities to find them after we talk to him."

Dani stared at his profile for several moments, considering his words. *Arrange for the local authorities to find them* seemed an odd way to frame it, but she merely asked, "Who is the man who chased after my sister and her kidnapper in the other van? Is he CSIS too?"

Interestingly enough, that question brought about a very long pause indeed before Decker said, "He used to be one of us."

Before Dani could ask another question, Decker slowed the van, and she glanced out the windshield to see that they'd reached the end of the street.

"How many bars now, Justin?" he asked.

"Three," came the grim response.

Decker turned the corner going left and drove up this new road, steering the van up a steep hill before slowing to a stop. "Now?"

"Four out of five bars," was the answer.

"Good enough," Decker decided, and steered the van off the road to park on the small stretch of grass between the pavement and the row of trees that sided it. "Give me the phone."

"Maybe I should call while Dani tends to your shoulder," Justin suggested quietly, and then pointed out, "She's a doctor. She's just going to pester you until you let her look at it, and it really is better if she does it sooner rather than later." He allowed a moment for that to sink in and then added, "Unless you'd like me to"—his gaze slid to Dani before he finished—"do my thing."

"No," Decker said sharply, and then glanced warily to Dani. Seeing that she was listening, he turned back and added, "I can make the call while she tends my shoulder. It was my decision to leave the keys in the SUV, I'll take the flack."

Justin shrugged and handed over the phone and then turned to Dani. "I didn't find a first aid kit when I searched the van earlier, so you'll have to make do with what we have. I have a pocket knife you can use to dig out the bullet, but I don't know what you'll use for a bandage and there's nothing to use to clean the wound."

Dani merely shrugged and accepted the pocket knife he dug out of his pocket and handed to her. She no longer really had any interest in looking at Decker's shoulder. There was something wrong here, and she was suddenly positive the two men weren't with CSIS or any other law enforcement organization. Dani was now afraid that she'd escaped one group of crazies only to land in the hands of two more.

However, she'd been insistent on tending to Decker's shoulder earlier, and demurring now would look suspicious, which was the last thing she wanted. It would be easier to get away if they thought she still believed she was in safe hands and was perfectly content to be there, so Dani merely glanced to Decker and asked, "Where do you want to do this?"

He hesitated and then shifted out of the driver's seat and moved to join her in the back. The bodies under the tarp took up most of the cargo space, leaving a very small area for the two of them. Dani turned and moved backward until she came up against the side door to make as much room as possible for him, and Decker shifted to kneel facing her.

When he began to unbutton his shirt, she found her eyes following the action, running over every inch revealed until Dani realized what she was doing and turned her attention to the knife she held, occupying herself with opening the blade. She then stared at it, her medical training reminding her that it wasn't sterile, and poking around in his wound with an unsterilized knife might do more harm than good.

Her gaze slid to the tarp, but Dani glanced back as Decker turned slightly so that the wounded shoulder was closer to her. She peered reluctantly at the bullet wound then, and found herself frowning and leaning closer for a better look.

"What is it?" Decker asked, tension in his voice.

"I— Nothing," she said quickly, but had trouble schooling her features. Dani didn't see a lot of bullet wounds in her practice. In fact, she had never seen one, but if she didn't know better she would have said the man had been shot at least twenty-four hours ago rather than the fifteen minutes or so since the shootout in the clearing.

"Why are you looking like that? Is there something wrong with the wound?" Decker asked before she could delve too far into the confusing questions plaguing her.

"No," she lied. "It just doesn't look as bad as I expected."

"I told you it wasn't bad," he reminded her.

"Yes, you did," she said quietly, her eyes refocusing on the wound. The glow cast by the overhead light wasn't very strong, but she could see the bullet just inside the wound. That couldn't be normal. Surely it should have traveled farther in than that?

"Just dig out the bullet and bandage it," Decker said when she simply sat there staring for another moment. "It will be fine."

Dani hesitated and then admitted, "I'm reluctant to use the knife to dig it out. It's not sterile."

"Neither was the bullet," he said with a shrug, and then turned his attention to punching numbers on the cell phone. Putting it to his ear then, Decker added, "Just dig it out and I'll have it cleaned up and get some antibiotics later."

Dani sighed and then picked up the knife again, but paused once more and glanced to Justin. "You don't happen to have a lighter or something, do you?"

"No, but I saw one in the glove compartment, hang on." He disappeared from view, and Dani heard him rummaging around in the glove compartment. After a moment she heard a satisfied grunt, and then Justin leaned around the seat and held out a small, disposable lighter.

Dani accepted it with relief. It wasn't ideal, but it was certainly better than nothing. She flicked the lighter and ran the flame it produced repeatedly over the blade, trying to move quickly enough that it wouldn't leave any carbon behind, but slow enough it would kill any germs or bacteria present. When she'd done the best she could, Dani turned to Decker, braced one hand on his shoulder to steady herself, and leaned in. Her mind was on what she was doing, but she couldn't help but inhale his natural scent as she worked. It was a spicy, woodsy smell that was quite pleasant and made her unconsciously close her mouth to inhale it more deeply through her nose.

"Lucian, Nicholas is up here," Decker said suddenly, nearly startling her into slicing his chest open.

He really should have left Justin to make the call, she thought with irritation, taking a deep breath to steady herself.

"No . . . there were complications," Decker said into the phone, and then glanced to her and nodded to his chest, saying, "Go ahead."

Dani pressed her lips together, thinking it would be better to wait until he finished his call, but shrugged and leaned in again. She soon found she'd been right and it was the bullet she could see just inside the wound.

"He was— he claimed he was tailing some ro— real bad guys," Decker said, his voice tight as she set to digging out the bullet. It was just below the skin and quick and easy to remove, which just didn't seem right at all. What kind of gun lodged a bullet just under the skin?

"Yes, you heard me right, he says he's still hunting down . . . bad guys even though he's . . . retired," Decker said.

Dani set the bullet on the floor of the van, but her attention was on what Decker was saying. It seemed obvious the man was editing his side of the conversation and she would have paid a lot to hear what he really wanted to say, Dani thought as she turned back to the wound. She had expected to find that it had started bleeding freely now that the bullet was out, but there was very little blood at all. It was enough to make her think she needed to go back to school and take a couple of trauma courses. This wasn't anything like she expected.

"Before I explain that, there are a couple of things I need you to get started on," Decker said as she glanced around for something to use to bandage the wound. While it wasn't bleeding, it did seem best to bandage it to at least make an effort at lowering the risk of infection. Unfortunately, there wasn't anything to use to bandage it.

"I need you to have Bastien track the SUV and see where it's headed," Decker said, and her gaze skittered to him. Tracking the SUV meant finding her sister, something she very much wanted to do, but she was also wondering if bad guys were organized enough to do something like that. It made her think that she might have been wrong and they weren't bad guys too, despite the odd treatment of the bodies in the van.

Decker suddenly covered the bottom of the phone and said, "That's good enough. Why don't you get out and stretch your legs a bit while you have the chance."

It was more an order than a suggestion, and there was no mistaking it. It seemed he wanted privacy for the call. Dani didn't hesitate; she nodded, turned to open the door behind her, and then slipped out of the van.

It seemed obvious he wasn't going to say anything revealing in front of her anyway, and she needed time to decide if she should be trying to escape or sticking with them.

Justin didn't follow her out of the van, but stayed to listen to the conversation, and Dani found herself standing at the side of the road without anyone to stop her from walking away. The problem was she wasn't sure she should.

Frowning, she began to pace up the road, considering the situation. It seemed obvious that things weren't as they seemed. It was doubtful these men were with CSIS. She was pretty sure they'd lied to her, and were withholding information.

On the other hand, Decker had risked leaving the cover of the woods and making a target of himself to pull her back up onto the cliff . . . taking a bullet in the process. That just didn't seem like the actions of a villain. And then there was the fact that Stephanie had been taken away in their SUV and these men had a way of tracking it. They were her best bet of finding her sister. Perhaps even her only hope of finding her.

She would stay with them for now, Dani decided . . . but she was going to proceed very very carefully with these men, watch and listen and learn what she could. Her life, and Stephanie's, might depend on it.

Chapter Three

"Goddammit, Decker, what the hell is going on? What do you mean track the SUV? You *lost* it? How the hell did that happen? And how could you let Nicholas get away?"

Decker grimaced at that roar in his ear as he watched Dani move a little away from the van, and then said, "It all got a little more complicated than expected."

"Explain."

Decker winced at the sound of grinding teeth that came over the line. The man was pissed . . . to the point that he was in danger of snapping off a fang if he wasn't careful. Clearing his throat, he relayed his conversation with Nicholas and everything that had happened.

A moment of silence followed when he finished speaking, and then his uncle slowly said, "Let me get this straight, Nicholas is still chasing rogues even though he's rogue himself?"

"So he said," Decker answered noncommittally.

"And you two helped with this nest?"

"Yes." Decker's gaze slid to the tarp-covered bodies. "There were six. They had a campsite in the woods and there's a little ravine next to it with two bodies in it. From the quick look I took, they're in a bad way. These guys butchered them . . . slowly."

"Tell me where it is and I'll have a cleanup crew go out and see if anything needs doing before the authorities can be led to them," Lucian said wearily.

Decker quickly told him the name of the road and gave directions to the ravine. When he finished, Lucian asked, "What about these rogues? Did you catch them?"

"Only four," he admitted grimly. "They had two new girls they'd just snatched and we managed to rescue one of them, but the sixth man got away using the second girl as cover. He—" Decker paused and cleared his throat before admitting, "I'd left the keys in the SUV in case Nicholas made a run for it and we needed to give chase in a hurry. The sixth rogue took advantage of that and stole the SUV for his getaway. Nicholas took off after them in his van while Bricker and I were taking care of the others."

Lucian cursed on the other end of the line and then snapped, "What about the other rogue? You say he got away too?"

"Yes. There were five down when I rushed after Nicholas. When we went back to the clearing, there were only four. Either the fifth one faked being hit, or we got bullets coated with a weak batch of tranquilizer and he recovered enough to get away in the few minutes we were gone."

"What did you do with the four still there?"

"We staked them to be sure they didn't recover and have them with us right now. It seemed better than leaving them for someone to find."

"Good, good," Lucian said, sounding calmer. "Okay, so you now have Nicholas and two other rogues to find?"

"That's why I asked you to track the SUV. If Nicholas *is* chasing it and we can catch up to the SUV, we can find both Nicholas and at least one other rogue."

"And rescue the second girl," Lucian muttered. "I'll call Bastien and have him track it. I presume you have a vehicle to give pursuit?"

"We took their van."

"What about blood?"

"In the SUV."

"Along with your weapons," Lucian said, sounding testy again.

"Yes," Decker admitted quietly. "We have a couple of guns each, but are low on ammo."

"All right. Sit tight. I'll call Bastien and get things rolling. I'll get back to you when I have coordinates and a plan for how to get a new SUV with blood and weapons to you."

Decker grunted and waited a moment to see if there were further instructions. When the only sound was the click of the phone disconnecting, he flipped his own phone closed with a sigh.

"Is he going to track the SUV and send someone to look after the clearing?" Justin asked as he watched Decker slip it in his pocket.

"Yes. And see about getting us another SUV with blood and weapons."

Justin's gaze moved to the tarp-covered bodies. "It will be nice to be rid of these guys. I keep thinking I catch a glimpse of the tarp moving out of the corner of my eye. I keep looking back, expecting them to sit up and start coming after us."

"You watch too much television," Decker said with disgust. "They've been staked. They aren't going anywhere."

"Yeah, well, I'll still be glad to be rid of them," Justin muttered, and then asked, "Will whoever brings us a new SUV take Dani too?"

Decker stiffened and shook his head. "No. She stays with us. She could be useful in helping to keep Stephanie calm when we get her back," he added, but knew Justin wasn't fooled into believing that was the real reason he wanted to keep Dani with him. They could control Stephanie as Justin had controlled Dani if need be.

Turning away to avoid the other man's eyes, he glanced out the window, looking for the woman in question, and then frowned. "Where is she?"

Justin followed his gaze, and then turned and peered through the windows on the opposite side. "There she is."

Decker twisted around and spotted Dani on the side of the road, a good hundred feet away.

"You don't think she's running away, do you?" Justin asked, sounding more curious than concerned.

"No." Decker opened the van door and slid out.

"I told you, you should let me keep her under my control," Justin said smugly. "She wouldn't even have had to get out of the van if I had."

"No," Decker repeated firmly, turning back to peer

through the open door. "No more controlling her. I don't like you being inside her head. Just stay out of her mind."

Justin arched an eyebrow. "And if she really does try to run away?"

"Then I'll stop her," Decker said firmly. He started to slide the door closed and then paused to peer at the kid grimly. "She's mine. Stay out of her head."

"I'm nearly a hundred years old, hardly a kid," Justin said dryly, plucking the thought from his mind.

Decker merely scowled, pulled the door closed, and started around the van to head after Dani.

Justin unrolled the driver's side window and leaned out to call softly, "Don't take too long. I think we should wait in town for the call."

Decker paused and glanced back. His tone was dry when he said, "Let me guess, you're getting hungry."

"I am," Justin admitted, and then added, "But you're also starting to look pale. You're going to need blood soon."

Decker shrugged that away and turned to continue after Dani. He wasn't terribly surprised to hear that he was pale. He had been shot twice, and his body had been working overtime to make repairs. It would be using up blood to do it and would soon need to replenish that blood. If Decker hadn't been distracted with everything going on, he would have long ago noticed the slight cramping in his stomach—his body's way of telling him it wanted more blood. He was certainly noticing it now that Justin had gotten him thinking about it, and it made him hope that Lucian was quick about getting another truck and blood to them.

A cool breeze against his chest brought Decker's attention to the fact that his shirt was still undone. Fortunately, Justin hadn't mentioned—and Dani hadn't gotten a look at his back to see—that he'd actually been shot twice. As he did up his shirt, Decker started to worry over what she must have thought when she tended to the one wound she had seen. It seemed obvious that she'd noticed something amiss when she'd removed the bullet. Decker's guess would be that the healing had been much further along than it would have been if he were a mortal. His kind healed much more quickly. It was why Justin had kept saying he should let her look sooner rather than later. Within twenty-four hours that bullet, along with the one in his back, would have been long pushed out of his body and Decker would have been fully healed.

As a doctor, even seeing it as quickly as she had, Dani would have noticed that the bullet was much closer to the surface than it should be. He had no idea how she'd explained that to herself, but she hadn't commented, and, he hoped, now that she'd done all she could by removing the bullet she would stop fussing over it.

Decker let that concern drop away as he reached Dani. He was about to tap her on the shoulder when she suddenly whirled in his direction. She jumped back with a startled little gasp as she saw him standing there.

"Where were you going?" he asked.

"I was just walking off some worry," she answered, and then moved past him to head in the direction of the van. "So, were they able to track the SUV? Are we ready to go?"

"They're tracking it now. They'll call when they have something," he answered, following.

She nodded. "Shouldn't we start out anyway? Head for town maybe? It might save us some time when they do call."

"Or it might add more time if we head in the wrong direction," he pointed out, and then shook his head. "We're better off waiting to hear back from Lucian."

"I suppose you're right," she said unhappily.

"It shouldn't take too long," Decker assured her gruffly, and then to distract her from her worry, said, "Tell me what happened."

When she paused and looked at him, he added, "It might help us figure out how to approach the situation when we catch up to your sister and the man who has her."

Dani was silent for so long that he thought she wasn't going to answer, but then said, "We came up for a family reunion. My uncle owns a house with several cottages on his property, and once a year has the whole family up for a weekend." She frowned and then admitted, "I'm usually too busy to come, but I managed to get some time off this year."

Decker nodded and didn't mention that he was very glad she had. He doubted very much if she was at the moment.

"We were supposed to leave tonight to avoid the weekend traffic. My idea," Dani added bitterly, no doubt thinking that if they'd left Sunday morning instead of in the evening, none of this would have happened. It was an excuse for her to take the blame for what had taken place, and Decker was searching his mind for something to say to take away that blame when she continued, "Anyway, Stephanie wanted to ride with me rather than crammed into my dad's van with our brothers and sisters."

"How many are there?" he asked curiously.

"Me, Stephanie, who's the youngest, and two brothers and two more sisters in between," Dani answered and smiled wryly as she pointed out, "The van was pretty packed with luggage and people on the way up, and I thought the company would be nice so I said sure."

Decker nodded.

"Stephanie wanted some snacks for the trip home, so I pulled into the grocery store." She let her breath out on an unhappy sigh. "I should have just stopped at the coffee shop or something. I—"

"What happened isn't your fault, Dani," he said quietly.

"Isn't it?" she asked huskily.

He shook his head. "You seem to be using every decision you made as a reason to blame yourself, but it isn't your fault."

Dani shrugged, her gaze on the ground ahead, and Decker knew she wasn't hearing him so he said, "It was your uncle's idea to have the reunion this weekend. If he hadn't, you wouldn't have been here. Do you blame him?"

"No, of course not," she said at once, and he nodded.

"Well, the fact you suggested everyone stay later to avoid traffic, or that you agreed to stop at the grocery store so your sister could get some snacks doesn't make it your fault either. If you want to lay blame, lay it where it belongs . . . with the men who took you."

Dani let her breath out slowly. "You're right, of course."

"But you're still blaming yourself," Decker guessed dryly.

"Maybe," she admitted wryly. "But I'll try not to."

Knowing that was the best he could expect, Decker let it go and asked, "Did they grab you on the way into the grocery store or on the way out?"

"Out," Dani answered, and then smiled as she admitted, "Stephanie had gone a little wild making her selections. My mother doesn't allow junk food in the house and Stephi went nuts, getting everything she loves but rarely gets. We were both laden down with bags when we came out. The van was parked beside the car when we came back. I didn't think much of it, and then . . ."

Decker's eyes narrowed on her face, noting the confusion and bewilderment there. "What is it?"

"I—We—The van door slid open and we just—Both Stephanie and I just dropped our bags and climbed into the van. I don't know why, but we just did," she said with bewilderment.

"And then what happened?" Decker asked, not wanting her to think about that too long. It was obvious the rogues had used mind control, but he could hardly explain that to her.

Dani hesitated, obviously still troubled by her own actions, and then continued, "Once we were in the van I suddenly knew we shouldn't be and I grabbed Stephanie's arm and tried to drag her back out. The men just laughed, and one knocked me back while another grabbed Stephanie and pulled her onto his lap and started pawing her. I tried to help her, but just got knocked back again. The man who hit me seemed to be enjoying it," she added angrily, and then her expression clouded with confusion and she said, "And then the one driving told them to stop playing with the *food*."

Decker's mouth tightened, but he merely said, "What happened next?"

"The guy holding Stephanie said something like 'Aw, Dad, we're just having a little fun.'"

This seemed to bewilder her even more. Decker wasn't surprised. All immortals looked to be about twenty-five to thirty. The father would look too young to be called Dad by the others.

"It must have been a nickname," Dani said, shaking her head. "They pretty much left us alone after that. They just kept staring at us with this eager, hungry expression that gave me the creeps. After a few minutes, Stephanie stopped screaming and then we got to the clearing. They dragged us from the van and made us sit on this log while they started a fire and stuff. That's when I found out my phone didn't get any reception there."

Decker nodded, recalling her telling him she hadn't been able to get a signal. That was probably why the men hadn't taken away her phone.

"When the men finished gathering wood and had a fire going, they joined us around the fire and I asked what were they going to do with us. They all started laughing and then one of them dragged me over to the cliff and threw a log from the fire down in the ravine and there were these two women—"

Her voice choked off and Decker caught her hand in his and gave it a squeeze. "You don't have to tell me. I saw them."

She nodded and fell silent, and Decker considered what she'd said. The men had obviously controlled her and Stephanie to get them into the van, but then had dropped the control and allowed them to struggle and be terrified for a bit. They hadn't had to. They could have kept them under their control and unaware the entire time they had them, but apparently enjoyed the horror their victims experienced.

"Those poor women," Dani said unhappily, "and their poor families."

"Yes," he said simply, and squeezed her hand again.

She glanced at him and said reluctantly, "I guess I owe you my life."

"You don't owe anyone anything," he said gruffly.

Dani shrugged and asked, "Did you already suspect these men were responsible for those other women going missing? Were you already following them when they kidnapped us?"

"Nicholas was tracking them," he admitted reluctantly.

"The one who went after my sister?" Dani asked.

He nodded.

"Did he see us get taken in the parking lot, or—"

"No. He was at a restaurant a good distance away when it happened," Decker said, and seeing the question in her eyes, explained, "I gather he put a tracking and listening device in the wheel well of the van. He heard when you were taken and used the tracking device to follow."

"And how did you and Justin end up there?" she asked.

"We followed Nicholas," he said shortly.

"Why were you following Nicholas?"

Decker shifted uncomfortably and merely said, "He was rushing out of the restaurant when we got there, so we followed."

The way her eyes narrowed suggested that it wasn't a very satisfactory answer. He wasn't surprised when she asked, "Who exactly is this Nicholas?"

Decker sought his mind for a way to answer and finally said, "He used to work with us."

"Then why hasn't he called you to tell you where he's tracked the SUV to so far?"

"He doesn't have my cell phone number," Decker said, glad to be able to answer at least that question and honestly. There hadn't even been cell phones when Nicholas had gone rogue. Before she could ask, he added, "And I don't know his number either."

"Does your boss know it?" she asked.

"No."

"Oh." Dani's shoulders drooped briefly and they started walking again, but they'd taken only a few more steps when she paused and turned to him excitedly. "The listening device."

"What about it?" he asked.

"Nicholas might still have the receiver on," she pointed out, and suggested, "You could speak into it and tell him your number and ask him to call you."

Decker raised his eyebrows at the suggestion. It was a clever one, or would be if there was any possibility of Nicholas calling. There wasn't, but Dani's words made him realize that he'd completely overlooked the presence of the bug and tracker. Nicholas might very well be listening to them. Justin had put both gizmos in one of the cup holders between the two front seats and they'd promptly forgotten about them. Nicholas had probably heard everything they'd said in the van, including his side of the phone conversation with Lucian, and the tracker would tell him exactly where they were right now. It's what Decker would have done had the situation been reversed and he should have thought of it, but in their rush to get things done and get going, both he and Justin had forgotten all about the two gizmos. At least he knew he had and suspected Justin had, or he would have said something.

"Come on." Dani hurried for the van.

Decker followed more slowly. He was pretty sure Nicholas wouldn't call, and Dani would be disappointed when he didn't. She'd also wonder why he wasn't calling and start asking more questions, which he didn't want or need. On the other hand, trying to dissuade her from her plan would just bring those questions earlier.

Justin was sitting sideways in the front passenger seat, the door open and his legs hanging out. He stepped down as they reached him and let the door swing closed, his eyebrows rising in question.

Dani smiled brilliantly and announced, "It just occurred to me that we don't have to wait for this Lucian person to track the SUV. Nicholas can tell us where it is. He's following it."

"Nicholas?" Justin asked doubtfully, his gaze sliding to Decker.

"Decker told me he doesn't know your cell phone

numbers, but what if you were to speak into the bug and tell him your numbers? Then he could call."

"But . . ." Justin began, and then paused when Decker caught his eye and shook his head.

"What?" Dani asked. When Justin remained silent, his gaze locked on Decker, she sighed and said, "You want to talk. I'll wait in the van."

Both men remained silent as she pulled the back door open and got in. The moment it slid shut, Justin urged Decker a few feet away from the van and then admitted, "I'd forgotten about the bug and tracker."

"Me too," Decker admitted, and then raised an eyebrow when Justin suddenly frowned and glanced back to the van. "What's wrong?"

"Maybe I should get them," Justin suggested. "Just to make sure she doesn't try to get a message to Nicholas."

Decker shook his head. "She doesn't know they're in the cup holder. She'll wait for us to try speaking into it."

Justin nodded, but then pointed out, "He won't call."

"No," Decker agreed. "But it's better to let her try than to have to come up with an explanation to give her for why he won't. I'm hoping Lucian calls quickly and she's sufficiently distracted by chasing after her sister that she doesn't notice when Nicholas doesn't call."

Justin was silent for a moment and then said, "We could let her try . . . or we could tell her they were broken and save the bug and tracker to set a trap for Nicholas later." When Decker's eyebrows rose, he pointed out, "If he is listening, by now Nicholas probably believes we've forgotten all about the bug and tracker because we've talked in front of them. If he continues to think this we might be able to use it to lay a trap to catch him."

Decker was shaking his head before Justin finished, and once he fell silent, said, "As you pointed out, Nicholas probably heard my phone call to Lucian and knows we're going to track the SUV. He'll know we're on his trail anyway and be on the lookout for us. Nicholas is one of the best. We are not going to sneak up on him without a damned good plan."

Justin paused briefly before suggesting, "After the next call you could tell me that Lucian said Bastien was unable to track the SUV, that the GPS isn't working for some reason. If we did that and deactivated the bug, Nicholas wouldn't know we were coming. Although," he added, "I wouldn't suggest trashing the bug, just trying to remove the battery if there is one. Bastien may be able to use the bug to reverse track Nicholas somehow."

"Could he?" Decker asked with surprise.

"I'm not sure," the younger immortal said. "I watch a lot of sci fi stuff, but I'm not a techie."

Decker stared at him with a frown. The ideas were good ones, and he wished he'd thought of them himself. First Dani had recalled the bug both he and Justin had forgotten about, and now Bricker had come up with a plan to use the bug to trap Nicholas. Where had his brain gone? He was usually the one to come up with these ideas.

"Don't be too tough on yourself," Justin said lightly, slapping a hand on his shoulder. He then added tauntingly, "Finding his life mate made Mortimer an idiot too."

Decker scowled. Finding a life mate had also made Mortimer so scattered that they had easily read his mind, he recalled. Decker decided he didn't like his mind being an open book to others and that he'd have to take greater care to be less distracted and keep his guard up.

"If you can," Justin commented, apparently still reading his thoughts. "Mortimer isn't very good at it anymore. I doubt you will be either."

Decker opened his mouth to tell him where to get off, but Justin forestalled him by asking, "Are you hungry yet?"

He almost said no, but in truth, his stomach cramps were getting worse, and in the end he admitted, "I could do with a bag of blood or four."

"Four, huh?" Justin chuckled. "Unfortunately, we don't have any handy right now. I meant for food."

"Oh. No, I'm not." He frowned at the realization. Aside from not being able to read the mate, and having difficulty keeping your thoughts your own, a reawakened appetite for food and sex and various other things usually came with finding your life mate. That being the case, the fact that he wasn't suddenly hungry was a bit worrying and he asked, "Why aren't I?"

Justin didn't look nearly as concerned. Shrugging, he said, "Maybe it takes longer for that to kick in. Or maybe you have to actually be around food. How long has it been since you ate, anyway?

"I stopped when I was one hundred and twenty," Decker admitted.

Bricker looked horrified. "That means I'll only be eating for another twenty years or so." He considered that and then shook his head firmly. "No way . . . although," he added with concern, "that last burger I had when we stopped at the café didn't seem quite as good as usual."

"That café was a dive," Decker said dryly. "The burger was probably roadkill."

"Hmm." He fretted over it briefly and then asked, "How old were you when you stopped having sex?"

"Eighty years ago," Decker answered.

Justin grinned. "Took you a little longer to get tired of sex than it did food, huh? I'm not surprised. I still don't understand how it's even possible to get tired of sex. I can't imagine a day when I will. I'm pretty sure I could do it every day, even twice or three times a day for the next millennia and not grow tired of it."

Decker shrugged, thinking the younger immortal would understand in another century or so.

"No, I won't understand in another hundred years or so," Justin said with certainty, still reading his mind. "I'm gonna want sex till I die. Women are incredible. Every one a different shape, size, color, even texture."

"Texture?" Decker asked, eyebrow rising.

"Sure. Some are softer, some harder, some in between, but all are beautiful in their own way."

Decker supposed he'd have to agree with that. His gaze slid to the van and the woman just visible through the glass, and he thought that while all women were beautiful, some were more beautiful than others.

Dani waited until Decker turned back to Justin to continue talking and then reached out and eased the window fully closed. She'd cracked it the moment the men weren't looking so that she could hear what they were saying . . . and had gotten an earful.

She sat back on her heels and considered what she'd heard. The last part had been worrisome. Decker had stopped eating at one hundred and twenty? And stopped having sex eighty years ago? The man couldn't be more than thirty years old. What nonsense was he spouting out there? And Justin's answer about having twenty more years before he reached one hundred and twenty and stopped eating? Dani didn't need her medical training to realize the two men were completely and utterly delusional.

A rustle of sound drew her gaze to the tarp-covered pile behind her as she shifted and brushed up against it. Dani grimaced. Okay, *delusional* was too mild a term. It seemed she was, after all, presently in the company of two crazy men. Not a happy thought, she decided, especially since their being crazy didn't change the fact that they were still her best chance of finding her sister.

Unless, Dani thought suddenly, her gaze sliding to the cup holder between the two front seats. It was where she'd heard Decker say the bug and tracker were, and she peered at it silently, her mind churning. According to Decker, he and Justin had followed Nicholas to where she and her sister were being held. So Nicholas was the one who had actually set out to save them, not these two. And Nicholas was the one now chasing after her sister. He was still trying to save her, while these two seemed more interested in catching Nicholas than helping her sister.

Nicholas had also been the one with a crossbow rather than a gun. He'd been holding the unusual weapon as he'd rushed after her sister and the man dragging her away from the clearing. But these two had been popping out from behind their trees firing guns, though she hadn't seen a single gun since waking in the back of the van. She didn't worry overmuch over that, however, and was more concerned with the fact that—as far as she knew—it wasn't legal for citizens to carry handguns in Canada. The only people who usually carried them were cops . . . and bad guys who bought them on the black market or various unsavory ways. Dani was pretty sure these guys weren't cops. From what she'd just heard, they'd never pass the psych exam . . . which meant they were probably also bad guys and Nicholas was the only good guy around.

She glanced out the window and—finding the men still deep in conversation—shifted forward until she knelt between the two front seats. She cast another nervous glance out the window and continued to watch them as she spoke close to the cup holder.

"Nicholas? If you can hear me, this is Dani, the other woman you saved tonight." She paused and licked her lips and then continued, "Decker and Bricker are going to set a trap for you using the bug and the tracking device you left in the van. They know you probably think they don't remember the devices are here and are going to try to use them to catch you."

Dani paused again and closed her eyes briefly before continuing, "I'm scared. Decker told me he works for CSIS, but there's no way he could. He's crazy. I overheard them talking and he seems to think he's hundreds of years old.

"I don't know what to do," she admitted. "I'm torn between fleeing for my life and sticking with them because they can track the SUV that Stephanie is in. I have to find my sister, but want to get out alive with her. If you're what I think you are, some kind of bounty hunter or private detective or something, please call me."

Dani rattled off her cell phone number, and then waited a minute and repeated it. She said it once more before finishing with "Call me right away if you can, I'm not sure if they'll leave me on my own again, and I need to know just how dangerous these men are. Hopefully you can tell me that."

Much to her amazement, Dani had barely stopped talking when her cell phone began to vibrate in her pocket.

Chapter Four

D ani?" The voice on the phone was a deep growl that Dani didn't recognize.

"Nicholas?" she asked hopefully.

"Yes. They probably won't leave you alone for long. We have to keep this short so listen to me. I don't know the younger kid, but I know Decker and you're safe with him. He would never hurt you, and I don't think the fellow with him would either. All right?" he asked. "You're safe."

"But they're crazy," she protested, and then bit her lip and glanced out the window, afraid she'd spoken too loudly. Justin and Decker appeared not to have heard, however. In fact, they were now walking as they talked, moving away from the van.

"They may seem crazy, but they aren't. You *are* safe with them. Trust me on this."

"You don't understand," Dani said with frustration. "They stuck branches in the bodies of those men who took us, and— Are they CSIS?" she asked abruptly.

"No, they *are* in law enforcement, but not any organization you've heard of."

"What organization?" Dani asked anyway, unwilling to accept that explanation this time.

After a hesitation, Nicholas answered. "They're Council enforcers."

"What are Council enforcers?" she asked at once.

"It doesn't matter. What matters is that you know that you are safe with them."

"But my sister—"

"She's alive and well. I'm still following them. Your sister should be all right. He can't hurt her while he's driving, and I don't intend to lose them so he can hurt her."

Dani closed her eyes with relief at his words.

"You haven't called your family on your cell phone, have you?" he asked suddenly.

Dani's eyes popped open as amazement shot through her. She should have called them at once . . . and the police. "No," she admitted finally, and then added fretfully, "I should have done that right away. I don't know why I didn't."

"They probably put the suggestion in your mind that you shouldn't," he said calmly. "I don't know why they didn't take the phone away at the same time."

She was frowning, wondering whose side the man was on here, and then he said, "Dani, I risked being caught to save your life, so trust me. Stay with them."

"Caught?" she echoed with a frown. "Why are they trying to catch you?"

The pause this time was very long before he said, "I made a mistake a long time ago. I'm afraid I killed someone. They were sent to find me and bring me in for judgment. They *are* the good guys Dani, I'm the bad seed."

"And you're asking me to trust you?" she asked dryly.

"Yeah," Nicholas said with what sounded like bitter amusement. "So who's the crazy one here, huh?"

Dani didn't say anything. She didn't know what to think now. He'd *killed* someone?

"I know you're scared, Dani, but you really do need to trust me and stay with Decker. And it would probably be for the best if you didn't try calling your family. At least not until we get your sister back, and I promise I *will* get her back for you, but in return you have to not contact your family. They'd just worry anyway. It's better they don't know until it's over and you're both safe. All right?"

She bit her lip, not sure what she should do.

"All right?" he repeated.

"All right," Dani responded quietly, though she wasn't sure she would keep her word.

Another moment of silence passed, and she suspected he was worrying that she wouldn't keep it, and then he sighed. "I won't call you again. They'll know we talked."

"No they won't," she assured him, not wanting to lose this connection with her sister. Nicholas was the only one who could reassure her that her sister was still safe and not lying at the bottom of a ditch like one of those women back at the clearing. "They're outside. I can see them. They don't know I'm talking to you."

"It doesn't matter. They'll know," Nicholas assured her solemnly and then added for good measure, "They'll read your mind and know everything you've thought and said and heard."

"Read my mind?" Dani asked uncertainly, beginning to wonder if the whole world had gone mad while she was in that grocery store.

"I know none of this is making sense to you, but you just have to trust me," Nicholas said firmly. "I'll do what I can to get your sister back, but they can do more. Tell them we just passed Georgian Bay on Highway 400. My guess is he's going to take the highway all the way to Toronto and try to get lost in the crowds there."

"Georgian Bay," Dani echoed faintly. That was almost an hour away. She frowned, confused by how they had gotten so far so fast. Surely she hadn't slept for that long, had she? And what had the men been doing during that time for her sister's kidnappers to get such a head start? Her gaze slid to the tarp-covered bodies behind her.

"Nicholas," Dani began, but before she could get any further she heard the click as he ended the call. She pulled the phone away and stared at it, her thoughts returning to his claim that he'd killed someone and that Decker and Justin had been sent to bring him in for judgment. Oddly enough, the claim didn't worry her as much as the one that Decker and Justin could read her mind. It seemed to suggest Nicholas was just as crazy as they were.

As for the bit about them having put the suggestion into her mind not to call her parents, that was just crazy too. She hadn't called because she'd been too distracted with other things, Dani told herself and began to punch in the number of her mother's cell phone. She had to call and tell them what was happening. They needed to know. She didn't look forward to explaining about Stephanie, but it was the responsible thing to do and—

Dani stopped and glanced up swiftly when the front passenger door opened and Decker slid inside. She immediately snapped her phone closed and slipped it quickly in her pocket, afraid it would be taken away if they saw it.

When Decker pulled the door closed and then turned to glance at her as Justin got in on the driver's side, she forced a smile and asked, "Is everything all right?"

"Yes," he said at once.

It was Justin who added, "I just wanted to talk to Decker about something. Guy type things."

Dani nodded and tried not to look like she had heard a good deal of their conversation and now knew they were crazy. She was relieved by the distraction Justin offered when he said cheerfully, "So, while we're waiting, why don't we go into town and get something to eat?

Before Decker or Dani could shoot down the idea, Decker's phone began to ring. The two men peered at each other silently, and then Justin reached for the tracker in the cup holder nearest him and began to fiddle with it as Decker pulled out the phone and placed it to his ear. Knowing Justin was removing a battery or otherwise deactivating the tracker, Dani concentrated on Decker as he said, "Hello" and then listened briefly, before saying, "Can you repeat that for Bricker?"

He held out the phone and Justin set the tracker back in the cup holder and then took the phone. He too said, "Hello" and listened briefly before saying, "All right."

Decker took back the phone and had a short conversation that consisted of mostly listening and the occasional grunt and then he snapped the phone closed. As he slid it in his pocket, Decker leaned to the side to glance back at her and said, "They weren't able to track the SUV. We're to head back to Toronto to coordinate and come up with a plan to track down the man who has your sister."

"I see," Dani murmured, and despite the fact that she'd expected it, found she was disappointed by his lying. Obviously, both men had just been told that the GPS on the SUV had been tracked and was on Highway 400, heading toward Toronto.

This was proven to her when Justin started the engine and asked, "You don't happen to know how to get to Highway 400 from here, do you? We had GPS in the SUV to get up here and I didn't find a map in the van when I searched it before we left."

Dani nodded and peered out the window as she said, "I can direct you. Head straight up here and I'll tell you when to turn."

Dani was staring blindly out the back side door window, lost in thought, when a curse from Justin made her glance curiously his way. She noted the frown on his face and the way his gaze kept dropping to the instrument panel.

"We need gas . . . like now. The warning light is on."

Dani's eyes widened in dismay at this news, and she sat up on her knees to peer out the windshield at the dark road ahead.

"Don't panic," Decker said firmly, noticing her anxiety. "I'm sure we'll find somewhere to stop before we run out."

"And if we don't?" she asked anxiously.

He didn't answer. Instead he turned and leaned forward in his seat to peer out at what lay ahead.

They rode in silence for a couple of tense minutes, and then Decker straightened, eyes squinting briefly before he let his breath out on a relieved sigh and said, "There's a sign up ahead."

"I see it." Justin nodded, relaxing a bit in his seat as he added, "An off ramp in one kilometer."

Dani squinted, trying to see what they claimed to, but all she saw was dark highway and taillights. She spent another moment straining before she could make out the green sign ahead, and it was a moment after that before she could read it in the intermittent lights of the cars preceding them and see that it was indeed an off ramp. Dani then sank back on her haunches, thinking that either the men had been lying to try to keep her from panicking, or she needed to get her eyes checked.

The moment they exited the off ramp, Dani rose up on her knees again, relieved when she spotted the gas station ahead.

"There's a restaurant right next to it," Justin pointed out as he steered them up the road. "If—"

"Jesus, Justin," Decker said with disgust.

"I was only going to say that if Dani wanted to use

the washroom, I'd drop her there, get gas, and come back for her," Justin said dryly, "This might be her only chance until we need gas again."

"Oh," Decker said with a sigh and closed his eyes. Dani took that opportunity to take a good look at the man in the illumination cast over them by the parking lot lights. She hadn't been able to really look at him before this tonight. Not in good light and not even in bad. It seemed to her that every time her eyes had moved his way it was to find him staring back, so her gaze had continually slipped away, gaining just an impression of a handsome man before she looked elsewhere. Now, however, with his eyes closed, she was able to really look at the man Nicholas had assured her she was safe with. He was a very handsome man, she thought as her eyes traveled over his straight nose and firm jaw. He had an interesting mouth, with a thinner upper lip but a full, sensual lower lip. However, he was—at the moment—extremely pale, unhealthily so. It reminded her of the wound he'd taken and made her worry that he'd lost more blood than she'd thought, or that it was infected.

"However," Justin added, distracting her, "now that you've mentioned it, if she wanted to grab me a burger or something while she was in there, she probably has the time and—"

"Bricker," Decker barked, silencing him.

Dani bit her lip, amused despite herself by the exasperation in Decker's voice. It was like riding with the odd couple in this van. While Dani had been staring out the window for most of the ride, she hadn't been completely lost in thought. Half of her attention had been on the brief spurts of conversation the two men had held. She hadn't comprehended all of what they said, she suspected they spoke in code a lot to avoid her understanding, but what she had picked up on was that Justin and Decker were complete opposites.

Justin appeared to enjoy the sound of his own voice and chattered a lot, while Decker was more quiet, speaking only when he had something to say. Justin had claimed at one point to love city life, enjoying the variety and the nightclubs, while Decker had responded that he preferred the peace and quiet of cottage country where he apparently had a second home. Justin enjoyed action movies and sitcoms, while Decker had said he didn't watch much of such things, preferring a good book and cozy fire.

Dani too preferred reading to television, and a cozy fire in a cottage beat out city life for her any day of the week despite—or perhaps because of—the fact that she'd been born and raised in a city and that's where her practice was. She'd also found herself in sympathy with Decker when it came to his obvious exasperation with Justin. It seemed apparent to her that Justin—who seemed younger even though they looked the same age—was deliberately taunting Decker and intentionally exasperating him.

"Dani?"

She let these thoughts slip away and glanced to Decker in question.

"*Do* you want to stop to use the facilities?" he asked.

Dani hesitated. She didn't really have to go to the bathroom, but knew it might be a good idea anyway.

Besides, it would be an opportunity to call her parents and the police, so she murmured, "Yes, thank you."

Decker nodded. He glanced around as Justin pulled into the restaurant parking lot, but then turned back to look at her again. He was going to get a crick in his neck from constantly turning to look back at her if he didn't stop that, she thought absently, and said, "You look pale. How are you feeling?"

"I'm fine," he assured her, waving away her worry. "I just need to feed."

"Then maybe you should get something to eat while we're here," Dani pointed out. She was too worried about her sister to be hungry herself, but could understand if Decker and Justin didn't feel the same way and they would be in the restaurant anyway.

"I'm not hungry," he answered contrarily, his gaze shifting to peer out the windshield as Justin slowed to a stop.

She was about to ask which it was, that he needed to feed or that he wasn't hungry when Justin distracted her by saying, "We'll pick you up as soon as we're done getting gas."

Dani hesitated, but then nodded and shifted across the floor to the door, her gaze sliding to the tarp-covered bodies as she went. While dead bodies didn't normally bother her, these ones were really starting to creep her out. She'd be glad to get away from them, Dani decided as she reached for the door handle. Before she could touch it, it began to move and the door slid aside to reveal Decker. She'd been so distracted she hadn't noticed him getting out of the front seat to help her disembark.

"Thank you." Dani accepted the hand he offered and gripped it as she got to her feet in a bent position and jumped to the ground. A sharp crack and skittering sound made her glance around to see what she'd dropped, and her eyes widened with alarm when she saw her phone lying on the pavement, its back off and lying several feet away beside the battery. She must not have gotten it all the way in her pocket earlier, and the jolt as she'd landed had dislodged it.

"My phone!" she cried with alarm, and, afraid the battery and phone back would be run over, she rushed to grab them first and then turned around to find Decker straightening from collecting the actual phone itself.

"It doesn't look too bad. I'll put it back together while you use the ladies' room," he said, holding out his hand for the items she'd rescued.

"It's okay, I can do it." Dani moved back to him intending to take back the phone.

"Decker, we have to move," Justin called from the driver's seat.

Decker hesitated, and then turned to the van and said, "Go ahead. I'm going to throw some water on my face."

Much to her dismay, he pocketed her cell phone and closed the van door, then caught Dani's arm and urged her toward the restaurant entrance.

"If you'll give it back, I can fix my phone," Dani said as he hustled her into the building.

"Later." Decker sounded distracted and his gaze slid over the people standing in lines at the tills as they moved past them. He escorted her around to the hallway leading to the washrooms and then gave her a little push toward the ladies' room door, saying, "I'll meet you out here when you're done."

Dani pushed her way reluctantly into the bathroom. It seemed she wasn't making the call this time . . . if she could make it at all. The phone looked fine other than the missing battery and backing, but if something had been jarred loose inside . . . She frowned over the possibility as she automatically joined the line of women waiting for a free stall.

"Why is there always a lineup in the women's washroom?" a redhead in front of her complained, drawing her attention. Dani stilled as she saw that the woman was punching out a text message on a cell phone.

"I don't know. I bet the men's room isn't this busy," a brunette responded, and then glanced at the message her friend was sending, and asked, "Telling Harry we're going to be longer than expected?"

"Yeah," the first woman said.

Dani was considering asking to use the woman's phone when she heard the low murmur of Decker's voice from the hall. It was followed by a high, feminine giggle. She glanced curiously in that direction, but the door was closed. When the male murmur she was sure was Decker's came again, she strained to hear what he was saying, but all she could make out was a low rumble of sound and then the female voice said what sounded like "broom closet."

"Hey miss? You're up."

Dani glanced around to see that the redhead was gone, only the brunette remained.

"I don't have to go. I was just keeping Sally company," the woman said when Dani glanced to her with confusion. "The third stall's free though."

"Oh, thanks," she murmured, and moved past her to the third stall. Dani went inside, quickly did her business, and then hurried out, hoping to catch the redhead and use her phone before she left. Unfortunately, Dani stepped out of the stall just in time to see the two women exit the washroom, laughing over something as they went.

Sighing, she moved to the sink, her gaze sliding around the room. It was as Dani washed her hands that it occurred to her that she might be able to borrow someone else's phone to make the call. She had a five-dollar bill and coins in her pocket, change from the grocery store. She could offer it to someone for the trouble. Unfortunately, there was no longer a lineup of women waiting for the washrooms. She turned off the tap and moved to the hand dryer, watching the stalls, waiting for someone to come out so she could ask.

The first person to step out was an older woman who, when asked, said apologetically that she didn't bother with "those things." The second was a middle-aged woman who said hers was in her purse at the table. Since she wasn't carrying a purse, Dani supposed it was probably true. She was about to ask a third woman who was stepping out of a stall with her purse on her arm, when the bathroom door opened and a dark-haired woman paused with it ajar to ask, "Is there a Dani in here?"

"Yes," she said turning to the door with surprise.

"There's a guy out here in the hall wondering what's

taking you so long. He was afraid he'd missed you while he was in the men's room."

"Oh." Dani hesitated, her gaze sliding to the girl she was going to approach about having a phone she might use, and then back to the woman at the door. The dark-haired woman raised her eyebrows, still holding the door open, obviously expecting her to rush right out. Grimacing, Dani decided now obviously wasn't the time and moved toward the door. As she started past the woman, she glanced up to murmur, "Thank you" and then paused with surprise.

"What is it?" she asked.

"There's blood on your neck," Dani informed her. "Just here."

When Dani pointed to the side of her neck, the woman gave a wry laugh and released the door to wipe at it. "Damned blackflies. They were crazy bad up at the cottage this weekend."

Dani opened her mouth to tell her that it didn't look like a blackfly bite to her and that there were, in fact, two of them a little more than an inch apart, but before she could, the woman said, "You'd best get going. It's not smart to leave a man as good-looking as that one waiting. He might decide he'd rather have a woman who doesn't keep him hanging around cooling his heels."

"We're not a couple," Dani said at once.

The dark-haired woman raised her eyebrows doubtfully. "Well, he sure seems to think you are."

Dani flushed, but merely moved past her and out into the hall to find Decker pacing as he waited.

"Oh, there you are." He smiled at her a bit tensely

and then caught her arm to lead her up the hall. "I was beginning to think I'd missed you and that you'd already headed out to the van, but didn't want to leave in case you hadn't."

"There was a line," she said.

"Oh." Decker shook his head. "They must put half the bathrooms in ladies' rooms that they put in men's rooms. We never have lines, and I'm always hearing the complaint that women's washrooms do."

"A lot of women suspect that very thing," Dani assured him as they weaved their way through the queuing people in the open area in front of the tills.

Decker actually chuckled, drawing her curious gaze his way, and she couldn't help but notice that much of his earlier pallor had gone. His cheeks were almost rosy. Apparently getting out of the van and splashing water on his face had helped. That or he had a fever, she thought as he ushered her out of the restaurant. When he drew her to a halt on the sidewalk and glanced around to see where the van was, Dani quickly reached out to place the back of her hand against his cheek.

Decker gave a start and caught her hand as he glanced at her in surprise, and she quickly explained, "I was checking to see if you have a fever."

He relaxed, but raised his eyebrows. "And do I?"

"No. You feel fine," she admitted.

"You sound disappointed," Decker said with amusement.

"No, of course not," Dani said and then admitted, "I'm just a little surprised. You weren't looking nearly as healthy earlier, and I was positive infection was setting in, but you look fine now and don't seem to be in pain."

Decker shrugged. "I'm not. I'm a fast healer and have a hearty constitution."

Before Dani could respond, the van slid to a halt in front of them and Justin leaned out the window. "Finally! I thought you two had set up house inside or something. Get in. We have to get back on the road."

Dani didn't resist when Decker caught her hand and led her around the van. He opened the front passenger door, but rather than get in, turned to catch her arm as she made to move past him to the back door. "I'll ride in the back. You take the front this time."

Glad not to be in the back with the bodies, she murmured thank you and allowed him to help her step up into the van. Decker closed the door as Dani did up her seat belt and then opened the back door and climbed in. Justin pulled away as soon as he'd slid the door closed, heading for the on ramp to the highway.

"What the hell is this?"

Dani glanced around at that irritated question from Decker and found him peering down at two large bags, two small bags, and a carton with three large drinks in it that all sat on the floor between the two front seats.

"What does it look like? It's food," Justin said dryly.

"Yeah, that's what I thought. I just can't believe you hit the drive-through," Decker muttered.

"I didn't. I had the drive-through girl bring it to me while I filled up at the gas station next door."

"How did you manage that?" Dani asked with surprise.

"I . . . used my charm," he muttered, and then added

dryly, "Though I wouldn't have bothered had I realized you guys were going to take so long. I could have gone through the drive-through twice in the time it took you to use the washroom."

Dani looked to Decker to find him rolling his eyes at this claim, and then Justin said, "Can someone unwrap a burger for me and hand it over?"

"You got enough food for an army here, Justin," Decker said with disgust as he pulled out a cheese-burger and began to unwrap it.

Dani didn't comment, but it really was an incredible amount of food for one man, and she had to wonder how she managed to keep in such good shape if he regularly ate like this.

"It isn't all for me," Justin reassured them. "I figured as soon as you saw my food, you'd find your appetites, so I got you each a burger, fries, and a drink. The rest are burgers for me. They're easier to eat while driving than anything else." He paused and glanced down at the food before saying, "Where is that burger?"

"Here." Decker held up the now half-wrapped burger.

Removing one hand from the steering wheel, Justin took it with a murmured thanks and then proceeded to eat the thing in two bites. Dani watched the process with amazement. She'd never seen anything like it. He was a human trash compactor.

Her gaze turned to Decker to see him shaking his head at the display. It was obviously something he'd seen before.

"Can I have another please?" Justin asked. "And maybe one of those drinks?"

Dani leaned over to retrieve the drink while Decker set to work unwrapping a second burger for Justin. She didn't hand it to him, but set it in the drink holder on his side.

"Thanks," he said, and picked up the drink, then paused and glanced worriedly to the second cup holder on her side. "You'll have to get the stuff out of your cup holder before you can use it."

Dani didn't ask what stuff. She knew he meant the bug and tracker, but she didn't have to remove them either. Decker did it for her, reaching in to scoop them out with one hand, as he held up another freshly unwrapped cheeseburger with the other for Justin to take.

"Watch the food," Justin cried, almost sounding panicked at the possibility that Decker might kneel on one of the bags.

"I'm watching," Decker said with exasperation as he dropped the two gizmos in his pocket and settled back on his haunches. He glanced down at the bags of food and asked, "One of these is for me?"

"Yeah," Justin said around a full mouth. "Try it, you might like it."

Dani glanced curiously from one man to the other. He made it sound as if Decker might never have eaten a burger before, which just seemed ridiculous. It was hard to imagine anyone never having at least *tried* a burger. Well, perhaps if he'd been raised a vegetarian, she supposed, but if he was a vegetarian he wouldn't be unwrapping the burger he'd just pulled out of the bag and be taking a healthy bite out of it.

She watched his face, noting the expressions that flitted across it, and would have sworn he really hadn't had one before. "Are you a vegan or something?"

Decker glanced at her with surprise. "No. Why would you ask that?"

"Well, it's like you've never had a burger before."

"He hasn't," Justin informed her. "Decker usually sticks to a liquid diet."

"Justin Bricker," Decker gasped, sounding as shocked as he was horrified by the revelation.

Ignoring him, Dani asked, "You mean protein drinks?"

"Something like that," Justin said evasively. "Their special liquid with lots of protein and—"

"Bricker," Decker snarled now.

"Well, you do," the man said, unrepentant, and then told Dani, "He claims it's too much fuss and bother to eat real food and sticks to a purely liquid diet as a rule."

"Goddammit, Bricker." Decker was nearly rabid with anger now, but the sound of a cell phone ringing made him forget about the man's teasing and start searching his pockets for his phone. His hello when he found and snapped it open was less than welcoming.

Dani watched curiously as he listened, and then he grunted what might have been a good-bye and put the phone away. "We stay on here until Vaughan. They're going to meet us in the parking lot at Outdoor World."

Justin nodded as he swallowed the cheeseburger in his mouth, she suspected without even bothering to chew it. "I know where that is."

"We're stopping?" Dani asked with alarm. Stopping meant Stephanie and the man who had her would just get farther ahead of them.

"Just a quick stop to switch this van for an SUV," Decker assured her.

Dani frowned, but then glanced to the back of the van and muttered, "I suppose it's better than driving around with five dead guys."

"Four," Justin corrected.

"Five," Dani repeated. "There were six in the clearing, and one got away with Stephanie."

The men exchanged a glance, and then Decker admitted, "One was missing from the clearing when we got back. We only managed to get four of them."

"Oh." Dani frowned. She'd thought there were five when she'd looked, but the light had been bad and the bodies were piled on top of each other. There might be only four.

"And don't worry, this won't slow us down much," Justin assured her. "We'll be able to go faster with the SUV. This old van doesn't get above one hundred and thirty kilometers an hour, but our SUVs are juiced up. They really move."

When Dani remained silent, Justin asked Decker, "Who's meeting us at Outdoor World?"

"Eshe," was the answer. "She's bringing a new SUV with supplies. Lucian and Leigh are on their way there too. It sounds like they're a bit behind us, though I don't know how they managed that."

Justin nodded again. "They really should have got there first, but his having to make phone calls probably held them up."

"Who are these people?" Dani asked curiously, twisting in her seat to glance at Decker. "Lucian is your boss, right? But who are Eshe and Leigh?"

"Eshe's another . . . er . . . agent like us," Decker answered, avoiding her eyes.

"She's one of the best. Eshe kicks ass," Justin said with a grin.

"Oh? Eshe is a woman then?" Dani asked, glancing at him curiously. She had a lot of patients with interesting and exotic names, but Eshe was one she'd never come across before this.

Justin nodded and said with admiration, "A whole lotta woman. Six feet tall, lean and mean and moves like a panther. I wouldn't want to go up against her. She's enough to scare a guy straight if he's even considering going rogue."

"Rogue?" Dani peered at him with bewilderment.

"Ignore Justin," Decker said grimly. "He's gone into his comic book fantasy mode. Tell me if he starts drooling and I'll find the napkins."

Dani managed a smile at Decker's words.

"Whatever," Justin said dryly, and then informed her, "Eshe is cool, and Leigh is nice."

"Is she an agent too?" Dani asked, just barely catching herself from saying *enforcer*.

"No. She's Lucian's life mate, though I hear she wants to help out on cases," Justin told her. "I guess it turns out she knows some of that martial arts stuff and can kick ass too."

"Life mate?" Dani asked. It was a term she'd never heard before.

"They aren't married yet," Decker put in.

"Oh."

"Leigh's nice. You'll like her," Justin said suddenly. "But Lucian's a bit of a hard-ass."

Dani shrugged that aside. "It doesn't matter. This is hardly a social occasion. We're just meeting up to switch vehicles."

"True, but I thought I'd better warn you," Justin said. "He can seem a bit harsh at times."

Dani didn't comment; her thoughts were on what she'd learned. Eshe was an agent too, or a Council enforcer as Nicholas had called them. Their boss, Lucian, was a hard-ass, and Leigh was his life mate. She shook her head, suspecting there was a lot about these people that she didn't know and should. Dani was less concerned with that, however, than with worry about her sister. She didn't understand why they had to switch vehicles at all. Did it really matter if they continued on in the van rather than switching for the SUV? While it would be nice not to be driving around with bodies in the back of the vehicle, the stop was going to slow them down, and the man who was holding Stephanie was already an hour ahead of them.

She didn't understand why those bodies were back there, anyway. Why hadn't they left them in the clearing for the police to find as they had the victims in the ravine? That was a question that should have occurred to her at the start, but somehow hadn't. There was a lot that hadn't occurred to her that should have, though. It was almost as if a veil had been drawn over her brain, making her thoughts fuzzy and slow. Perhaps she'd been drugged, she thought suddenly. Perhaps that was why she'd slept and didn't recall dropping off to sleep. Perhaps Justin or Decker, or both, had drugged her.

The possibility made her wonder once again if she shouldn't be trying to get away from these men, but the fact still remained that they were her only link to her sister at the moment. They could track the SUV Stephanie had been taken in, something she didn't think the police could do without more information than she had to give them.

Dani sat fretting over these thoughts as they raced along the highway. Justin was driving much more quickly than was legally allowed, not to mention much more swiftly than was safe, but she didn't comment. The faster they went, the faster they'd catch up to Stephanie, so she merely checked that her seat belt was securely fastened and prayed they didn't get pulled over.

She'd barely had the thought when Justin announced, "We've picked up a cop."

Dani peered into the side mirror to see a police car approaching at speed, lights flashing.

"I've got it," Decker assured him, and barely a heartbeat later, the flashing lights shut off and the police cruiser slowed and began to fall behind. She stared at the disappearing vehicle in the mirror with confusion, not sure what had just taken place. It was just something else for her to fret over as they rushed along the highway. She was so wrapped up in her thoughts that time seemed to fly by, and it was a bit of a shock when she spotted the sign that read Vaughan Mills.

"Here we are," Justin announced as he took an off ramp a few minutes later. "You'll get to meet Eshe and Lucian now."

Chapter Five

Outdoor World was long closed and the parking lot virtually empty as they pulled in. Decker eyed the lone silver SUV there, noting the three people inside. He could make out the distinctive shape of Eshe in the driver's seat, but there were also the bigger, bulkier forms of two men—one in the front passenger seat and one on the back bench seat. It brought a frown to Decker's lips. Lucian hadn't mentioned the woman would have company.

"Eshe's not alone," Justin commented as he turned the steering wheel to park two spots away on the driver's side of the other vehicle.

"Who are the men with her?" Dani asked curiously.

Decker glanced her way to see she was squinting out her window at the neighboring vehicle.

"I don't know," Justin admitted. "I've never seen them before."

When he and Dani then turned to peer back at Decker

in question, he merely shook his head. He'd never seen the pair before either.

"Probably just more enforcers," Justin decided aloud, and Decker turned sharply on him for the slip, but neither he nor Dani appeared to have caught it. Shaking his head, he eased closer to the van's side door and opened it. He got out, grateful not to be on his knees anymore, and then turned to open the door for Dani, noting that Eshe and the men were getting out of the other vehicle as well.

"Thank you," Dani murmured, dropping to the ground in front of him.

Decker nodded and closed the door, then took her arm to lead her toward the approaching trio.

"Jeez," Dani breathed as they neared, and he smiled wryly to himself at the impression she must be getting. Eshe, by herself, was pretty amazing. She was six feet tall as Justin had said, and presently wearing a tight, black leather bodysuit that showed just what he'd meant by lean and mean, but that's not where Decker's attention was. Eshe often sported interesting and unusual hairstyles, always short and often fitting her mood of the moment. Judging by her hair tonight, she'd had a rough week. The tight black curls that usually lay close to her head were standing up in short, kinky waves that had been dyed intermittently blond and red so that it looked almost like fire. Her large, intelligent eyes were flashing gold and black, and the smile of greeting she offered was hard and sharklike, revealing pearly white teeth that contrasted sharply with her lovely mahogany skin. The woman was beautiful and—Decker had noticed—intimidating as hell to most people who met her, both mortal and immortal alike. It seemed Dani was no different.

Either that or it was the men who had her eyes going so wide, he thought, his gaze now moving to the mirror images on either side of Eshe. Paler-skinned and obviously twins, the men too were dressed in leather, but tall as Eshe was, they had a good four to six inches on her. They both had long dark hair; one wore it pulled back in a ponytail, while the other was wearing it loose around his face. However, it was their build that was most startling; the men were a pair of powerhouses, wide and bulky with muscle.

Individually, each of the three people approaching would attract attention; together it was impossible not to gawk, Decker thought, and then noted that each man carried a small black case by its strap. He eyed them curiously, suspecting they held computers, though he wasn't sure for what purpose.

"Did you run into any trouble on the way?" Eshe greeted them when they reached each other.

Decker left Justin to answer the question, sorry he had when the younger immortal seemed to forget Dani's presence and said, "Nah. We had a cop jump on our tail at one point, but Decker did the mind-control thing and sent him on his way."

Eshe nodded and then gestured a bit irritably to the two mountains on either side of her. "This is Dante and Tomasso. They were in the office when Bastien called me, and they insisted on accompanying me."

The one with the ponytail that Eshe had introduced as Tomasso shrugged. "We were bored."

The other, Dante, nodded in agreement. "Yeah.

Christian is always off with Marguerite and Julius, and we've had nothing to do but hang around the office bugging Bastien."

Decker's eyebrows rose at the mention of his aunt Marguerite, her husband, Julius, and their son Christian. It suddenly clicked in his mind who these men were.

"You're Nottes," Justin said with realization even as he thought it. "You're Christian's cousins from Italy. The twins."

The two men nodded, and Dante said, "And you're Justin Bricker and"—his gaze shifted to Decker— "Martine's son, Decker. You weren't at the family gathering."

"I was on a job when Marguerite got everyone together," Decker said quietly.

"She said as much," Tomasso assured him, offering his hand. Decker accepted it, and as they shook in greeting, Tomasso admitted, "That's part of the reason we came out with Eshe. To meet you."

"Yeah," Dante said as he next shook hands with him, and then, sparkling eyes darting to Eshe, he added, "Besides, we couldn't allow the little lady to drive all the way out here by herself in the middle of the night."

He received an elbow in the stomach from Eshe for his effort. It was no playful jab, but a blow that made him double over in surprised pain. She glared at Tomasso when he started laughing, and snapped, "If the two of you boys don't stop talking like that, I'm going to show you what this *little lady* can do."

This didn't seem to curb their amusement any. Decker had worked with Eshe several times and knew the woman well. He could have warned the men that they were playing with fire, but then decided to let them learn the hard way. It wouldn't be a lesson soon forgotten and would make for one hell of a show.

"What's in the cases?" Justin asked Dante and Tomasso curiously.

"Portable computers set up to track the stolen SUV," Eshe explained. "One is for Lucian and one is for Mortimer. We're to wait for both men here to hand them over. There's a third one in the SUV for you guys."

"Nice," Justin commented.

"Better than hunting blind," Eshe said with a shrug. "Though, if you two hadn't let your ride get stolen—"

"Their eyes," Dani said suddenly, distracting Decker from the irritation that Eshe had managed to stir with the start of her comment. Turning, he peered down at her as she swiveled to frown at him with confusion. "Their eyes shine like a cat's in this darkness. They . . ." She paused, eyes widening, and then said with amazement, "So do yours. They look all silver-blue."

Decker caught the way Eshe's eyebrows rose, but muttered, "It must be a trick of the light."

"This is the woman we're supposed to take back, then?" Eshe asked. "Why aren't one of you controlling her?"

"I would, but Decker won't let me," Justin announced, and then added significantly, "And he *can't*."

"No one controls me," Dani said grimly. "And I'm not going anywhere."

Catching the way Eshe's eyes flashed a deep gold with black flecks, Decker caught Dani's arm and hurried her away from the group, managing to get her a good distance past the SUV before she began to struggle. Deciding it was far enough, he turned her to face him.

"It might be better if you waited here and let me handle this," he suggested quietly before she could get out the words that were trembling on her tongue.

Dani hesitated, her eyes sliding back to the group by the vehicles. Decker glanced back as well to find that everyone was watching them with curiosity as Justin said something. Suspecting he didn't want to know what that was, Decker sighed and turned back to Dani, reclaiming her attention by saying, "I'll talk to them. I won't leave you behind."

Dani's eyes narrowed rebelliously, and he wasn't terribly surprised when she said, "You'd better not. I know you've been lying to me and aren't with CSIS, and the only reason I'm not at a police station right now screaming bloody murder is because you can track the SUV. You're my only link with my sister at present, Decker, but if you leave without me, I'll go straight to the police and tell them everything I know."

"I understand," he said with a solemn nod, not bothering to mention that she wouldn't get the chance to call anyone. Eshe would take control of her mind and see to that if he didn't convince the woman to leave Dani with him. He was hoping that wouldn't come to pass, however. He really didn't have any intention of leaving her behind or letting anyone else sift through her thoughts and control her actions, so he added, "But please stay here and let me handle it. All right?"

Dani crossed her arms angrily, but gave a stiff nod.

Just as he turned away, she pleaded, "Just hurry. The more time we waste here, the further away Stephanie gets."

Decker merely nodded as he made his way across the parking lot to the group.

"You've found your life mate," Dante said quietly as he rejoined them. "Congratulations."

"Thanks," Decker muttered, and then glanced to Eshe.

"My orders were to bring her in," the woman said, voice hard.

Decker shook his head. "She stays with me."

"Then you'd better call Lucian, because I do what I'm told and I was told to bring her in."

Decker snorted. He was about to point out that she only did what she was told when she felt like it when Dante said, "No need to call him. Lucian is here."

Turning, Decker glanced in the direction Dante was looking and watched a second SUV park, this one on the other side of the van.

Decker scowled. He would have fought Eshe if necessary to keep Dani with him, but you just didn't argue with Lucian. Or, at least, you did your best to avoid it. Decker feared in this case he was going to have to argue the point. No one, not even Lucian, was getting between him and Dani.

"Lucian's found his own life mate now," Eshe commented as they watched him get out and walk around the vehicle. As Lucian opened the passenger door for Leigh, she added, "He may understand and let you keep her with you."

Decker frowned at the comment. He'd heard a few

say the man had softened since finding Leigh. But he hadn't seen anything to suggest that was true. His uncle was still a hard-boiled rock as far as he could tell.

"Why is everyone standing around?" Lucian growled as he reached them. His eyes skated over the group before coming to rest sharply on Decker. "Where are the rogues?"

"In the van," he said at once, following when his uncle abruptly turned and ushered Leigh to the back of the vehicle. Once there, Lucian grasped the door and then paused and turned to glare at Decker. "It isn't closed."

"What?" Decker moved up beside him and saw that it was true, the door wasn't shut tight.

"Sloppy," Lucian snapped. "You're lucky it didn't fly open and spill bodies out on the highway. Wouldn't that have been fun to explain?"

Decker held his tongue. It *had* been sloppy, he acknowledged as he watched Lucian pull on the door, but while it wasn't quite closed, it had caught enough that it didn't pop open until he pushed the button to release the catch. He swung the door wide and then opened the second door as well, and everyone crowded around as he grabbed one corner of the tarp and threw it back. They were all silent as he peered over the bodies. "How long have they been staked?"

"Since we left the clearing," Decker said. "I didn't want them recovering and causing trouble."

Lucian nodded and murmured, "The stakes will have to be removed soon so they can survive for their trial."

Decker just nodded, knowing the Council would insist on their thoughts being read to find out just how much trouble they'd caused before they would pass sentence. The enforcers usually had a good deal of information on a rogue and what they'd been up to before going after them. If they had enough information, sometimes they could exterminate the rogue on the spot and start cleanup right away as had been done in the most recent case in Kansas, but they knew nothing about these men and the damage they might have done. That would have to be found out before anything else could be done.

"Who are they?" Leigh asked, slipping her hand into Lucian's as she peered at the bodies.

"They bear a striking resemblance to Leonius," he murmured, a troubled expression claiming his face.

"Leonius?" Decker asked, not recognizing the name.

"Leonius Livius," Lucian clarified. "He was one of the few original Atlanteans who escaped when it fell."

"Edentata," Eshe breathed, apparently recognizing the name.

"What is edentata?" Leigh asked with confusion.

Lucian shifted and then said, "*Edentate* is Latin for no teeth. Edentata are immortals who have no fangs to help them get what they need to survive. The ones who are sane are called edentates. However, the ones who are plagued with insanity and go rogue are usually called no-fangers to differentiate the two. Leonius Livius was a no-fanger." Lucian paused before adding, "But he fell in battle a couple millennia ago."

"Maybe he had children before he died," Decker suggested.

"He did, but they all fell in the same battle with him.

We made sure," Lucian muttered, and then leaned in to examine one of the men more closely. He peered at his face, then opened his mouth to peer inside, and reached in to push on the palate behind the canine teeth. After a moment he straightened and shook his head. "No fangs."

"How can you tell?" Justin asked curiously, making it obvious he'd never dealt with an edentata before.

Decker wasn't surprised. They had been killed off over time and were pretty rare these days. Decker had only ever run into one himself in his two hundred and fifty-nine years. He explained, "If you push on the roof of your mouth behind the canines, they'll slide out on us whether you want them to or not, but with the edentata there are no fangs to come out."

Justin reached into his own mouth. He must have pushed on the palate behind his right fang, because that's the one that slid forward and down.

"Cool," he said, removing his finger and allowing the tooth to slide back into place. "I never knew we could do that."

"Why didn't they develop fangs?" Leigh asked. "And how did they survive?"

"I'll explain later," Lucian assured her, and then turned to Decker. "Where's the girl?"

Decker turned and gestured to where Dani was pacing under a lamppost and casting glares their way. She was impatient to be off, he knew.

"What is she doing over there?" Lucian asked with dismay. "And why isn't someone controlling her?"

"She's Decker's life mate," Justin said quickly, no doubt trying to head off Lucian's mounting temper, but all it did was make Lucian turn on Decker and start to shuffle through his thoughts. Decker could feel it happening, but didn't try to block him, if he even could.

"CSIS?" Lucian asked with disbelief, bringing curious glances from everyone but Justin. Decker squirmed inwardly as his uncle continued to sift through his thoughts, and then Lucian shook his head with disgust. "And you haven't explained to her about us? First Mortimer, and now you . . . Am I the only one who made it through this life mate business with my brains still intact?"

From what Decker had heard, Lucian had been a bit befuddled too, but he kept that thought to himself and merely said, "I was waiting for the right moment."

"Right. Well, that's now," Lucian announced, and glanced in Dani's direction to bark, "Girl!"

Dani was in the process of pacing away and didn't turn at the shout. She probably had no idea it was she he was shouting at, Decker thought.

"What's her name?" Lucian asked impatiently, and then shook his head. "Never mind."

His eyes narrowed with concentration on Dani. She came to an abrupt halt, and then turned and walked over to stand in front of Lucian.

Decker waited, aware that his uncle was no doubt now controlling and reading Dani. He knew exactly when his uncle released her by the confusion that immediately clouded her face as she peered around at them.

"What—?" Dani said uncertainly and then paused, concern crossing her face.

"Your mind isn't faulty and you're not losing time,"

Lucian said, apparently reading that concern in her mind. "The reason you don't remember walking over here is because I took control of your mind to bring you here . . . And I can do that because I'm an immortal . . . or as you people seem to insist on calling us, a vampire," he said with disdain. "Everyone standing here is one . . . including Decker, who is the only one here who can't read or control your thoughts. That makes you a possible life mate for him, but you'll be the one to decide."

Now that he had Dani standing there with her mouth open, Lucian held out his hand in front of Eshe. When she placed the keys to the SUV in his palm, he turned to hand them to Decker saying, "Right! Now that I've got the hard part out of the way, get her in the SUV and get your asses moving. You can explain the rest on the way."

"Just a minute," Dani protested when Decker took her arm to lead her to the vehicle. "I—"

"There is no just a minute," Lucian said coldly. "We still have a pair of rogues and a young girl in peril out there. Your sister, I believe. Either get moving now, or you will be going with Eshe."

Decker suspected threatening her with Eshe hadn't been necessary; Dani had stopped trying to make him drop her arm the minute her sister was mentioned. He led a much subdued Dani to the new vehicle, opened the side door and ushered her in, then turned and handed the keys to Justin. "You drive."

Justin accepted the keys without question and turned away to walk back around to the driver's side. Decker was about to climb into the back with Dani when

Lucian called out his name. Pausing, he walked back around the vehicle to find his uncle walking to meet him halfway.

"Is there something else?" he asked stiffly, annoyed with him for his treatment of Dani.

Lucian nodded. "I gather you and Justin had some plan to trap Nicholas using the bug and tracker from the van?"

Decker's eyebrows flew up. They'd planned to talk to the others and tell them about their idea when they got here, but had forgotten. "How did you know?"

"I read it from her mind."

Decker glanced back toward the SUV when Lucian gestured toward it. "From Dani? But she doesn't know—"

"She eavesdropped on your conversation with Justin, and then proceeded to speak into the bug and give Nicholas her number to call. He did, and she told him all about your plan."

"Why would she—?"

"Because she doesn't trust you," Lucian interrupted. "She knows Nicholas was tracking these men and is the reason she and her sister were saved. She also knows he is even now chasing after her sister, trying to save her. Everything she knows about you, though, is confused by lies. You've made such a shambles of trying to keep what you are a secret, she doesn't trust you as much as she trusted Nicholas who she hadn't even talked to." He let that sink in, and then added, "You need to explain things and gain her trust if you want her as your life mate."

Decker nodded solemnly.

"Now, get going. We have work to do."

Decker turned away and jogged back to the SUV.

Justin had the computer up and running and was talking on his cell phone when Decker stepped up into the back of the vehicle and pulled the door closed.

"Thanks, Bastien. I think I've got it now." Justin ended the call and slid his cell phone into his pocket. He then smiled at Decker and said, "Look at this stuff. Talk about cool. I guess Bastien hired some techno geeks after all the rigmarole they had to go through to get Marguerite's cell phone tracked in Europe. They came up with this. Look." He pointed to the screen. "That blue dot there is us, the green one beside it is Lucian's vehicle, and the black one is the stolen SUV." Justin frowned. "It's on Highway 427 nearly to Etobicoke rather than heading into downtown Toronto like we expected."

Decker nodded silently, wondering where the rogue holding Stephanie was headed. They'd all been sure he'd try to lose himself in the city. Lucian had several immortals, including enforcers and volunteers, waiting at different spots in Toronto to converge on the vehicle when it did.

"Etobicoke?" Dani asked, leaning forward to peer at the screen. "That's not an hour from here, is it?"

"It's only half an hour from here. I caught up a bit," Justin said cheerfully.

Decker noted the wry expression on Dani's face and guessed she wasn't terribly surprised. Justin had been driving like a bat out of hell since leaving Parry Sound.

"Who are those other colored dots?"she asked now.

"Other enforcers," Justin answered. "That yellow one is my usual partner, Mortimer, and his life mate, Sam." His eyebrows drew together as he noted the position of the dot. "They're still a good hour or more behind us. I hope your pickup hasn't been giving them trouble."

"My pickup is not giving them a hard time," Decker assured him, and then, catching the curious look Dani cast his way, he explained, "The vehicle that was stolen was a company one Mortimer and Justin drove up from Toronto. Mortimer and Sam are in my personal pickup, which has a company GPS in it."

"It has a cab on the back with a bed too," Justin said, eyebrows wiggling. "And they're new life mates, kind of like newlyweds only times a thousand. They'll need the bed."

Decker rolled his eyes and told Dani, "Yes, it has a bed, and that's why I suggested they take it, but not for the reason Justin is hinting at. Sam is mortal, which means they can double-team it. Sam could show Nicholas's picture around during the day while Mortimer slept and he could do it at night while she slept."

"He spoils everything, doesn't he?" Justin complained, turning in the driver's seat to start the engine.

Decker settled on the backseat next to Dani and buckled up and then turned to peer at her as she did the same, wondering what she must be thinking. She hadn't said a word about Lucian's revelations yet.

Finished with her seat belt, Dani turned to him and asked, "Lucian is your uncle, isn't he?"

"Yes."

She nodded, her expression thoughtful, and then asked, "So insanity runs in the family then?"

Justin burst out laughing from the front seat, and Decker turned a scowl on the younger man. He took a deep breath for patience before returning his attention to Dani. It was obvious she hadn't believed a word his uncle had told her, and he briefly considered what he might say that could possibly convince her. And then he had an idea.

"What are you doing? Stop that," Dani said when Decker began to undo his shirt.

"I'm just showing you my gunshot wound," he said soothingly.

"Oh," Dani relaxed a little, but not completely. She couldn't have said for sure why she found the idea of seeing his naked chest more disturbing this time than when she'd taken out the bullet. Possibly it was because, despite everything, she found she was starting to like him, but whatever the case, she was having difficulty pulling on her professional persona this time. Instead she sat watching him undoing button after button, her eyes eating up inch after inch of pale flesh revealed until she had to force her eyes away.

"Okay," Decker said a moment later.

Dani turned back reluctantly to find he'd tugged the shirt open and off the injured shoulder. Her eyes skated over all that pale marble flesh and then froze. She leaned closer, and then snapped, "I need a light."

Justin immediately flicked on the overhead light, casting a strong, harsh glow over everything, including Decker's bullet wound. Dani peered at it closely, noting that it had shrunk in size and was knitting itself together. Were someone to ask her how old the wound was, she would have guessed several days, possibly a week. Her mind immediately began running around in circles, searching out all her medical training and trying to find an explanation for how it could possibly have healed that quickly, but nothing was presenting itself.

Dani sat back and peered at him silently for a full minute and then said quietly, "That's not humanly possible."

"It's not *mortally* possible," he corrected, just as quietly.

"Show her your teeth," Justin said from the front seat.

Decker opened his mouth, and she watched with sick fascination as his canine teeth slowly shifted forward and down, becoming what could only be described as fangs. When she then turned to the rearview mirror, Justin raised his head slightly and allowed his own teeth to push out of his mouth. Dani swiftly turned her head back, caught sight of Decker's teeth retracting, quickly dropped her eyes to his chest and the nearly healed bullet wound, and then turned and reached for the door handle, fully intending to make a jump for it.

Only her forgotten seat belt prevented it. She managed to get the door open before Decker could react, but the seat belt held her in place when she tried to jump.

"Dani!" Decker grabbed her with one hand as she began to try to undo her seat belt and pulled the door closed with the other, then forced her around to face him. "Look at me. I need you to listen. You're safe. I won't harm you. You must realize that. If I wanted to hurt you I would have done it long ago. You're safe."

He repeated the words over and over until she stopped struggling and forced herself to be calm in his hands.

"It's okay," he said then. "I know this is hard to accept, and scary for you, but you have to let me explain. You owe me that much at least, don't you think?"

"Owe you?" she asked with surprise, finally raising her face to peer at him again.

It was Justin who pointed out judiciously, "Well, he did take a couple of bullets back there when we saved you. Surely you should at least let him explain?"

Chapter Six

A couple of bullets?" Dani asked, turning back to Decker.

"It doesn't matter," he said quietly.

Dani frowned, but then decided he was right and it didn't really matter. What mattered was that this was the oddest nightmare she'd ever had in her life and she wished it would end. She wanted to wake up and assure herself everything was all right, that Stephanie was at home with her parents or even at the cottage, safe and unharmed.

"Dani?" Decker said, eyeing her uncertainly.

Her gaze focused on the face of the dream man before her, and she found herself wondering where her imagination had come up with that handsome visage. Had she seen him around Windsor or up at the cottage, thought him attractive, and inserted his face in her dream? If so, she really should have made him a cop or some other good guy rather than a fang-bearing vampire.

"Are you calm enough to listen to me?" the dream Decker asked, taking her hands. He looked pretty doubtful on that score.

However, Dani felt perfectly calm, though that was a relative term, she decided, and glanced down at her hands. She tried to shake off his hold, intending to pinch herself, but he merely tightened his grip, watching her with concern. Not seeing any other recourse, Dani suddenly threw her head backward, slamming it into the not-a-dream SUV's rear side window.

"What are you doing?" Decker bellowed, reaching for her.

"Trying to wake myself up," she muttered wryly as he caught her by the shoulders as if to keep her from doing it again. He needn't have bothered; the pain presently radiating through Dani's skull was enough to convince her she wasn't dreaming. It seemed she was awake and in an SUV with two men who claimed to be vampires . . . and who also had the fangs to back up the claim.

"She thinks she's dreaming," Justin said quietly from the front, his usual amusement notably absent. "I think she's realizing the truth though."

"Stay out of her thoughts," Decker said, but his voice was more resigned than angry, and Dani wondered what he was talking about when he said it. She didn't really care though, except that it was a bit annoying not to know what they were talking about half the time.

"Dani," Decker said firmly. "Trust me, this is not a dream."

"Why is it you men always say trust me before spitting out something completely unpalatable?" she asked, irritation flickering through her. "Vampires aren't supposed to be real. And how come you had to be a cute vampire? You should be a dog. All evil, vile people should look as ugly as they are inside."

"We aren't ev—" Decker halted his denial, and then he did something she hadn't yet seen him do and lifted his lips in a very rare—and in her opinion, totally inappropriate—grin as he asked, "You think I'm cute?"

"Earth to Major Decker," Justin said dryly. "She thinks you're a cute *evil bastard*."

"Right." He frowned and shook his head as if trying to shake her words out of it, and then said, "We're not evil or vile. We aren't even vampires."

"But you have fangs, and that Lucian fellow said—"

"He said your people insisted on calling us that," Decker reminded her firmly. "But we aren't."

"Well, we kind of are," Justin corrected. "We just don't like to be called that. At least the old bloodsuckers don't. I don't know why. I think it's kind of sexy myself." Taking on a bad fake accent he said, "I am a vampire, and I vant to suck your—"

"Justin," Decker said with thinly stretched patience. "You aren't helping here."

"Sorry," he muttered. "But we do have fangs and drink blood and—"

"Bricker," Decker snapped, turning to glare at him.

"Right. Sorry, I'll zip it." He met Decker's gaze in the mirror and mimed zipping his mouth shut. But the moment Decker stopped glaring at him and turned back to Dani, he piped up again. "Tell her about Atlantis."

Decker sagged, his eyes closing briefly, and then he took a deep breath and said, "Yes, Justin, I was just about to do that."

"Atlantis?" Dani echoed with bewilderment.

"Or maybe you better start with the nanos," Justin said, changing his mind. "She's a doctor. She'll understand the science part of it better."

"Yes, I know. Thank you, Justin, *I can handle this*," Decker said grimly, obviously on the edge of really losing it. He then turned to Dani, eyed her with a sigh, and asked, "Will you at least listen to me?"

Dani nodded. It wasn't like she really had any choice, not after having seen those fangs.

"Okay," Decker said with relief. "We're human. If you were to cut me open you'd find everything exactly the same as any other man, except that all my organs and tissue would be remarkably healthy and undamaged."

"Everything is exactly the same but our blood," Justin put in.

"That's true," Decker acknowledged. "Our blood is different. It has nanos in it. At least that's as good a description as any." When Dani simply stared at him, he explained, "You see, our scientists were trying to develop a way to repair or remove things like cancer, infection, and serious injuries without resorting to surgery and inflicting further trauma on the body. What they came up with were nanos, little bio-engineered gizmos that were programmed to travel through the bloodstream. They used the blood both to fuel and regenerate themselves, as well as to make repairs in the body, regenerate tissue, or surround and kill off any infection or illness that may be present."

Dani nodded to encourage him to continue. So far what he'd told her wasn't anywhere near crazy. She had read about recent experiments using just such technology for a similar purpose.

"They succeeded beyond their expectations," Decker continued. "The nanos did go in and perform repairs and kill off infections and cancer, and anything else that attacked the body. It was hailed as a medical breakthrough. The sick and injured lined up in droves to receive it. My mother's parents were among those first infected with them."

"Whoa, back up," Dani interrupted at once, "Your mother's parents? Your *grandparents*?"

Decker nodded. "My grandmother, Alexandria, had what is now called cancer and my grandfather, Ramses, was seriously injured in an accident. Both were terminal. They were subject one and two, both treated at the same time. It's how they met. They were married three months later, and my uncle Lucian and his twin brother Jean Claude were born a little less than nine months after that. They were the first born infected."

"Oh, see now." Dani sat back, shaking her head. "You were doing really well right up until the grandparents bit. Before that you had me suckered, but there is no way they had this kind of technology fifty years ago."

"Fifty?" Justin snorted, meeting her gaze in the rearview mirror when she turned his way. "Try several thousand."

Decker took a moment to toss a glare in his direction and then turned back to Dani. "This is the part that's hard to believe." He paused and took a breath and then said, "Our ancestors came from Atlantis."

"Atlantis," she said with open disbelief. "*Atlantis*, Atlantis? The legendary lost land?"

"Yes. As the legends claim, Atlantis was highly advanced technologically. Unfortunately, it was also terribly insular and didn't share that technology with anyone. They didn't share anything with anyone. They lived surrounded by sea on three sides, with mountains between them and the rest of the world, and it was how they liked it. So when Atlantis fell, those who survived crossed the mountains to find themselves in a much more primitive world. They had no way to store blood or perform transfusions."

"Wait a minute," Dani interrupted. "You skipped from a miracle cure to no blood and transfusions. Why the need for bl—?"

"The nanos used a lot of blood to support themselves and make repairs. More than the human body can create. Transfusions had to be given to those who had been treated with the nanos. That was fine in Atlantis, but when Atlantis fell . . ."

"No more transfusions," she said, struggling now with whether to believe him or not. Some of it actually made a mad sort of sense.

"Right, and that's when the nanos began to change our people. They had been programmed to repair and regenerate and basically keep their host alive and at their peak condition physically. Without blood, our ancestors would have died, so the nanos changed them in ways that would help them stay alive and at their peak health-wise. It made them fast and strong so that they could get the blood the nanos needed."

"The eyes," she murmured with realization. "Your eyes reflect light like a cat or raccoon."

"Because we are nocturnal hunters like them," Decker said quietly.

"You said this Sam is a mortal so she can canvass during the day while Mortimer slept. You can't go out in sunlight?"

"We can," he admitted. "But as a doctor you know that the sun causes damage, which means the nanos have more work, which means a need for even more blood. We feed on bagged blood now, but before blood banks and bagged blood, we were forced to feed off our neighbors and friends. And we did our best to minimize how much feeding we needed to do."

"And the nanos brought on the fangs too?" she asked.

He nodded. "They gave us all the physical attributes needed to make us better hunters."

"I see," Dani murmured, glancing down to her hands and trying to take it all in. It was a lot to swallow, almost as hard to believe as the old legend about dead, soulless creatures cursed to walk the earth for some past sin. The science was one thing, but Atlantis? Thousands of years ago? True, she'd come across legends about the fabled Atlantis over the years, but those were just myth. Weren't they?

"Would it be easier for you to believe if I claimed we were the cursed undead?" Decker asked wryly. As if reading her mind, she thought, and that reminded her about Nicholas and Lucian's claim that they could read and even control her.

"You say they gave you the physical attributes needed to make you better hunters. Is that all?" she asked, eyes narrowing on him.

He hesitated and then admitted, "No. They also developed our ability to read thoughts and control minds too. It helps us to—"

"What am I thinking right now?" she interrupted abruptly.

Decker shook his head. "As Lucian said, I can't read you, Dani."

"I can," Justin said, drawing her gaze. "You're thinking of your sister."

Dani turned to frown at the man. "That was too easy. Of course I'd be thinking of her. Try again," she ordered, searching her mind until she came up with something else.

"A giraffe," Justin said.

"Again," she demanded.

"A purple elephant." This time he answered almost before she finished asking. "Shall I control you now?"

"Can you?" she asked, eyes narrowing, and then glanced down with shock as her hands rose and clapped several times.

"Enough," Decker barked, taking her hands in his.

"She asked," Justin said defensively.

Dani stared at Decker, her hands unmoving in his, and asked a little shakily, "How? Why can't you if he can?"

He met her gaze, and then glanced away without answering. It was Justin who said, "Because you're his life mate."

Dani's gaze flickered to the man, her mind recalling Lucian mentioning this earlier, but she turned to Decker when she asked, "What is a life mate?"

He let his breath out on a sigh. His gaze dropped to their hands, rose to meet hers again, and finally he said, "The nanos don't just allow us to read mortal's minds. We can read each other too if we don't keep our guard up to block others from intruding on our thoughts. It makes life somewhat . . ." Decker shook his head. "It can be exhausting. So much so that some immortals avoid others as much as possible just so that they don't constantly have to be on guard. But isolating oneself can lead to depression, rage, and madness, and an immortal going rogue." He paused briefly, and then explained, "A life mate is that very rare person whom we can't read and who can't read us. They can be mortal or immortal, but being with them is like an oasis of calm. We can relax and be ourselves around them without fear that they'll hear every thought we have. And, since we can't read them, we aren't bombarded with their thoughts either. They can be a true mate, someone we can't read or control and whom we can spend our long lives with, happily."

Dani stared at him, recalling exactly what Lucian had said: *I'm an immortal . . . or as you people seem to insist on calling us, a vampire . . . Everyone standing here is one . . . including Decker, who is the only one here who can't read or control your thoughts. That makes you a possible life mate for him, but you'll be the one to decide.*

He'd said *possible* life mate and that she'd have to decide. Did that mean she might not be? Or that she was Decker's life mate, but that she could reject him if she wished? Before she could ask, Justin suddenly said, "Decker?"

He turned reluctantly away from Dani to glance at Justin. "What?"

"Sorry to interrupt, but I'm speeding and we've picked up a radar cop. I could try to handle him myself, but I don't want to take my concentration off the road."

"I'll handle it," Decker said, and glanced out the rear window.

Dani twisted in her seat to watch what could have been an instant replay of their first encounter with the other officer. The flashing lights on top of the cruiser were suddenly shut off and the car slowed and dropped away. When she could no longer see it anymore, Dani turned back to Decker. "You controlled him and the other officer who was on our tail earlier."

When he nodded solemnly, she asked, "But you can't control me?"

He shook his head, and Dani's eyes narrowed. "But Justin can?"

His nod this time was almost reluctant, as if he suspected a trap.

"So it was Justin who made me sleep in the back of the van after the incident in the clearing?" Dani asked, already suspecting she knew the answer. It would explain why she couldn't recall actually getting into the van and going to sleep.

Decker winced at her sharp tone, but nodded.

"What else has he made me do?" she asked, her voice going cold.

"Nothing," he assured her solemnly.

"Why should I believe that when you've done nothing but lie to me from the minute I met you?"

"I only lied because, had I told you the truth, you would have thought us mad . . . and you were already shaken up after your encounter with the rogues and were hardly in the mood to trust us," he said firmly. "We are Council enforcers, Dani. Vampire cops, if you like. Our people have laws and we have to enforce them. We hunt rogue immortals that break our laws."

"What kind of laws?" Dani asked, relaxing a little. She could hardly argue that he should have told her the truth from the start. Decker was right. She hadn't been in any condition for this little revelation then. Heck, she wasn't sure she was ready for it now, but she was beginning to accept it, and a lot of her fear was slipping away with every passing minute.

"The first and most important one is not to feed off of, or harm, mortals."

She liked that law, Dani decided. "What else?"

"Couples are allowed to have only one child every hundred years."

That one made her frown. "Why?"

"It's intended to keep our population low. We need blood to survive. Having too many of us with that need could be a problem."

She understood that, but the rule still made her uncomfortable. What did they do to immortals who had more than one child in a hundred years? What did they do with the child? Before she could ask, Justin announced, "I think our rogue has just taken the Dixon Road exit."

"Dixon?" Dani swiveled her head to peer at the screen, alarm bells going off in her head and drowning out any worry about immortal babies. "That's where the airport is."

Decker cursed and unbuckled his seat belt to shift to his knees between the front seats so he could better watch the computer screen. Sure enough, the little black dot had taken the Dixon turnoff.

"He couldn't be thinking to try to catch a flight or

something, could he?" Dani asked from beside him, and Decker glanced around to see that she'd unbuckled as well and was moving to join him.

"Get your seat belt back on," he growled, very aware that at the speed Justin was driving, she'd probably be killed if they were in an accident.

Dani ignored him, her eyes locked on the computer screen. "He can't be thinking to take Stephanie on a plane. She has no passport, or—"

"I'm sure he's not," Decker assured her, even though he wasn't at all certain of that himself. Lack of a passport wasn't an issue when you could control the minds of the people asking for it. "Now get back in your seat and put the seat belt on."

"It's hard to see this. It's too small," Dani said, ignoring him again, and glanced to Justin. "Is there a way to make the image bigger?"

"I'll do it," Decker grumbled, not wanting Justin to be distracted. He used the portable's mouse pad to zoom in on the section of map where the black dot was, and then sat back. "There."

"Oh God, he *is* on the off ramp," Dani said with horror as the image came into focus on a much larger scale. "He has to be going to the airport. If they leave the SUV we have no way to track them."

"Don't panic," Decker ordered, and then pointed to a brown dot that was also on the ramp. "Look, one of our guys isn't far behind him. And Nicholas is probably still on his tail. Besides, I don't think there are flights out at this hour."

"There are flights until half past midnight," Dani said tensely.

Decker glanced at his watch, frowning when he saw that it wasn't even midnight yet. He was a bit surprised it was so early. It felt like a lifetime had passed since he'd realized he couldn't read or control Dani.

"They'll get him, Dani," Justin said. Fortunately, he kept his eyes on the road ahead as he spoke. "We're like Mounties, we get our man. His stopping just means it could all be over and you could have your sister back soon."

Dani didn't respond. Her eyes were glued to the computer screen, watching the little dot as if taking her eyes off might mean it would disappear, taking her sister with it. Decker wanted to tell her to get back in her seat and buckle up again, but knew she would fight him on it. He almost had Justin take control of her and make her do it, but Bricker was driving so fast, Decker didn't want to risk taking his attention away from the road even long enough to perform that small task. So instead he sat silent, his worried gaze shifting between Dani, the screen, and the road ahead to take in the other cars on the highway. It wasn't as busy as it would be during the day, but it was busy enough, and Justin was weaving in and out of traffic at a scary rate.

Decker's gaze slid back to Dani and his gut clenched at the idea of losing her to an accident if one of those cars should suddenly cut them off. It made him shift a little closer to her, and raise one arm behind her back to brace it on Justin's seat. He then moved his other hand in front of his stomach, preparing to grab her and hold on if anything should happen.

Sitting so close to Dani, Decker found himself immediately enveloped in her scent. It was an aroma not dissimilar to strawberries, and rolled over him, sweet and delicious. He'd noticed it earlier while she'd tended his gunshot wound, but had been distracted at the time with both the phone call to Lucian and worry over her noticing something amiss with his wound. He was noticing now, however, and without thinking, he moved in closer, his head turning to allow him to inhale the slightly intoxicating scent more fully. It was like wine, sweet yet pungent, and for some reason, it made him hungry.

"He's turning," Dani said tensely.

Decker started to glance at the screen, but his gaze didn't make it that far. It paused on her profile as she anxiously licked her lips. He found himself watching with fascination as the pink tip of her tongue slid along a mouth that looked incredibly soft and full.

"How close are our guys?" Justin asked, glancing around.

"Keep your eyes on the road," Decker growled, his hunger adding gravel to his voice. His gaze slid reluctantly to the screen and he peered at it closely. The brown dot representing one of their SUVs was now on the ramp. A gray one was still on the 427, but only minutes behind. His gaze slid back to the first two dots and he murmured, "It looks like he's turned into the car park. Our guy isn't far behind."

"I think he's stopped," Dani said with concern.

Decker leaned in and made the image bigger still. "No, he's just going slow."

"Maybe he doesn't realize he's being followed and is looking for parking?" Justin suggested.

Decker grunted. "Our guy's right behind him now

and the others are coming off the ramp and catching up."

"Who is in the SUV following him?" Dani asked.

"I don't know," Decker admitted. "Lucian didn't tell me who else he was able to call in at such short notice."

They both watched silently as the gray dot caught up to the other two and all three dots came to a halt, almost overlapping one another.

"They're stopped," Dani said anxiously.

"They probably have him then," Justin said with certainty.

"Do you think so?" she asked, hope trembling in her voice.

"If not him, then they probably at least have your sister," Justin said, and then pointed out, "She's mortal. She'd slow him down. He'll either have to let her go or try to run for the airport to get lost in the crowd with her, and there's no way he could outrun our guys on foot dragging her along. Besides, it's late, the airport can't be that crowded at this hour. When we get there they'll either have both of them, or one will have her and the other will be chasing down the rogue in the airport."

Dani seemed to fold into herself with relief at those words, and Decker let his hand drop to rub her back soothingly, his head instinctively ducking to inhale her scent again.

"Hold on, some idiot just—" Justin didn't finish the sentence; he was too busy braking hard and swerving to avoid whatever "idiot" had interrupted his speedy pass up the highway. The action threw Decker forward, and he instinctively caught Dani as he went, crushing her to his chest and holding her there as they were then thrown to the side and into the passenger seat. He turned them so that he would take the brunt of the blow as they hit the chair, and then Decker was falling backward, taking Dani with him as Justin accelerated and swerved back, presumably to miss another obstacle.

"Sorry about that. Everyone all right?" Justin glanced around, squinting as he tried to pierce the darkness now cloaking them where they lay on the floor of the vehicle.

"We're fine. Eyes on the road," Decker reminded, worried that another vehicle might cruise into their path. He then glanced to Dani. She had ended up splayed on his chest in the cramped space between the front seats and the bench seat they'd been sitting on. "Are you all right?"

Dani raised her head. Even with his exceptional sight, Decker could barely make her out in the darkness. From what he could tell, she was more dazed than anything, though. He relaxed and closed his eyes with relief, planning only to take a moment to calm down, but found himself slowly becoming aware of the smell and feel of her. The image of her wide eyes and bemused expression was imprinted on his mind. She was soft and warm in his arms, and she thought he was cute, he remembered. Dani also smelled good enough to eat. She was a feast to his senses that Decker couldn't resist, and without even thinking about it, he caught her upper arms and pulled her up his body until her face was above his. His head then rose of its own accord; he claimed her lips and was lost.

Decker was vaguely aware of her initial stiffening, but she didn't struggle, and when she opened her mouth, probably to protest, he took full advantage and slid his tongue inside her, tasting the sweetness that was Dani.

Still shaken by being tossed around the vehicle, Dani was so startled when Decker kissed her that she didn't at first react. By the time she regained enough of her good sense to think of pushing him away, it was too late. She was already enveloped in his warm, strong arms, his body hard beneath her, his mouth covering hers, his tongue filling her and his scent assaulting her.

Decker smelled good. Dani had noticed that earlier while removing the bullet from his shoulder, but that had been only a teaser, a faint whiff compared to the full-on assault she was getting at this moment. It was overwhelming now that she was in his arms, and that, combined with the taste and feel of him, was enough to keep her quiescent in his arms. But when his hands began to move over her body, smoothing over her back and then moving down to cup her behind to urge her more snugly against him, she gave up that quiescence and began to kiss him back. The moment Dani did, a storm of desire poured through her. It was incredibly strong and felt slightly foreign, but was overwhelming, carrying her along on its crest as it beat against the shore of her brain. It then receded, only to strike again, this time joined by another wave of the raw emotion. The assault left Dani breathless and filled with a mindless need.

Decker groaned into her mouth, the vibration of sound making her moan in response, and then they both completely lost any sense of who or where they were. At least, Dani did. She forgot that they were lying cramped in the back of an SUV with Justin inches away. She forgot that this was not just a stranger who had told her several lies, but someone who claimed and truly seemed to *be* a vampire. She forgot her anger with him, her worry for her sister . . . and pretty much her own name. Dani forgot everything and threw herself into the moment, clutching at his shoulders and shifting excitedly against the hardness she could feel pressing against the apex of her thighs as one of his hands pushed down on her bottom, urging her closer.

She was vaguely aware that his other hand was moving up her side, but wasn't prepared for the excitement that jolted through her when it brushed lightly along the side of her breast. Dani sucked in a surprised breath and found her upper body instinctively twisting and arching to press her breast invitingly into his palm. He accepted the invitation, hand closing over the mound and kneading it briefly before slipping away to move under the hampering cloth of her T-shirt. She felt him tug the delicate material of her bra aside and froze briefly, then turned her head and pressed her mouth to his shoulder, biting into it to smother her moan as his warm hand closed over her eager flesh.

His own mouth now free, Decker immediately began trailing kisses to her ear, making her shudder with surprised pleasure as he briefly nibbled there. Dani bore the combined assault as long as she could, but hunger was beating at her brain, and she finally turned her face back to find his lips once more. The kiss this time was almost vicious with their mounting need, and then

Decker began to shift beneath her, his hands stopping what they were doing to grasp her hips and lift her.

Dani didn't, at first, understand what he was doing, and then his knee slid between her legs and he let her settle back against his thigh. She was now riding his leg, her body farther up his. It forced her to bend her head at an awkward angle to maintain their kiss, but she managed it. When his upper leg pressed more firmly against her where all the strings of her desire were culminating, Dani began to suck at his tongue. She then shifted one hand to the carpeted floor beside his head and pressed herself back into the caress, grinding herself against his thigh, at the same time rubbing her own upper thigh across the hard proof of his excitement.

Decker's response was to release a low growl and squeeze her breast almost painfully, and then he eased his hold to pay special attention to her nipple. It was too much for Dani; she felt like she was drowning in the pleasure assaulting her and she tore her mouth away, throwing back her head to gasp for air. But Decker was relentless; he simply continued to rub his leg against her and caress her breast, and then raised his head to press his mouth to the neck she'd unthinkingly offered him. He ran his lips and tongue along the vulnerable skin, pausing to suck and nip and suck again. Dani never felt any pain, nothing to tell her that his teeth had sunk into her flesh; pleasure had filled her up and left her completely oblivious. It wasn't until her vision began to blur that she realized something was wrong.

It was only when Dani went limp in his arms that Decker realized what he was doing. Cursing himself, he retracted his teeth and caught her as she slumped against him.

"Is she all right?"

Decker turned a fierce glare to Justin just as he turned back to watch the road ahead. "Why the hell didn't you stop me?"

"I didn't know you were biting her until I heard your curse and looked just now," Justin said quickly, and then added, "I thought you were just . . . you know . . . groping each other."

Decker's mouth tightened at the crude description of what had been—until a moment ago—a beautiful, passionate moment, but Justin wasn't done.

"I figured after eighty years without, you probably needed to let off a little steam so I just kept my eyes on the road . . . and tried not to hear all the grunting and groans back there."

"Thanks," Decker said dryly, easing to a sitting position and raising Dani as he went. Decker then tilted her head back to peer at her face. She looked a little pale, but her breathing and heartbeat seemed normal. Hopefully it was just a faint.

"No problem," Justin said. "Though you do owe me one; it was hard to resist peeking. It sounded pretty H and S."

"H and S?" Decker glanced to him with confusion.

"Hot and steamy," he explained, and then added almost enviously, "It sounded like you two were really tearing it up back there."

Decker frowned at the words, his eyes dropping to the two puncture wounds on her throat. No tearing, just a case of his getting too caught up in the moment and not only biting her, but not even remembering to be careful about how much blood he was taking.

Shaking his head, he shifted to lift her back onto the bench seat.

"We should have had some blood the minute we got in the SUV," Justin said regretfully as Decker pulled Dani's seat belt around and buckled her in. "Speaking of which . . . why didn't you? You should have been ravenous after that gunshot wound."

"I had a nibble at the restaurant while I was waiting for Dani to come out of the bathroom," Decker admitted, his eyes shifting from Dani's pale face to the rearview mirror.

"Yeah?" Justin met his gaze and then said, "It's been a long time since I had anything but bagged blood."

"Let's hope you never do," Decker said at once. His being low on blood from the gunshot wound and without bagged blood available was one of those emergency situations when biting a mortal was allowed. He'd originally intended to just suffer the cramps attacking him and wait it out until they met up with Eshe and could claim the replacement SUV with its supplies, but when Decker had found himself just a little too fascinated by Dani's neck as he'd helped her out of the van, and then felt his fangs trying to push themselves out and down as he'd walked her through the mass of bodies in the busy fast-food restaurant, he'd realized waiting wasn't an option. After seeing Dani to the ladies' room he'd waited for the first lone person to come up the hall and lured her into the broom closet between the two bathrooms for a little snack. He hadn't taken much, just enough to take the edge off his hunger, and then had put it in her thoughts that she had blackfly bites on her neck, and had sent her in to see if Dani was still in the washroom.

"How was it?" Justin asked as he steered them onto the off ramp.

"Fast food," Decker muttered, reaching out to brush away a stray strand of hair that had fallen across Dani's face. His gaze then dropped to her chest, and he noticed that there was something wrong. Her chest looked kind of lopsided. It took him a moment to recall that he'd tugged her bra aside to free her breast for his caresses. It was still out under the T-shirt.

"Fitting," Justin said with amusement. "It was a fast-food restaurant after all."

Decker hardly heard him. His eyes were shifting between Dani's face and her chest. He was hesitant to touch her while she was unconscious, but it would just take a second to pop her breast back in her bra, and he feared she'd be embarrassed if she woke up and noticed it herself. Besides, maybe if he tucked it back in she'd think the whole thing had been some erotic dream . . . including the bite part.

Not that Decker wanted her to forget their moments of passion. It was mostly the part when he'd sunk his teeth into her neck and sucked out her lifeblood that he wouldn't mind her forgetting. He suspected she was going to be pissed at him again when she remembered that, and deservedly so, he thought soberly as he took in her pallor and unconscious state.

Decker cast a glance toward Justin to be sure he wasn't looking, then leaned forward and quickly lifted her T-shirt. He'd intended to just tuck her back into the silky cloth and then lower it again. It didn't quite work out that way. First, the sight of her naked breast was just too fascinating to cover right away. Decker found himself just sitting there staring at it for a moment, before his good sense reminded him of Justin's presence. He glanced to him to be sure Justin was still watching the road, and then reached out to perform the tucking part.

"You're awfully quiet back there. What are you doing?"

"Nothing," Decker said, jerking guiltily upright without the tucking. He met Justin's gaze in the mirror and scowled. "Watch the road."

"Yes, boss," Justin said dryly, and shook his head as he turned his attention forward again.

Decker waited to be sure he continued to watch the road and then turned back to Dani, scowling when he saw that in his panic not to be caught groping an unconscious woman, he'd left her slumped there with her T-shirt still up.

Muttering under his breath, Decker leaned forward and grasped the edge of the bra cup, only to release it and snap upright with alarm when Justin spoke again.

"What's wrong? What are you doing back there?"

"Nothing," he said innocently. "Why?"

"Because you keep muttering and bending over Dani like there's something wrong. Is she all right? You didn't kill her, did you?" Apparently unable to see her in the mirror, he twisted his head around, trying to get a look at her.

"Goddammit, Justin! Eyes on the road," Decker

snarled, shifting to block his view of Dani. "I'm just
. . . checking her pulse."

When Justin turned around again, Decker immediately turned to Dani to tuck her back in her bra before
quickly dragging her T-shirt into place. He then sank
back on his side of the bench seat with a sigh, relieved
to have the task done with until Justin said, "I got news
for you, Decker. You don't take a mortal's pulse from
the boob."

Decker sat up and met his gaze in the mirror with
alarm.

"Oh, settle down. Your mind's an open book at the
moment, remember?" Justin said, rolling his eyes when
his gaze met Decker's in the rearview mirror. "I know
you weren't groping her."

Decker slumped back again with relief.

"Even though you really wanted to," Justin added
with amusement.

Decker scowled at the back of his head, considering
what physical violence he could perform on the man
without causing an accident.

"None," Justin said, obviously still reading his
thoughts. "Besides, we're here."

Decker immediately peered out the front windshield
at the scene ahead. They were pulling into the parking
garage and he could see three SUVs parked side-by-
side near the back, but not a single person around. He
let his breath out on a sigh, knowing this couldn't be
good.

Chapter Seven

Dani woke slowly from a rather pleasant dream in which she and Stephanie were walking down a flowered path. She was smiling at the memory of it as she stretched in bed. Then she opened her eyes, and the smile was replaced by a frown as she found herself in a barren, cream-colored room that held nothing but the bed she lay on. While it was a large, comfortable bed with fresh, fluffy pillows and sheets that were obviously new and still creased from being packaged, it also rested on the floor without a frame to support it.

Sitting up, Dani peered around with confusion and then pushed the sheets aside. She paused as she realized she wore only her panties . . . and didn't recall undressing. The last thing she remembered was— Dani stiffened as the last day's events washed through her mind, a kaleidoscope of bright, sparkling memories of a happy, sunny day with her family, followed by dark terror and anxiety that finished with an almost equally dark and desperate passion.

Dani pushed herself off the mattress and glanced around frantically for her clothes. Relief slid through her when she saw that they lay folded in a neat little stack on the floor. She quickly donned them, and then hesitated, her gaze moving to the windows. Not a single one had any kind of covering on it.

Hoping she might at least get some idea of where she was by looking outside, Dani walked to the closest one and found herself peering out on a balcony. This room was on the second floor, and a long terrace appeared to run the length of the building. Anyone walking along it could have watched her sleeping, but she didn't see anyone about, and Dani turned her attention to what lay beyond it. The backyard, she assumed, if it could even be called a backyard. The house was on a slight hill that ran for about a hundred feet. It was covered with grass and had several shady trees, as well as a little pagoda. Beyond those first hundred feet, however, was also what appeared to be a landing strip for airplanes that ran straight out between two lush green fields of what might have been soy. Dani took in the sight with awe and a little alarm. There must have been a hundred acres of field spread out before her on either side of the airstrip, and all of it was bordered by woods.

"Where the hell am I?" she muttered, and then turned to survey the room, searching for an exit. There were three doors in the room, one in the wall straight across from her and one in each wall on either side of her. Dani suspected the one directly opposite was the exit, but half afraid she'd find it locked, couldn't resist testing the others first. The one on her right led into a walk-in closet as barren as the room itself, the other to a bathroom with a sink, toilet, and huge tub. Suddenly aware that she had to go to the bathroom, Dani stepped inside and pulled the door closed.

It was as she washed her hands that she noticed the dark, ugly mark on her neck. Dani leaned forward to get a better look, her eyes widening as she recognized it for the hickey it was.

Dear God, she hadn't had one of those since high school, Dani thought, straightening as dismay coursed through her at what people would think when they saw it. She was supposed to be a professional, a grown-up doctor, not a teenager. Frowning, she slid her fingers over the discoloration, her mind moving past that initial reaction as memories of how she'd gained the bruising slithered into her mind like an apple-bearing snake. Dani suddenly distinctly recalled the smell and taste of Decker as he'd kissed her. She could feel his hands sliding over her body, his fingers plucking at her nipples, his thigh rubbing between her legs, and then his mouth moving to her neck . . . The echo of their moans and panting almost seemed to ring in her memory, and she briefly closed her eyes as her body responded, her nipples beginning to pebble and ache as excitement pooled between her legs.

Giving her head a shake, Dani forced the memories away and leaned closer to the mirror again to examine the rest of her neck for hickeys, and that was when she found the two puncture wounds. She froze, staring at them with a sort of horrified fascination, her fingers instinctively brushing over those as well. They didn't hurt, which made her wonder, and they appeared to be already healing, but the sight of them took her back again to the night before, and she recalled how overwhelming their passion had been, and how she'd broken their kiss and lifted her head to gasp for air, stretching her neck out before Decker like a sacrificial offering.

Jeez, how stupid could she be, Dani thought with dismay. The man had *told* her he was a vampire, showed her his fangs, and yet not only had she been foolish enough to indulge in what was pretty much a roll in the SUV with him, she'd done so without even first donning a turtleneck or scarf or something to protect herself. And then she'd as good as invited him to bite her by unthinkingly offering him her neck. Dani supposed it was like offering a steak to a dog. What half-bright dog would stick its nose in the air and refuse?

Shaking her head at herself, she let her hand drop away from her throat and turned from the mirror. She had more important things to worry about than her own complete lack of common sense. She needed to find out where she was and what had been done with her sister after they'd rescued her from the airport last night. At least, Dani presumed it had been only last night. But the truth was, for all she knew, several days might have passed since she, Decker, and Justin had been rushing to the airport after her sister and the man who had taken her.

Frowning at the possibility, Dani hurried quickly out of the bathroom and to the only door she hadn't yet opened. Much to her relief, it wasn't locked. She took that to be a good sign. At least she didn't appear to be a prisoner here. Wherever *here* was, Dani thought as she slid into a long, alien hallway and peered uncertainly one way and then the other. She had no idea which way to go, so simply started out heading right.

As it turned out, this direction led her to a set of wide stairs descending to the first floor of the house. Dani moved slowly down them, her eyes sweeping over the empty entry at the bottom and peering through the open doors on either side to find those rooms completely barren of furnishings. That along with the silence was beginning to creep her out a bit.

Dani paused on the bottom step, listening, but couldn't hear a sound. From where she stood she could see out the long, narrow windows on either side of the front double doors, and once again was confronted with a wide expanse of grass and what could have been a tarmac airstrip, but what she suspected was a driveway. While there were no fields here, the front yard too was bordered by woods on all sides. They looked thick and deep, and the driveway disappeared into them without any sign of a road being visible.

"Alex?"

Dani turned in surprise, but there was no body to go with the voice that had spoken. It wasn't until it spoke again that she realized it was a woman's voice and wasn't coming from nearby, but had carried through the empty house.

"Yes, of course I'm fine. We just wanted to spend another day together. Besides, Mr. Babcock owed me at least an extra day after making me work on my holiday," the voice said.

Dani slowly started up a hall on the right, following the voice.

"No, he wasn't mad about my taking an extra day,"

the voice assured this Alex, and then added, "At least not until I gave him my notice."

Several doors lined the hall Dani moved along, and she glanced into each, finding yet more empty rooms.

"I have a new job," the woman continued. "And I'm moving in with—"

The voice suddenly died, and Dani at first suspected it was her arrival that brought it to a halt. But then she saw that the speaker stood at the opposite end of the room with her back to her. She was tall and slender, with long, dark hair pulled up in a bun. She wore a dark business suit of jacket and skirt and was talking on the phone, or listening at the moment as the case might be.

Not wishing to interrupt, Dani glanced curiously around the kitchen. As with the rest of the house, this room appeared pretty barren. It did have a refrigerator, stove, and microwave, but the glass-faced white cupboards were empty and the small breakfast nook that overlooked the backyard was bereft of the table that should have been there.

"No, I have not lost my mind," the woman said with exasperation, reclaiming Dani's attention. "Look, I have to get to work. I'll swing by the restaurant tonight and explain, okay?"

The woman grunted at the response of whomever she was talking to and said good-bye. It wasn't until she turned to move to the phone base on the side counter that she spotted Dani. She paused briefly, a startled expression widening her large eyes, and then continued to the counter.

"My sister," she explained, setting the phone back in

the cradle. She then turned to peer at Dani as she added wryly, "She thinks I've lost my mind. Now I just have to come up with a way to reassure her I haven't without telling her the truth."

When Dani just stared at her silently, not sure what to say to that, she grimaced and said, "I'm sorry, Dani. Of course you don't have a clue who I am, do you?" Her high heels clicked on the floor as she moved forward, holding out her hand. "I'm Samantha Willan. Call me Sam."

Dani straightened slightly as the name sparked a memory. "Mortimer's Sam?"

"Yes." The woman smiled happily as they shook hands, her face transformed from almost plain to almost pretty. When Dani smiled uncertainly back, Sam tilted her head and said sympathetically, "It must have been unsettling to wake up in a strange bed in a strange house. Especially one that's half empty," she added, glancing around before explaining, "Bastien bought the house, but only purchased minimal furnishings."

"Bastien?" Dani asked, vaguely recalling Justin and Decker mentioning that name as well.

"Yeah. I'm pretty new to all this myself, but apparently he's the go-to guy if you need anything done," Sam explained and then sighed. "I guess Lucian told him to buy a house for the enforcers to use as a headquarters and he found this one. He also bought beds, a fridge and stove, and the other appliances, but said he thought he should leave the furnishings to whoever ended up living here and running it . . . which is going to be Mortimer and me." She paused to peer at the empty upper cupboards surrounding them and grimaced. "I guess it was nice of him in a way, but I so don't have the time to shop right now."

Dani merely stared at her with confusion.

"You don't have a clue where you are, do you?" Sam asked suddenly, and shook her head before adding, "And I don't have the time to explain. I'm already late for work." Sam tapped her fingers impatiently on the marble countertop and then blew out an exasperated breath and started to move past her. "I guess we'll just have to wake Decker. I hate to do it, but it's his own fault. I told him he should wake you up last night, but—" She shrugged.

"It's all right," Dani said quickly. "If you're running late, just tell me where he is and I'll find and ask him myself."

"Oh, thank you," Sam said with relief as she swung back. She immediately headed for a purse that sat perched on the empty counter next to a door at the far end of the room. "He's in his room. Sleeping. They all are. It's daylight and they were up all night searching for your sister."

"Stephanie?" Dani asked with sudden alarm, and when Sam nodded, asked, "Wasn't she at the airport?"

Sam paused with her hand on her purse, her expression troubled, but then she simply said, "I really have to go to work, Dani, and this isn't going to be a fast-and-easy-answer kind of deal. I think Decker should explain to you."

"Where is his room?" she asked abruptly, anxious to learn about her sister.

"The room next after yours," Sam said with obvious relief that she hadn't insisted that Sam explain. She picked up her purse and slipped the strap over her shoulder as she added, "He wanted to be close in case you woke up. Not that it made much difference."

Nodding, Dani turned back the way she'd come.

"Dani?" Sam called, stopping her.

She turned back in question.

"Don't be too mad at Decker. He's a pretty good guy from what I know of him. And finding a life mate can apparently put a person off their stride to say the least." Sam smiled wryly as she said that and then turned and headed out the door behind her.

Dani caught a glimpse of the interior of a garage with three vehicles parked inside and then the door closed. She waited until she heard an engine start, and then turned and headed back up the hall, her temper rising with each step. She was furious that she'd been allowed, or possibly *made*, to sleep through the events of last night and now didn't know what the heck was going on. Other than the fact that her sister was apparently still missing, she had no idea what had happened. The last thing she recalled was rolling around in the back of the SUV with Decker—a rather poor description of what had taken place, Dani acknowledged. Those few moments of passion had been like nothing she'd ever before experienced. They were burned in her brain, as was the image of the puncture marks on her neck. Even so, they still didn't burn as brightly as her anger by the time she retraced her steps, passed her room, and moved to the next door up.

Dani stopped there and raised her hand to knock, and then paused. She'd had every intention of rapping furiously at the door to wake the man, but mindful of the fact that Sam had said *they all* were sleeping, she hesitated. Dani had no idea who *they all* were, but if *they all* had been up all night searching for her sister, she had no desire to repay them by disturbing their sleep. Decker, however, was another matter. She'd really like to smack him . . . and decided she would as she reached for the doorknob.

Decker had had trouble getting to sleep and didn't think he'd slept long at all when he was attacked by what he was at first sure must be a wildcat. It was hissing and snarling as it knelt half on him and raked sharp claws over his face.

Snapping his eyes open, he grabbed at the creature, instinctively rolling to wrestle it to the mattress so that he could press his lower body over it to keep it from trying to scratch with its back legs. Decker had dealt with wild felines before.

Only once he'd come down on her body and forced her arms to the floor on either side of her head did he wake enough—and his bleary eyes clear enough—for him to realize it wasn't a cat but a woman.

"Oh. Dani." Decker let his forehead drop to rest briefly on her chest as he regathered himself. He then raised it to offer her an apologetic smile. "Sorry. I was asleep and thought you were—"

"You bit me!" she snapped, interrupting him.

Decker's eyes dropped to her throat to see the proof of his naughtiness the night before and he stared at it, very aware of the feel of her body beneath his as he recalled giving her those puncture wounds . . . and the hickey, he realized, spotting that as well.

Damn, Decker thought as he peered at the bruising. That was a good one, but he hoped the men didn't see it. They might start calling him Hoover.

"You bit me," Dani repeated, hissing the words in what he suspected was an effort not to be overheard. It explained why he'd thought she was a cat, he supposed, and then stiffened as she began to wiggle beneath him, struggling to be free. Decker slept naked and could feel the cool air on his bare behind where he lay on her with only the sheet caught between them. He could also feel himself hardening as she shifted about, trying to dislodge him.

"You might want to stop that," Decker warned.

"You'd like that, wouldn't you?" she growled, sounding amazingly like a wet, angry cat.

"Actually, I'd rather you kept wiggling about. It's you who I don't think would enjoy the consequences," he said wearily, shifting his hips to press his erection against her and make his point. Satisfied by the way she suddenly stilled, he added solemnly, "I am sorry about biting you. I'm afraid I just got a little overexcited. But to be fair, you did bite me too."

"I did no . . ." Dani paused mid-denial, her eyes flickering as she apparently remembered sinking her teeth into his shoulder. It had been a good bite too, not some little nip. The woman had left marks. Fortunately, he'd been so excited himself he'd barely felt it.

Decker saw her eyes slip to his shoulder with worry, and knew she was concerned she'd done more damage to his gunshot wound. He wasn't surprised when her eyes widened incredulously.

"It's gone," she breathed with amazement.

He didn't glance down, knowing Dani was talking about the bullet wound. It had been completely healed and gone by the time he'd lain down to sleep this morning. There wasn't even a scar anymore.

"Dear God," she breathed, sounding dismayed, and he thought she was still reacting to his healing abilities when she suddenly screeched, "You're *naked*!"

Decker smiled wryly. "Good of you to notice."

Dani merely stared at him, her eyes moving over his naked chest and then to the side to peer down the length of his side and back. A slow, burning heat entered her eyes, and her tongue slid out to lick her lips. It was an unconscious action, he was sure, but was enough to make more blood rush to his groin and have him hardening further. Growling under his breath, Decker lowered his head to kiss her, but found himself kissing her fingers as her hand suddenly appeared over her mouth.

"Stephanie," Dani said when he raised his head, her voice hard and cold again.

Decker hesitated briefly, and then sighed and rolled off her, taking the sheet with him. He then closed his eyes, trying to gather his thoughts as he felt the bed shift as she sat up beside him.

"Sam said you were up all night looking for . . ."

Made curious by her sudden pause, Decker opened his eyes to find her staring at his groin with a wide, startled gaze. Following her glance, he wasn't surprised to find a small tent resurrected there, but she apparently was. He didn't know why. Surely she'd felt his erection while he was lying on her?

"You were saying?" he prompted dryly.

"What?" Dani turned to peer at his face, then flushed and cleared her throat before continuing, "What happened at the airport? Didn't they get Stephanie?"

"No," he answered simply.

She frowned at the unhelpful answer, worry tugging at her features, and then asked, "And the man who took her?"

"He got away too," Decker said on a sigh.

"Too?" Dani asked, frowning over his choice of words. "You mean with her, don't you? He took her with him. It's not like she fled on her own."

"We aren't sure," he said, and then sat up on the bed to lean against the wall as he explained, "When Bricker and I got there, the three SUVs were all stopped in the middle of the lane at the back of the parking garage, but there was no one in sight. We didn't know where everyone was or even which enforcers belonged to those two SUVs. You were still asleep and I didn't want to leave you there alone, so we decided to check the SUV."

"What did you find?" she asked tensely.

"Nothing," Decker assured her.

Dani closed her eyes with obvious relief, and he knew she'd feared there might be blood or something else to suggest Stephanie had been hurt. He was glad he could reassure her that much. Nothing else he had to say was likely to.

"Lucian showed up just as I was about to call Bastien," he continued. "He knew who the volunteers were and called them himself. They'd just finished searching the airport and were on the way back so we waited there for them."

"Volunteers?" she interrupted sharply before he could continue. "You mean enforcers, don't you?"

"No. I mean volunteers. Toronto is huge, and there weren't enough enforcers in the area to cover everywhere. Bastien called in volunteers to help in the search," he admitted tightly, thinking that if the men in the first two SUVs had been enforcers rather than volunteers, things would have gone much differently and they would no doubt have Stephanie there safe and sound right now. Unfortunately, that wasn't what had happened.

"What happened to Stephanie?" Dani asked impatiently when he remained silent.

Sighing, he ran a hand through his hair and recounted what they'd been told. "When the first SUV caught up to the stolen one it was already in the parking garage. They followed it, and then our second SUV showed up and they were able to force it to a halt. But when they rushed it, there was only Stephanie inside."

"What?" Dani gasped with amazement, and then shook her head. "No way, Stephanie just turned fifteen. She doesn't have a license. She hasn't even tried a practice run or know how to drive," she said firmly, and then sighed as she added, "I was going to take her out to the country to teach her this summer."

"She was driving, Dani," he said quietly, and then added, "He was probably controlling her."

"Oh," she said unhappily, and then frowned and asked, "How could they possibly lose her?"

Decker continued grimly, "When they asked her where her kidnapper was, she told them he'd ordered her to turn into the parking garage and keep driving around in circles and then jumped out as she slowed to turn in."

"And she did it?" Dani said with confusion. "Why didn't she immediately drive off to find help? Why—?"

"He could have been still controlling her, Dani," Decker said gently.

She swallowed and nodded. "Go on. What happened next?"

"The men were afraid the rogue was trying to get away by plane, so they told her to stay put, that they'd take her to her sister as soon as they got back, and then ran into the airport to hunt for him."

"They didn't just leave her there alone," she said with disbelief. "Volunteers or not, they couldn't have been that stupid."

Decker hesitated again. He'd rather hoped to avoid telling her this part, but finally he admitted, "Not alone, no. There was a security guard in the area. They brought him over, told him they were the police and that Stephanie was a kidnap victim and that they needed him to stay with her and keep her calm while they went after the kidnapper."

He paused and peered down at the sheet lying across his body, not at all surprised to see that the tent had fallen.

"And he believed them?" Dani asked with surprise. "They don't have badges, do they?"

"They don't need them," Decker pointed out.

"Oh, right. They used that mind-control business," she muttered with realization and then frowned. "Then where is she? What happened? He didn't just let her wander off, did he? She might be out there in shock somewhere—"

"He didn't exactly let her go," Decker interrupted, avoiding her eyes. This was the hardest part to tell her, but there was no hope for it. "When they came back out, and told us Stephanie and the guard should be there, we spread out to search the parking garage. We didn't find Stephanie."

"And the guard?"

"Dead," he said bluntly.

As he'd feared, Dani's eyes widened with horror and fear. "What—? How—? Did—?"

"His throat was slit," Decker answered before she could finish the question.

Dani sat back, her face paling sickly. "The rogue killed that poor man and took Stephanie."

"That's what we think," he said carefully.

"What do you mean *think*?" she asked coldly. "Of course he did. She wouldn't have gone with him willingly."

"No, probably not," he acknowledged. "But we don't understand why he bothered to take her with him when it would be easier for him to slip away on his own."

Dani frowned at his words and then looked thoughtful for a moment before saying, "The one who has her watched her a lot."

"Watched her?" he asked curiously.

She nodded. "I noticed him watching Stephanie in the van, but at the clearing he was left to guard us and he couldn't seem to take his eyes off her. He just stood there, his expression really intense and locked on her like his life depended on it. It was creepy. I wanted to . . ." Dani shook her head unhappily and waved that away. They were both silent for a moment and then she said, "So you're still chasing him?"

He nodded.

"But then why are we here?" she asked with a sudden burst of frustration. "We should be on the road following him."

Decker caught her arm as she started to get off the bed. "He didn't take the SUV."

"Didn't . . . ?" Dani stared at him with incomprehension, and then a new horror began to rise in her eyes as she realized the state of things. "You've lost her."

Decker winced, but said quickly, "We'll find her."

She didn't look as if she believed that was likely, and then sighed and glanced around. "I need to call my parents. They'll be worried sick."

"It's all right. Lucian sent a couple men over to take care of them last night," Decker told her, and her eyes widened with alarm.

"Take care of them *how*?"

Dani asked the question as if suspecting their people might have gone and shot them down like dogs in the street or something. The reaction irritated the hell out of him. "They just eased their minds and made them think that you and Stephanie stopped in Toronto for a couple days to see the sights and visit Wonderland. It was so they wouldn't worry. If you call them, you'll just upset and confuse them. They're happy and calm right now." And not likely to call in the mortal police and blow this up into a "situation," he thought, but didn't say that out loud.

Dani stared at him for several moments, looking uncertain, and then shook her head and said dully, "You should have woken me."

"There was no need. You couldn't do anything to help either situation."

"I could have helped look for Stephanie," she argued. "Another set of eyes wouldn't have hurt. Besides," Dani added, getting upset again. "None of you even know what she looks like."

"Every man has a picture of her," he assured her solemnly.

That made her frown. "Where did you get a picture of her?"

Decker hesitated, knowing she wasn't going to like this, but finally admitted, "From your memories."

"What?" She gasped.

"We got a photo from your parents too," he added quickly. "But those are posed and often don't look much like the person, and the images of her in your memory are better. They're more recent and natural and told us what she's wearing too."

"You mean to say you let a bunch of your men poke around inside my head?" Dani breathed with a horror that suggested it was tantamount to rape, and Decker understood her feeling. Lord knew what they might have inadvertently seen while in her thoughts. Lucian had ordered them to stick to her most recent surface memories, and Decker trusted the enforcers he worked with to have done so. However, a lot of those memories included him, and one of them was something he would have preferred to keep private, that being the incident in the back of the SUV.

Decker would never tell Dani, but he was pretty sure

it no longer was private. He hadn't asked any of them, but judging by the low whistles and looks cast his way by a couple of the enforcers and volunteers as they'd finished reading her thoughts, pretty much everyone had been witness to it.

"It was necessary," he said now, forcing those thoughts aside. "We had to have a clear and recent image of both Stephanie and the rogue who took her. I only caught a glimpse of them as they escaped. You know and have a lot of clear visual images of Stephanie and the rogue who took her. Now they know exactly who and what they're looking for, and they've been out all night searching for them."

Her shoulders and head drooped with defeat, and Dani stared down at her hands briefly, apparently accepting the necessity, and then she raised her head. "They were searching all night, but is there anyone out there now looking for them? Probably not, right?" she answered herself. "You guys have to avoid the sun."

"We have specially coated windows on the SUVs. Most of the men are still out there looking. I was too until—" Decker's head swiveled to look for a clock, but the room was barren of all but the mattress and box spring on the floor. That would change soon enough, but for now . . . He reached for his watch, which lay on the floor beside his jeans, and grimaced when he saw the time. "A half hour ago. I came back because I thought you might wake soon and wanted to tell you what had happened. When I learned you were still sleeping, I decided to crash until you woke up."

"Well, I'm awake now. Let's go."

"Right." Decker sighed wearily.

"I'll drive and you can sleep. I'll wake you if I find—" Dani stopped suddenly and said, "Nicholas."

"What about him?" he asked with a frown.

"Has he called? Did he lose them too? Has he called?" she repeated impatiently.

"No. We haven't heard from him," Decker answered.

Dani bit her lip and then asked abruptly, "Where's my cell phone?"

"Still in my jeans. Wh—" The word ended on a surprised "oomph" as she suddenly shifted to her hands and knees to climb across him to get to his jeans beside the bed. Decker would have stopped her, but got distracted by her derriere, which was suddenly in front of his face as she bent over him, her knees on one side of his thighs, one hand on the other, bearing her weight, as she reached for the pile of his clothes.

It was a very nice derriere, Decker decided as it waved around in front of his face, swaying a bit as she patted his jeans for the lump that would be her phone.

"Aha!" Dani's derriere suddenly dropped out of his line of vision as she straightened, cell phone in hand. Decker sighed with disappointment. It had been a rather pleasant view and he'd been tempted to grab it again as he had in the SUV and—

He was distracted from his less than sterling thoughts by a muttered curse from Dani.

"What is it?" Decker asked, forcing his eyes to her face as she settled back on her haunches.

"My battery," Dani said, feeling her pockets. "It must have fallen out when—" Pausing abruptly, she turned sharp eyes on him. "Who undressed me?"

"Sam and Leigh," he said at once, not bothering to mention that he'd intended to do it himself, but they'd shooed him away and taken over the task.

"Hmm," Dani muttered, not looking as if she believed him. Then she was suddenly off, launching to her feet and rushing off the bed to scamper to the door.

Decker watched her race out of the room and then glanced down at himself with a small sigh. The sheet had tented below his waist again as he'd watched her bottom dance before his face. On the one hand, it was nice to know he could get erections repeatedly like this after eighty years without even a spark of interest in that area. On the other hand, it seemed a terrible shame that they were going to waste. Sighing again, Decker tossed the sheets aside and stood up to don his jeans and go after her.

Chapter Eight

Dani scanned the floor around the mattress, but didn't see the battery anywhere. She had resorted to crawling around on the bed, checking under the pillows and sheets and blanket when Decker spoke from the door.

"Can't you find it?" he asked. He didn't sound terribly surprised.

Sitting back on her haunches, she shook her head unhappily. "No. I don't know where it could be. I put it in my pocket."

"Maybe it fell out," Decker suggested, avoiding her gaze. "Your phone did."

"Yes, it did," she said slowly, and then stood to move past him into the hall.

"Where are you going?" he asked, following her.

"To check the SUV. Maybe it fell on the floor in there while we were—" Dani cut herself off, aware that she was blushing over what they'd been doing on the floor of the SUV.

"The SUV isn't here."

"What?" She whirled around at that softly spoken announcement. "Why not? Where is it?"

"Mortimer and Sam brought my personal vehicle back, so it was taken back to Argeneau Enterprises. They plan to build a parking garage for them out here, but until they do, they're still kept at the compan—"

"Well, then we'll have to go to Argeneau Enterprises," Dani said, cutting him off. But when she turned to continue toward the stairs, Decker caught her arm to stop her.

"There's no use doing that, Dani. It probably won't be there. One of the other men will be using it to search for Stephanie and the rogue."

She frowned over that possibility and then said, "Well, we'll just have to call Bastien and find out who he gave it to so that we can—"

"Bastien will be sleeping," Decker said at once. "Why don't we just wait until—"

"I'm not waiting. We're waking him up," Dani snapped, and then shook her head with bewilderment at the resistance she was meeting. "Jesus, Decker, my sister is—"

"I know," he said soothingly, trying to calm her . . . and probably quiet her down, she realized, noting the way his eyes slid to the doors in the hallway.

Dani didn't want to wake everyone up, just Bastien, if it meant she might get a lead on her sister, so turned and led the way up the hall to the stairs. She jogged swiftly down them, and then continued on into the kitchen before turning to face him. But as Dani opened her mouth to speak, it occurred to her that they didn't have to wake anyone up.

"We don't have to wake Bastien," she announced, and Decker immediately relaxed, his relief obvious. Until she added, "We'll just take your vehicle and go to town and buy a replacement battery."

Decker closed his eyes and shook his head. "Dani, Nicholas isn't going to call you. He—"

"You don't know that," she protested, her voice rising with frustration, and then she asked, "Why are you trying to stop me? And why didn't you wake me up last night? Or was I even really in a natural sleep? Did you have Justin control me and keep me asleep on purpose?"

The guilt on his face was answer enough, and Dani felt rage and frustration explode within her.

"You bastard," she yelled, grabbing the cordless telephone—the absolutely only thing there was in the kitchen to grab—and swinging it back to throw it at him. That was when Dani learned how quickly immortals could move. Suddenly Decker was there in front of her, grabbing her by both wrists. He squeezed the one that held the phone until she dropped it and then gave her a little shake.

"Listen to me," he snapped. "Nicholas isn't the hero you think he is. Fifty years ago he killed a woman."

"What the hell's going on down here?"

Both of them froze and jerked their heads to the door as Lucian barked that question.

Decker released Dani and stepped away. "I'm sorry. Did we wake you?"

"Hell no . . . you woke up the whole house," Lucian growled, and stepped into the room to allow two other men to join them.

Dani bit her lip as she watched them enter. She recognized Justin, but had no idea who the second man was, though she thought it might be Mortimer. It didn't matter, though; she was sorry they'd woken them with their argument.

"Now," Lucian growled, "tell me what is happening."

"Dani wants to get a battery for her phone," Decker explained wearily. "She thinks if her phone was working, Nicholas would call her. She thinks if he's still following her sister, he might be able to tell us where they are."

Dani said firmly, "He *would* call me. He knows I will be worried."

"Dani," Justin said pityingly. "Nicholas is a rogue. He can't afford to call again. He only got away with it the first time because we didn't know you had the phone."

She ignored him and stared at Lucian as she said, "He promised he'd get her back for me."

Lucian considered her silently and then asked, "And you believe him?"

The question was not sarcastic or dubious, simply curious, and Dani didn't hesitate to nod.

"Why?" he asked at once.

"I don't know," she said, and then sighed and admitted, "Maybe I just *want* to believe him because he's Stephanie's best hope." When Lucian continued to stare at her without speaking, Dani added, "I know he's what you guys call a rogue and that he's killed someone. He told me that, but—"

"Afraid," Lucian murmured.

Dani paused and tilted her head uncertainly. "I don't understand. Afraid what?"

"Nothing," he said at once, and then added, "Well, if he was trying to call, I'm sure he's given up by now. There's no use—"

"My phone has call display and he didn't block his number."

"What?" Decker almost gasped the word, he was so shocked.

Everyone in the room appeared to be, they'd all frozen on the spot, their eyes locked on her, but Dani ignored everyone else but Lucian. "His number will be in my phone memory."

"Why didn't you tell me that?" Decker asked, stalking toward her, anger clear on his face. "You knew we were hunting him. Why the hell wouldn't you tell me that you could give me his number? Bastien could have used that to track him down."

"That's exactly why I didn't tell you," Dani said at once. "The man is trying to save Stephanie. There's no way I'm going to repay that by turning him over to you."

"He's not a *man*, he's a vampire and a rogue one at that," Decker said harshly, and then added, "And you have no idea if he's trying to find Stephanie or not. He's rogue, Dani. Why would he risk his life for some girl he doesn't even know?"

"I don't know," she admitted, and then asked, "Why did you take a bullet for me before we'd even met? And why did he put himself in jeopardy to save us the first time?"

"We don't know that he *did* try to save you the first time," Decker said, ignoring the comment about himself. "Maybe he was running with that group, and lied to save his own hide when we got the drop on him. Maybe he just put us on to those guys hoping we'd be distracted and he could escape . . . as he did," he added bitterly.

"Or maybe he's not the man you think he is," Dani countered.

"Give me the phone," Lucian said.

"Why?" she asked suspiciously.

"Give me the phone, woman!" he snapped.

Dani hesitated, but then reluctantly handed it over. She didn't really have much choice. The man could have controlled her and taken it anyway.

Lucian grunted what might have been approval when she held it out. He then took it and immediately handed it off to Justin. "Take it to Bastien and have him see if one of his people can fix it. Tell him to send it back to Dani at once if they do."

Dani's eyes widened. She'd expected that would be the last she'd see of her phone, that they'd take it and use it to catch Nicholas and that would be that.

Lucian saw her expression and merely shrugged. "It's you he'll be calling. He might hang up and toss his phone if anyone but you answers."

Dani scowled at the words.

"Now, I am returning to my bed. I suggest the rest of you do the same. Decker, keep an eye on her," he ordered, and then turned to Dani and added, "And you will remain right here waiting for your phone to be returned."

"Of course," she said calmly, and then just so he

didn't think it was because he'd said so, added, "I wouldn't want to be stuck in traffic an hour away from here when the phone starts ringing."

Much to her surprise, Lucian Argeneau looked amused. He turned to Decker and said, "I like her. You have my blessing. But I suggest you stop thinking with your dick and use your brain before you lose her. Explain the situation. I know you don't like talking about Nicholas, but it's the only way she'll understand and see that she can trust you and perhaps not Nicholas."

Dani frowned at the words. She didn't care if she had his blessing and—despite her body's rather alarming response to Decker in the SUV last night—had no interest in being his vamp ho. She did, however, want—no, need—to trust in Nicholas. Right now Dani was pretty sure that he was her only hope of seeing Stephanie alive again.

"Dani," Decker said quietly as the other men left the room.

She cast a resentful glare in his direction, not really wanting to talk to him at all, but said, "You shouldn't have had Justin put me to sleep."

"He didn't. You fainted. I just— When you started to stir, I had him help you to keep sleeping. I shouldn't have done that, and I'm sorry I did," he added quickly when she opened her mouth to speak. Decker then shrugged helplessly and tried to explain, "I wanted to save you some worry. I was hoping we'd find her before you woke and—"

"I'm not some brainless twit who needs coddling, Decker. She's my sister. You should have woken me up," Dani snapped, and then added with frustration,

"It's not your place to save me worry. The phone could have been fixed by now, Nicholas could have called, and we could have Stephanie back safe and sound. Instead she's out there God knows where having God knows what done to her . . . if she's still alive," she added bitterly.

"Dani, I'm sorry, but he won't call," he repeated solemnly.

"You don't know that. And *I'm sorry* doesn't get my sister back, does it?" she asked, shaking his hand off and moving out of the kitchen. She headed up the hall and then took the stairs to the second floor, aware that he was following, but trying to ignore that fact. It was hard to ignore it when she walked into her room and tried to close the door behind her, only to have him stop her.

Dani glared at him briefly and then shook her head wearily and said, "Go away, Decker. I need time to think."

He ran a weary hand through his hair as he followed her into the room. "I can't."

She hadn't forgotten Lucian's order that he keep an eye on her, and Dani was too weary to argue with him, so she glanced around in search of an escape. Her eyes settled on the door to the bathroom. "Then stay. But I'm going to take a bath. I trust you don't have to be in there with me?"

"No, that's fine," Decker said in subdued tones.

Nodding, she crossed to the door and slid into the bathroom. Dani closed the door, but rather than start running a bath, leaned back against the panel of wood and lowered her head briefly. She'd only just woken up a short while ago, but felt as if she hadn't slept at all. The morning's events had been terribly draining, and all she wanted to do was curl up on the floor, go to sleep, and not wake up until Stephanie was back safe and sound.

Her lips twisted at the thought. That was exactly what Decker had hoped to do for her by keeping her asleep last night and she was mad at him for it. She supposed it wasn't really what she wanted at all. What she really wanted was to get Stephanie back right then, whether she was alive or dead. Obviously, she would prefer to have her back alive, but if the rogue had already killed Stephanie, then it was better to know now than to suffer the agony and anxiety of bouncing between hope and fear as she was. That, she found, was unbearable.

But you don't always get what you want, Dani told herself grimly, and forced herself away from the door to start running a bath.

She had pushed the button to drop the stopper and turned on the taps to start the water running when a knock sounded at the door. It made her scowl.

Knowing it was Decker, she was about to tell him to go away when he said, "Dani? I fetched you some soap and towels."

She blinked in surprise at the words, glancing around to see that while the small hand towel and bar of soap she'd used that morning were there, they were the only things that were, besides toilet paper. There were no towels hung over the rack, no washcloths either, and no soap by the tub. A quick search of the cupboards proved that those were completely empty.

"Dani?" There was concern in his voice now at her silence.

Grimacing at the realization that she'd have to answer the door after all, Dani called, "It isn't locked."

There was a pause and then the door opened. Decker entered, a stack of towels and various other things in hand. He eyed her warily, and then moved to the counter, explaining, "I guess Bastien didn't think to purchase things like this for the house, but Sam ran out to the twenty-four-hour drugstore last night and picked up a few sundries and then swung by her apartment for the towels. I didn't remember until you came in here or I would have mentioned it so that you could choose what you needed yourself." Decker set the items down and added, "If there's anything I didn't think of, let me know and I'll get it for you."

Dani's face softened at the thoughtful gesture, but she only murmured, "Thank you" as he turned to move back out of the room. She stood there for a moment after he left, part of her wanting to go out and say something to end this awkwardness between them, but she had no idea what to say. He'd been wrong to keep her asleep, even if it had been with good intentions. Decker hadn't set out to hurt her, and it had been sweet in a way, but . . .

Dani shook her head and glanced to the tub to find that it was already half full. She moved to the counter to collect the bubble bath, one of the sundries he'd brought her. She poured a generous amount into the tub and began to strip.

The water was warm and inviting when Dani stepped into it. She eased slowly to sit, sighing as the water and bubbles enveloped her. She reclined back in the tub and closed her eyes, hoping the warm, bubble-filled water would soak away some of her tension and worries, but knowing it wouldn't.

The sound of rushing water died and Decker stopped pacing the bedroom to peer toward the bathroom door, very aware that his Dani was on the other side of it. His life mate . . . who presently hated his guts, he thought grimly. It was a depressing thought. Decker knew he hadn't done much right since meeting her. First there had been that stupid CSIS business, and then biting her, and now he felt as if he'd personally failed her by not saving Stephanie. Intellectually, Decker knew that there was nothing he could have done, but that didn't stop him from feeling responsible. And it wasn't even the reason she was angry with him at the moment. It was his having Justin control her to make her sleep. That had seriously pissed her off.

I'm not some brainless twit who needs coddling. She's my sister. You should have woken me up. It's not your place to save me worry. Her words ran through his head, and Decker scowled at the bathroom door. Of course it was his place. She was his life mate.

Irritated now, he glanced around for somewhere to sit, but the only piece of furniture in the room was the bed. Decker moved to it and dropped to lie flat, his legs crossing at the ankles and hands resting on his stomach as he listened for sounds from the next room.

Was she in the tub yet or just now undressing? He wondered and wasn't terribly surprised when his thoughts immediately moved south, producing an image of her tugging her T-shirt off over her head and letting it drop to the floor as her hands moved around to her back and rose to undo the clasps of her bra.

Decker could still recall the silky feel of it as he'd tugged it away from her breast to touch her warm skin. He remembered the smell of her too and savored the memory as what she might be doing continued to play in his head, and she allowed the bra to glide down her arms and slip to rest on her T-shirt. In his imaginings, Dani then paused to twist her hair up on the back of her head so that only little wisps hung around her face. That done, she reached for the button of her shorts. Those shimmied to the floor the moment they were undone, and she stepped out of them, then slipped her thumbs beneath the elastic on either side of her panties and drew them slowly, lovingly, down over her hips, thighs, and knees until she could step out of them one foot at a time. They fluttered to the bath mat as Dani stepped carefully and oh so slowly into a tub full of bubbles.

A little moan of disappointment slipped from Decker's lips as the water and bubbles embraced his dream Dani, hiding her from view. He grimaced at the ceiling, telling himself that she was his life mate and it would all work out. The day would come when he would simply walk in there while she reclined in the bath. She'd smile at him welcomingly and crook her finger to bring him to the side of the tub, then reach out to run her hand slowly up his leg before slipping it around to caress him through the cloth of his jeans and ask, "Care to join me? The tub's big enough for two."

"Oh yeah," Decker breathed aloud as his Dani sat up and reached for the button of his jeans. She unsnapped it with a hand that had bubbles clinging to it, and then raised her eyes to watch his face as she drew the zipper down in a leisurely fashion. He pushed his jeans off his hips the moment she'd finished, letting them pool around his ankles, and she reached down to help him step out of them, then turned her attention to his boxers. Dani pulled those down much more slowly than he had his jeans. The elastic waistband got caught on his emerging erection so that she had to lift it over his shaft. A smile played about her lips, and she leaned forward to press a kiss to the tip before helping him to step out of those too.

Dani raised her head to peer up at him then, her eyes just skittering over what she'd revealed as she murmured, "Your shirt."

Decker reached to tug that up over his head. The moment his face was enshrouded in the soft cloth and he couldn't see what she was doing, Dani caught his erection in a suddenly soapy hand and squeezed gently as she ran her fingers along its length.

Shuddering at the explosion of desire that shot through him, Decker ripped the shirt off to toss it over his shoulder and then urged her hand away and stepped up to the top of the tub. Dani scooted forward, leaving room for him behind her as he stepped into the water. Decker sat down behind her, the warm water sliding over his skin like a caress as he settled, then Dani eased back to sit between his spread legs, and reclined to rest against his chest.

"I was waiting for you," she murmured, running her hands along his outer thighs under the water.

"Were you?" Decker asked. He'd been waiting for her for two hundred and fifty-nine years. His hands moved to her arms and smoothed down over the soft skin to her elbows, his fingers brushing the inside crook of her arms in a feathery touch that made her shiver against him.

"Yes," she breathed, wiggling against him. "I was hoping you'd wash my back."

Decker smiled faintly as he grabbed for the bar of soap. He slid it briefly under the water, and then began to rub it between his hands to make lather. He urged her to sit up and began to run his hands over her back, running them in circles until every inch of skin there was covered in the soapy lather. He then reached for the soap again and worked it for another minute before returning to the chore, his circles becoming wider and wider until they included her sides.

"Oh." Dani sighed as Decker let his fingers roam to where they wanted. His hands closed warm and soapy over her breasts, squeezing and kneading under the pretense of cleaning. When she leaned back against him, her foam-covered back sliding across his clean chest, Decker peered down her body, watching his hands cup and knead and then catch her nipples between thumb and finger and pinch lightly.

The action drew a long moan from Dani and had her tilting her head back and twisting toward him in silent invitation. Decker lowered his head at once, his lips covering hers and his tongue sliding eagerly out to fill her mouth. She tasted as sweet as he remembered, and his fingers tightened on her breasts briefly, then he let one drift away to find the washcloth, and dunk it in the water. He used it to rinse away the soap so that he could caress her without the slippery lather. The moment the last bit of soap was gone, Decker dropped the cloth and covered her breasts again, thrusting his tongue into her mouth as he tweaked her nipples lightly.

"Oh!" It was a half gasp, half groan as she covered his hands with hers, urging him on. When he then slipped one hand out from under hers, she moaned her disappointment. But that was followed by a startled hiss of sound when his hand dropped down over her stomach to slip between her thighs.

Dani stiffened against him briefly in surprise, and then spread her legs as wide as she could inside his to try to accommodate him. She then groaned into his mouth as he caressed her, her own tongue wrestling with his as she arched and twisted in his hands. Dani reached up and back then to slide the fingers of one hand into his hair and clutch his head to urge him on, but then slid the other behind her back between their bodies and into the water to find his erection once more. Decker froze, his hands stilling as he groaned into her mouth and bucked into the caress.

With the second stroke, he recalled himself and resumed kissing and caressing her. His kiss was more demanding now, though, and their caresses more urgent. When they were both panting and breathless with need, Decker broke their kiss and withdrew his hands again, this time to lift and turn her. The moment he had her settled sideways in his lap, he began to trail his mouth down her cheek and then along her neck and lower to find and clasp one damp nipple.

Dani breathed his name, a sound of need and pleading as her hand found him again under the water's surface and closed. It was no gentle caress, but one determined to bring him to the brink. Afraid he would explode there in the water, Decker reached down and forced her hand away. Dani allowed it, but also rose up in the water to shift until she knelt with knees on either side of him. She then reached for him again as she settled herself on his lap, using that hold to direct him into her.

Decker's breath left him on a hiss as her warm, moist heat closed over him and he had to bite his tongue hard to keep from exploding right then. Dani appeared to know this and smiled wickedly as she released him to grab the sides of the tub and slowly eased herself down and then just as slowly raised herself back up. Decker ground his teeth helplessly for a minute, and then reached between them to find the nub between her legs. He caressed her, running his finger around and over it until the smile left her face to be replaced by an almost pained look as Dani began to move more swiftly into the stroke. Decker began to raise his hips, thrusting into her almost violently as she lowered herself, and she shifted one hand to his shoulder to steady herself as he drove them both over the edge.

The sound of sloshing water, joined with violent coughing, was enough to wake Decker from the slumber he'd dropped into. Leaping off the bed, he rushed to the bathroom door and nearly thrust it open before he caught himself and knocked instead.

"Dani? Are you all right?" he called loudly, frowning at the deep violence of her cough. "Dani?"

"I'm fine," she got out between hacks. "Just swallowed some water. Go away."

Decker hesitated, but while she was still coughing, it didn't sound as violent as it had, and after a moment, he turned and walked back to the bed, wondering how she'd managed to swallow water.

He was about to lie back down on the bed, but paused as he became aware of a quickly cooling damp spot on the front of his jeans. He stared at the dark patch, grimacing as he recalled the dream he'd had. It had started out just plain imagination, but he must have drifted off to sleep because it had quickly felt, smelled, and seemed real. If he hadn't awoken on the bed, startled from sleep by Dani's coughing, he could almost believe it *had* been real. That he'd actually walked in that bathroom and—

Decker paused and stood a little straighter, his head slowly turning toward the bathroom door as he recalled another symptom of finding a life mate—shared dreams. In his case, wet dreams.

Dani gave one last cough and then sagged in the tub. Despite having slept nine hours, she'd somehow managed to fall asleep in the tub and nearly drowned herself. She couldn't believe she'd done that. More than that, she couldn't believe the dream she'd had when she'd fallen asleep. It had featured her and Decker-Maybe-Argeneau-Maybe-Pimms indulging in some pretty hot sex.

Good Lord, Dani thought with disgust, she was having erotic dreams about a man whose last name she didn't even know. She then recalled that she'd nearly had real sex with the man whose last name she didn't even know in the SUV the night before. She covered her face with the damp washcloth, wondering what was the matter with her.

Obviously she was losing it. Dani was no prude, but . . . Gad! She'd never been promiscuous either. She'd been too busy studying and trying to keep her grades up to bother much with dating at university and medical school. Then she'd had her internship, which had been years of hell where sleeping alone didn't happen much, let alone sleeping with someone else.

Not that she was a virgin. She'd had boyfriends and dates and such, but she'd certainly never before indulged in a hot humping session in the back of an SUV speeding up the highway.

What was the matter with her? This just so wasn't like her at all. She didn't lust after men she'd just met. So to lust after this one, who happened to be a vampire . . .

Dani closed her eyes as that word ran through her brain. *Vampire. Life mate. Rogue.* She was gaining a whole new vocabulary and wasn't at all sure it was one she wanted. Although she wouldn't mind a few more explanations. Especially about the life mate business. Lucian had said she was Decker's, and Decker had told her that a life mate was that rare person whom a vampire could relax with. Just how rare? And *was* she Decker's life mate? If so, what exactly did that mean?

Did she even have the right to wonder about this stuff when Stephanie was kidnapped and in peril? Dani didn't feel like she did and felt selfish and uncaring for doing so.

Sighing, she pushed the button to allow the tub to start to drain and stood up to reach for a towel, making a silent vow as she did. From now on, she would concentrate on the most important matter at hand. Finding Stephanie.

Chapter Nine

Decker paced to the windows, peered out over the fields behind the house, and then paced back to the bed, only to repeat the circuit. He'd made a quick run to his room to change into clean jeans and arrived back in the room to hear splashing from the bathroom. It hadn't been the violent sounds that had accompanied her coughing earlier, however, so he'd begun to pace as he waited for her to finish.

The sound of the bathroom door opening brought Decker's pacing, and thoughts, to an abrupt halt. He turned as Dani stepped into the room. She was rosy-cheeked, her damp hair brushed back and flat to her head. The sight was endearing, he decided, and then noted that she had been forced to redon the clothes she'd worn earlier. They would have to look into getting her some more clothes.

"You look adorable." The words tumbled from his mouth unbidden. They brought a suspicious glint to Dani's face, as if she thought he was being sarcastic.

"Thank you," she muttered finally and added, "You look like hell."

It surprised a laugh from Decker, and he smiled wryly and said, "Thank you."

"I mean you look tired," she added quickly, flushing.

Decker grimaced, but nodded and admitted, "I am."

"Well, for heaven's sake, go to sleep then," Dani said, sounding exasperated.

Decker sincerely wished he could. He was exhausted, but shook his head. "I can't."

"Oh right. You have to keep an eye on me," she said with irritation, and then exploded with annoyance. "This is stupid. I'm not going anywhere, I have to wait for my phone. And if you don't sleep now, you'll be useless when Nicholas calls and we have to move."

Decker cleared his throat and said, "Speaking of Nicholas—"

"I don't want to hear it," Dani cut him off sharply, and immediately hurried to the bed to drag the soft wool blanket off it. She then rushed for the door.

"Where are you going?" Decker asked in a hissed whisper as he hurried after her into the hall.

"To sunbathe," Dani hissed back, apparently no more eager than he was to wake Lucian and the others again.

He opened his mouth to argue with her, but then snapped it closed and rushed down the stairs after her. Decker waited until they'd moved into the kitchen before opening his mouth again, but she beat him to it.

"I'm only going to be on the lawn. You can keep an eye on me from the house . . . or am I not allowed to go outside at all?" Dani added, and paused at the door next to the breakfast nook to turn a glare on him.

Decker hesitated. He didn't want her to feel like a prisoner, and he *could* keep an eye on her from the house, but he really wanted to talk to her about Nicholas. He knew Dani didn't think she wanted to hear it, but she had to. Lucian was right, it was better if she understood the true situation.

At least, Decker hoped his uncle was right, because he sure as hell didn't know what was best anymore. The problem was he was torn by several different motivations. Part of him wanted to protect Dani from the knowledge he had to impart, and keep her hopes alive by allowing her to count on a man who just might not be that dependable. Another part was irritated as hell that she appeared to trust Nicholas more than she did him. And yet still another part thought it might be best to tell her because, while it would shatter her illusions, it would also prepare her for the worst if it turned out Nicholas wasn't on their side.

Decker was torn from his internal struggle by the sound of the door closing. Glancing up, he saw Dani through the door window, stomping off across the deck toward the grass, dragging the blanket with her. It appeared she'd grown tired of waiting for him to make up his mind and made it for him.

Cursing, he moved to the door, peered out as the sun peeked out from behind a cloud, and then ground his teeth together and pushed the door open to follow her.

"What are you doing out here? You guys are supposed to avoid the sun," was Dani's irritated greeting when he caught up to her halfway down the yard. It was obvious she'd hoped to escape him by coming out here. For some reason that just made him more determined to stick with her.

"We do, but not all the time," Decker said. "Besides, there's plenty of bagged blood in the house."

Dani glared at him, obviously annoyed and then snapped, "Fine," and turned to continue walking.

"Where are we going?" he asked, smiling despite himself. She really was quite adorable when all huffy like this.

"*I*"—she emphasized the word—"am trying to find a dry spot to lay out the blanket."

Decker's gaze slid over the dew-kissed lawn. While it was hot and muggy out, it was still early and the sun wasn't making a very good showing. Decker smiled as he eyed the clouds overhead. If he wasn't mistaken, they were storm clouds. Mother Nature was on his side, it seemed.

His gaze slid back to Dani. He'd allowed her to rush ahead a couple of feet and now found himself staring at her behind and the backs of her thighs and even her shapely calves as she hurried along. Distracted as he was by the view, Decker was completely unprepared when she stopped abruptly and turned around. He nearly crashed into her before he could stop himself, but managed and—ignoring the scowl she was giving him—lightly asked, "Giving up?"

"Not in this lifetime," Dani assured him, grim-faced as she headed back toward the house. "Just giving the grass more time to dry so I don't ruin the blanket."

Decker nodded, trying not to show his relief. Despite what he'd said, he didn't like being out in the sun. The damage would be minimal for her and simply add to the aging process over time, which wasn't the case for him. His skin was a little more sensitive due to lack of exposure, and would take on more damage because of that. Decker was old enough to have been trained from birth to avoid such an occurrence. More sun meant more blood needed, which meant more risk of discovery.

Despite the fact that they now used bagged blood from blood banks, they still tried not to use any more blood than necessary. The mortal blood banks were often notoriously short on supplies, and the blood banks the immortals ran were really no different. Wasting blood made him feel guilty and uncomfortable, Decker acknowledged to himself as he followed Dani back to the house.

He'd thought she intended to return inside, but learned his mistake when she laid the blanket over the railing surrounding the deck and then turned to the left and began to walk away.

Grimacing, Decker quickly followed. "Where are we going now?"

"To explore," she muttered, and then asked, "Where are we anyway?"

Dani glanced over her shoulder as she asked the question, catching him eyeing her behind and legs again. Decker raised his eyes, but shrugged unrepentantly. He was a man, and if the woman was going to charge ahead of him, he was going to be looking at her butt. There wasn't much else to look at out here.

"Just outside Toronto," he said, answering her question.

"Hmmph," she grunted, though whether it was at his ogling her or his answer, Decker couldn't tell.

"What are we going to explore?"

"The barn," Dani muttered. "You can't see it from my room. I didn't realize it was here."

Decker glanced to the barn ahead, not that there was much to see. It was a barn; old, red, rectangular, and huge, with large sliding doors on both the front and back and a small swinging door in the middle of the side facing them. Dani headed for the smaller door.

Decker automatically moved ahead as they neared, to open it for her, his gaze moving curiously over the interior as she walked past him. It appeared to be filled with empty stalls that lined the opposite wall for two thirds of the way before stopping to leave an open area. This side was the same except that the middle stall was missing to make way for the doorway they were entering through.

"They're going to tear it down and build a garage here for the SUVs," Decker announced as he followed her inside.

Dani's response was another grunt as the door swung closed behind him, leaving them in darkness.

"Hang on," Decker said. While he could still see well enough to move around, he knew she was probably now left as blind as the proverbial bat. He moved back to the door and swung it open again, but all the way this time, until it banged against the outer wall. When it stayed open, he nodded his satisfaction and stepped back inside, but Dani was no longer where he'd left her. His head turned, eyes searching the shadows anxiously until the squeal of metal on metal drew his gaze to the huge double, sliding doors at the front end of the building. She had braved the darkness to approach and slide one open. It moved along the rusty track for perhaps four feet before coming to a grinding halt. Dani gave it another shove, putting her whole body behind it, but the door wasn't going any farther.

"Here, let me try," he offered.

"That's all right. It's fine," Dani decided as she turned to see the effect.

Decker followed her gaze. It was much lighter in the barn now. There were still dark corners, and it was a bit dim overall in comparison to outside, but good enough, he supposed, and moved away from the door to follow as she set out to explore.

"There's still hay in here," Dani commented with surprise as she peered at the half a dozen fresh bales stacked against the wall. At least two more lay broken open on the ground in front of them. He couldn't tell if they'd been deliberately put there, or had simply been knocked off the others and broken open themselves, but they had made a small mound of fresh-smelling hay.

"It's a barn," he said with a shrug. "Barns have hay."

"Yes, but why didn't the previous owners take it with them?" Dani asked curiously as she glanced around and added with surprise, "And the saddles."

Decker turned his head until his eyes settled on two saddles that had been left hanging on the wall. He moved closer to examine them, noting the poor shape they were in. "They're pretty old. They probably aren't much good anymore."

"The hay looked pretty fresh though," Dani commented, and he glanced around to see that she'd started moving along the stalls. Peering curiously into each one as she went, she added, "I would have expected they'd take that with them."

"Maybe they were getting out of farming and had no use for it," he suggested, trailing after her.

"You don't usually farm horses," she said, sounding amused. "At least I don't think you do. I guess they could have been breeders."

Decker didn't comment, and he wasn't looking around much either. It was a barn. Wood walls, wood stalls, the smell of hay, and motes of dust floating in the pools of light spilling from the open doors. It wasn't really very interesting to him. Decker was more concerned with how to tell her what he had to . . . and make her listen.

"Dani," he began.

Dani sighed to herself with irritation. She just knew Decker was about to bring up Nicholas again, but she didn't want to hear it.

She began to walk a little faster along the stalls, asking, "How long do you think it will take for Bastien's men to fix the phone?"

"I don't know," he muttered. "But while we're on the topic—"

"Oh look, more hay," Dani interrupted as they reached the end of the stalls.

Decker sighed and moved up behind her to peer in at the bales stacked in the end stall.

"They must have kept them in here so they didn't have to drag hay all the way from the front for these back stalls," Dani guessed, but was just talking to keep him from being able to. She began to walk quickly back toward the front of the building. "I always wanted a horse when I was growing up. I suppose most little girls do. I'd get one now, but I don't know how to ride and—"

"He ripped her throat out," Decker blurted.

Dani came to a shuddering halt at the end of the stalls, her eyes locked on the open door ahead. She stood just on the edge of the pool of light spilling through those doors. All she had to do was cross the open area with its hay and saddles and she'd be out, able to rush somewhere else to try to avoid hearing what she suspected was going to at least shake, and possibly topple, all the hopes she'd placed on the shoulders of one Nicholas Argeneau, rogue vampire. Instead she turned slowly to face him, her voice defeated as she said, "Tell me."

Decker glanced away, regret flickering across his face, then shifted to lean back against the stall behind him and crossed his arms over his chest. Peering down at the ground then, he said, "Her name was Barbara Johnson. She was a housewife, eight months' pregnant. Both she and the baby died. She was an only child. Her father had a heart attack when they gave him the news, her husband hung himself after the triple funeral, and her mother became an alcoholic and drove her car into a tree before the end of that year." He raised his head and added bitterly, "The man you're counting on not only killed a woman, but also wiped out a family.

"And that's just the victim's family. Ours was torn apart by it too. His younger brother, Thomas, won't talk about him, and his little sister . . ." Decker shook his head. "Jeanne Louise really looked up to Nicholas and wouldn't at first believe it, but when she finally did . . . she won't even admit to his existence. As far as she's concerned, she only has and ever had one brother."

Dani had moved to stand opposite him as he spoke and now leaned weakly back against the stall she'd stopped in front of. His words swam around inside her head, carrying vivid images. And then she began to shake her head, her voice bewildered as she said, "But he risked being caught to save Steph and me. And he used to be one of you. Are you sure he—?"

"Yes." Decker rubbed the back of his neck wearily. "I was the one who caught him afterward. Her blood was all over him, even still coating his teeth and tongue."

Dani felt her heart sink at this news and shook her head with bewilderment. "Why did he do it?"

Decker shrugged unhappily. "His life mate died in a car accident a couple weeks before. They hadn't been together long, and she was pregnant. I think he just went crazy. Everyone knew he was in a bad way, and we all tried to help, but he was so damned bitter and angry—" Decker shook his head. "He locked us all out of his life. He stopped working as an enforcer, wouldn't see anyone . . ." He paused and then admitted, "Nicholas is my cousin on my mother's side. His father, Armand, is her brother. Nicholas was also my partner before it all happened, and despite the age difference we were good friends as well as cousins. I went to his house that day to try to get him to go out. I knocked, but got no answer and nearly left, and then I heard a woman's scream."

Decker grimaced and admitted, "I was stupid enough to try knocking again before deciding to break down the door or I might have been in time to save her. I just never imagined . . ."

Dani moved to his side, drawn by the guilt and pain reflected on his face. But once there, she had no idea what she could do to soothe him and merely raised her hand to rest it on his crossed arms, offering silent comfort.

It seemed to be enough. Decker took a deep breath, blew it out, and then continued almost mechanically, "I broke down the door, but by the time I found them in the basement it was too late. Nicholas was sitting on the floor with her lying across his lap and—as I said—her blood was all over him."

"I see," Dani said quietly, watching his face. It seemed obvious Decker blamed himself for Barbara Johnson's death, as well as what it had done to her child, father, husband, and mother. The very fact that he knew so much about the family told her that.

Decker, Dani realized, had taken on the responsibility for what Nicholas had done, much as she had been blaming herself for her and Stephanie being kidnapped.

"None of it was your fault," Dani said firmly, wanting to help him see that just as he had helped her. "Nicholas is the one who—"

"I let him go," Decker interrupted.

She stiffened. "What?"

"I let Nicholas go," he repeated. "When I saw what he'd done, I just turned right around and said I was going upstairs to call Lucian. When I got back downstairs he was gone."

"You were probably in shock. You didn't mean to—"

"Didn't I?" Decker interrupted grimly.

Dani raised her eyebrows and asked solemnly, "Did you?"

He turned his face away and admitted, "I've spent fifty years trying to figure that one out." Decker pushed himself away from the stall and paced, adding, "At the time, I didn't know who Barbara was or what had happened. She was just a strange dead woman in his arms. Nicholas was my cousin. He'd been like a big brother when I first moved here from Europe, putting me up, helping me find a place and settle in. He was the one who showed me the ropes when I became an enforcer. Maybe some part of me did know he'd run . . . and let him."

Dani shook her head. "You're second-guessing your motives, Decker, when the truth is, there might not have been any. If you thought that highly of him, you had to have been in shock over what he'd done. Anyone would be."

"But—"

"And even if you weren't, even if you did know he would run, it doesn't make you responsible for the deaths of Barbara Johnson, her child, husband, or parents. That deed was down to Nicholas, and it was done before you got to him. You aren't responsible for those deaths."

"And what about the mortals he may have killed since then?" Decker asked quietly.

Dani hesitated, a frown claiming her lips. She didn't really believe Decker had intentionally let Nicholas go. She suspected he just felt so guilty the man had escaped that he was blaming himself for all of it. She understood that, but it didn't make it right. The only one responsible for anything Nicholas had done that day and since was Nicholas himself.

"And what about those women in the ravine and your sister?" Decker added, drawing her from her thoughts. "What if Nicholas *was* running with that group and just claimed to be hunting them to get the opportunity to escape?"

Dani immediately began to shake her head. "I don't know what happened that day when he killed Barbara. Maybe he snapped, maybe he ripped her throat out, but I still don't believe the man I talked to on the phone was running with those animals, or had anything to do with our being kidnapped and taken. He led you to us, Decker," she said almost pleadingly. "He helped save me, and chased after the rogue when he took my sister. I have to believe that . . . It's all I've got to hang on to."

Decker sighed, his shoulders sagging under the weight of a guilt she knew she couldn't remove. It would be a monkey on his back until he caught his cousin, or perhaps even until he died.

"Right," he said wearily, moving past her to head out into the open area. "I guess we should head back to the house."

Dani followed slowly. There was no reason to avoid him anymore. He'd told her what she'd tried so hard to avoid hearing. They might as well go back to the house. Perhaps once there she could persuade him to sleep, she thought, and then noticed that he'd stopped in the open door and was peering out with a frown. That was when she became aware of the steady ping of rain on the metal roof overhead. She'd been so caught up in their conversation and her own thoughts that she hadn't noticed it when it started. Now she wondered how long it had been coming down.

"We're going to have to make a run for it," Decker said as she reached his side. "I think it's about to really pour."

Dani nodded and took the hand he offered her, and then glanced up wide-eyed as the steady ping suddenly turned into a loud drumming. She turned her gaze out the door to see that it was now almost as dark as night outside, and that the rain was coming down in sheets.

"Maybe we should wait until it slows down again," she suggested.

Decker hesitated, watching as the sky lit up with lightning. It was followed shortly afterward by a loud crack and then a rumble as thunder rolled overhead, and he nodded. "Yeah. We'll wait it out."

Taking back her hand, Dani turned to lead the way to the bales stacked against the wall. She seated herself on one and plucked a piece of straw from it, then watched him slowly move to join her.

They sat in silence for several minutes and then— unable to stand it any longer—Dani asked, "Is your last name Argeneau or Pimms?" When he glanced at her with surprise, she added, "You didn't seem to be sure when we first met."

He smiled wryly and then plucked a bit of straw out of the bale and began to toy with it. "I was born Decker Argeneau Pimms. My mother is an Argeneau. The Pimms comes from my father. But we've always switched between the two names."

When she raised her eyebrow in question, he ex-

plained, "Our kind tend to have to move every decade
or so. People get suspicious when you don't age after
that period, so we move. Our family also switched between the name Argeneau and Pimms every century or
so too. This century they're using Argeneau. At least
my parents and sisters are. I'm not sure about my
brothers."

Dani wondered about that comment, unable to imagine not knowing what names her brothers and sisters
were going by, but merely asked, "How many brothers
and sisters do you have?"

"Three younger sisters and three older brothers," he
answered easily.

"You have an even larger family than we do," she
said with a smile.

"Only one more," Decker said with a shrug. "And we
aren't as close as your family appears to be. It's the age
difference," he explained.

"How old are they?"

"Let's see." He paused to think and then said, "Els-
peth was born in 1872 and Julianna and Vicki—
they're twins," he explained. "I think they were born
in 1983."

Dani stared at him blankly. "1872?"

Decker nodded.

"But that would make her over a hundred and thirty
years old."

"About one hundred and thirty-seven or thereabouts,"
he said, and then reminded her, "The law about leaving
at least one hundred years between each child causes
the large gaps."

Dani closed her eyes as everything clicked into place

in her head. Decker telling Justin that he hadn't eaten since he was one hundred and twenty, his saying in the van that his grandparents had been treated with the nanos in Atlantis, and his telling her just moments ago that his family was using the name Argeneau *this* century. They called themselves immortals, and she was beginning to realize it wasn't because they were quick healers. Dani didn't know why she hadn't worked it out before this. She supposed she'd been too stressed out and worried about Stephanie, but she was beginning to understand now.

"Your people don't age and die," she said.

"We don't age," Decker agreed, "But we can die. I did mention that it was Nicholas's life mate's dying that pushed him over the edge."

"I assumed she was mortal," Dani murmured with confusion. "Sam is mortal, and I thought—"

"Sam is only mortal because she isn't ready to turn yet," he explained, and then shook his head and muttered, "I guess I didn't explain things very well last night." He paused and took a deep breath and then said, "The nanos will repair any damage including that caused by aging. They also kill off illnesses, but they travel through the bloodstream, so if you rip out the heart, they aren't going anywhere or repairing anything. The blood will die and so will they."

"So Nicholas's wife died in an accident that ripped out her heart?" she asked with disbelief. "What kind of accident rips out your heart?"

"No. Nicholas's wife, Annie, burned to death in a car accident."

"So fire can kill you too."

He nodded. "And decapitation."

Dani supposed that made sense, and asked, "But otherwise you don't die or age?"

Decker shook his head.

"And your sister is one hundred and thirty-seven?"

"Thereabouts," he agreed.

"And she's younger than you?"

Decker seemed to realize where her questions were leading. Lips twisting wryly he said, "I'm two hundred and fifty-nine years old, Dani."

"Two hundred and . . ."

"Fifty-nine," he finished.

Finding it just too hard for her poor brain to accept, she asked weakly, "You're pulling my leg, right?"

"No," Decker said solemnly, and then worry crossed his face. "Does the age difference bother you?"

Dani gave a short disbelieving laugh and then frowned and peered at him with concern. "Decker, you've told me about life mates, and I know you think I'm yours, but—"

"I don't think, I know," he said firmly, and then reminded her, "Dani. I can't read you."

"Yes, but—"

"And we're sharing dreams."

She stared at him with bewilderment. The only dreams she'd had since meeting him were the one where she'd been walking a flowered path with Stephanie, and— Dani froze, and then asked with dismay, "The tub?"

"I'm afraid so," he said with chagrin. "I fell asleep on the bed while waiting for you to finish your bath, and . . ." He shrugged.

She felt herself flush with embarrassment, but asked, "So I experienced what you were dreaming?"

"Not exactly," Decker said slowly.

"Well what exactly?" she snapped.

"From what I understand it's a shared sort of thing. Your brain was supplying what you were doing and my mind controlled me, so while I was soaping your breasts, it was you who turned and raised your face to kiss me and you who reached back to grab my—"

"I wonder if the rain's stopped," Dani interrupted in a strained voice.

She started to slide off the bale of hay, but he caught her arm to stop her, pointing out, "You can hear it's still pounding down."

"Oh yes," she murmured, licking her lips and avoiding his eyes. His words had taken her right back to the excitement of those moments, and his voice had deepened as he spoke, becoming so damned sexy . . . She wanted him to kiss her. She wanted to kiss him back. She wanted— Giving her head a shake, Dani pulled her arm free and slid off the bale. She immediately started walking for the open doors.

"It could rain for hours. We should probably go back and . . ." She paused in surprise as Decker caught her arm and spun her around.

"Don't run from me, Dani," he whispered, his expression intense. "I'll just give chase."

"I'm not running," she whispered, her eyes on his mouth.

"Yes," he growled. "You are." And then he did exactly what she wanted and kissed her.

Chapter Ten

A small explosion went off in Dani's head as Decker's mouth covered hers. She didn't resist or try to pull away. Instead her hands slid around his neck and her mouth opened for him without any urging. Dani moaned as his tongue accepted the invitation and slid in. It rasped across her own tongue, wrestling with it as he began to walk her backward, hands at her hips, guiding her as if they were dancing.

Eyes closed, Dani blindly followed his lead, absorbed in the sensations erupting to life in every corner of her body. They came to a halt when she felt something press against her back, and then Decker's hands began to roam. When they found and cupped her breasts, she rose up on tiptoe and moaned into his mouth, and then pulled her mouth away on a gasp as he began to knead them. Decker immediately ducked his head to press his mouth to the curve of one breast visible above her scoop-necked T-shirt.

Dani opened her eyes and watched his tongue slip

out to glide along the edge of her top, riding over the pale flesh and then dipping to lick her cleavage. He squeezed and pushed one breast a little higher and turned his mouth to close over it through the material. She closed her eyes on a moan, and leaned back over the bale of hay he'd backed her into, her hands tangling in his hair. Dani felt him tug at the neckline of her shirt, and opened her eyes as he roughly pulled that and her bra aside to reveal one breast. This time when his mouth closed over it, there was nothing between them, and she cried out, her eyes closing again as his tongue swept over her nipple, urging it to an excited peak.

As quickly as he'd claimed the breast, Decker abandoned it, raising his head and catching her behind the neck with one hand to force her upright for another kiss. Dani went willingly, her response eager and urgent, her own hands slipping from his hair to his shoulders and then to run over his chest. She measured the wide expanse with sweeping caresses that ran over his pecs and then down across his tight, flat stomach, before riding back up to investigate his nipples through the cloth of the T-shirt he was wearing today. Dani flicked her nails lightly over the little excited nubs, surprised to find it made him groan into her mouth with excitement. She was even more surprised when it sent little jolts of pleasure through her own body as if she were experiencing the caress.

She felt Decker's hands at her waist, and then a tugging as he pulled her T-shirt free from her shorts, so wasn't surprised when he suddenly urged her away to draw it up over her head. He dropped it on the mound of hay beside them, and was immediately reaching around for the clasps at the back of her bra. Dani shuddered, goose bumps rising on her flesh as they snapped free, and he drew the bra off her shoulders and down her arms. His hands were covering her exposed flesh even before the bit of lace had fluttered down to join her T-shirt, and Dani reached for his head, tugging his face back so she could kiss him.

This time she was the aggressor, thrusting her tongue between his lips and urging them apart as he tweaked and caressed her breasts and nipples. Decker allowed it, briefly, and then took over the kiss, forcing her head back as he ravished her until she was gasping for breath and clutching at his shoulders to stay upright. Then his mouth broke away and traveled down her throat, just skating over the skin in passing. Decker paused to nip and nibble at her collarbone briefly, making her moan and squirm, and then continued on his way, following a trail to her breast. He divided his attention between each, licking and suckling at one and then turning to do the same to the other as his hands slid away, fingers trailing down over her stomach.

Dani sucked in a startled breath, stomach muscles contracting, but caught at his hands when they reached the waistband of her shorts. Decker let her nipple slip from his mouth then. When he raised his face in question, she lowered her own to kiss him. It wasn't that Dani wanted him to stop exactly, but she was already standing there topless, and he still had all his clothes on.

Decker kissed her back, straightening as he did, and Dani immediately placed her hands on his lower stomach. She caught the material of his T-shirt in her fingers and began to drag it out of his jeans. She felt Decker smile against her mouth and then he was helping, pulling at the cloth and breaking their kiss to lean back as they removed it together. It fell to join her clothes, and Dani stepped closer and pressed her mouth to one of his nipples to give it the same treatment he had given hers.

Decker groaned with pleasure, his arms closing around her, hands sweeping up and down her naked back as she worked, and once again she was startled to find that the act of pleasuring him seemed to roll through her as well. Caught up in the moment, Dani didn't pause to analyze it, but continued what she was doing until Decker claimed her mouth again.

Now his naked chest was against hers, the short, crisp hairs brushing across and tickling her nipples. Caught up in his kisses as she was, Dani didn't consider that it meant his other hand had stopped caressing and gone elsewhere until she felt it slide between her legs. She gave a little start of surprise, and then groaned into his mouth as he rubbed her through her shorts.

Decker groaned in response and then his hand dropped away, only to slide up under the hem of her shorts and brush against her with only the silk of her panties between them. They groaned in unison then. Dani shifted her hips into the caress, offering herself to him, and Decker immediately pushed the silk aside to touch her properly. She began to suck frantically on his tongue as he stroked once, and then twice, and then reached down to find and caress him through his jeans. He was hard, his erection pressing against the cloth as if trying to escape, and Dani left off touching him to quickly unsnap his jeans and yank down the zipper so that she could slip her hand inside his boxers and find him. The excitement building inside her seemed to double as Dani closed her hand over the hot shaft and stroked him, and then Decker removed his hand again. This time she didn't try to stop him when he reached for the button of her shorts, and then he was pushing her panties down.

Decker dropped to squat, forcing her to leave off touching him as he helped her step out of both. He tossed them to the side to join the rest of the clothes on the mound of hay. He didn't, however, straighten again, but instead turned back to examine what he'd revealed. Dani had the sudden urge to cover herself with her hands, but didn't get the chance when Decker reached out to urge her legs apart and leaned forward to press a kiss to one inner thigh.

"Oh—I—" Dani stammered breathlessly, grabbing at the bales of hay behind her to steady herself. She was glad to have it to hold on to when he then caught her by one leg behind the knee and lifted it to draw it over his shoulder. She was left standing on one leg, her behind pressing into the slightly prickly straw as he kissed a trail up the tender skin. When he reached the apex of her thighs and pressed a kiss there, the leg Dani was standing on went weak and nearly buckled. Decker's hand immediately tightened on it, holding her up as he ran his tongue over her tender flesh, and then he raised that leg over his shoulder as well, leaving her sitting on his shoulders, facing him and leaning back into the hay to keep her seat as he buried his face between her thighs and alternately kissed, nibbled, and lathed the core of her with his lips and tongue.

Dani threw her head back and cried out, one long ululating sound as wave after wave of pleasure assaulted her. Her brain had disengaged and she was pure sensation as she bucked in his hands, her body straining for what it wanted. Decker shifted his hands to her behind then, controlling the situation, forcing her to remain still as he pleasured her. Just when she thought she was about to reach the satisfaction they were both working toward, Decker suddenly stopped what he was doing and swung around with her still on his shoulders, one of his hands quickly shifting to her lower back to support her as he lowered her to lie on top of their clothes on the mound of hay on the floor in front of the bales.

Dani managed to scrape together enough brain function to marvel at how strong he must be to do that, but it was all she could muster. In the next moment her thoughts scattered as he settled back into his rhythm, scraping over her with lavish strokes and then pausing to suckle briefly before running his tongue around the center of her excitement. When his hands slid up her stomach to find her breasts, Dani covered them with her own, squeezing him even as he squeezed her.

This position gave her more of an opportunity to move and she did, her back arching and hips rocking. Her legs shifted restlessly until Decker pinned one of her legs with his body and then grabbed the other thigh to spread her wider and hold her still. A moment later that same hand moved down to join his mouth, the fingers rubbing over and then into her, and Dani lost it. She screamed his name, her body bucking wildly, back arching up off the hay as pleasure and release exploded within her. They hit in wave after inundating wave until she didn't know where one began and another started, and then it didn't matter and Dani felt herself falling back to the hay as her vision went dim.

Dani woke to birdsong in her ears, a vision of dusty old barn beams above her, and a cat-that-got-the-cream smile on her face. She felt absolutely fabulous, and for one moment didn't wonder why. And then she had the urge to stretch and started to move her legs, only to find them weighted down by something heavy.

Raising her head, she peered down along her body to find Decker lying with his legs on one of hers, his elbow pinning down the other, and his face buried in her lap. She stared at him blankly for a moment as she recalled how they'd gotten there, and then dropped back on the hay.

"Now you've gone and done it, Dani McGill," she muttered. "Not only have you had an almost roll in the SUV, you've had a *real* roll in the hay . . . Well sort of," she added with a frown as she realized it had been only a half roll. After all, Decker had pleasured her, but she hadn't done a thing for him, and apparently his pleasuring her had taken so much out of him that he'd conked out directly afterward.

Dani raised her head to peer down at him again. The man was dead to the world. She blew her breath out on a sigh, then closed her eyes and shook her head, wondering when her life had gotten so out of control . . . and how she was going to get out from under Decker without waking him up. Dani so did not want to be here when he woke. How was she going to face him? What could she say? *Thank you, Decker, that was wonderful. So sorry I fell asleep on you without reciprocating?*

Jeez, she thought with disgust and then stiffened as a sigh sounded and the warm weight of Decker's head was removed from between her legs. Biting her lip, Dani raised her head and glanced down to find him peering up with sleepy, silver-blue eyes.

"Hi," she said weakly and tried for a smile.

"Hi yourself," Decker responded in what was really a very sexy growl, and then he was suddenly crawling up her body. He settled on his side in the hay, one leg splaying over her lower body, one hand moving to rest on her stomach, and the other propping up his head as he peered down at her.

"I'm sorry I fell asleep," Dani said quickly, flushing with embarrassment as she forced the words out. "I—"

"You didn't fall asleep," Decker said, a smile widening his mouth. "You fainted."

Dani's guilt fled, chased out by the pure male satisfaction on his face. "Yes, well," she began with disgruntlement, only to have him interrupt.

"It's another sign of a life mate."

"It is?" she asked, relaxing a little.

Decker nodded, the hand on her stomach beginning to move in a rather distracting manner. "The shared pleasure is just too much for the mind to handle at first, so the brain winks out."

"Well . . . it *was* pretty awesome," Dani admitted shyly and then grimaced and said apologetically, "But it wasn't exactly shared. I was getting most of the pleasure."

"No, you weren't," he assured her at once. "I experienced it too. That's why it's called shared pleasure."

"You mean you . . ." She paused, unsure how to say what she wanted to ask.

"I mean when I do this . . ." Decker bent his head to catch her nipple between his lips, his teeth scraping over the bud and making Dani close her eyes as a sleepy shiver of excitement reawakened within her, and then he lifted his head, releasing the nubbin, and growled, "I experience your pleasure as my own. It flows through you and into me and back, and each time I do that"—he rasped his tongue over her nipple in another quick caress, sending another lazy wave of excitement through her—"it happens again," he whispered. "The waves build up, bouncing back and forth and growing in force until the mind can't take it."

Dani forced her eyes back open and peered into his face, noting that the silver had overtaken the blue of his eyes. She reached up to brush her fingers over the skin by his eye, but shook her head and said, "I can't believe you gave up sex eighty years ago if it was like what I just experienced."

Decker's eyebrows slid up his forehead. "So Uncle Lucian was right, you *were* eavesdropping when Justin and I were talking," he said with laughter in his eyes.

"Sorry," she muttered, withdrawing her hand, but he just caught it and raised it to his mouth to kiss her knuckles.

"It's all right," Decker assured her. "But the sex I gave up eighty years ago wasn't like this. I told you, shared pleasure is another symptom of being a life mate. I've never experienced it until you."

Dani felt pleasure wiggle its way through her at that announcement. It made her feel special, and she smiled and murmured, "Man, it's almost enough to make a gal want to be a vampire if she can experience that."

His eyes glowed briefly, but then Decker said seriously, "I'd like that. But as you know, you don't have to be immortal." When she didn't hide her confusion at his words, he frowned, "Surely you *did* experience what I'm talking about?"

Dani hesitated and then admitted, "I did notice something strange when I was toying with your nipples and . . . er . . . stuff," she added, blushing as she recalled caressing his erection, and then she rushed on, "but you made me stop so quickly and the rest of it was just so overwhelming, that I . . ." She shrugged helplessly.

"Ah." Decker relaxed a little, but still looked troubled and then asked uncertainly, "Do you want to try and see if you experience it?"

Dani hesitated. Did she want to know if she was truly his life mate? Experiencing what he'd just described would certainly convince her. But then what? Did they marry and live happily ever vampire after? And how was she supposed to explain that to her parents? *Mom, Dad, I'd like you to meet my fiancé, Count Great Sex.*

On the other hand, Dani told herself, she was dying to experience what he'd just described. Not the overwhelming passion, of course; she'd already experienced that, although it would be nice to experience again, but the pleasing-him-would-please-her part was fascinating.

It was undoubtedly her scientific curiosity wanting that, she thought, and nearly snorted aloud at her own lie.

"It doesn't matter," Decker said suddenly. "We'll find out eventu—" The words ended on a sucked-in breath as Dani gave a silent answer by reaching down to clasp his penis. It was soft and limp at first, but inflated like an airplane life jacket at her touch. She hardly noticed; Dani was too distracted by the shock of excitement that shot through her. She ran her hand experimentally over his growing penis several times, sending more shock waves through herself as the first one receded and rolled back and knew there was no doubt that she was experiencing this shared-pleasure business.

With her eyes closed as they were, she was startled when Decker's mouth suddenly covered hers, but it was a good startled and she opened eagerly to accept him as her hand continued to play over his now-hard shaft, steadily increasing their shared excitement. But it wasn't enough, she wanted more, and pressed against his chest with her free hand as she turned her head away, breaking the kiss.

When Decker lifted his head, Dani urged him backward, sitting up even as he allowed her to push him down. This was like a drug and she wanted more. She wanted to ratchet the experiment up a notch.

The moment he was flat on his back, Dani shifted to her knees beside him and leaned forward to close her mouth over the tip of his shaft and then groaned along with him as her mouth followed her hand downward, sending shock waves of pleasure through them both. It was the most incredible thing she'd ever experienced, and urged her on as she worked over him. Dani could actually feel what felt best to him, knew which lick, nip, or suck where and at what speed had the most impact.

Her earlier guilt about what she'd thought was Decker's pleasuring only her dropped away like a silk scarf as she laved him with her tongue. He'd experienced the pleasure and excitement along with her just as she was experiencing his mounting passion now.

It was amazing! she thought faintly, and then lost the ability to think when his hand slid over her behind and the back of her thigh, before dipping around to find her own pleasure center. Now she was bombarded by both the pleasure she was giving him as well as what he was doing to her, and it wasn't long before they both cried out their release and the lights blinked out again.

Dani woke with a little sigh and a smile and her head between Decker's legs.

She stared at the penis lying sleeping before her eyes and could have kissed its little head. She was feeling very close to the little guy, and not just because it was about an inch from her nose. Dani had a feeling they were going to be good buddies.

A hand running up her thigh distracted her from thoughts of her new best friend, and Dani forced herself to move. She eased to a sitting position and turned to peer at a sloe-eyed Decker. She couldn't have stopped the smile that spread her lips then had she wanted to, and when he smiled back, she suddenly blurted, "Let's do it again!"

"Hello?"

Decker blinked his eyes open and raised his head slightly to peer around. It took his bleary, still sleep-befuddled mind a moment to realize where he was, and then he recognized that the weight on his chest was Dani, and memory came rushing in.

They were in the last stall at the back of the barn, the one with the hay in it. Decker had insisted on moving the party there after the third time they'd passed out. He hadn't wanted to be caught bare-arsed in the hay in the open front of the barn should anyone come upon them while they were unconscious. He hadn't wanted anyone to come upon them bare-arsed while they were awake either. So when he'd woken up after finally making love to her for the first time, he'd scooped up their clothes and carried her back here where they would at least have a little privacy.

"Hello?"

The second call sounded a little closer, and this time Decker recognized Sam's voice. It was time to move. He eased Dani off his chest, eliciting a little sigh and moan from her. He then grabbed his jeans and T-shirt and quickly tugged them both on while trying to stay bent over and unseen. With that accomplished, Decker hurried to slip out into the barn before Sam could reach the stall and discover them.

"Oh, Decker." Sam paused halfway down the barn and smiled as he walked quickly to join her. "I saw the barn doors were open as I drove up so came to see what was happening. It's too early for you guys to be out and about and I thought Dani might be in here."

Decker glanced at his wristwatch, noting that it was half past six o'clock. The men probably were up, but as she'd suggested, would avoid coming out until later.

"I was going to ask Dani if she wanted to go shopping with me," Sam added.

"Oh, yes, she's . . . er . . ." Decker floundered, not knowing quite what to say.

"Indisposed?" Sam suggested, tilting her head slightly to the side as she eyed him. "Is that straw in your hair?"

Decker reached for his head, running his fingers quickly through his hair as he muttered, "I was taking a nap."

Sam nodded, but then asked, "Why are you wearing Dani's T-shirt?"

"I'm not," he began, but glanced down to see that he actually was wearing Dani's scoop-necked white T-shirt, and he was stretching the hell out of it. He'd thought it seemed snug when he'd pulled it on.

"And inside out," Sam added, barely able to hide her mirth now. Shaking her head, Sam turned away and headed for the door. "Ask her if she'd like to go shopping. If so, I'm leaving in about twenty minutes. That should give her time for a quick shower if she likes. You're welcome to join us too," she added as she left the building.

Decker stared after the woman and sighed. So much for discretion.

"Decker?"

He turned as Dani's head appeared above the stall. "Oh, there you are," she said, smiling when she spied him. "I can't find my T-shirt. Did you . . ." Dani paused, eyes widening as he started back along the stalls. "Is that my T-shirt?"

"Yes," Decker admitted on a mutter as he reentered the stall to find her standing with shorts on, bra in hand, and at least half a dozen pieces of straw sticking out of her tangled hair in different directions. "Sam came looking to see if you wanted to go shopping. I dressed quickly to stop her from finding us and donned your T-shirt by mistake. Sorry," he added, though it came out muffled as he tugged it off over his head. "Here you are."

Decker held it out, but Dani was too busy laughing to take it, which just added to his disgruntlement until he noticed how it set her breasts bouncing. The frown left his face as his eyes locked on the two moving targets.

"Oh no," Dani said suddenly, her laughter dying. "Don't you be looking at me with your eyes all glowy silver, Mr. Pimms. We have to stop now, I want to go shopping. Actually, I *need* to now that you've stretched my top out," she added, slipping on her bra and reaching back to do it up.

Decker remained silent, watching the way her breasts rose slightly as she performed the maneuver, barely hearing her words when she added, "Besides, it must be past noon at least, and I want to make sure the phone didn't arrive while we were out here messing around."

"Six," Decker said absently, his eyes traveling over her body as she finished with her bra and took the T-shirt from his hands.

"Six what?" Dani asked absently as she tugged the cloth over her head.

"It's after six," he explained. "Six-thirty actually."

"What?" she squawked as her head popped out of the neckline of the T-shirt and into view. Pausing then, she stared at him wide-eyed and then said uncertainly, "You're joking."

Decker shook his head, a little surprised by her shock.

"Dani, we've made love at least ten times," he pointed

out, not adding that it had been in several interesting and innovative positions he'd never imagined. Decker had thought he'd done it all before sex became too dull for him to bother with, but Dani was very creative, especially with a saddle.

Her eyebrows had risen with surprise. "That many? It's all kind of a blur for me after the fifth time." She shook her head and then finished tugging her T-shirt into place, muttering, "You must have a Viagra pump where your heart should be."

"It's the life mate thing," Decker informed her. "I gather most life mates are insatiable when they find each other."

Dani didn't comment. She was peering down at her shirt and frowning at its new Deckerized shape. It had been stretched out so much, the neckline was pretty much indecent, and it draped her like a blouse rather than the snug fit it had been. Clucking under her tongue, she tugged at the neckline, trying to make it more acceptable, and then pulled it off one shoulder so that at least it didn't reveal the silky cups of her bra anymore. She then tied a knot in the hem at her hip so that it looked like some sort of eighties fashion style. Apparently deciding that was the best she could do, Dani then tried to rush around him and out of the stall, but he caught her arm, forcing her to a halt.

"Decker, let me go," she complained. "I have to go see if the phone is back. "

"You have straw in your hair," he said with exasperation and quickly plucked the bits out and then tried to smooth the wild mass into some sort of order so she wouldn't be completely humiliated if anyone saw her.

Decker then caught her face between his hands and pressed a kiss to her impatient lips before releasing her.

"Thank you," Dani murmured, and ran for the door as if afraid that he might start ravishing her again . . . and that she might respond despite her worries of the moment. It wasn't that silly a notion. Decker's body was beyond satiated, and yet just the smell of her as he'd neared and the sight of her half naked had been enough to wake little Decker. He'd been hard-pressed to keep the kiss he'd given her to a quick peck and hadn't missed the way desire had flamed in her own eyes before she'd rushed off. They were definitely life mates.

Sighing happily, Decker bent to snatch up his T-shirt and tugged it on as he headed after her.

Chapter Eleven

"Sorry we took so long," Dani gasped, rushing up to the small table in the food court where Sam sat patiently waiting. She dropped the half a dozen bags holding her purchases with relief. "Decker insisted I needed more than just the T-shirt, shorts, and underwear and made me try on oodles of clothes."

"That's all right, I just got here myself," Sam said as Dani finally settled in the seat opposite her. "I only intended to get more sheets since the ones on the beds now are all that are at the house. Then I realized the half a dozen towels I grabbed from my place last night weren't going to last long, and then I thought of linens for the kitchen, and . . ." She shrugged wryly. "A salesperson had to help me carry it all to the car. I just bought a coffee and sat down not two minutes ago myself."

Dani nodded and asked, "I don't suppose anyone called from the house to say my phone was back?"

"No," Sam said solemnly. "I would have hunted you down and told you."

Dani nodded. After rushing from the barn to the house and learning her phone hadn't yet returned, she'd reluctantly agreed to the shopping trip. It wasn't that she hadn't wanted to come, but she'd feared the phone would arrive the minute she left. However, after Mortimer had promised to call Sam the moment it arrived, Dani had allowed Decker to chivvy her into the shower and then hustle her into Sam's car to come to the mall.

They'd split up on reaching the mall, Sam heading off in search of linens for the house and she and Decker popping in to pick up a couple of spare outfits. At least that had been Dani's plan, until Decker saw the one small bag of items she'd purchased. He'd immediately insisted she'd need more clothes than that. He'd then insisted she try on each item and model it for him before buying it.

The whole business had left her annoyed and flustered until Decker had slid into the dressing room to "help" her get out of the last outfit. The mall's air conditioner was obviously on overdrive because Dani's nipples were still erect from the cool air that had assaulted her as he'd stripped the clothes away.

She shivered and pretended to fuss with one of the bags as she recalled what he'd done to her in that little room. He'd had to cover her mouth with his hand to muffle her excited cries by the time he'd finally pulled her onto his lap on the chair in the corner and thrust himself into her. It had been terribly exciting. As had waking tangled with him on the floor, stirred from unconsciousness by the salesgirl rapping on the door and asking loudly if she was all right, though *excit-*

ing wasn't perhaps the right word for that part. *Panic-inducing* probably fit better.

Dani didn't think her heart was going to survive this . . . whatever this was she was having with Decker. The man was insatiable . . . and so was she with him. If they continued like this she was likely to have a heart attack.

"Where's Decker?" Sam asked, bringing her from her thoughts.

Dani gestured vaguely toward the restaurants surrounding them, searching, but unable to spot him right away. "He went to grab us a couple of drinks while I brought the bags over and let you know we were here."

Sam nodded and then asked, "How are you doing?"

"Okay," Dani answered quietly. "Concerned about Stephanie, but Decker keeps trying to reassure me they'll get her back, and does his best to distract me." Dani flushed as she said that, feeling guilty because once they'd hit the barn her mind had been somewhat distracted with Decker's revelations and then by the man himself. She'd thought of her sister several times in the barn and since, but all it took was Decker's touching or kissing her to push the worry out of her mind.

There was something wrong with that, she thought unhappily. This life mate shared-pleasure business was like a drug and it was addictive as hell. She was already jonesing for him to hurry up and get to the table so she could see and touch him.

"It's pretty bad, isn't it?" Sam said suddenly, watching her closely.

Dani forced a smile. "Having Stephanie kidnapped is

bad enough on its own, but by this animal it's just . . ." She shook her head helplessly, trying not to think what her sister might be going through.

"I didn't mean that, though that's bad as well," Sam said when Dani turned to her. "I meant this life mate business. Mortimer and I can't keep our hands off each other either." She shook her head. "I've never experienced anything like this. It's like a temporary madness."

"So it's not just me and Decker it affects like this?" she asked with relief.

"Oh, good Lord, no," Sam said firmly. "Apparently all life mates are . . . well—"

"Walking horn dogs and doggettes," she suggested dryly.

Sam burst out laughing, but nodded. "I was going to say wildly absorbed in each other, but your description is more fitting."

Dani smiled faintly.

"I'm ashamed to admit it, but it's really a good thing that Lucian assigned us to check the Penetanguishene area rather than where Decker found you or you'd still be in the clutches of those rogues too. Mortimer and I were pretty useless during the search. I couldn't think straight for wanting to touch him, and he was no better. I'm amazed we're even alive, or at least that I am since a car accident probably wouldn't have killed him." Her eyes were turned inward, and Sam murmured, "I still don't know how he avoided that little Toyota."

"The Toyota?" Dani couldn't resist asking.

Sam blinked and flushed at the question, and then sighed and admitted, "We got a little carried away at one point . . ." Her lips twisted with guilt as she admitted, "Well, we got carried away a lot and spent a good deal of time parked on the side of the road, rocking the pickup rather than doing what we were supposed to be doing, but the incident with the Toyota was different." She closed her eyes, looking dismayed by what had occurred, and then blurted, "We were driving down the highway and I just reached over to run my hand over his leg—you know, affectionately." She grimaced. "The next thing you know his pants are undone and I'm in his lap."

Dani's eyebrows flew up her forehead.

Her tone was dry when she suggested, "I recommend neither of you driving while the other's in the vehicle until the worst of this passes." Sam made a pained face and reached to rub her lower back, adding, "I probably still have the imprint of the steering wheel in my back. I know I'm going to be bruised for a long while."

Dani flopped back in her seat with amazement. That definitely beat her and Decker rolling around in the back of the SUV while Justin drove. Good Lord, if Sam and Mortimer couldn't even find the sense to pull over before she crawled in his lap, what chance had she had?

"That's way too much information, isn't it?" Sam dropped her face into her hands as if hiding from her.

"No." Dani reached out to touch her arm reassuringly. "I'm glad you told me. I've been feeling horribly guilty for enjoying Decker when Stephanie is out there somewhere suffering Lord knows what. I feel like I should be doing something to find her and instead am—"

"You shouldn't feel guilty. There's nothing you can

do," Sam assured her firmly, raising her head. "From what I understand, Mortimer and Lucian think your phone is the best bet they have at the moment."

"They do?" she asked with surprise.

Sam nodded. "Trying to find them when he doesn't want to be found, especially in a city the size of Toronto, is like looking for a needle in a haystack. And they're not even sure they still are in Toronto. Mortimer said your phone and Nicholas are really the only chance we have of finding Stephanie and the man who took her."

Dani frowned. "Decker keeps trying to tell me not to count on Nicholas."

Sam considered that and said slowly, "He's probably afraid of getting your hopes up and then you taking a big fall if Nicholas lets you down."

"Maybe," Dani murmured, and then met her gaze and said, "I guess they used to be pretty close. It sounded to me like Decker was closer to Nicholas than his own siblings. They were partners too."

"Were they?" Sam asked with surprise. "Mortimer didn't mention that to me."

Dani was silent, her thoughts on the possibility that Decker might also be keeping her hopes down to keep his own down as well. She was pretty sure he'd been devastated by the man going rogue, and didn't think it was just because he blamed himself for letting him escape. She knew she'd be terribly upset if someone in her family had killed someone.

"I guess I'm not surprised," Sam commented.

Dani lifted a blank gaze. She'd been so distracted by her thoughts that she'd lost the thread of the conversation.

"That they were closer than siblings," Sam explained. "Not that they were partners."

"Oh." Dani tilted her head curiously. "Why is that?"

"Well, from what Mortimer said, every sibling would be at least one hundred years apart. That's quite an age difference," she pointed out. "I mean, I know people with brothers or sisters only ten years apart that you can hardly tell are related. I can't imagine having one a hundred years older."

Dani just shrugged. She was the oldest child in her family, more than fifteen years older than Stephanie, who was the youngest, but they were close. She had been her main babysitter when Stephanie was a child, and now that she was older, often had her over for sleepovers, or took her shopping. Knowing her thoughts were sliding perilously close to the worry and fear she felt for her sister, and that a mall food court was no place to let them loose, she pushed those thoughts aside and glanced to Sam. "Decker said you are mortal?"

"Yes. I'm not ready to turn," she admitted quietly. "I suppose I'll have to someday, but for now I'm happy to straddle both worlds."

Dani raised her eyebrows. "We can be turned? You mean into an immortal?"

"Sure. I gather it's just a transference of their nano-carrying blood to an individual." Sam frowned. "Didn't Decker tell you that?"

"No," she said, and Sam patted her arm.

"He will," she said with certainty. "He's probably trying not to overwhelm you with too much information at once."

Dani nodded, but thought it was possible he just hadn't thought of it yet. The explanations had come in fragmented bits since they'd met; a little here, a little there. He might not even be aware of what he'd left out. It didn't matter though. She wasn't really keen on the idea of being turned herself. In theory it sounded all right. Who wouldn't want to be young and healthy for . . . well . . . possibly forever? It sounded good until you factored in giving up everyone else you loved, plus the career you put your heart and soul into in ten years. No, she wasn't keen on turning, Dani thought. But perhaps she too could straddle the line between both worlds and hold off on the change like Sam was. The possibility made her glance to Sam and ask, "Is it hard?"

"What?"

"Being a mortal with an immortal mate," she explained.

"Not so far," Sam said wryly, and then pointed out, "But we haven't been together long."

Before Dani could ask how long, Decker arrived at the table.

"Here we are," he said, sliding into the seat next to her and setting a tray piled high with food on the table.

"This is for you." He set the coffee she'd requested on the table before Dani. "And this . . . and this . . . and this . . . and . . ."

"Good Lord, Decker, I can't eat all that," Dani said with dismay as she stared at the cheeseburger, fries, and donut he'd already set before her and then glanced to the chocolate sundae he was adding to the growing mound. There was another of each still on the tray for him, plus two pitas, two slices of pizza, and two plates with chicken on them. It looked like the man had hit nearly every restaurant in the joint.

"I wasn't sure what was good so I got a selection. Just eat what you want," he said easily, picking up a slice of pizza and biting into it. Concentration on his face, Decker chewed the bite of food and then nodded as he swallowed. "This is good, much better than those burger things. You should try this."

Pushing her cheeseburger aside to make room, he set the other plate holding a slice of pizza before her, then picked it up and held it before her mouth, urging, "Try it."

"I—" Dani had been about to say she knew what pizza tasted like, but found her mouth full of the tip of it as Decker apparently set himself the task of feeding her.

"Bite," he ordered.

Dani rolled her eyes and bit as Sam burst out laughing. Seeing the ridiculousness of the situation, she let a small smile curve her own lips as she chewed the food.

"See, I told you you'd like it," Decker said, noting her smile. He set the pizza on her plate for her to continue feeding herself and turned his attention to his own food.

Swallowing the bite in her mouth, Dani noticed Sam glancing at her food and said, "Be my guest. I can't eat all this."

Decker nodded. "Go ahead, Sam, I got plenty enough for everyone."

The woman took one of the plates of chicken, saying, "I shouldn't be hungry. I ate dinner at my desk while going over affidavits for my boss, but I have been using up a lot of energy lately."

Dani smiled faintly at her chagrined tone, suspecting she knew exactly how she'd been using up that energy, and then asked curiously, "You work at a law firm here in Toronto?"

"Yes. Though not for much longer. I've served my notice. Two weeks and I'm free," she said, smiling, and then added. "Actually two weeks less a day now."

Dani grinned at her pleased smile. "Decker told me you'll be running the enforcer house with Mortimer. How long have you two been together?"

"We met a little more than two weeks ago," Sam admitted, and then sighed and added, "I was hoping he'd come with us tonight, but he has so much to do to get things organized at the house, he couldn't."

Dani nodded sympathetically, but her mind was on the fact that Sam didn't really have much more experience of this life mate business than she did. She found that a bit disappointing. She'd hoped Sam could tell her how long she could expect this driving need for Decker to last. Surely they couldn't maintain this level of hunger for each other forever? Passion was nice, but this all-consuming need that drove everything out of her head was somewhat overwhelming. It was also hampering her thinking processes, pushing worry for her sister out of her head, and that just left her feeling guilty afterward. Surely it had to calm down at some point soon, didn't it? Dani didn't know, and doubted Sam could answer the question either. She supposed she'd have to ask Decker when they got back to the house.

They chatted a bit as they ate, but finished up quickly, eager to complete their shopping expedition. Dani wanted to get back to the house and Sam seemed equally eager to get back. Dani suspected it was because Sam wanted to see Mortimer, something she could understand completely, Dani thought as they got up to leave the table and Decker took her hand in his. Just that simple touch sent a shiver skimming up her arm, and she thought that he would be a difficult man to give up. Not that she was sure she would have to, but Dani hadn't really had a chance to consider the matter much.

How did this relationship work in with her life? She was a doctor, had worked hard to become one. Dani had a flourishing practice, a busy and what she'd thought until now fulfilled life, and was mostly happy with things. However, from what she'd learned, she'd have to give that all up to have Decker. At least she would in ten years or so.

Decker tugged Dani suddenly to the side, drawing her attention to the fact that she'd nearly collided with another shopper not watching where she was going. Realizing this was neither the time nor the place to worry about all this, she murmured, "Thank you" to Decker for preventing the collision, and then began to pay attention to where she was going.

"Oooh, I love these."

Decker raised his head from the package containing something called a shrimp ring that he'd been examining with interest, and glanced to where Dani bent over a section of the frozen food area ahead. She turned to Sam, saying, "These are so good."

"I know," Sam agreed. "I love those. Mix up a salad to go with it and you have a meal. They're great. We better grab a lot of them."

Dani nodded and placed the box she held in the cart, then turned to collect several more. "The best part is they're healthy for you too and only take ten minutes in the toaster oven to make."

Decker was about to turn back to the box he held, but paused when Dani suddenly straightened and turned to Sam with a frown. "Is there a toaster oven at the house? I saw a microwave, but . . ."

"No," Sam muttered. "Not only is there not a toaster oven, there aren't any pots or pans or dishes or silverware."

Decker didn't need to see the dismay on Dani's face to realize what that meant. It seemed they had another store to hit after this one. Or at least he thought that's what it meant until Dani turned and replaced the boxes she'd just picked up.

The moment she'd finished, Sam turned the cart around and headed his way. Since the girls had already covered this section, he assumed they were coming back for him to place his latest selection in the cart and proceeded to do so, his eyebrows flying up with surprise when Dani immediately took it out and set it back where he'd gotten it as Sam continued past him.

"Hey!" Decker protested. "I wanted that."

"We'll pick some up later," Dani assured him and hurried after Sam. He stared after her, watching as the women removed several items from the cart and returned them to where they'd found them, and then shook his head with bewilderment and moved to join them.

"Ladies," he said as he reached them. "You seem to have the concept of shopping a little confused. I believe you are supposed to put items *in* the cart, not take them out."

"We need pots and pans and things to cook with," Dani explained, setting a box of frozen chicken in the freezer.

"So?" Decker asked, not seeing the problem. "We'll stop at a store and buy some after this."

"We can't," Sam informed him. "It's hot out and we don't have a cooler. The food will go bad sitting in a closed-up car while we buy the other stuff."

"Oh," he murmured, realizing that *was* a problem. They'd come to the mall in Sam's car rather than one of the SUVs, which would have had a cooler in it. He grimaced and then did so again as his gaze slid over the almost full cart. It would take forever to put everything back. "Can't we just leave the cart here and—"

"No." The two women gasped the word with horror as they turned on him.

"Decker," Dani said as if talking to a not very bright child. "The food will go bad just sitting here in a cart too. The frozen food especially, the ice cream will melt and—"

"Okay, okay, I get the point." He glanced around. Spotting a fellow in the store uniform and apron near the meat counter ahead, Decker slid into his mind and made him come over.

"What are you doing?" Dani asked suspiciously, eyes narrowing on his face.

"Getting us a little help to save time," he answered. When the store worker stepped up to the cart, Sam moved out of the way, watching wide-eyed as he silently began to take over returning the food from the cart.

"There." Decker caught each of them by the arm and ushered them away. He noticed Dani glancing guiltily back toward the store clerk, but didn't slow his step for a minute.

"Where can we buy what you need?" he asked in businesslike tones as he hustled them out of the store.

"The department store will have everything," Sam answered promptly. "It's up and to the right at the far end of the mall."

"Of course it is," Decker said dryly, and hurried them along. So much for thinking they were nearly done, he thought wryly, positive the women would take forever in the department store.

Decker soon learned he was wrong about that. Dani and Sam seemed as eager to get the task done and get out as he was, and he found himself pushing the cart along at a quick step as they piled things in. He watched dishes and silverware and pots and pans fly into the cart at an almost dizzying speed. There was very little fuss or discussion. They would walk along the aisle, eyes scanning the options, and then one would say, "Those look nice, good, or well-made" depending on the product, and the other usually agreed. It seemed obvious the women had very similar taste. Decker wasn't surprised. They were both around the same age and both professionals. He suspected they'd become good friends in time.

"This looks like the best of the lot," Dani said as she read the side of a box holding a coffeepot. "It's got a timer, automatic shutoff, and the works." She frowned and then glanced to Sam to add uncertainly, "It's bit pricey though."

Sam stepped to her side to examine the writing on the box and nodded. "We'll take it."

Dani asked, "Are you sure?"

"Bastien gave me a company credit card to buy things for the house," Sam announced.

"Ah." Dani and Sam exchanged a smile that Decker fancied was a touch evil, and then the coffeepot went into the cart and the two women continued to the tea-kettle section.

"Women," Decker muttered, his eyes dropping to Dani's derriere as he followed.

"What about women?" Dani asked, apparently hearing him. When she and Sam both turned back in question, Decker found his gaze lifting to Dani's breasts, to the curve of her shoulder sticking out of her top, and then, finally, to her face.

"Incredible creatures," he answered finally. "Beautiful, sexy, smart, know what they want and how to get it."

"And how to spend money?" Dani suggested, apparently not taken in by his words.

Decker hesitated, and then nodded as he added, "But worth every penny they spend and more."

"Good answer," Dani said with a grin before turning away to continue up the aisle with Sam. He saw them glance at each other and then heard Dani comment in an amused whisper, "Didn't take him long to come up with that, did it?"

"Nope," Sam agreed, her voice just as hushed. "Mortimer has his smooth moments too. I think it's because they're so old."

"Geriatrics," Dani agreed with a solemn nod.

"I'm amazed they have so much vim and vigor at their age."

"It's probably only temporary," Dani assured her. "The vim will no doubt fall off from overuse within a couple weeks and the vigor will die off without it."

"No doubt," Sam agreed on a sigh and added, "Such a shame. It's really what they're best at."

Decker was just stiffening up at the insult—there were a hell of a lot of things he was good at besides vim and vigoring—when it occurred to him the women might realize he could hear them and be teasing him.

He was absolutely positive that was the case when Dani commented, "That and eating. You did eat most of that food you bought, Decker."

She hadn't turned her head or raised her voice, but she had addressed him directly.

Sam was chuckling now as she said, "Mortimer has a healthy appetite too."

"And like Decker, not just for food, I gather. How's your back?" Dani asked, and the two women burst into peals of laughter.

He had no idea what they found so damned amusing, but merely shook his head and moved up between them with the cart. "All right you two. Enough, let's get this done and get back to the house."

Sam and Dani began to move a little faster again, but they were still chuckling as they selected a teakettle and set it into the cart.

Decker shook his head and asked, "How much more is there to get? This cart is pretty full."

Sam paused to consider the cart and then frowned and said, "We'll need another cart."

"I'll get it," Dani offered, but Decker caught her arm to stop her and tugged her in front of the cart they already had.

"You stay with Sam. I'll get it," he said, and then slipped away.

The first cart was stacked ridiculously high with appliances by the time he got back, and so was the second one by the time they headed to the checkout. The clerk rang everything up, stacking box after box on her counter as she went until both carts were empty. She then read out the total. Decker winced and almost groaned at the amount, but Dani and Sam didn't even blink.

As the clerk began to help stack the boxes back in the two carts, Decker commented, "This stuff needs to go to the car. Why don't you two head over to the grocery store while I take care of that?"

"Thanks," Sam said, handing over her keys.

Decker nodded as he took them and then bent to press a quick kiss to Dani's lips. At least it was supposed to be a quick kiss, but Dani sighed against his mouth and he found himself urging her lips open so that his tongue could slip in. He felt her hands creep up to his shoulders, and then Sam said with amusement, "Maybe you should help him take this lot out, Dani."

"Yes," Dani breathed as Decker broke the kiss to hear her answer.

"All right. I'll be in the grocery store," Sam said with a chuckle as she turned away.

Decker was just imagining what they could do after they got everything stowed away in the car when Sam called out, "Just watch out for the steering wheel."

He didn't know what the hell that meant, but Dani had suddenly gone stiff in his arms.

Dani blinked her eyes open at Sam's parting warning, her gaze taking in the silver fire in Decker's eyes. There was absolutely no doubt in her mind what would happen if she went out to the car with him. They might get the appliances and dishes in the car, but she was positive they would end up in it as well, probably in the front seat since all these boxes weren't going to fit in the trunk and at least a couple would have to go in the backseat. Dani suddenly had a vision of Sam coming out to find them unconscious in the driver's seat, she having fallen back, draped over the steering wheel, and Decker with his head slumped on her chest, both of them oblivious of the car horn blaring beneath her back and the crowd of curious onlookers it had drawn who were spread around the vehicle looking in.

Groaning, Dani shook her head and pulled away from him.

Decker frowned and raised an eyebrow in question.

"It might be better if I went with Sam after all," she said, flushing.

Decker looked disappointed, but nodded and said easily, "Okay. I'll catch up in a couple minutes."

Smiling with relief that he wasn't angry, she started to lean up to give him a quick kiss and then caught herself and shook her head. "Better not."

Decker chuckled and then bent to press a kiss to her forehead before turning her by one shoulder and giving her a gentle push in the direction Sam had taken. "Go on . . . Before I decide to try to change your mind."

Dani headed out of the store, glancing over her shoulder as she went. Her eyes traveled down his body as he turned to speak to the store clerk. Decker really was a fine figure of a man. Not as strapping as his uncle, who looked like he wielded broadswords for a living. Decker was leaner, but muscular for all that, she thought, recalling running her hands over his rippling stomach and wide chest. And he was super strong. Good Lord, she wouldn't have believed some of the positions they'd explored that afternoon were even physically possible . . . and they wouldn't have been for anyone but Superman. And Decker, she thought on a smile, finally turning her head away once he was out of view . . . just in time to see the wide chest she was crashing into.

"Sorry," she apologized, and tried to step around the man, but he'd caught her by the arms and held her in place. Dani lifted her head then, her smile dying as she stared into the face looking down at her and breathed in horror, "You."

Chapter Twelve

"Thanks." Decker slipped a tip into the store clerk's hand and sent him on his way with the two now-empty carts. He didn't bother to watch him go, but turned back to close the rear passenger door and the trunk. Decker then hit the button on the remote to lock Sam's car and headed for the nearest entrance to go find the women in the grocery store.

Sam was in the dairy aisle, reading the back of a yogurt cup. He had no idea why. The woman didn't need to worry about her weight; she was tall and Twiggy thin.

Sam glanced his way, her eyebrows rising when she spotted him. Setting the yogurt in the cart, she smiled and commented, "Well, that was certainly quicker than I expected."

Decker shrugged as she turned back to the yogurt shelf, not sure why she'd think it would take long, but asked, "Where is Dani?"

Sam turned back with confusion. "She went with you."

"No, she changed her mind and decided to shop with you while I took care of getting the other stuff to the car. She left right behind you," he added, and then frowned and asked, "Are you saying she hasn't got here yet?"

"No." Sam bit her lip. "Maybe she just stopped to get something on the way."

"She can't. She doesn't have a purse." Decker glanced worriedly around, hoping to see her rushing toward them.

"Where could she be then?" Sam asked, sounding bewildered.

Cursing, Decker turned and started back the way he'd come, glancing up each aisle he passed, but she was down none of those. Sam had been chasing around behind him with the cart, but paused when he did and suggested, "Maybe she went to the car."

"I told you, she was coming to shop with you," he said impatiently.

"I know," she said soothingly. "But she doesn't know this mall and it's big and somewhat confusing. Maybe she got turned around, couldn't find the grocery store, and went to see if you were still at the car."

Decker considered that briefly, and then said, "I'll go check. You stay here in case she finds her way here."

The moment Sam nodded agreement, he hurried off. He rushed through the halls, scanning the crowds he passed for Dani as he made his way out to Sam's car.

Decker could tell before he reached it that it was empty, but approached anyway to peer inside in case he'd not locked the doors as he'd thought and she'd crawled inside and fallen asleep.

No such luck. Straightening, he swiveled his head

left and right, checking the parking lot to see if she was approaching, and then pulled out his phone and called Sam's cell phone number.

"Is she there?" he asked the moment she answered.

"No," Sam said almost apologetically and then asked, "What do we do? Should I call Mortimer?"

Decker stood still for a moment, experiencing the panic trying to break free inside him and then said, "No. We'll search the mall ourselves first."

He closed the phone without saying good-bye, his eyes scanning the parking lot once more, and then he started back toward the building. They would find her, Decker assured himself as he walked. They had to. He couldn't lose Dani now.

"There he goes: your hero."

Dani ignored that comment from the man in the driver's seat beside her, her attention instead on Decker as she watched him walk away. She wished she could throw open the pickup door and scream, wished she could move at all really, but the ugly bastard next to her had her firmly under his control. At least physically; he was leaving her to her own thoughts, though.

He was probably listening to them, Dani thought bitterly. It hadn't escaped her notice that he had seemed to be enjoying her terror when he and the others had kidnapped her and Stephanie up north, and he'd seemed equally entertained by it as he'd made her walk out here to this beat-up old brown pickup truck. Dani was sure the people they'd passed hadn't noticed a thing amiss, none of them could have known that she was screaming with terror inside her head.

"I *am* actually enjoying your delightful responses to everything," he agreed, proving she was right and he was poking around in her head listening. "Although I will have to take exception to the ugly bastard bit. I am, and have always been, quite handsome. Don't you think?"

Dani's head turned without her input, her eyes remaining open when she tried to close them as he forced her to look at him.

"Now, tell the truth," he insisted chidingly. "Is this not a handsome face?"

She stared at the face, resentment and anger temporarily sinking her fear and making her silently curse his hide. He was an extraordinarily good-looking man with a charming smile, sparkling yellow-gold eyes, and a glorious mane of golden hair that was brushed back off his face and fell to almost his shoulders . . . and he was still an ugly bastard, Dani thought grimly.

"Oh ho!" He laughed at her thoughts and turned to start the pickup, saying, "You're going to be so much fun to play with. I can hardly wait."

Dani tried to control the fear that wanted to rise up in her at that comment. She didn't want him to have the satisfaction of knowing he'd caused it.

This was obviously the fifth man from the clearing, the one who had gotten away. He was the one the others had called Dad in the van when she and Stephanie had been taken. Dani had thought then that it must be a nickname because surely he was too young to be the father of the others. But back then—one whole day ago, Dani realized with amazement—she hadn't known about immortals and how they didn't age. All she'd known was that he had sat in the passenger seat at the front of the van, watching his sons terrorize her and Stephanie with a small smile that suggested he approved. Since Mortimer had explained that an immortal could completely control a mortal, and that they could have taken Dani and Stephanie without their even being aware or suffering, it seemed obvious that he wanted the suffering. That being the case, she was going to do her best to keep from giving it to him.

"Oh, now, that's just being a spoilsport," he complained, turning to glance at her, and then he gave her a grin that made her skin crawl. "I guess it will be a challenge to see if I can get a response out of you, won't it? Maybe I'll make you dance naked for me when we get to the house. Or I wouldn't mind trying out some of those interesting positions you and Decker tried in the barn. Wouldn't that be fun?"

There was no way Dani could prevent the horror those words sent soaking through her mind, and she was helpless to do anything but stare, her mind writhing at the very thought.

"There we go. Now you're getting into the spirit of things," he congratulated on a laugh. "But you're far too distracting to me right now, so it's time for you to go sleepy bye. I'll wake you when we get to the house," he promised.

Dani expected him to simply put her to sleep mentally as she knew he could, but instead he punched her. She saw his fist coming and couldn't do a damned thing to escape the blow, and then pain exploded in her head and everything went dark.

* * *

"Well?" Decker stopped pacing beside Sam's car as Mortimer, Justin, and Lucian approached. A curse slipped from his lips as his uncle shook his head.

"Everyone's checked in and there's no sign of her anywhere," Mortimer announced.

Decker turned to look out over the quickly emptying parking lot. The men Lucian had called in, men who were supposed to be looking for Stephanie, had been searching the mall for the last hour. They'd spread out like a swarm to find her, and apparently come up with nothing. It was now nearly ten o'clock, the stores would all be closed soon, and then the lot would be completely empty.

"Is there anywhere she's mentioned that you think she might have run to?" Mortimer asked.

"She didn't run," he growled. "She has no reason to run from me."

"Sorry," Mortimer said, and then shrugged and added, "It's just that she didn't seem too happy with you this morning and I thought perhaps she had—"

"Things have changed," Lucian interrupted calmly. "Decker and Dani have sorted out their differences and mated."

"Get out of my head." Decker scowled at his uncle.

Lucian merely smiled at him and then turned to Mortimer to say, "Have men watch her family's home and her clinical practice just in case, but I suspect Decker's right and she hasn't run."

"What are you thinking?" Mortimer asked.

"I'm thinking that her disappearance is connected to her sister somehow," he said. The words were the very last thing Decker wanted to hear, and immediately brought an image into his head of the bodies in the ravine.

"You're not thinking the rogue and Stephanie somehow turned up here and she gave chase, are you?" Justin asked with disbelief.

"It's not impossible," Lucian murmured thoughtfully. He considered it briefly and then shook his head. "But it's just as possible that the rogue that got away in the clearing may have followed you to Toronto and taken her in the hopes of trading her for the others."

"But he didn't have a vehicle to follow us in," Decker said quickly.

"The woods were at the end of a road," Lucian pointed out. "Presumably there was something on that road to cause it to be there. There may have been cottages, or a business with a vehicle for him to steal."

"There were cottages," Justin said quietly.

Decker grunted. He hadn't noticed, but he'd been preoccupied with navigating the dark, bumpy lane without headlights. The rogue who had disappeared from the clearing might very well have stolen a vehicle and followed them. He'd certainly had the time to do it. It had taken a while for them to clean up things at the clearing and then they'd waited on the road to find out where they should be headed. Decker felt his heart sink as he accepted this, but then rallied. If the rogue hoped to trade Dani for the other rogues, it meant there was still hope for her, and that they would receive a call soon.

"There's no use staying here. The men have searched and Dani isn't in the mall," he said, moving to Sam's car. She'd left it for him so that Dani could find it if she was just lost. Sam herself had caught a ride home at least half an hour ago with one of the men. The appliances and clothes had gone with her. The groceries had never gotten purchased.

"Decker is right. Leave two men to wait here in an SUV until the mall closes just in case Dani is lost in there and we missed her," Lucian ordered as Decker unlocked the car and got in. "Have the rest return to looking for the rogue and Stephanie."

Decker pulled his door closed and stuck the key in the ignition. He was starting the engine when the passenger door opened and Lucian slid in to settle beside him.

When Decker raised an eyebrow, he said, "I am riding with you. Justin drives like a horse's arse."

Decker's mouth twitched at the acerbic comment, mostly because it wasn't true. Justin didn't hesitate to use speed when necessary, but was really a very good driver. However, that wasn't the real reason his uncle had chosen to ride with him. Decker suspected it was because he was worried about how Decker was taking all of this.

"I never worry," Lucian growled, doing up his seat belt.

Decker gave a harsh laugh of disbelief. "Yeah, I know. You're a coldhearted bastard . . . and you're still reading my thoughts."

Lucian didn't respond.

"Wake up."

Dani blinked her eyes open to find herself sitting slumped in the front passenger seat of the pickup. She felt weak, a little nauseous, and there was a terrible pounding in her head. Wincing, she sat up, closing her eyes quickly when the interior of the vehicle began to swim in a rather alarming manner.

"Yes, I know. I hit you too hard and now you feel nasty," came the impatient comment from her right side. "But we all have our trials to bear. Now, come on. Rouse yourself and get out. We're here."

"Where's here?" Dani asked fuzzily, forcing her eyes open again. Much to her relief, the world didn't move around her this time. Turning cautiously then, she peered at the man standing outside the vehicle, holding the door open. "Who *are* you?"

He raised his eyebrows at the question, and then clucked his tongue with feigned dismay. "I forgot to introduce myself, didn't I? That was most remiss of me. Leonius Livius the Second at your service." He gave a sweeping bow that reminded her of movies of Renaissance times and then straightened and gave her a wink as he added, "You can call me Leo."

"Let me guess," she said wearily. "You were born and raised during the Renaissance?"

"A very good guess, but no. Alas, I was born much earlier," he assured her. "I did enjoy that era though. The long ball gowns were very elegant and helped to hide any cuts I made in search of food. I could keep a woman for months before having to find a replacement if I was careful not to take too much blood."

Dani recalled the shape of the bodies in the ravine and wondered if that was what had happened to them, kept alive for months, their blood being drained, their life slipping away while this man and the others abused and taunted them. It could be what was happening to Stephanie right now.

"Of course, with the skimpy clothes you girls wear nowadays, that isn't possible."

Dani glanced down at her stretched-out top and shorts and supposed he was right. Thinking back to the brief, shadowed glimpse she had of them, she thought there had been cuts at all the major arteries on the women in the ravine.

"To keep a woman any length of time now, one has to either keep them hidden or dress both them and yourself as punks. My sons don't seem to mind, but I find it a rather rough and distasteful style." He shrugged, and then added, "But one does what one must."

"The men in the clearing were all your sons?"

"Yes they *are*." He emphasized the present tense.

Dani ignored that. "And the one who took my sister too?"

"Ah yes, sweet Stephanie. She's prettier than you," he commented, glancing her over. "And quite the screamer as well. Twenty-one took a real shine to her. I could tell."

"Twenty-one?" she echoed, confusion and worry for her sister tumbling through her.

"Leonius the Twenty-first," he explained. "Twenty-one for short."

"You named all your sons Leonius?" Dani asked slowly, struggling to understand.

"Of course. I was named after my father and it only seemed right to continue the tradition, so my first son was Leonius the Third, and so on."

"Yes, but—"

"But, but, but," he interrupted impatiently. "We were talking about the sweet, screaming, Stephanie."

Dani closed her mouth.

"Aren't you going to ask me if she's all right?"

"You couldn't know if she is or not if you've been following us around," she said quietly. Decker had said they'd removed everything from the men's pockets while searching for keys to the van, so Dani knew he didn't have a cell phone to call or be called on and probably had no better idea where his son, Twenty-one, was than she did.

"Ah, but I wasn't in the clearing to be searched and Twenty-one fled before that," he pointed out, apparently having dipped into her thoughts. He allowed her to get her hopes up that he might know where her sister was and if she was all right, and then happily squashed those hopes by saying, "However, I did lose my phone somewhere along the way. Probably down in the ravine with the girls," he said with a frown. "I do hope they don't run up my minutes on me. You women are so yippy."

Leonius burst out laughing at his own words, but Dani merely stared, not finding his little joke the least bit amusing. After a brief moment, he stopped and peered at her with a little sigh. "I fear you are lacking a funny bone, Danielle. We shall have to work on that. In the meantime, while I don't have my phone, my boys and I do have a system for contacting each other should we get separated during one of our little adventures. No doubt Twenty-one has left a message by now . . . As well as his brothers if they've managed to free themselves. I'll check after I get everything rolling here."

"But the others are dead," Dani pointed out, feeling like she was Alice and had just fallen through the looking glass.

"No. Decker and Justin staked them through the heart, it's true, but I unstaked them. Not enough to make it obvious. I only pulled the stakes out enough to be sure they were no longer piercing the heart."

"You were under the tarp when we were driving to Toronto," she said with realization. She'd thought she'd counted five bodies, but Decker and Justin had assured her there were only four.

"Yes, I was. I'm very old, you know, and strong. I recovered more quickly from the tranquilizer than even I would have expected. Not fully, mind you, but enough to roll myself out of the clearing and down into the ravine with the girls. I was recovered enough to walk and talk by the time they were moving my boys to the van. I waited until they turned their attention to putting out the campfire and collecting you, and then got under the tarp with them. I managed to raise the stakes on two of them before Decker started the van and set out, but had to be much more careful once they decided to wake you. Justin was constantly looking back to talk to you."

Leo pursed his lips. "I fear the delay may have cost one or two of my boys their lives. You can't leave the stakes in too long if you wish to preserve life. If the blood dies from lack of oxygen, the nanos die, and there is no hope for the host. But I'm not sure how long that actually is."

Dani couldn't help noticing that while he looked displeased, Leonius didn't actually look torn up about the loss . . . and hadn't been willing to risk being caught to unstake them. "You were gone when we switched vehicles at Outdoor World."

She had seen Decker and the others crowded around the back of the van and assumed they had been checking the bodies. Decker would have noticed an extra one.

"I left your delightful company while Justin was busy getting gas and Decker escorted you into the restaurant to use the facilities," he announced. "While my sons were showing no signs of regaining consciousness yet, I knew I couldn't wait for them and slipped out while I had the opportunity. I then hitched a ride with a lovely pair of young women. The brunette drove, following you, while I fed on the redhead in the backseat. She was an exciting little bundle; a real screamer like your sister. I actually had to concentrate hard to keep her friend under control and driving while I drained her life away. Sally was her name. I believe the three of you met. At least the brunette had a memory of speaking to you briefly to tell you a stall was available in the ladies' room."

Dani blanched, recalling the two women with the cell phone in the fast-food restaurant.

"You are so delightfully expressive," Leonius said with a chuckle. "I really don't even need to read your mind to know what you're thinking."

"Why *aren't* you reading my mind?" she asked, only now realizing that he seemed to dip in and pluck things out intermittently. He wasn't in there constantly, though, and wasn't controlling her either.

"I don't wish to share your headache or try to decipher thoughts that are obviously as slow as molasses. I'll wait until you're more recovered, thank you. Now, shall we get out of the pickup?"

Dani hesitated, but supposed there was little point resisting right now. She was too weak to run, and he would simply take control and make her do what he wanted. Besides, the sooner he "got things rolling," the sooner he would see if he had a message from Twenty-one, and she might learn how Stephanie was.

Wincing at the pain that immediately stabbed through her head, Dani shifted on the pickup's bench seat and slid out of the truck. The jolt as her feet hit the ground sent a pain so sharp through her head that nausea followed, and she had to close her eyes and clutch at the truck, taking deep breaths to try to keep down the food she'd eaten at the mall.

"Oh my, tsk tsk. You really are in a bad way. I hit you far harder than I'd intended, but then you *were* trying my temper. You must try not to spark my temper so this doesn't happen again. I wouldn't want to accidentally kill you in case my sons haven't managed to escape and are still with the enforcers. I might have to trade you for them."

"Me?" Dani straightened slowly and just as slowly turned her head to peer at him with disbelief. "They won't trade your sons for me."

Leonius was silent, his gaze concentrated on her face, and then his eyebrows rose. "You actually believe that," he marveled, apparently having suffered sharing her headache long enough to read her mind. "You have no idea of your value, do you? How charming."

He broke out in laughter, making Dani wince as the sound grated on her nerves and aggravated her pounding head.

"Now listen," he said suddenly, the laughter dying as

abruptly as it had started. "Let Daddy teach you a thing or two that you can use." Leonius paused until she met his gaze and then said, "A life mate is more valuable than anything else on this earth. Most immortals would give up any and all wealth they'd accumulated, their family, and even their own lives for a life mate. You are a precious jewel. Do you understand?"

Dani nodded slowly, but only because he expected her to. She didn't really believe that she carried that high a value for Decker. She simply couldn't. They had only met the day before. Dani liked him . . . well, more than liked him, she acknowledged; she liked him *a lot* . . . And she was definitely in lust with him and—judging by his performance that day—thought he might be in lust with her too, and maybe liked her a lot as well, but that didn't mean he was going to turn over this man's murdering sons for her. At least, she hoped not. Dani didn't want them free. How could she enjoy any peace of mind knowing those animals were out preying on innocent women because of her?

"Are you feeling recovered enough to walk?" Leo asked solicitously. "We should really go inside. We mustn't keep our hosts waiting."

Dani turned her head slowly to the building they were parked beside, her gaze sliding over an old Victorian house with a wide, white front porch. She then swiveled to peer at the outbuildings and fields of corn and felt her heart sink. She was sure this was not his house. She was also sure their "hosts" weren't willing ones, and she feared this was all going to get much worse before it got better.

Chapter Thirteen

"Come, I have a couple of surprises for you, and I know we're going to enjoy them mightily." Leonius took Dani's arm and half dragged her up the steps to the porch of the old farmhouse when she didn't move quickly enough for his liking. She winced at his bruising hold, but otherwise didn't react. She had no intention of saying or doing anything that might add to his enjoyment of this nightmare.

"Here we are." Leo leaned past her to push the front door open and then forced her inside.

Dani closed her eyes briefly as the bright, overhead light sent shafts of pain through her head. The smell of cinnamon and apples teased her nose and brought her eyes slowly open. They stood in an old country kitchen with white cupboards and a wide-planked, hardwood floor that was undoubtedly as old as the house itself. Her gaze slid over a rooster-shaped teapot on the table, cow figurine salt and pepper shakers, and finally to the source of the sweet smell; a pie, not long from the oven. It sat on a cooling rack on the far end of the old, long, butcher-block table before her.

"I was watching from the woods in front of the house when you and Decker went into the barn," Leo said beside her. "When you stayed there so long, I approached under cover of the rain. Once I saw what the two of you were up to, I knew I'd have time to search for a place close by, somewhere near enough to keep an eye out, and to bring you to after I captured you." He paused to explain, "I didn't expect you to go shopping or even to really leave the grounds. I expected I'd have to steal you from the house while the others were sleeping.

"Anyway," Leo continued, urging her to the opposite end of the table. "I was very pleased when I found this place. It's nice and cozy, with only the mister and missus to worry about . . . I was a little worried about it being right next door, but—" He brought them both to a halt in front of the pie and ran one finger lightly over the crust. As light as his touch appeared to be, some of the crust flaked away. It made him smile, and he continued, "When I came in the old woman was just taking the pie out of the oven. I decided to take that as a good omen and risk it."

Dani frowned at the mention of an old woman, wondering what had become of her, but then his words sank in and she realized how close they must be to the enforcer house. Right next door. If she could just get away—

"Your heart rate has picked up," Leo commented with amusement, and when she cast a startled glance his way, he explained, "I have very good hearing. We all do. And your heart is racing. What could you be thinking, I wonder?" He leaned close and whispered by her ear, "Could you be thinking of escaping? Running away to your Decker?"

He burst out laughing at the thought, then shook his head and said, "So amusing" as he turned and led her to an archway leading to the next room.

It was a living room. With no lights on it was dark enough that she had trouble making out much. Leo didn't seem to have the same problem, and she was reminded that Decker had said the nanos improved their night vision when he asked with distaste, "Very colonial, don't you think?"

She glanced to his face and thought he was wrinkling his nose, and then he confided, "I despised the colonials. A bunch of jumpy redneck idiots with guns who shot first and asked questions after. It was hard for a self-respecting no-fanger like me to get a meal without getting a chest full of buckshot in the process."

Yay, colonials, Dani thought grimly, although she hadn't a clue what a no-fanger was.

Leo was apparently reading her mind again because he turned on her and said, "Oh, see, now that's the kind of thing that's going to make me have to punish you again. If you don't learn a little self-control, this could be even more painful than I planned."

Dani remained silent. There was nothing else she could do.

Nodding with apparent satisfaction, Leo led her through the dark room to a door. He opened it, flipped a switch to turn on the lights, and then urged her down into a laundry room in the basement.

Dani glanced around at the concrete floor, cheerful pale yellow walls, and then to the washer and dryer against the wall as he led her the few steps to and through an archway into a much larger room. It was obviously the husband's workshop. The wall opposite them was covered with pegboard. Tools of every description hung from hooks slotted into its holes. The wall on the left was taken up with a long workbench. The wall on the right had shelves holding sanders and paint cans lined up on either side of a wide archway into what appeared to be a small, dark room taken up by a large boiler and the other workings of the house. But Dani barely gave all of this a glance. Her attention was on the three chairs set in the center of the room and the elderly couple, each one bound and gagged and tied to an end chair, leaving the one in the center empty.

"Come. Let me introduce you to our hosts."

Dani stumbled forward when he tugged her arm, her gaze shifting between the couple. They were older, perhaps in their late fifties to early sixties. The husband had skin darkened and leathery from years in the sun, and a grimly determined expression that refused to show fear. The wife had wide eyes full of tears, fear, and pleading as she gazed at Dani from above her gag.

"This is Mr. Dani's-Dinner and Mrs. Dani's-Midnight-Snack," Leo announced, bringing her startled glance to him as he explained, "They're my surprises. They're going to help you through the turn, my dear."

"Turn?" she asked sharply. "I thought you were going to trade me for your sons?"

"I am," he assured her in a soothing voice, and then grinned. "Actually my original plan was to kill you to punish Decker for staking my sons, but then I realized he was only following Lucian's orders and a lesser punishment would do . . . for him," he added darkly. "Lucian is another matter entirely. He's lorded it over the rest of the immortals for far too long. It's time he—" Leonius stopped suddenly, his anger falling away. Shrugging, he said, "But I digress. We were talking about you. Come sit."

He urged her toward the center chair, taking control of her and making her sit between the older couple when she resisted.

Dani sank onto the seat and turned to look first at the husband and then at the wife. The husband peered at her pityingly, the wife with despair. She turned back to Leonius and said the first thing that popped into her head, "But I don't want to be a vampire."

"I know," he murmured, smiling down at her in a way that suggested that didn't bother him at all. "So sad really. Don't you realize there are women all over the world who would pay good money to be one?"

"Well go turn them then," she said at once.

Leo burst out laughing. "You are so adorable. No. I fear it's you or no one."

"Why?" Dani asked with frustration.

"Because Decker has to be punished," he explained patiently.

That logic just bewildered her. "But I'm his life mate. He'd probably turn me himself if given the chance. He'll hardly think it a punishment for you to turn me."

"He wants to turn you into one of *his* kind," Leo said. "I'm going to turn you into *my* kind. You'll be a no-fanger, and he won't like that at all. In fact, I'm afraid he and the rest of them despise our kind, my dear, so don't expect a warm reunion should you be foolish enough to escape. Lucian and his bunch have hunted us ever since Atlantis, nearly to extinction at one point. They killed my father and all my brothers. The only reason I survived is because they didn't know about my mother or that she was carrying me in her womb. So"—he smiled cruelly—"this *will* be a punishment to Decker. I have taken his beloved life mate and am turning her into one of the despicable no-fangers he and his kind loathe so much. He'll really want to kill me then . . . and you."

Dani stared at him with a combination of confusion and fear. "I don't—"

"You don't know what a no-fanger is?" he asked, apparently plucking the rest of the thought from her head. "Oh my, Decker has been very remiss. But I suppose he was busy doing other things, wasn't he?"

Dani flushed at the insinuating way his eyes traveled over her, and recalled his saying earlier that he'd seen what they'd gotten up to in the barn.

"Is that a bite mark on your neck, Dani?" He suddenly bent at the waist to bring his face closer to look, and then he asked in a stage whisper, "Are there any other places he bit you, I wonder? More . . . intimate places perhaps?"

She caught the hand that was suddenly sliding up her thigh and leaned her head back to glare at him. The man was crazy as a loon. One thought could make him suddenly angry, while another that should be insulting amused him. She had no idea what he was talking about when he said no-fanger, but she wanted none of it.

"It's an immortal without fangs," Leo said, apparently poking around in her head again.

Dani frowned at the announcement and asked with confusion, "But you have the nanos?"

"Oh yes. We have the nanos and need the blood."

"Then how do you . . ." She paused as she recalled the women in the ravine with their cuts and wondered if his blow hadn't done some brain damage that she would be so slow.

"Like this."

Dani glanced down as the hand that she'd used to grab his was suddenly being held by him in turn, and then he produced a short, sharp knife and flashed it across her wrist. It all happened so fast that it took a moment for her to realize what he'd done, and then the pain set in and she drew in a hissing breath as she watched blood rise, rich and red, to spill out of the wound.

Leo immediately lifted her wrist to his mouth to catch the liquid and began to suck greedily.

Dani stared with revulsion and tried to pull her hand away, but he merely tightened his hold painfully and continued with his meal, sucking at the wound until it stopped bleeding. She ground her teeth together to keep from crying out when he then used his tongue and teeth to dig at it to encourage it to bleed more.

When he couldn't seem to extract another drop, Leonius raised his head and sighed with pleasure before glancing at her to announce, "There's just nothing as sweet as fear in the blood. All that adrenaline and noradrenaline and the extra oxygen just make it perfect." He tilted his head and gestured to the bleeding cut, asking politely, "You didn't mind, did you? It seems only fair since I'm going to give you some of mine."

"You're insane," she said weakly.

"Yes, isn't it marvelous? It's in the blood, you know," Leo announced, and then his smile took on a cruel edge and he used the knife to slice his own wrist, adding, "And now I'm going to share that blood with you."

Dani jerked back, trying to avoid him when he reached for her, but there was no escape. Leonius was fast, strong, and determined. Before she knew it, his hand was at the back of her head, grabbing a handful of her hair. He yanked viciously so that she cried out in startled pain, and then his wrist was immediately against her open mouth.

"Swallow," he ordered.

Dani pushed desperately at his wrist, feeling the blood pouring in, but refusing to swallow it as she fought to get out of the chair and get away, but she was held in place by the hand at the back of her head. When her mouth was full and blood began to leak out around his arm, he suddenly released her hair and pinched her nose closed with thumb and finger. Dani gasped in panic, swallowing convulsively as she tried to get air, and then again, choking on the thick liquid that poured down her throat. But no air followed, just more blood.

Dani was sure she was going to drown or suffocate, and then she was suddenly free. Choking loudly and spitting up what was left in her mouth, she gasped for air and peered around to see that the farmer had tried to help. Bending as far forward as he could, tied up as he was, he'd launched himself at Leo, chair and all, ramming him in the stomach and forcing him back from

Dani. As she realized this, Leo roared with fury and swung out at the man.

Standing bent over, and panting, the chair still tied to his back, the farmer was helpless to avoid the strike. Dani screamed in horror, hardly noticing the wife's muffled shrieks as the blow picked up the farmer and sent him flying into the wall. A loud crack filled the basement as he struck the stone wall chair-first, and then man and what were now chair pieces tumbled to the cement floor.

Dani slid weakly from her seat and onto her knees on the cold concrete, still trying to catch her breath, and then glanced worriedly to the woman when Leo's angry gaze turned to her. She was making frantic little sounds through her muffle and scraping her chair across the floor, trying to get to her husband.

"No," Dani gasped desperately as he moved to the woman, his arm rising again.

Leonius paused and turned to peer at her, one eyebrow arched. "*No* is a word I dislike very much."

Dani bit her lip and then winced when he turned back and hit the farmer's wife. The blow had much less anger and strength behind it, however. While it sent the woman's face jerking to the side, and blood began to pour from a cut on her mouth above her gag, she at least stayed in her chair and remained conscious

Dani bit her tongue, afraid to say anything in case it just angered him and caused him to inflict more pain on the woman, but had to dig her nails into her palms to keep her mouth shut when he bent to lick away the blood trail from the shrinking woman.

"Mmmm." He straightened slowly, eyes closed as he

savored the flavor, and then he smiled at Dani. "Afraid *and* diabetic, an unbeatable combination. You're going to love me for leaving you such a treat."

"Never." The word—full of disgust—slid from her lips before she could stop it.

Fortunately, in his usual unpredictable manner, Leo was amused rather than angered further. Laughing loudly, he shook his head. "You say that now, but trust me, when the hunger hits, you'll tear these two to pieces to suck out every last drop of blood."

Dani stared back with silent horror at the very possibility, and shook her head.

"Yes," he assured her as he moved back to catch her by the arms and lift her up into her chair. He paused then, bent over and face-to-face with her as he added with delight, "It will take less than an hour for the need to get so bad they start looking like a couple of big juicy steaks on legs." He straightened and then continued, "Not long after that you won't be able to control yourself. The pain and hunger will be so strong you'll start gnawing on them."

Leonius grinned at her expression and gave a little shiver. "I can hardly wait and only wish I'd thought to get a camera to film it for you to watch afterward." He sighed. "All this talk of food has given me the munchies. Those two gals from the restaurant weren't very filling yesterday, and I'm afraid in all the excitement today I neglected to feed myself."

His considering gaze turned back to the farmer's wife. As the woman shrank back into her chair, Dani said quickly, "You said she was mine."

Leo turned back, eyebrows rising again, but this time

a wry smile joined them. "You're only saying that to try to save her, but you'll understand the irony of that in an hour or so. I, at least, have a knife. You will be tearing into her with your teeth."

When Dani shook her head again, he smiled and shrugged. "However, I did say she was a gift to you. Besides, I'd just have to run out and grab you another. You'll need at least two to get through the turning. So . . ." Swinging away, he headed for the arch and the stairs beyond. "I guess I'll just have to run out and pick up some fast food. I do want to be back in time to watch the fun when it starts, and, unfortunately, Lucian did choose a spot to hell and back for this new headquarters of his. I might take a bit of time, but I promise I'll get back as quickly as I can. Do try to wait for me so I can watch, won't you?"

Leonius paused at the stairs and turned back. When she merely stared, face expressionless, he let his eyes slide over her and added, "Perhaps I'll find myself a nice plump little blond like yourself." He smiled. "Watching you and Decker earlier today has put me in the mood for some fun and games, and I haven't bothered with that in a very long time. But I promise I'll save that until I get back so that you can join in too if you like." Turning away, he continued upstairs, calling, "Back soon."

The door closed behind him, but Dani waited, listening to the footsteps cross the floor above. The moment she heard the yawn of the screen door opening, then the clack of it slamming shut, she got swiftly to her feet and moved to the farmer on legs that were a bit shaky. Kneeling beside the unconscious man, she examined him quickly, assuring herself that nothing seemed to be broken. Other than a head wound, he appeared uninjured, though he would no doubt be bruised and battered by the abuse he'd taken.

She set his head gently back on the floor and started to glance toward the wife, but paused and raised her hand to her forehead as a wave of dizziness swept over her. The smell of blood immediately overwhelmed Dani and she stiffened and pulled her hand back. The shallow cut on her wrist was no longer bleeding; Leonius had sucked every bit of blood out of it that he could. However, a stain of fresh red liquid covered her palm from her examination of the farmer. The blood glistened on her skin in the fluorescent light in the room, its smell oddly sweet and rather pleasant.

Horrified as that thought wafted through her mind, Dani pushed herself to her feet. The room spun, but, desperate to get away from the bleeding man, she stumbled across the workshop and up the stairs to try the door. It was locked, of course.

Panic immediately overwhelmed her, but Dani leaned her head against the wooden panel, forcing herself to take deep breaths in an effort to calm down. She was panicking about nothing. The dizziness was the result of stress and the wound on her wrist. She couldn't be turning this quickly, Dani assured herself, and then Leonius's words whispered through her head. *It will take less than an hour for the need to get so bad they start looking like a couple of big juicy steaks on legs. . . Not long after that you won't be able to control yourself. The pain and hunger will be so strong you'll start gnawing on them.*

She closed her eyes on a moan. She had to escape and get the couple as far away from her as she could, Dani thought, and turned away from the door to start back down the steps, alarmed at how shaky her legs had grown in so short a time. Doing her best to ignore it, Dani glanced around the laundry room, but since there didn't appear to be anything she could use to pick the lock, she moved into the workshop.

The husband was still unconscious and the wife was looking at him with worry, but one glance at the woman's bloody lip made Dani avoid her and instead head toward the pegboard with its lined-up tools. She grabbed a hammer, then a pry bar, and started to turn back, her eyes running over the archway into the boiler room as she did.

A glimpse of what appeared to be the corner of a door made her pause. Dani peered at it for a moment, then set the tools on the corner of the workbench and moved to the archway. Sure enough, there was a door there, half hidden on the other side of the boiler. She moved closer before opening it, and found herself staring into darkness.

There was a light switch on the wall and she flicked it up, blinking as a bare lightbulb winked on overhead. It was a strange room. Two feet deep and running the length of the basement. It smelled damp and felt chilly. A pump and water softener were at one end, and empty shelves took up the other, suggesting that it had at one time been used as a cold storage room, but the wall across from her was covered with sheet after sheet of hard Styrofoam insulation boards. There was no exit.

Disappointed, Dani stepped back and closed the

door, then turned away, only to sway and grab for the boiler as the room spun around her. She closed her eyes, assuring herself yet again that this had to be because of the blood Leonius had taken. Surely the turning couldn't start affecting her this quickly?

Then why are you avoiding the couple? Why haven't you dared get close enough to untie the wife? some part of her mind asked tauntingly, and Dani moaned unhappily as she acknowledged that they were in real trouble. Leo had forced her to drink his blood and presumably she was turning, becoming like him.

A no-fanger, she thought unhappily. Even though Dani still really didn't know what that was, the possibility that her being one might make Decker despise and apparently want to kill her was gut-wrenching. While she hadn't been sure if she'd wanted to make a life with him before this, having that possibility taken away was enough to sweep aside the uncertainty. It certainly would have been preferable to what she was now faced with.

Leonius had ruined her, she accepted sadly. He had utterly destroyed her and might as well have killed her, because it was the only acceptable end she could now see for herself. Dani was not going to allow herself to become like him, killing innocent people to revel in their blood. She had become a doctor to save lives, not to destroy them.

Becoming aware of an unpleasant acidy feeling in her stomach, Dani closed her eyes, took a deep breath, and forced herself to think calmly. She needed to find a way to get this couple out of here so that they were out of both her and Leo's reach by the time he got back . . .

and then she had to figure out how to kill the no-fanger and herself. She'd rather be dead than a monster.

Her mind made up, Dani opened her eyes again and moved carefully back to the archway. She was about to head back to collect the tools she'd set on the workbench, hoping to use them to force the upstairs door open, but paused at a moan from the farmer. Her gaze slid to find him rolling onto his side. Dani started to go to him, but had taken only one step when the acidy feeling in her stomach increased to a brief stabbing pain. Sucking in a shocked breath, she stumbled, bumping into the arch. She grasped it, and then slid down its length when pain stabbed through her again. By the time the second one passed, she was on her hands and knees, panting heavily.

Finally she lifted her dazed eyes to find the farmer now grunting and making other sounds trying to get her attention. The man was also squirming on the floor, appearing to be trying to move closer to her, his head bobbing. It took her a moment to realize the head bobbing was a silent gesture meant to get her to come to him. Her eyes slid to the blood still dripping from his head, and Dani shuddered as she recalled Leo's claim that in less than an hour the couple would look like big juicy steaks to her.

They didn't have much time. She had to get them out of there, Dani thought faintly. She had to get them untied so they could help her find a way out. Even if they couldn't come up with anything, it would be better if the couple were untied and could at least fight her off if she did lose control of herself.

Determination coursing through her, Dani started to

shift to stand, but groaned and fell back to her knees as the action brought the stabbing pain again. Whimpering, she took a moment to wait for it to ease and then crawled across the floor to the husband. Tears were bleeding from her eyes by the time she reached him, but she ignored that and untied his hands. The moment she'd accomplished the task, he brushed away her clumsy hands and took over the job of freeing himself.

Dani fell back with relief, finding the sight and smell of his blood disturbing. She rolled away from him, curling into a ball on the floor and hugging herself around the waist. She heard him grunt and a rustle she suspected was his getting to his feet, but didn't look. Instead she pressed her hands into her stomach, wishing she could dig out Leo's blood and stop all the pain.

The farmer moved past her, coming into her line of vision again as he moved quickly to his wife. Dani watched him untie the rope that bound the woman to the chair, but when he set the rope aside on the floor, she said, "Tie me up."

The farmer and his wife both turned to glance at her with surprise.

"Tie me up," she repeated. "You'll be safer."

They exchanged a glance, and then he returned to untying his wife, concentrating on the rope around her wrists now.

"If we can't get out of here," she began desperately, "I might—"

"Don't worry, girl," he interrupted. "I know a way out."

Dani felt a moment's hope, even thinking for one moment that she too might escape and perhaps find a way to stop what was happening to her, or to at least get help from Decker and the others. There would be a better chance of their stopping Leo and ensuring he never did this to anyone else than she had by herself . . . and they would keep her from hurting anyone too, Dani thought, but then closed her eyes and shook her head. She couldn't risk going with them. There was no way to know how long she could control herself. Her gaze slid back to the farmer as he finished untying his wife's hands and she said, "Tie me up and you two go without me then."

The wife reached up to remove her gag now her hands were free and said firmly, "We're not leaving you here for him to abuse."

"You need to get away from me. If what he said is true, I could attack you."

"What? That blood and vampire business he kept going on about?" The husband snorted as he straightened and helped his wife to stand. "The man was high on something. It was all bunk."

"What did he give you, dear?" the wife asked with concern, moving toward her as her husband rushed off through the boiler room to the long narrow room with the pump and water softener.

"His blood," Dani said on a sigh. "Now I'm becoming a vampire too."

The woman stopped beside Dani, her mouth opening to speak, but she paused and glanced around as her husband reappeared and rushed to the workbench. They both watched him grab the claw hammer Dani had set there, and then he rushed away again. There was a squeal of nails being torn from wood, and then the wife said, "What's your name, dear?"

"Dani," she answered wearily.

"Well, Dani, my name is Hazel Parker and that is my husband, John." Hazel knelt beside her and added sensibly, "I have to tell you, dear, vampires aren't real. That man must have drugged you somehow before he brought you down here."

Dani closed her eyes. She wasn't terribly surprised they didn't believe it. She hadn't when Decker had told her, and he'd had fangs to flash. To Hazel and John, Leo must have just seemed your normal, everyday psychopath, she thought. Unless—

"Who tied you up?" Dani asked, suddenly.

Confusion flashed briefly on Hazel's face, but she said, "I tied John and then the young man tied me up."

"Why did you tie up John? Did Leo threaten you?"

"No," she admitted, her confusion deepening. "He didn't even tell me to do it, and I didn't want to . . . I just . . . did." Something like panic flickered in her eyes. "I tried to stop myself, but it was like someone else was controlling my body."

"Someone else was," Dani said firmly. "Leo. He's a vampire."

Hazel peered at her with uncertainty and then turned with relief as her husband hurried back into the room.

"I got it open," John announced, rushing to them. "I didn't think I would be able to. I nailed it shut a good twenty years ago, but the nails pulled out with a little elbow grease."

He paused to peer from his wife to Dani, and then set

his mouth and bent to catch Dani's arm and lifted her. "Come on. He could be back any minute."

Dani resisted briefly, but her struggles were weak at best. She didn't seem to have any strength left in her body, and that was what made her give in and add what little strength she had to helping him get her to her feet. There was no way she could take Leo like this. If she stayed, he would simply bring her more innocents to feed on, and the way it was going, Dani feared she wouldn't be able to resist.

She would get out of the house with them and then send them next door to the enforcer house for help while she hid in the bushes or something. Then Decker and the others could come back and take care of her and Leo. It seemed like a good plan to Dani, and under John's urging, she took a faltering step forward, only to gasp and bend over as the movement made her pain increase again. Panting like a woman in labor, she stared at the floor and told herself she only had to get outside. Then they would drive off safely, leaving her— Dani stopped and glanced to John sharply, asking, "You don't drive a brown pickup, do you?"

"Yes," John answered, urging her forward another step. "Why?"

"Because that's what he was driving and is probably driving now," Dani told them miserably, ready to give up and find some way to force them to leave without her.

"Then we'll have to take his car," John said staunchly. "It's in the barn. I was out there putting away the new tractor when he drove it right in and—" John cut himself off abruptly, his mouth tightening at some unpleasant memory. "Come on, let's go, or we'll still all be standing here arguing when he gets back."

Dani bit her lip, but started to move again. She did her best to ignore the pain the activity sent shooting through her as they made their way to the cold room she'd examined earlier. She noticed the hammer and long nails lying abandoned on the concrete floor, and then raised her head to see that one of the boards of Styrofoam had been removed to reveal a stone wall with an old window in it.

The sight made her heart sink with despair. There was no way she was going to be able to get out through that in the shape she was in.

Chapter <u>Fourteen</u>

Y ou can do this, girl."

Dani turned her head toward the old farmer. Apparently her expression had given her away, but he wasn't giving up even if she was.

"We'll help you," he added when she began to shake her head, and then he snapped with impatience, "At least try, dammit! You might as well walk back into the next room and use one of my tools to slit your wrists if you won't try."

She ground her teeth together at those blunt words. He was right, and she *could* do this, or at least she could give it a damned good try. Dani had never been a quitter, firmly believing that the only failure was not trying. That belief had seen her through medical school and the grueling hours she'd worked as an intern afterward. She'd made it through all that; she could make it through this stupid window too, Dani told herself firmly. And if she didn't, it wouldn't be for lack of trying.

Relaxing a little, John helped her forward to stand

in front of the window. They paused then, and John reached out and undid the rusty old hook-and-eye fastening. He swung the old-fashioned window out and up to slip the hook through a second eye in the low ceiling, holding the window out of their way.

The lower ledge of the window was about level with Dani's chin. It was about two feet wide and two feet high and was three quarters underground. She found herself looking out at a metal window well with grass poking up over the top and the star-filled night sky visible above it from where they stood.

"We'll need a chair or something to get out," Hazel said, and turned to rush out of the room.

Dani eyed the window and said unhappily, "I'm going to slow you down."

"We have a little time," John said with a shrug. "We're a good ways out in the country. It's half an hour to the nearest fast-food restaurant."

Dani didn't bother explaining that wasn't what Leo had meant by fast food.

"Here."

John turned and then stepped back, taking Dani with him as Hazel rushed in carrying one of the chairs from the workshop. She set it down in front of the window and then turned to eye them both uncertainly.

"You climb out, Hazel," John said. "And then I'll help the girl up and you can pull on her from outside."

Hazel nodded and scrambled onto the chair. She was spry for her age and size, Dani noted, watching as the matronly woman managed to wiggle herself through the window and huffed and puffed her way out into the well.

When Hazel paused on her knees and turned to peer back at them, John said, "Get out on the lawn. If you lie on the grass and reach down you can pull from above while I help the girl from this end."

"My name's Dani," she murmured as they watched Hazel heft herself out of the window well.

"Nice to meet you," John responded absently as he watched his wife with concern, and then he urged Dani to the chair. With his help, she managed to climb to stand on it and brace herself against the ledge. Hazel's hands immediately appeared from the top of the well, and Dani reached to clasp them, holding on as John grasped her lower hips and put his shoulder to her behind, and she began to move up. There was a lot of grunting and panting, and Dani was sure at least two layers of skin were scraped from her stomach when her T-shirt rose up, but after what seemed like forever she found herself crumpled in the bottom of the well.

"You're gonna have to try to stand to help Hazel get you out, girl," John said breathlessly, and Dani turned to see him standing on the chair inside the window. They were all out of breath from the effort expended, but his face was alarmingly red. Her eyes slid to his forehead where blood was drying around the wound there, and she felt her stomach dance, and then Dani groaned as pain knifed through her again, a terrible agony. If she could just get a little blood, just a little, she knew it would ease. Just a taste. Maybe she could just lick his forehead as Leo had done his wife's face, just a lick.

"Dani?"

She shook her head and raised her face to peer at

Hazel. It was dark out, but the light seeping around John's form from inside was enough for her to see the sudden alarm on the woman's face.

"You've gone terribly pale, child," she said, sounding shaky. "Are you all right? Can you try to stand?"

Shame rolled through Dani as she realized what she'd been thinking, and she briefly closed her eyes. She needed to get out of there and get as far away from these people as she could. From any people. She needed to get to help, but not just any help. Someone who knew what was happening and could stop her. She needed— "Decker."

"What was that, dear?" Hazel asked.

"We have to move," John said, prodding her leg. "You have to stand."

Dani drew her knees up in front of her, placing her feet flat on the ground. She reached for the top of the window well and felt Hazel's hands close over hers. As Hazel began to pull, Dani stopped fighting the pain eating at her and instead used it to find the strength to push herself upward. She rose, at first vaguely aware that Hazel was pulling and John doing what he could to push her, but she was doing most of the work herself, forcing her muscles to move. The action made the pain in her stomach spread outward, shooting into her limbs like acid and hitting her brain like a hammer. The agony forced everything else from her thoughts as she crawled out of the well. The moment she felt the cold grass beneath her hands and knees, Dani flopped to the ground and rolled away from the window well, curling into a ball and clutching herself.

She was barely aware of the sounds from behind her

as Hazel helped John climb out. He muttered, "I'll go see if the car will start. Try to get her up." And then Hazel was leaning over her, asking her if she was all right. Dani could hear the woman's heartbeat above her ear, could almost hear the rush of blood running through the woman's veins, and found herself rolling over.

Hazel slipped her arms around Dani, raising Dani's head and shoulders to rest in her lap. Hazel then lowered her face to peer at her.

"You're so pale." The words were anxious and carried the faintest hint of blood with them.

The still-functioning part of Dani's mind told her that it was from the bloody lip Leo had given Hazel, but she didn't care, the scent started her body screaming with want.

Moaning, she turned her head to the side, her eyes landing on the crook of the arm Hazel had slid beneath her head. The creping skin was thin with age, and in the soft light coming from the window well, Dani could see the spidery blue veins creeping up her arms. Veins that carried blood, her mind told her, warm sweet blood that would take her pain away. Just a little, enough to take the edge off . . .

Dani thrust herself away from the temptation, rolling up against the wall. Feeling the brick, cool and gritty against her face, she raised a hand and began to claw her way upright, digging the fingers of one hand into the small indents between bricks and pushing at the ground with the other.

"Let me help you." Hazel was at her side again, taunting her with her smell. Without thinking, Dani caught her by the front of her blouse and dragged her closer so that she could inhale the scent.

"Your eyes," Hazel breathed, voice shaking. "They've gone all silvery."

The words were like a slap in the face to Dani. She immediately got control of herself, released the woman's blouse, and pushed her away.

"Run." The word was a desperate plea. "I'll hide in the bushes. You can send help back for me."

Hazel peered at her uncertainly, obviously battling a real desire to flee, and then the sound of a low, rumbling engine sounded from the back of the house. Hazel glanced toward it, relief obvious in the set of her body, then grim determination settled in her face and she stepped back to Dani's side.

"We aren't leaving you behind," she announced, catching Dani under the armpits and dragging her upward with a surprising show of strength. "We are all three getting out of here, little girl. So you'd better set your mind to it and get your feet moving or I'm just going to drag you around the house to the car on your back."

Dani shook her head, not helping when Hazel shifted to her side to draw one arm over her shoulder and then tried to urge her forward.

"It's just around the house to the barn and then we're on our way," Hazel said almost pleadingly. "Five minutes and we'll be safe. Please, Dani, try."

Five minutes. Dani let the words tumble around inside her head. She only had to control herself for five minutes and then Decker would take over everything. He'd keep the Parkers safe from her, he'd put her out of her misery, and then he'd come take care of Leo. Five minutes. Surely she could manage to control herself that long?

Dani forced her legs to straighten and took a staggering step forward with Hazel's help. She heard, but ignored, the woman's gasped "Thank God" as they headed for the corner of the house.

"I heard that Leo fellow say we're right next door to where you were," Hazel grunted breathlessly as they crossed the lawn. "I'm thinking he must have meant the Sanderson place. It sold a couple weeks ago. Are the people there friends or relatives?"

Dani had no idea who had owned the house before, but doubted if the houses on both sides of this one had been put up for sale and sold, so nodded weakly.

"Do they have a phone yet? If so, we can use it to call the police."

"Yes," she rasped, knowing that wasn't likely to happen. Hazel and John would probably be put under someone's control the minute they reached the house, and then the men would come after Leo themselves. She hoped they tore him limb from limb, but suspected they'd merely stake him and decapitate him or something to make sure he was dead. Then they'd probably remove every trace of what had happened from this home and remove everything from John and Hazel's memories so that they continued on in what had most likely been a peaceful and content life. After that they'd no doubt turn their attention to her.

"Oh, John." Hazel sighed with relief as they stumbled around the corner.

Dani glanced up to see the man hurrying toward them.

"Here, let me help." John took Dani's other arm over his own shoulders and they began to move more quickly as he explained, "There were no keys for the car and I don't know how to hot-wire the damned thing so we'll have to take the tractor."

Dani let her head drop back down to rest her chin against her chest. She was afraid of what might happen if she saw or smelled the bloody wound on his fore-head again, so it was Hazel who answered.

"That's fine," the old woman yelled to be heard over the engine as they drew near the farm vehicle. "We're going to the Sandersons' old place anyway. We can cross the field on the tractor and not risk running into him on the road."

"Good thinking, wife," John yelled back as they reached the side of the tractor. When he came to a halt then, and hesitated, Dani risked lifting her head to peer at the vehicle. The first thing she saw was a green metal two-step ladder used to climb onboard. Her gaze then slid to the open glass door and the cab. It was obvi-ously pretty new, the interior looked as fancy as an air-plane cockpit with a cushioned seat, gears, and buttons, and even a little screen that made her think of the GPS on her car. But she couldn't help but notice there also wasn't enough room for all three of them inside.

"Get in Hazel," John shouted. "You'll have to drive. I'll set the girl on the floor once you're in and stand on the step to be sure she doesn't fall off."

Hazel slid out from under Dani's arm to climb into the cab. Dani glanced to John then, to see him watch-ing his wife. He wasn't a very tall man, and his face was just above hers, leaving her staring at the trail of blood that ran from his forehead and down his cheek to his throat. She swallowed and turned her head away, so was caught by surprise when he suddenly turned, grasped her by the waist, and lifted her to sit on the floor of the cab with her legs dangling out.

"Hang on," he yelled.

Dani sagged against the door frame, clutching at it as he reached up to grab the frame of the open door on each side and climbed up to stand on the steps in front of her. It blocked her in and left his face level with hers. John smiled at her almost kindly before glancing to Hazel.

"Go on, Hazel," he yelled. "Let's get out of here before he gets back."

Five minutes, Dani reminded herself. All she had to do was hold out for another five minutes. Or maybe less now, maybe only four, she thought, and then the tractor lurched forward and she fell against John, grabbing at his shirt to keep from falling over. She held on for a moment, and then became aware of a tantalizing smell coming from the cloth. Lifting her head a little, she peered at the bit of shirt caught in her left hand, spotting a dark stain on the tuft of material that stuck out of the circle made by her clenched thumb and first finger.

It was blood that had dripped down from his head wound and dried there, Dani realized, and found herself inhaling deeply, drawing the sweet scent with a metallic tang into her nose. She closed her eyes at the dizziness that overcame her as the blood in her body began to jump, bubbling as if on the boil, and then before Dani quite realized what she was doing, her mouth closed on the dark stain and she was suckling at it, drawing every bit of blood from the cloth that she could.

The tractor suddenly bumped and shuddered and then bumped again, making her lose hold of the shirt as she fell back, and John quickly looked down at his damp shirt as it fell to rest against his chest. He glanced to Dani then, frowning as he took in her face.

"Are you all right?" he yelled. "You're pale as death and sweating."

Dani groaned and peered past him to the field beyond to see that they'd moved behind the house and bumped their way into the field. Hazel was headed in what appeared to be a straight line for the neighboring property, picking up speed as she went. Judging by the direction they were moving, it seemed the Parkers owned the farm to the right of the enforcer house. As Dani recalled from what she'd seen that day on the way to the mall, this field was as long as at least one city block, possibly two . . . and then they'd meet the woods.

She wasn't going to last it out, Dani thought with despair. The field was so long and there was no way they could drive the tractor through the woods. They would have to cross those on foot. None of that would be a problem were she not losing control so quickly. She had already been reduced to sucking dried blood off a shirt. What was next?

Dani turned to try to see how far they had gotten and what lay ahead, but John's body was blocking the way. Then he too turned away to look ahead, leaving his neck stretched before her. Dani found herself forgetting about the crops and the worry of the woods and staring with hungry fascination at the vein pulsing in his neck.

Realizing what she was doing, she forced her eyes away, only to find herself staring at his inner wrist as he readjusted his hold on the door frame and grabbed it a little higher as he leaned out to get a better look ahead.

"Take us to the edge of the woods and I'll run to the house to get someone to come help us get the girl there," John yelled suddenly, startling her attention away from his wrist.

"All right," Hazel yelled back.

John turned to glance at Dani, frowning when he got a look at her. He let go of the frame with the hand closest to her and jarred his shoulder against it to keep from losing his position so that he could feel her forehead. He then glanced beyond her to Hazel, leaning in a little and placing his forehead closer as he yelled, "The girl's flushed and feels feverish. I think—"

He paused abruptly as Dani suddenly turned her head, leaned forward, and licked the hand he'd pressed to her cheek.

"Hey, now!" John jerked his hand away. "Nobody licks on me but Hazel, girl. Behave yourself."

"Sorry, there's blood on it from when you wiped your forehead," she mumbled.

"What was that?" He leaned closer, eyebrows rising in question, and Dani found her attention focusing on his forehead. His head wound had started bleeding again, and fresh, sweet-smelling blood was seeping out. She watched it slowly trail down, making a path through the dried blood from earlier, and felt saliva gathering in her mouth. Dani swallowed thickly and then licked her lips, finally leaning forward a little to better inhale his scent, amazed to realize he smelled as delicious as a nice juicy steak as Leo had said he would.

"What did you say?" John asked, leaning even closer, and Dani took the opportunity to lick his forehead. He immediately jerked back in shock, and then scowled at her and snapped, "Stop that!"

"What did she do?" Hazel asked.

"She keeps licking on me, Hazel. She's worse than that damned cat of yours," he growled, glaring warily at Dani now.

Dani wanted to apologize, but she was busy savoring the blood she'd managed to get in the quick lick, moving it around inside her mouth before swallowing it. She'd never thought so before, but blood was really quite delicious, and Dani was wondering how she could lure him in for another lick when Hazel asked with amazement, "She *licked* you?"

"Yeah, she keeps—" John broke off to lean back away from Dani as she tried to lick him again. The action made him lose his grip on the door frame with the hand by her head and he shouted, the free arm pinwheeling as his upper body started swinging outward.

"John!" Hazel cried.

"I've got him," Dani yelled, and was slightly amazed to find she did. Her hands had reached out instinctively to catch him by the front of the shirt and had dragged him half into the cab so that his chest rammed into her knees and his face was directly in front of her. She didn't know where the strength had come from, it was just suddenly there, but so was the pain, ripping through her and urging her to drag him closer so that she could lick his forehead again.

"Hazel!" John roared, pushing at her, but unable to break her grip. "Help me!"

Dani was distracted by a smack on the head as Hazel yelled, "Stop that! Bad girl! Leave him alone! Stop licking my husband!"

Decker heard the door open and lifted his eyes sharply to see Lucian appear in the entrance, a dark form against the moonlit background.

"There you are." Lucian peered into the lightless barn. "Sam said she thought she saw you come out here."

"Any news?" he asked sharply.

Lucian shook his head.

Decker sighed. He then slid off the bale he'd been sitting on and crossed to the door. He'd been sitting out there ever since arriving at the house. It had made him feel closer to Dani to be where they'd last been together, but he'd sat torturing himself with memories of the brief interlude and the possibility that it might be all they had. It was better if he returned to the house, even if it was only to pace his room like a caged tiger and fret.

He reached the door and paused, expecting Lucian to step out of the way for him to leave. When he didn't, Decker noted the way his uncle stood, his head raised slightly in a listening attitude and a frown playing on his lips.

Decker arched an eyebrow. "What is it?"

"I think I hear a tractor," Lucian muttered, turning

his head to glance around with displeasure. "Who the hell would be working the fields at this hour?"

Decker shrugged. "A farmer?"

Lucian turned a look of disgust his way. "Of course it's a farmer. But what idiot farmer would be working this late?"

Decker shrugged again with disinterest. Lucian didn't notice, however; he'd released the door and was moving away. Decker caught the door as it swung shut and stepped out to see him walking around the side of the building. His gaze slid to the house, moving over windows glowing with light, and then he turned to follow his uncle.

Lucian had disappeared when he reached the back of the barn, but Decker could hear the soft rustle of his passage through the woods and followed. The forest was only twenty feet deep here. Decker made his way through the trees almost soundlessly, and paused at his uncle's side on the edge of the field to peer out at the dark shape of the tractor stopped halfway across. There were no lights on the vehicle, or if there were, they weren't on, but the engine was running.

"What—?"

"Shh," Lucian hushed him. "Listen."

Decker turned back to the field and listened, picking up the faraway sounds of a man yelling and a woman shrieking in high, alarmed tones. "No!" and then, "No Dani!"

Decker's feet were moving even before the name had died. Aware that his uncle was on his heels, he flew across the field, moving so fast his feet hardly seemed to set down on the dirt as he tore through the plants.

The scene he arrived on was one Decker thought would stick in his mind for a very long time. Dani had an elderly man in jeans and a checkered top pinned to the ground, her knees resting on his shoulders as she held his head still and madly licked at his forehead. She appeared completely oblivious to the man's struggles, and even to the equally elderly woman in a cotton dress who was on Dani's back, trying to drag her off, screaming, "Stop that! Stop licking my husband. Have you lost your mind? Leave him alone!"

Decker lifted the woman off Dani, turned to hand her to Lucian, and then turned back to find Dani had given up on the forehead and was now following the dried blood trail down his cheek to his neck.

"Stop her!"

Decker didn't need that shout from Lucian; he was already catching Dani by the arms and yanking her away from the man she was assaulting.

"No," she moaned, struggling weakly to shake him off. "I want more."

"Dani," he said sharply, spinning her around.

She raised her head, her eyes settling on his face and widening. "Decker," she breathed with relief. "You found us. Thank God. Now you can kill me."

When Dani then sagged against his chest, Decker closed his arms around her. His eyes moved to the elderly man as he got shakily to his feet, and then to the older woman before he asked grimly, "What happened?"

The woman rushed to her husband's side as Lucian released her. Slipping a supportive arm around his waist, she peered at him briefly, and then glanced to Decker.

"I don't know," she admitted, her worried eyes shifting to Dani. "That man must have drugged her or something. She was sick when we broke out of the basement, but then as we were escaping on the tractor she started licking on John. When I tried to make her stop, she tossed him off the tractor like a rag doll and leaped out after him. By the time I got the tractor stopped and jumped out, she was on him like a dog on a bone." She shook her head and repeated, "He must have drugged her. There's something wrong with that girl."

"Leonius," Lucian said suddenly, and Decker turned to see his eyes concentrated on Dani. He'd obviously been reading what had happened from her mind. His uncle shifted his gaze to him and announced, "Leonius took her from the mall and brought her to their house." He gestured to the house visible across the field. "He forced her to drink his blood, and then left her in the basement to make a meal of them while he went in search of another victim for himself, but they escaped."

"Jesus," Decker breathed, peering down at Dani. She was leaning heavily against him, her knuckle in her mouth, rocking slightly and moaning with what sounded like pain.

"Get them to the house and get Dani strapped down. I'm going to their place to wait for Leo," Lucian ordered. He then turned and sprinted across the field toward the house next door.

Decker watched him go, and then tugged Dani's finger from her mouth, wincing as he saw the damage she'd done to it.

"No," she moaned, and tried to raise it to her mouth

again, but Decker caught her hand in his and twisted it behind her back as he scooped her into his arms. He managed to trap her other hand between their bodies so that she wouldn't then start gnawing on that one. Dani immediately began to struggle, but he merely crushed her closer and turned to the couple.

John and Hazel Parker, Decker plucked the name from their thoughts as he glanced over the man. He appeared to have recovered from his run-in with Dani. Decker nodded toward the woods ahead and said, "That way."

Nodding, the man took his wife by the hand and began to lead her toward the woods.

Chapter Fifteen

Something cold dripping onto Dani's closed lips stirred her from the exhausted, almost unconscious state she'd worked herself into as Decker had carried her through the woods. Opening her eyes, she found him kneeling over her and glanced around with confusion to see she was tied down to the bed in her room. Since the bed was without a bed frame or headboard, the rope had simply been tied to one wrist, somehow passed under the bed, and then brought up to tie to her other wrist. The same had been done with her ankles. Primitive, but effective, she decided as she tugged at the rope and found the weight of the bed held her in place.

Dani didn't recall how she'd gotten there and realized she must have zoned out for a bit. She remembered fighting frantically to make Decker put her down, or at least just release her hand so she could suck her knuckle again, but he had ignored her as he'd herded the Parkers to the house. By the time they'd gotten

there, she'd been really out of it. She had vague recol-
lections of Sam, Mortimer, Justin, and Leigh crowding
around them, thought Mortimer had ordered Justin to
take care of the Parkers while he went to help Lucian,
and then all she could recall were walls and ceilings
swimming overhead and now this.

"Open up."

Rolling her head, Dani peered up at Decker, noting
that his expression was grim and closed as he held a
bag of blood over her mouth. "I don't want—"

The words died in her throat as he tipped the bag
of blood, pouring some of the cold, red liquid into
her mouth. The moment the cool, life-giving blood
splashed onto her tongue, Dani forgot about telling
him she didn't want to be an animal like Leo and
that he should just kill her now. Instead she opened
her jaws wider and swallowed greedily as the liquid
flowed in.

It was like a cool cloth on a burn, easing her agony
and beating it briefly back, but all too soon the bag
was empty and the pain came roaring back like a riot
of hoodlums charging up through her body demanding more. Dani was gasping under the attack when the
door opened and Sam and Leigh rushed in, carrying
three bags of blood each.

"We brought more," Sam announced as the two
women rushed forward, their worried gazes on her.

"Thank you." Decker took a bag from Sam and used
his teeth to rip off one corner. He then leaned over Dani
to tip it over her mouth. She opened her lips eagerly,
sighing as the cold blood slid down her throat, taming
the riotous crowd inside.

They went through this four more times, five bags of blood altogether gushing into what had become the bottomless pit of her stomach, and then Dani stiffened as her body went still. There was no more rushing in her ears, no more acidy cramping in her stomach, and her heartbeat slowed to almost a stop. Dani felt trepidation creep over her then. It felt like the calm before a storm, and she just knew when it hit it would be a hurricane, devastating everything in its path.

"What is it?" Decker asked. He was eyeing her face with worry, another bag held, but unopened, in his hands.

"You tell me," she said tightly. "You're the expert here."

"I'm not an expert. I was born an immortal. I've never sat through a turning before," he admitted, and then turned to glance at Leigh in question.

"I'm afraid I haven't either," Lucian's life mate admitted, worry clear in her expression.

Dani heard Decker sigh, and then he turned back to her and said, "Tell me what's happening."

She opened her mouth to speak, and then cried out as it all charged back. The rushing in her ears returned, but was now a roaring, making her deaf to everything else. The acidy cramping returned in earnest and then became an invisible bed of knives slamming down from the ceiling, stabbing through her stomach and chest and then shooting off in all directions through her body. And her heartbeat began racing, charging, thudding so hard she feared it would explode out of her chest. But worse still was the blast that went off in her head. Pain as she'd never experienced ripped her skull apart. Her body then began to convulse, and Dani lost the ability to see or even think. She was pure sensation now, aware only of the agony tearing at her.

"Dear God, what's happening?" The question screamed through Decker's head, even as Sam asked it aloud when Dani began to convulse on the bed.

"Maybe I'd better call Lucian and see if this is normal," Leigh said.

"No. Lucian can't do anything," he said at once. "Call Bastien and tell him to send over drugs and an IV."

Leigh nodded, but before she could go in search of a phone, Dani suddenly began to thrash.

Decker turned back to the bed just in time to see her jerk her hands toward her chest. She appeared to be trying to grab at her stomach, or perhaps her heart, but the rope stopped her . . . for half a second, and then the sound of the box spring frame's snapping reached his ears just as her hands continued toward the middle and up. The edge of the destroyed box spring and mattress on the side Decker wasn't sitting on curled upward as Dani grabbed not for her chest or stomach, but for her head. Her fingers raked into her hair, catching handfuls and then fisting around them as she pressed against her skull, and then just as quickly she began to tug outward.

Had Decker not launched himself to grab her hands and stop her just then, he was pretty sure Dani would have torn whole hanks of hair out of her scalp. Fortunately, he did grab her and then struggled to hold her down and keep her from hurting herself, but her legs were now moving too, her whole body bucking. Decker was more than grateful for Leigh's help when she launched herself on Dani's legs, but when he saw Sam in his peripheral vision, coming up the side of the bed to help by taking one of the arms, he roared, "No! Stay back. She's too strong. She could kill you right now without even realizing it."

"But you two can't hold her alone," Sam pointed out, her eyes frantic.

Decker didn't respond, but knew she was right. While he and Leigh were strong thanks to the nanos, the combination of nanos and the pain Dani was suffering was making her unmanageable. He was about to suggest Sam call Justin upstairs when the bedroom door opened and he saw his cousin Etienne, and Etienne's redheaded wife, Rachel, rush into the room carrying two large duffel bags.

The moment the pair saw the state of things, they dropped the bags and rushed to the bed.

"What happened?" Rachel asked, moving up on the other side of the bed to catch at that arm even as Etienne moved to help Leigh hold Dani's legs.

"She's turning," Decker muttered. Even with the four of them holding her down, they couldn't keep her still.

"Yes, we know that," Rachel said. "We were at the office when Lucian called asking Bastien to send out an IV and some drugs for a turning. We offered to bring them over and help out," she explained, and then added, "But I meant why is she like this already? Lucian said she'd been given the nanos only an hour ago, and Kate took three or four hours to get to this stage."

Decker frowned. "You were at Kate's turning?"

"I may work in a morgue, but I'm still a doctor," she

pointed out dryly. "Knowing that, Kate asked me to be on hand in case anything went wrong."

"And it didn't go like this?" Decker asked with worry.

She shook her head, grimacing as Dani nearly got loose, and she had to pretty much sit on her arm to keep it even close to still.

"This started after the fifth bag of blood," Sam said, moving a little closer to the bed.

"You've already given her blood?" Etienne asked. "How?"

"Her mouth," Decker answered. "I opened the bags one after another and poured them in."

"Oh."

That soft sound of understanding drew his eyes to Rachel to see her biting her lip. "What is it?"

"I— Well, I think that's probably sped things along a bit," she admitted. "According to Marguerite, they've found that using the IV slows the process a little because it takes longer for the blood to get into the body. But it also reduces the risk of the turnee injuring themselves or someone else. However, if you poured five bags down her throat one after the other, then the nanos have probably gone into overdrive and are doing everything at once."

Decker cursed.

"It's all right," Rachel assured him. "It just means she'll get through it more quickly." She then glanced to Sam and, her voice vibrating as Dani's thrashing bounced her around, said, "Hi, I'm Rachel Argeneau."

"Sam Willan," Sam said, tearing her gaze from Dani and offering a distracted smile. "Mortimer's life mate."

"Bastien told us," the redhead assured her. "Sam, do you think you could go look in the smaller bag and bring one of the little black cases inside it to me?"

Sam nodded and rushed to the bags, seeming happy to have something to do to help the situation. When she returned with the little black case, Rachel shifted to a more stable seat on Dani's arm and then took the case and opened it to reveal two needles and two ampoules inside.

"What's that?" Decker asked with concern.

"A combination paralytic and numbing agent," Rachel answered as she retrieved one needle and one ampoule and prepared a shot. "It won't completely remove the pain, but it will ease it considerably and paralyze her so that she can't hurt herself or anyone else."

"How long will it take to work?" Decker asked as Rachel gave Dani the shot.

"Pretty quickly," she announced. "Fortunately, Bastien's boys have come up with some pretty powerful stuff. This shot would kill a mortal, but the nanos will prevent that on her. Unfortunately, they'll also make it so that the drug is only effective in the short term and will have to be administered at regular half-hour intervals."

Decker nodded. The nanos tended to try to fight off the effects of, and remove, any chemicals in the system that weren't there naturally. It made it very difficult for one of their kind to be an alcoholic or drug addict. The immortal that went down that route had to continually be taking in large amounts of alcohol or drug-soaked blood from a mortal to stay high or drunk. Even the tranquilizer on the bullets they used was effective for only half an hour to forty-five minutes, which was more than long enough to get the rogue chained up and subdued. At least, that was normally the case, Decker thought, recalling that Leo had been affected for only a matter of minutes.

"It's starting to work," Etienne commented, drawing his attention to Dani. Her thrashing had calmed down considerably, and her face was no longer contorted with pain and horror.

"Dear God," Rachel breathed suddenly, her gaze locked on Dani's face. "Bastien didn't tell us who it was. This is Dr. McGill."

"You know her?" Etienne asked with surprise.

Rachel nodded. "She trained in Toronto and interned at our hospital for six months before opening her own practice . . . in Windsor, I think." She frowned and turned to Decker almost accusingly. "What the hell is happening?"

"She's my life mate," Decker said quietly.

"Oh." She relaxed. "So you turned her?"

He shook his head. "Not me. Leo did."

"Christ," Etienne breathed, drawing Rachel's confused eyes his way.

"Who's Leo?" she asked with bewilderment.

"He's the no-fanger that disappeared from the clearing up north when they found Nicholas," Etienne said. Apparently they'd been filled in briefly on at least part of the recent events and Rachel had merely forgotten the name, because she said, "Oh," and nodded again.

"Did you know about Nicholas being Thomas and Jeanne Louise's brother?" Leigh asked curiously.

Rachel nodded. "I had trouble drinking blood when

I was first turned. Thomas helped me out. He said his sister-in-law used to have the same problem, but they found a fix for it and he hooked me up with a couple of straws. I didn't think anything of it until I was talking to Jeanne Louise at Kate's wedding shower and asked her about brothers and sisters. She said there wasn't anyone else, just her and Thomas."

Leigh nodded, "We had a similar conversation where she told me the same thing. I guess she took it badly when Nicholas went rogue."

"Yes," Rachel murmured, and then finished, "I didn't confront her then on what Thomas had said, I wasn't sure if I'd misunderstood him or something, so I waited until I could ask Etienne about it and he told me about Nicholas."

Silence fell in the room for a moment, and then Leigh asked, "Why is it so awful that Leo turned Dani?" When everyone turned to glance at her, she shrugged and added, "I mean, Morgan was a rogue and he turned me and no one seemed bothered by it, but everyone seems super upset that this rogue, Leo, turned Dani."

"Because Leo isn't just a rogue, he's a no-fanger," Decker said quietly.

"I know, but do the fangs really matter?" she asked. "I mean, we use bagged blood anyway."

"It's not that," Rachel explained, "According to Bastien, being turned by a no-fanger is dangerous."

"Why?" Sam asked curiously.

When no one else answered, Decker said grimly, "Because it means she only has a one in three chance of coming out all right, an edentate, just missing the fangs but otherwise like us."

Sam's eyes widened with horror. "You mean she could die?"

He hesitated and then admitted, "One in three do."

"So, one in three die, and one in three come out all right." She paused and raised her eyebrows. "What happens to the other one in three?"

"They come out a no-fanger, crazy like Leonius," Etienne answered when Decker remained tight-lipped.

Decker found himself swallowing back the fear suddenly lodged in his throat as they all turned to peer at Dani. He'd rather have Dani die during the turn itself than see her become like Leonius. If that happened, she would either have to be put down like a rabid dog, or be kept locked up and restrained for the rest of her life, which could very well be eternity. Decker didn't want to see Dani locked up, but didn't know if he had it in him to take her life if she was one of the one in three who went mad. She was his life mate. She was also someone he'd come to care for and even love during the short period they'd been together. There was so much to admire in Dani, he hadn't been able to help himself . . . and now he was faced with the possibility of losing her.

There was a horrible taste in her mouth. That was Dani's first awareness as she began to wake up. That and the fact that her mouth was so dry, her tongue felt like a roll of used-up sandpaper. Moving it around in her mouth, she tried to work up some saliva, but what little she did manage to draw out merely made the taste in her mouth worsen.

Grimacing, Dani opened her eyes and peered around

the bedroom she'd used the first night at the enforcer house, and then she recalled everything and sat up abruptly. Something brushed against her arm and she glanced down, a scowl claiming her lips as she saw the ropes fastened to her wrists and trailing away across the mattress. Dani tugged at them, a little surprised when the frayed ends came snapping up and nearly hit her in the face.

She had a vague recollection of waking to find herself tied down, but—judging by the frayed ends—it looked as if the rope had been worn away. Her eyes slid to her feet to find that there were two more pieces of rope attached to her ankles. She was also still wearing the clothes she'd worn when taken from the mall.

Ignoring the rope for now, she peered around. The room was as empty as it had been the first day she'd woken here . . . except that the bags of clothes from their shopping trip sat neatly stacked against the wall.

She could change into clean clothes, Dani thought, and then grimaced at the idea of pulling nice clean clothes on her less than clean body. She felt greasy, as if she'd just worked an eight-hour shift over a fryer.

Dani grimaced and started to crawl to the edge of the mattress. She then braced one hand on the wall and forced herself to her feet. She was as unsteady as a newborn foal when she finally straightened. She closed her eyes briefly and leaned against the wall until the trembling this little bit of activity had caused eased slightly. She then walked carefully to the bathroom door, her hand sliding along the wall as she went, ready to press against it and keep her upright should her legs buckle.

When she made it to the bathroom door, it raised her confidence a little. She went straight to the bathtub, turned the taps to start the water running, and then manipulated the button to switch it to shower mode. Water immediately began to surge down, catching her head and shoulders, but Dani merely closed her eyes, turned her head, and opened her mouth to let it gush in.

A memory from the night before immediately flashed across her mind, and Dani stiffened as she recalled Decker pouring the blood into her mouth. Groaning, she turned her head down again and forced the memory away, unready to contend with what had happened yet. She then straightened and started to pull off her shirt, but saw the ropes on her wrists and paused to remove those. One came off easily, but the knots on the other were tight and resisted her efforts. Leaving it on, she turned her attention to the ropes at her ankles and quickly removed those, then tried the last rope on her right wrist again.

Dani fumbled with it briefly, but finally gave it up and simply stripped off her clothes, stepped under the shower, and tugged the glass door closed. The water was colder than she normally liked, but it was bracing as well and she stood under it, allowing it to pound down over her head briefly before adjusting the temperature. She then reached for the soap and began to clean herself, washing away the film of greasy waste that had apparently been forced out of her body by the nanos. It was the only explanation she could think of for it, but since thinking about it forced her to think about last night, Dani pushed these thoughts away and simply concentrated on soaping herself clean.

It wasn't until she was washing her hair that Dani began to consider her situation. She was now one of the dreaded no-fangers. At least she presumed she was, though in truth, other than the weakness still plaguing her, she didn't feel any different. She didn't now have a mad urge to cut up people to get their blood, or leap on them to lick open wounds.

Dani grimaced at the memory of assaulting poor John Parker. She was pretty sure she wouldn't be doing that were he to walk into the bathroom right now. In fact, the idea of lapping up blood from his forehead, or even drinking it from a glass just seemed gross to her . . . much as it would have before Leonius had forced his blood on her. It made Dani wonder if perhaps the nanos hadn't taken. Perhaps she hadn't gotten enough to bring about the turn, or perhaps her body had fought off the nanos somehow.

The thought had barely entered her mind before Dani's more sensible side slapped it down. It wasn't very likely that her body had fought off the nanos. It was more probable that she was just full of blood right now and not craving madly for it as she had last night. But even that gave her hope. She seemed to be thinking clearly, her thoughts didn't strike her as insane or unusual. Perhaps if she kept herself full of blood, she might still be able to live a relatively normal life.

Dani considered that as she rinsed the shampoo out of her hair, and had almost convinced herself that it would work, that she could get blood from the Argeneau Blood Bank as Decker claimed immortals did, keep herself well-fed, and continue working at her practice . . . perhaps even continue her relationship with Decker. That fantasy melted away as she recalled Leonius's claim that immortals hated no-fangers, that they hunted them down and killed them, and that Decker would want to kill both Leonius and her when he found out.

Leaning against the tiled wall, Dani closed her eyes and tried to think over the sudden howling in her mind at the very thought of Decker despising and wanting to kill her. She tried to tell herself that he wouldn't, that he could have killed her last night, and hadn't, but her stupid mind immediately pointed out that while he hadn't killed her, he'd tied her down like an animal and had been grim-faced and cold as he'd poured bag after bag of blood into her mouth.

As those memories assaulted her, Dani feared Decker might very well loathe her now, and while he hadn't killed her yet, it might only be because he thought they might use her. Maybe they thought she had some information about Leonius and his son that they could use to hunt them down if they hadn't caught and killed Leonius already.

She had to get out of there, Dani realized. She had to get out of that house before someone realized she was awake and tried to tie her down again. Pushing away from the wall, she turned the water off and pulled the door open. The towels she'd used after her bath the first morning hung over the towel rack. Dani grabbed one and quickly dried herself, ignoring the way the now-wet piece of rope still attached to her wrist slapped against her. She then swiftly rubbed her hair to get the worst of the water out before tossing the towel aside and heading for the door. Finding the bedroom still empty, she rushed to the bags against the wall and tipped up the first one to empty its contents on the floor.

Several silk panties and a summery blue halter dress tumbled to the floor. Deciding that would do, she grabbed the nearest pair of panties and pulled them on, then tugged the halter dress on over her head, yanked it into place, and tied the halter around her neck as she headed for the door. Once there, she paused to listen, but when she couldn't hear sounds coming from the hall, Dani eased the door open and peered out, relieved to find it empty. She wasted no time, but tiptoed out and to the stairs. When no sounds of movement reached her from the main floor, Dani headed silently down to the entry. It was when she saw the bright sunny day outside that she slowed.

The fact that it was daylight explained why the house appeared empty. Dani supposed that meant Sam would be at work, and everyone else would be asleep in their beds, completely unaware that she'd broken free at some point during her turn and was now awake and escaping. That was a good thing. However, it caused other problems, she realized, recalling Decker saying that immortals avoided going out in sunlight because it caused damage and increased the need for blood.

That was a definite problem, Dani acknowledged. She felt fine right now, but feared she might not be after an hour or so walking along a dusty country road under a baking sun. She shifted on her feet, unsure what to do, and then thought of the vehicles in the garage. Perhaps she could take one of those. It would be stealing, of course, but she could leave it somewhere and call later to tell them where it was. Besides, better a thief than ending up attacking someone in a frenzy for blood.

Dani turned and was about to head for the kitchen when she heard the soft click of a door closing upstairs. When footsteps followed, moving quickly toward the stairs, she ducked into the empty living room and pressed herself to the wall, eyes locked on the archway to the hall. Her heart beat rapidly with the fear of discovery as she listened to someone jogging lightly down the stairs. She held her breath then, but the footsteps merely moved away toward the kitchen. She let her breath out with relief and glanced around, looking for a proper hiding spot.

That was when Dani saw John and Hazel Parker. The couple were seated on the lush carpet, upper bodies slumped against each other on the far wall, both apparently asleep, she realized as John let out a loud, snuffling snore. The sight of the couple answered one question for Dani. Leonius hadn't been caught. If he had, the couple would have been returned to their home with their memories altered.

John Parker let loose with another loud snore, and Dani began to worry that it might draw whoever had come downstairs into the room to check on the couple. She would definitely be discovered then. It was time to move. Easing up to the archway leading to the hall, she started into the entry, planning to check out the room across the hall for a possible haven where she might think. But she was only halfway across when the person in the kitchen started out and up the hall once more.

Panic yanking on her, Dani changed direction and slid into the empty coat closet next to the front door, easing the door carefully shut in an effort not to make a sound.

Chapter Sixteen

Decker moved quickly out of the kitchen, a cold bag of blood in each hand; one for him, and one for Dani. He wasn't sure how long she would be knocked out, but he planned to feed her another bag whether she was awake or not. He'd done that intermittently through the night as she went through her ordeal. Sometimes it hadn't gone too well and his clothes had suffered for it. When he'd seen the bloodstains covering his shirt and jeans as he'd stood to head for the kitchen, Decker had decided it might be better to change first. He didn't want the first thing Dani saw on opening her eyes to be him covered in blood.

Decker had headed to his room, just planning to change, but several yawns and a weary scrub at his eyes along the way had made him think a swift shower might be good too. He'd intended to be quick about it, but thoughts of Dani had slowed him somewhat and he'd found himself simply standing under the beating water as his mind crowded with worry for her. Decker thought the worst of the turn was over and was pretty sure Dani was going to survive it. Now there was just the question of whether she would come out of it sane or not . . . and what he would do if she didn't.

It was concern that she might wake up alone and afraid that had forced him to get out of the shower. Decker had dried himself, dressed in clean clothes, and headed for her room, only to recall that his original intention had been to fetch some blood from the kitchen. He'd come down to the kitchen then, grabbed two bags, and was walking up the hall intending to head back upstairs when he caught sight of the coat closet door closing ahead.

For one moment Decker thought he must have imagined it, but then he heard a soft thud and a grunt from behind the door. He paused in the hall, staring at it for a moment, then took a couple more steps forward and stuck his head into the living room. His lips turned down in a frown when he saw the Parkers still there, sleeping soundly. It hadn't been one of them closing the closet door from inside.

Decker straightened and turned to approach the closet, thinking that it couldn't be Mortimer, Lucian, or Justin. They were all at the Parker house waiting for Leonius to show up. And Leigh, Rachel, and Etienne had headed to bed shortly after Sam had left for work. That left only— He caught a glimpse of the frayed end of rope sticking out under the door and then it disappeared, tugged inside the closet.

"Dani?" he called uncertainly, and shifted the bags of blood into one hand so that he could open the door. He'd turned the doorknob and pulled the door open a bare couple of inches when she said, "No," and the door was pulled out of his hand to slam shut.

Recognizing her voice in the short word, Decker found a smile plucking at his lips at her denial and nearly chuckled until it occurred to him that the woman was in a closet, denying it was she. That wasn't exactly sane behavior. It wasn't psychotic either, at least he hoped not, but . . .

Worry gnawing on his nerves, he reached for the door again. "Dani, are you all right?"

This time he got it open six inches or so before she snapped, "Go away," and yanked it closed.

Really worried now, Decker set the blood down beside the door so that he could use both hands on the knob, but Dani must have been using both of hers as well on the other side. He had to put in some real effort to turn the knob and then pull the door open. He had it nearly a foot ajar when she suddenly released her hold. Unfortunately, Decker hadn't expected that, was still pulling with all his might, and slammed himself in the head with the damned thing. Cursing, he stumbled back a step, grabbed for his head, and saw her tug the door closed again.

Sighing, he let go of his head and moved up to the door to ask wearily, "Dani, what are you doing?"

"Hiding. What does it look like?"

Decker considered that. She sounded odd, like she was crying and trying to sound angry so that he wouldn't know. He was about to ask her again if she was all right when she suddenly said, "I'm not an animal."

He blinked at those words, his head jerking back slightly at the pain evident in her voice.

"I don't want you to tie me up again," she added, and then cried almost desperately, "I'm not like Leonius. I don't even want blood. I just want—" Her words died on a gasping sob, and Decker reached for the door-knob. This time he met no resistance and found out why when he saw that Dani had backed into the corner and turned to press her face there.

Decker hesitated and then stepped inside, pulling the door closed with one hand as he reached to rub her back with the other.

Dani stiffened at his touch and cast a quick glance over her shoulder, revealing that she was indeed crying. She then turned back to the corner, her voice watery as she asked, "What are you doing in here?"

"Hiding with you."

The words made her crumble and she sagged against the wall, her shoulders shaking with soft sobs.

Aching along with her, Decker caught her shoulders and turned her unresisting body to press her against his chest. He saw the piece of rope dangling from her wrist, realized she must not have been able to remove that one since the others were gone, and almost offered to remove it. But then he decided to ignore it for now, and slid his arms around to hold her as he rocked her in that dark, airless closet. He rubbed her back and mur-mured reassuringly, and eventually her crying slowed and stopped. After a moment she whispered, "You hate me now."

"No," he said quietly, and she lifted her head to peer up at him.

"But I'm a no-fanger."

"No, you're not," he assured her.

Dani shook her head sadly at his denial. "Yes, I am. I'm a no-fanger, and immortals hate them."

"You're Dani," he repeated firmly. "And you are *not* a no-fanger, you're an edentate. Immortals don't hate edentates."

"Edentate?" she asked with confusion.

"It's what sane immortals without fangs are called," he explained. "You're an edentate, Dani. Only the insane, rogue fangless ones are called no-fangers."

"Edentate," she said slowly, but then shook her head. "But Leonius said you would hate me, and you tied me down last night like a dog. You—"

"We tied you down last night so you wouldn't hurt yourself," Decker assured her quickly. "You were biting yourself and thrashing around, Dani, it was necessary."

When she raised her head, hope in her eyes, he added, "And we don't despise any race. We hunt down and kill rogues only, both immortal and edentata alike."

When she peered at him doubtfully, he reluctantly admitted, "Unfortunately, half of the edentata who survive the turning come out no-fangers like Leonius and go rogue so, in the past, enforcers had to kill a lot of them in comparison to immortals, but not much anymore," he added. "I've only ever even heard of one no-fanger besides Leonius and his sons since becoming an enforcer sixty years ago, but I know an edentate. He works as an enforcer."

"Really?" she asked, almost eagerly.

Decker nodded, and when she leaned against him with a sigh, asked, "Are you ready to get out of here now? I fetched some blood from the kitchen to take upstairs. It's outside the door. We could go to the kitchen and—"

"I don't want it," Dani interrupted on a mutter. "I'm not— I don't—" Shaking her head, she pressed her face to his chest again and repeated, "I don't want it."

Decker peered down at the top of her head, slowly realizing Dani was still struggling to accept what she was. There had been shame and even despair in her voice as she'd refused the suggestion. He understood, but denying it wasn't going to make it go away, and neither would refusing to feed. And judging by the way her face glowed palely in the dark of the closet, she was in need of blood whether she admitted it to herself or not. The longer she left it, the more likely the chances she would be leaping on some poor unsuspecting mortal in search of food. Decker considered the problem briefly, and then urged her away from his chest, saying, "Come. Let's sit down."

Dani hesitated, but then sat down on the floor with her back to the wall when he did. The moment she was settled, Decker reached to open the door, grabbed first one bag of blood and then the other, and dragged them into the closet before pulling the door closed again.

"Here, can you hold this for a minute?" He handed her one of the bags. "I'm afraid of kneeling on it and bursting it."

Dani reluctantly took the bag, and he immediately popped the other to his teeth. He didn't look at her, but could feel her eyes watching him in the bit of light creeping under the door as his teeth began to drain the bag. Decker had hoped seeing him feed would encourage her to do the same, but she merely watched him silently. When the bag was nearly empty, Decker tipped it up, deliberately allowing the last few drops to dribble out and run slowly down his chin. He tore the empty bag away and set it in the corner, then turned to face her.

"Kiss me," he said softly.

Dani swayed toward him, nostrils flaring and eyes locked on the droplet of blood and the trail it was leaving, and then she caught herself and leaped to her feet, dropping the bag of blood as if it were on fire. She reached for the doorknob, but Decker grabbed the discarded pouch of blood and launched to his feet, catching her hand to stop her.

"Kiss me," he repeated.

"I don't want to," Dani said, but he could hear the lie in her voice.

"I want you to," he said softly, drawing her closer and lowering his head above hers. "Just one kiss."

Decker saw her swallow, her eyes shifting between his lips and the blood, and then he lowered his head the last few inches and pressed his mouth to hers. She managed to remain completely still and unresponsive for perhaps a heartbeat, and then Decker slid his tongue out to urge her lips apart, and she moaned and opened for him. He knew she could taste the blood he'd just consumed, knew it was like waving a glass of scotch under the nose of an alcoholic, and hoped to God this worked as he slid his arms around her and drew her against his body.

When she began to suck on his tongue, drawing off any remnants of blood remaining there, he hoped it might work, but when she then broke the kiss to lap up the blood on his chin and the blood that had trailed down his throat, he knew it had. When she'd cleaned up the last of the blood remaining, Dani pressed her head to his chest with a defeated sigh.

"You're hungry," he said quietly.

Her head nodded against his chest.

"Do you want me to open the bag?" When she stilled against him, but didn't respond, he added, "I'll turn my back if you like."

Dani sagged against him with a sigh, and then burst out, "I know this is stupid, but I don't want you to see—"

"It's all right," he said gently. "This is all new and upsetting. We'll take it slow."

Dani nodded, a little sigh slipping from her lips, and then she stepped away. Decker used his teeth to tear off a corner of the bag, holding it carefully to be sure he didn't spill any. He then handed it to her just as carefully. The moment Dani took it, he turned his back and waited. A soft sigh told him when she was done, but he gave her another moment before turning around.

"Thank you," Dani murmured as he took back the empty bag.

"Feel better?" Decker asked as he bent to set this bag with the other. She nodded her head as he straightened.

"I didn't think I—" She shook her head, unwilling to say that she'd needed blood.

Decker slid his arms around her and drew her back to rest against his chest. "I know. You'll soon learn to recognize the signs."

"I wish I didn't have to," she muttered.

Decker ran one hand up and down her back and then cupped her head and urged it up so he could see her face. "I'm sorry this is so upsetting to you, but I'm not sorry you're now an immortal. I would have turned you myself when you were ready for it."

"But now I'm—" She shook her head unhappily.

"You're Dani," he said quietly. "The nanos don't change that. You're Dr. Dani McGill. And fangs or no fangs, you're an immortal." He let that sink in and then added, "My immortal, my life mate, my hope for the future, and the woman I love."

Dani's head shot back at those words. Her heart leaped, but she stared wide-eyed at him through the dark and shook her head from side to side. "You don't love me, Decker. You can't."

"No?" he asked.

"No. We just met."

Decker nodded, but asked, "What do you know about me?"

"Not much," she muttered, and then realized that wasn't true. They had managed to talk a little between lovemaking sessions in the barn. She knew he had a house on the outskirts of Toronto not far from an aunt named Marguerite that he was quite fond of, but that he didn't get to stay there much because he was always traveling for work. She knew he had a cottage up north where he occasionally got to go to enjoy the peace and quiet, that he preferred reading over television, and plays to movies. She knew he had six brothers and sisters—three older brothers and three younger sisters. She knew he liked food, loved sex, at least with her, and found Justin exasperating. And she knew he devoted his life to keeping mortals and immortals safe from those vampires, fanged or fangless, who chose to go rogue and wreaked havoc. Dani also knew he was calm in a crisis, strong, considerate . . .

"In here." Decker tapped her chest when she remained lost in her thoughts. "What do you know about me in here? Do you trust me?"

Dani considered the question. While she hadn't trusted him when they'd first met, that was because he'd been lying to her. But once he'd explained the lies and who and what he was . . . At the Parkers, the one person she'd wanted to see was Decker. She'd trusted that he would take care of things. She'd trusted him. Dani nodded. "Yes."

"Then believe me when I tell you, Dani McGill, that I love you. I love your independence, your determination, your love and concern for family, your intelligence, your wit, your—"

She covered his mouth with her hand. "I believe you. But it would never work between us. Even if you don't despise me for being a no-fanger—"

"Edentate," he corrected.

She nodded and continued, "Your family might. Leo said—"

"He lied. Or he truly believes those things, but he's crazy. My family will love you," Decker added, drawing her back into his arms. "And regardless, I love you, Dani. I'd give my life for you."

She gave a small laugh. "You almost did before we had even met in that clearing."

Decker shook his head. "You know getting shot wouldn't have killed me. I wasn't risking much there, but I *would* give my life for you, Dani. I'd give it to save your life, and even to just reverse what's happened and make you mortal and happy again if it would."

Dani snorted at the thought and unthinkingly muttered, "Well, that would hardly make me happy if you were dead."

She saw the smile curve his lips and realized what she'd said, and then his mouth was on hers. She felt his hand at the back of her head, angling her to where he wanted her, and then his tongue was inside her mouth and Dani let her hands slip up around his shoulders as she began to kiss him back. The passion that swirled up through her was breathtakingly sudden. It tore a moan from her mouth and had her shifting eagerly closer, pressing herself against him from calf to lips. She could feel his erection pressing against her and was completely caught by surprise when he suddenly tore his mouth away and leaned his forehead against hers, his hands dropping away.

Dani wanted to pull his head back to her, but forced herself not to and waited uncertainly, half afraid that despite his claims, Decker was repulsed by her now that Leonius had turned her. His body certainly seemed willing enough, but his mind apparently wasn't, she thought unhappily, and then he said, "I'm sorry."

"For what?" she asked warily.

He gave a half laugh, as if it should be obvious, and then said, "For this. You've just woken up after being turned. You're upset and we're squeezed into a closet, for God's sake, yet I was about to yank up your skirt and—" He broke off and shook his head.

Dani felt relief slide through her, and caught his hand.

She drew it down to her outer leg where the hem of her skirt ended and said huskily, "Yank up my skirt."

Decker pulled back to peer down at her, but she merely caught his head with her other hand to draw his mouth back to hers even as she slid his other hand up her outer thigh, pushing the skirt upward. She whispered, "I want you to."

It was all she had to say; Decker took over then. He began to kiss her, his tongue thrusting into her mouth, but he didn't continue raising her skirt. Instead he shook off her hand and reached for the halter of her dress. It soon dropped down, baring her breasts, and Dani groaned as his hands covered them, squeezing and kneading as he kissed her, sending wave after wave of passion through them both. He then broke their kiss and ducked his head to catch one nipple in his mouth. That hand free now, he slid it between her thighs, pressing the cloth of her panties and gown against her as he found and rubbed her core.

Dani groaned into his mouth, her own hand moving to work at the button and zipper of his jeans. Despite her desperate distraction, she managed to undo both. She then jerked down the front of his boxers and his penis sprang out. The moment it had, Decker caught her leg behind the knee and drew it up and around his hip. He then pushed her skirt up so that he could reach between her legs again. This time, it was to tug her panties aside.

Dani's groan as his fingers ran over her was followed by one from him, then Decker caught her other leg up, shifted his hands to her bottom, and raised her up a little before lowering her onto his erection. He was hot and hard, and the feel of him filling her made her tear her mouth from his with a gasp. She almost then turned to bite his shoulder, but caught herself at the last moment. Dani wanted to bite something terribly badly, not for blood, just because the feelings exploding over her were too intense, but that was dangerous now.

Trying to reduce the risk that she might get overexcited to the point that she couldn't stop herself, Dani released the hold she had on his shoulders and grabbed for the bar that ran the length of the closet. She clutched at that with both hands and leaned her head back away from him as he withdrew himself and began to drive back into her.

Decker claimed her lips again then, kissing her deep and hard before breaking away. When it ended, she found herself pinned to the wall, his shoulder far too temptingly close. She closed her eyes and shook her head, clutching desperately at the bar as he drove into her over and over again, sending wave after wave of excitement coursing through her. And then just when she reached the breaking point, she spotted the rope still dangling from her wrist and lunged for it, sinking her teeth into the thick cord as he drove into her one last time and then cried out as he exploded. The waves that washed over her then were enough to push her over the edge too, and she was aware of actually biting through the rope before unconsciousness claimed her.

Chapter Seventeen

It was the hard slam of his back on the floor that woke Decker. Blinking his eyes open, he saw that the closet door he and Dani had collapsed against had been opened. Justin, Mortimer, and Lucian now stood in a circle around his head, peering down at him with surprise. At least Mortimer and Justin appeared surprised, he thought with a sigh. Lucian looked stone-faced as usual, with just the slight arching of one eyebrow to suggest it might be unusual to open a closet door and have two half-naked people fall out.

"Well," Justin said finally when no one else seemed eager to speak. "I thought you'd never come out of the closet."

The younger immortal then burst out laughing at his own joke. When no one else joined him, he glanced from Decker's grim face to Dani, who lay still in a faint on his chest, and then to both Mortimer and Lucian. Shaking his head, he muttered, "You guys really need to go buy yourselves a sense of humor."

Turning on his heel, he stalked off to the kitchen.

Lucian watched him go, and then turned back to eye Dani briefly before telling Decker, "Get her up and into the kitchen. I need to ask her some questions."

"Did Leonius show up?" Decker asked at once.

Lucian shook his head and turned to head for the kitchen with Mortimer following.

"At least he didn't lecture me on our choice of spots," Decker muttered to himself as he watched them go.

"Are they gone yet?"

Eyes widening at that whisper from Dani, Decker caught her by the shoulders and raised her up slightly. Her face was completely bereft of any sign of sleepiness. "You've been awake the whole time?"

"Falling out of the closet woke me," she admitted on a sigh.

"Why didn't you get up or—" The question died as she glanced meaningfully at herself. He followed her gaze to see that the halter of her dress was resting on his chest, leaving her breasts completely exposed. His mouth began to water at the sight, and Dani immediately pushed herself upright to kneel between his legs and grabbed the ties of the halter to pull them up and around her neck.

Decker sighed as she covered all that loveliness, but knew it was for the best. It also reminded him that he had a bit of tucking and straightening to do as well, and he quickly took care of that before getting to his feet and offering her a hand.

"They didn't get Leonius, did they?" she asked quietly as they started up the hall.

"No," Decker answered. Lucian had merely shaken

his head in answer to the question when he'd asked it. Dani, of course, hadn't been able to see that from her position facedown on his chest, but had guessed the answer. She looked so unhappy that he added, "We will. We won't stop until we get him."

Dani nodded, but didn't look as if she believed it.

Justin was sitting on the island beside the sink, Lucian was leaning against the counter across from him, Mortimer stood between the two men facing the door, and all three had a bag of blood to their teeth when Dani and Decker entered.

Decker felt Dani's fingers brush his as they paused, and he glanced down to see her watching the men with silent envy. Whether she envied the fact that they had no qualms about feeding in front of others, or that they could use their fangs to do it while she had to drink it like a mortal would, he didn't know, but Decker took her hand in his and gave it a gentle squeeze of reassurance.

Dani turned to meet his gaze, and smiled slightly.

Lucian suddenly tore the now-empty bag of blood from his teeth with a curse. When everyone turned to peer at him, he said, "We were wasting our time waiting there. Leo's already been and gone."

Everyone looked startled by this announcement, but it was Dani who asked, "How do you know that?"

"Because I just read your mind," Lucian answered unapologetically. "According to your memories the house was in perfect array when you arrived, and he walked straight out after leaving the three of you in the basement."

When Dani nodded a silent acknowledgment to this,

he added, "But when I got there the rooster teapot lay smashed on the floor with tea everywhere, the salt and pepper shakers lay in pieces by it, and the apple pie had been smashed by a fist." He shrugged. "Leonius must have come back while you were crossing the field."

"He would have heard the tractor," Mortimer pointed out. "Why wouldn't he head straight after it rather than—"

"He would have checked the basement first," Lucian said with certainty. "He probably found it empty and just smashed the pie and swiped everything else off the table on his way back out. Leo probably did check the field then, but we may have either been on the scene or running to the tractor. Our presence would have scared him off."

"Is there a brown pickup at the house?" Dani asked tensely.

Lucian shook his head.

"Oh." She sounded relieved, and then explained, "That's what he was driving. I was afraid he might have set out on foot to watch the house again." She turned to Decker and explained, "He was watching us in the barn that first day."

Decker felt his mouth tighten, but merely slid his arm around her waist and drew her to his side.

"He was going to try to trade me for his sons," she added.

"His sons are dead," Decker said quietly.

"All of them? How?" she asked, surprise lifting her eyebrows. When no one answered right away, she said, "Leonius was in the van from the clearing to the restaurant where we stopped while Justin got gas. He was under the tarp and said he pulled the stakes out on two of his sons. He said it was enough that they should recover."

Decker exchanged a glance with his uncle, and then admitted, "The Council had them taken care of as soon as they finished reading them, Dani. They had to. We have no prison facilities, and rogues are like rabid dogs. They have to be put down to protect others."

Dani didn't comment on that, but announced, "Leonius said the tranquilizer didn't work on him, but did on his sons. He said he was too old and strong and it only affected him for a few moments."

"That's good to know," Decker said grimly. "We'll have to stick with arrows for Leonius then."

The other men nodded in agreement, and then Lucian shifted and glanced to Mortimer. "You may as well call the boys and tell them to start cleaning up everything so we can wipe the Parkers' memories and send them home."

"What if he does come back?" Dani asked, and then pointed out, "He might try to use the house as a spot to watch from again if he thinks you've cleared out."

"I doubt it," Lucian said, but turned to Mortimer.

"I'll put a couple men over there to keep watch until we catch him just to be sure," Mortimer said before he could say it, and then added, "I'll also send a couple over to our neighbor's on the other side to be sure he hasn't set up camp there instead."

Lucian nodded his satisfaction and then headed for the door. "I'm going to catch some sleep. Wake me if anything happens."

"You both look like you could use some rest," Mortimer announced suddenly, drawing Decker's gaze. "If you want to sleep I'll call you if the phone arrives."

Decker hesitated; he hadn't slept much in the last two nights and he *was* tired. Dani was looking a little wilted as well and could probably do with a rest. While she'd been unconscious all night, it hadn't been what you could call a restful sleep. Nodding, he turned Dani toward the door to usher her out.

She didn't resist, and he noticed as they walked up the stairs that her expression was troubled. It made him wonder what she was thinking.

He got his answer when Dani glanced at him as they entered her room and asked, "How exactly did edentates come into existence? Are they just a mutation of immortals?"

Decker closed the door before saying, "The edentata, both edentates and no-fangers, are the result of the first experiments with nanos."

She had started across the room, but stopped to turn on him with surprise. "I thought you said your grandparents were the first?"

"They were the first *successful* trials with the final batch of nanos," he interrupted, moving away from the door. "But there were unsuccessful trials beforehand."

"Unsuccessful how?" she asked as he urged her to the bed.

"Apparently the first batch used for human trials, the batch that produced the edentata, was tested on six individuals. Two died, two went crazy, and two seemed fine and didn't show issues until after the fall of Atlantis when blood transfusions were no longer available."

Dani watched him settle to sit on the ruined bed with

his back to the wall and then moved to join him before saying uncertainly, "And Leo is one of the four who survived?"

"His father, Leonius the First, was," Decker corrected." He was one of the two who went crazy during the turn."

"Why did he go crazy?"

"I don't know," he admitted. "I'm not sure even the creators of the nanos knew why, but having two thirds of the test subjects die or go mad was enough for them to cancel the trials and try to improve the nanos. They apparently did some tweaking, and the final result is what my grandparents got."

"What did they do about Leonius and the other no-fanger who was driven crazy by the faulty first batch?"

"They were locked away where they couldn't harm themselves or others."

She nodded slowly, but her mind had apparently gone back to what he'd said earlier and she asked, "What were these issues that showed up in the other two after Atlantis fell? The two of six who didn't go crazy? Was it just the lack of fangs?"

Decker hesitated and then said, "That was the most apparent difference. Some edentates also don't have the improved night vision, but otherwise they are pretty much the same. They have the increased strength and speed and the ability to read and control minds like us."

"So I will be able to read minds and control people?" She seemed surprised.

He nodded. "It takes a little time to learn those things, but yes, you'll eventually be able to do both."

"Hmm." Dani was silent for a moment, considering that, and then frowned. "If Leonius was locked up, how did he father Leo? I mean, they didn't allow conjugal visits or something, did they?"

"No." Decker chuckled at the idea, but admitted, "No one knows for sure, it's assumed that when Atlantis fell either someone let him and the other subject loose, or he simply escaped in all the chaos." Decker grimaced. "Whatever the case, he survived."

"And the other?"

Decker shook his head. "It's believed the other died in Atlantis."

"I wish Leonius had too," Dani said bitterly.

"Then I wouldn't have met you," he pointed out quietly. "You wouldn't have been kidnapped, wouldn't have been there for us to rescue from the clearing, wouldn't be here with me now."

Dani lowered her head. She wanted to say she'd prefer that to being what she was, but it wasn't wholly true. She couldn't say she loved Decker yet, she wasn't sure if she did or not, but she did care for the man. Certainly her heart ached at the prospect of never seeing him again. Perhaps had Stephanie been rescued from that clearing too, it would be a different story entirely, but she hadn't, and Dani couldn't be pleased to be what she was or fully enjoy the relationship forming between her and Decker. It seemed her mind was constantly slipping back to worry about Stephanie.

Sighing, she shook these thoughts aside and said, "So Leonius managed to escape Atlantis, wreaked havoc, but also met his life mate and had Leonius the Second?"

"Leonius had several sons and he more than wreaked havoc, but I'm not sure if he ever met his life mate."

"Then how—?"

"Leonius didn't just attack mortals, but immortals as well," Decker explained, expression grim. "He had a real liking for kidnapping immortal women and forcing them to bear his children. Leonius had a lot of sons."

Dani raised an eyebrow. "No daughters?"

"Apparently he had no use for them and usually killed daughters at birth."

"Nice," she muttered.

Decker continued, "Leonius is part of the reason for the hundred-year rule. He was having children by the dozen, keeping mortals like cattle to feed them, and it began to look as if he were creating an army of his own offspring. That's when the first Council of immortals was formed. My grandfather Ramses got several other immortals together to try to figure out what to do about Leonius and his brood, and after much deliberation, it was decided that they had to be stopped. The immortals formed an army of their own, attacked Leonius and his brood, and thought they'd wiped them out. It appears they missed one."

"Leo," she said on a sigh.

He nodded.

They were both silent for a minute, and then she asked, "I have the faulty first batch of nanos now, right?"

"Well, yes, not the original ones, but clones that have been recreated over time."

She hesitated, and then asked, "Is there any way to fix it? Maybe give me a transfusion of your nanos, or . . ." She let her voice trail off when he began to shake his head.

"I'm sorry, Dani. I don't know much on this subject, and you'd have to talk to Bastien. He'd know more, but I'm pretty sure that wouldn't work. Your nanos would see mine as invading bodies and kill them as they do cancer cells and viruses."

"Right." She let her breath out on a sigh, and, playing with the now much shorter rope on her wrist, asked, "So, if I were to have a child, would that child have only a one in three chance of not being stillborn or insane?" Children were a consideration. Dani was over thirty and had been recently thinking she would like to get married and have a baby or six like her parents.

Decker was silent so long she stopped fiddling with the rope and turned to peer at him. The answer was in his expression, a shocked look of dismay that told her that yes, it would, and that he was only now considering this.

"We don't have to be life mates," she said softly. "I won't blame you if you . . ." She paused when Decker turned on her sharply.

"We are life mates, Dani," he said firmly. "And I want to be. Nothing will change that. We'll just put off having children for a while. Bastien has people working on this kind of thing. He'll come up with something."

"And if he doesn't, or I'm already pregnant?" she asked.

Decker blinked, apparently not having considered that they'd just had sex in the closet downstairs without any kind of protection, not to mention several times in the barn the day before that, but she'd been mortal then and there had been no worry about her being an edantate.

Dani watched Decker close his eyes with dismay and sighed to herself, then glanced to the door when Mortimer shouted for them from downstairs. She turned back to Decker as he blinked his eyes open; he hesitated briefly and then stood and helped her to her feet, saying, "We'll cross that bridge when we get to it."

And definitely be using protection from now on, Dani thought as he tugged her out of the room and down the stairs.

"What is it?" Decker asked as they reached the bottom of the stairs, where Mortimer stood with a man Dani had never seen before.

It was the newcomer who answered. Stepping forward, his gaze locked on her, he said, "Bastien asked me to bring this for a Dani?"

She glanced down, and her eyes widened as she saw what he held out.

"My phone!" Dani took it from him and offered a grateful smile. "Thank you."

He nodded, expression solemn, and then turned to slip back out through the still open front door.

"Call Nicholas," Mortimer said at once, and when she hesitated, pointed out, "You'll find out if he knows where your sister is . . . if he answers."

Dani opened the phone, looked up her call list, and found Nicholas's number. As she engaged the call, she wondered why Nicholas hadn't blocked his number so that it wouldn't show up, but then the phone picked up, and she forgot about it as she waited for him to say hello. Instead what she heard was a recorded message.

Dani closed her eyes, snapped the phone shut with a disappointed sigh, and said, "The number's no longer in service."

Decker hugged her close and murmured, "I'm sorry. I know you were counting on him."

Dani nodded, but didn't say anything. She was aware that Mortimer was slipping away, allowing them time alone. Sighing, she slipped her phone back in her pocket and raised her face to ask Decker what they should do now to find Stephanie when the phone began to vibrate in her pocket.

Chapter Eighteen

"Dani?"

"Nicholas?" she gasped in shock, recognizing his voice from their first call. Her eyes flickered to Decker as he moved in closer, and then to Mortimer as he suddenly paused and turned back. Both men looked grim, and she could feel the tension filling the air.

"I'm sorry I didn't call sooner," Nicholas said. "I know you've probably been worried sick, but I didn't want to call until I had some good news for you."

"My sister?" she asked eagerly, encouraged by his mention of good news. "Do you have her?"

"No." He sounded apologetic. "But I know where she is and that she's alive."

Dani closed her eyes. Alive was good. She'd take alive. Everything else could be repaired either with counseling, or by having Decker or one of the other men wipe Stephanie's memory.

"I imagine you aren't alone?" Nicholas asked.

Dani opened her eyes. Judging by their expressions,

Mortimer and Decker could hear both sides of the conversation. It was that nano-hearing of theirs, she supposed as she admitted, "No. Decker and Mortimer are here."

Both men looked put out, but she ignored them.

"Does your phone have speakerphone capabilities?"

"Yes," Dani said, for the first time grateful that she'd allowed the salesman to talk her into getting it.

"Put me on speaker then," Nicholas requested.

Dani did, then held the phone out in front of her. "Go ahead."

"Decker?"

"Yeah?" he asked grimly.

"The Four Seasons Hotel, room 1413," Nicholas said. "I'll give you five minutes to get on the road and then I'll call back." The phone clicked as he hung up.

Dani was moving before the sound died, hurrying down the hall toward the kitchen and the garage beyond. She was aware that Decker was on her heels and that Mortimer was following him, but her mind was on getting to the garage and a vehicle.

"We can take one of the SUVs," Mortimer suggested.

"A van would be better," Decker said quietly, and then added, "We don't know what shape Stephanie is in."

"He said she was alive," Dani announced, almost smiling with relief.

Her desire to smile died, however, when he pointed out gently, "*Alive* covers a whole lot of ground, Dani."

The image of the women in the ravine immediately rose up in her mind, and Dani bit her lip, her worry pouring back through her. Stephanie's mind could be healed or her memories erased, but she might still bear scars from this experience.

"We don't have a van," Mortimer pointed out, tugging them back to the matter at hand.

"I do."

They all paused and swung back at that announcement as Lucian stepped off the stairs and turned into the hall.

"What's happening?" he asked, moving toward them.

Dani continued on into the kitchen as the men paused to answer. She didn't really care if they took a van or a go-cart as long as they got to her sister. Her gaze landed on Justin as she entered the kitchen. The man was just closing the refrigerator door, a disgusted expression on his face. Turning to see her, he said, "We don't have a single thing to eat in this house. I should—"

He paused abruptly as he noticed her expression and then glanced to the men when they entered behind her. "What's up?"

"Nicholas called. We have to move," Decker announced, catching up to Dani and taking her arm to usher her to the door to the garage.

Justin nodded, all thoughts of food apparently driven from his mind as he fell into step behind them.

Dani thought Lucian would drive since it was his van, but he tossed the keys to Decker and then paused to open the passenger side door, gesturing for her to get in. "You can ride up front with Decker."

She didn't hesitate. By the time she'd fastened her seat belt, Decker and the others had climbed in. She watched Decker push the button on the remote to open the garage door and start the engine, and then turned in her seat to glance curiously into the back of the van. Her eyes moved over several custom-built cupboards and chests lining the side walls in the back. The men had no seats, but it didn't seem to bother them; they were busily flipping up chest lids and pulling open cupboard doors. At least Lucian and Justin were; Mortimer had stopped to pull out his cell phone and was making a phone call. Probably sending the other enforcers and volunteers to the hotel, Dani thought, her eyes sliding to the other two men as they began retrieving weapons. Lucian's van was a rolling arsenal, she saw with amazement . . . and wardrobe, she added as Lucian drew a long leather coat out of a cupboard and began to shrug it on.

"Isn't it kind of hot for that?" Justin asked, loading bullets into a gun. Dani had no idea what the gun was, but it certainly looked impressive.

"Yes," Lucian acknowledged. "But it will be less conspicuous. This coat hides a lot of sins."

Dani understood what he meant when she saw him shift to a chest to pull out a small one-handed crossbow that he then tucked into the inner left side of his coat. A quiver of arrows followed and was installed in the inner right-hand side. While Justin was going for guns, it seemed Lucian, like Nicholas, preferred the old-fashioned weapons.

Her gaze slid to the guns the other two men were tucking into their jeans out of sight. The crossbow wasn't really necessary this time. While Leonius had been resistant to the tranquilizer on the bullets, his sons hadn't been. The guns would do.

"What do you want in the way of weapons, Decker?" Mortimer asked, putting his phone away and glancing in their direction.

"My usual," he growled.

"Use silencers," Lucian ordered, and then the phone rang and an expectant silence filled the van.

Dani glanced down, automatically answering her phone and switching to speakerphone before saying, "Hello? Nicholas?"

"Yes." There was a pause, and then he apologized. "I'm sorry he got away with your sister at the airport, Dani. It's my fault. An enforcer SUV was one car behind me when we got off the ramp. Unfortunately, I thought they could handle it. I parked to watch what unfolded to be sure." His voice was angry as he added, "It was stupid of them to leave the girl behind. As enforcers they should have known better."

"The men who reached the airport first were volunteers, not enforcers," Lucian said, and then asked, "Did you take her?"

"Well, hello to you too, Uncle," he said dryly. "No I didn't take her. What were you thinking, Lucian? That I killed the security guard?"

"Did you?" Decker asked grimly.

"No." The word was short, and then he continued on topic, "Apparently the sixth rogue didn't go into the airport."

Dani immediately said, "Stephanie told the men that he jumped out as she turned into the parking garage."

Nicholas grunted. "That makes sense. They were out of my sight then too. He apparently picked a vehicle with an older woman in it. He must have taken control of her and then watched when your men arrived." Nicholas continued, "As soon as the enforcers left, Stephanie and the security guard walked to a car. I saw the girl get in the passenger side. The guard walked around to the driver's side and then he bent out of sight. A moment later the car backed out . . . There were three people inside, and I thought it was the girl, the guard, and Six, and knew he'd pulled a fast one. I started my engine to follow and saw the guard lying on the ground as I drove by.

"I followed them to the hotel in the city. He was three cars ahead of me when he turned in. He didn't bother to park, just left the car at the entrance. By the time I pulled in he was out and was ushering Stephanie and an older woman inside. When I hurried into the lobby he and the women were already on a packed elevator and the doors were closing." The frustration in his voice was palpable. "The damned thing stopped on eight floors. I couldn't search any of them without risking their being on one floor and slipping away while I searched another, so I've sat in the damned lobby watching that elevator ever since."

"Without blood?" Lucian asked.

"Oh, heck no, Uncle, I've been biting every mortal who's walked past," Nicholas said sarcastically. "That's what we rogues do for fun."

"You should have called me, I would have brought blood over for you," Decker said silkily.

"I just bet you would have, cousin." There was a dry chuckle, and then Nicholas said, "I was about to give up on watching this morning and try searching the floors the elevator had stopped at when the sixth rogue walked right past me and got on the elevator."

"He got past you to get out and then returned?" Lucian asked.

"Yeah. Though I don't know how. I didn't take my eyes off the damned elevator," Nicholas muttered with obvious irritation. "He had to have slipped out using the stairs."

All four men grunted at this suggestion.

"Fortunately there weren't many hotel guests around at that hour and there was only one person on the elevator with him and they went to the same floor; fourteen. I took the same elevator up when it came down. There was a maid setting up for the day in the hall. She'd seen him come up, and I managed to read her mind to get what room they're in."

"1413," Dani said, the number burned on her brain.

"Yes. He's probably down for the day. But I'd still hurry. He wasn't alone when he came back. He had a blond with him," Nicholas announced.

"You haven't approached the room?" Decker asked sharply.

"I haven't eaten in two days chasing this bastard, cousin. I've done the hard work. Now you get to do the cleanup . . . Are you downtown yet? You should be. I imagine you took the Gardiner Expressway. Where are you?"

Dani quickly blurted the intersection ahead, gaining a glare from Lucian. She ignored him.

"Turn right, Decker," Nicholas said quickly.

Decker cursed and cranked the wheel, tires squealing as he took the corner at the very last possible second. Teeth grinding together, he said, "You're not at the Four Seasons, are you? You're at a different hotel."

"Very good, cousin. Nice to see you're as sharp as ever. You should see the correct hotel up ahead. I realize you probably have a small army of men already circling the Four Seasons, but you didn't really think I'd stand here waiting to be captured by one of the enforcer teams, did you?"

There was a grim silence in the van.

Nicholas continued, "I wouldn't wait for the men to make their way from the Four Seasons to here. I suggest you hit the room at once."

"Why?" Decker asked sharply.

"I told you, he had a blond with him, and judging by his pissed expression, she's not in for a good time."

"Then perhaps you should go in there right now," Lucian suggested.

"I'm too weak, I need blood," Nicholas growled. "I've been standing at the end of the hall listening ever since I found the room. There have been no sounds to suggest he's started in on her yet." He paused and then added, "By my guess you're pulling up to the hotel now."

"Yes," Dani said, glancing out the window to see they were pulling in.

"Good. It shouldn't take you long to get up here. I guess I'll head out." There was a brief pause and then he added, "And Decker?"

"Yeah?" he asked as he pulled up to the doors.

"If you don't save this girl after all the trouble I've gone to, I'm going to kick your ass."

"Anytime, cousin," Decker said grimly as he threw the van into park and shut off the engine. He was out of the van with Dani and the rest of the men following before the click sounded, ending the call.

She slid the phone into her pocket and then jogged the few steps to catch up to Decker and took the hand he was holding out behind him. The moment her fingers slid into his, he glanced back and said, "I think you should wait in the lobby."

"She's my sister," Dani said grimly. "Besides, I'm an immortal now too, right?"

Decker's mouth compressed, but he didn't try to argue with her.

"Do you want Mortimer and me to look for Nicholas while you and Decker go after the sixth rogue?" Justin asked the question of Lucian, but it was Decker who answered.

"No. Getting Dani's sister back comes first. We'll just have to go after Nicholas later."

Dani hardly heard Lucian's grunt of concession. Her eyes were on Decker as he pulled her through the lobby, and she thought she must love him after all. How could she not? This immortal had taken a bullet for her before even knowing her name, had driven her to heights of passion she'd never imagined, had watched over and nursed her through the turn, and then comforted her afterward. This was an immortal who had been tortured by guilt since the events resulting in Nicholas's escape, and yet was putting the life of a young girl he'd never met ahead of finding a rogue he'd been hunting for fifty years. He was a good man, an immortal. Her immortal if she wanted him . . . and she did, Dani acknowledged, and then glanced around when Decker slowed and drew her closer to his side.

They'd reached the elevators and were pressing their way through the large crowd of people gathered there waiting to take the lifts up. Dani was quite sure they'd be waiting a while, but when an elevator arrived and the people began to crowd toward it, the ones closest miraculously stopped, blocking the others from entering so that Decker could lead their party through and get on board. As the doors closed on the disgruntled people trying to get past the human blockade, Dani decided she couldn't wait until she could read and control minds. It had certainly come in handy just now, she acknowledged, wondering which, or how many, of the men had caused that little miracle.

"Find a maid and get a pass key," Lucian ordered Justin as they headed out of the elevator and turned into the hall holding room 1413. The younger immortal nodded and turned away to accomplish his task as the rest of them continued forward for several feet, but then Decker paused and turned to her.

"She's my sis—" Dani began in a whisper, but he cut her off in a whisper of his own.

"You can come in as soon as we subdue the rogue."

Dani hesitated, but then nodded reluctantly.

Relaxing, Decker pressed a quick kiss to her forehead and then turned to follow Lucian and Mortimer. The three men reached the door and paused to pull out their weapons as Justin raced past Dani. She saw him hand Lucian something and then reach for the gun he'd slid into the back of his jeans.

Heart in her throat, Dani watched as Lucian unlocked the door and swung it open, and then Decker pushed past him to charge into the room with the other three men following. She heard a woman's screaming first. It was followed by several muffled popping sounds that she thought must be gunshots filtered through the silencer, and couldn't stop herself from rushing up the hall.

"This one's alive," Mortimer said, and Decker glanced up from the older woman he'd been checking.

"So is this one," he admitted, and then straightened to frown at the couple on the bed; an older woman with salt and pepper hair, and a younger man with dark hair. The woman was probably the one taken from the airport garage, but Decker had no idea who the man was. Both of them were pale, unconscious, and had been cut several times.

His gaze slid to the blond Leonius's son had been feeding on when they'd entered, the woman he'd brought up in the elevator that morning. She'd been shrieking hysterically as they entered and struggling to escape the man sucking at the wound on her arm, but she was quiet and blank-faced now as Justin wrapped her cut to try to stop the bleeding.

"Neither of the women is Dani's sister," Lucian growled.

Decker didn't need his comment to realize that. A quick glance at everyone in the room as he'd entered had been enough for him to know the girl wasn't there.

"What do you think he did with her?" Justin asked.

Decker shook his head even as Lucian did and then glanced to the younger immortal to see he'd finished bandaging the blond, and was now scooping her up to carry her over and set her on the bed with the other two mortals.

"Dani's not going to take the news well," Justin said unhappily.

"No," Decker agreed quietly, and didn't know how he was going tell her. Rubbing the back of his neck wearily, he turned to take the few steps to the door out into the hall, thinking the sooner he got it over with the better. She was probably driving herself crazy with worry out there. He was rather amazed that she wasn't already banging on the door to be let in, and could only think she was afraid of what she might find.

As it happened, she had a right to be afraid, Decker thought grimly as he pulled the door open. His gaze slid to where he'd left her, and Decker paused with one foot still inside the room, surprise widening his eyes when he saw she was no longer there.

"What is it?" Justin asked, moving up behind him.

"She's gone," he said with disbelief and then started up the hall, eating up the distance with long, quick strides.

"This is weird, Decker," Justin said, hurrying along beside him. "Dani wouldn't leave."

"I know."

"She was too worried about her sister."

"I know," he repeated grimly.

"Someone must have taken her," Justin added, speaking Decker's fears aloud. "Do you think it's Leonius? He could have been following us again."

He didn't comment, but quickened his stride, trying to think how much time had passed since he'd left Dani in the hall, and how far she could have been taken. They turned the corner, and both came to an abrupt halt as they saw the bank of elevators ahead and that there was no one in front of them. Decker cursed and turned back.

"What are we going to do?" Justin asked quietly.

Decker thought and then said, "The men should be here by now. They're probably stationed at the exits. We'll have to start searching the hotel."

"I'll tell Mortimer to start calling the men and put them on the alert," Justin said.

When he nodded, the younger enforcer burst into a run and raced back up the hall to 1413. Decker continued at a quick clip, but didn't try to keep up. He was trying to coordinate things in his head, trying to think of every possibility and ensure they didn't miss something. Justin disappeared into the room where the other men waited just as Decker was passing the door to the room next to 1413. Moving fast, Decker almost missed the sound of something hitting the floor that was almost completely muffled by the carpet and door. But he did hear it, and instinctively stopped and moved closer to listen.

Dani couldn't move. Leonius held her completely immobile with one hand covering her mouth, the other at her throat, almost choking her, and his body pinning hers to the wall. He'd been holding her there like that ever since he'd reached out into the hall and yanked her into the room as she'd run past.

She had no idea why he wasn't just controlling her with his mind as she knew he could, but supposed it was because he took such great pleasure in the physical act of terrorizing her. However, she was grateful he wasn't, as she shifted her eyes sideways to try to see into the room.

Leonius looked in that direction too, she noticed, his

mouth turning down with displeasure. He then dragged her away from the wall and forced her the few steps out of the hall and into the open bedroom area.

Dani spotted Stephanie at once. The pretty young girl was seated half bent over on the edge of the bed, swaying and trying to get to her feet, but she appeared too weak to manage it. What looked to have been a full glass of water now lay on the floor, and a clear liquid was soaking into the carpet in a wide puddle. Dani supposed its hitting the floor had been the thud she'd heard.

She looked over Stephanie quickly, relieved to see that there didn't appear to be any cuts or bruises on her, at least not on the parts she could see. Dani had feared that when they found her, Stephanie would be covered with them as the bodies in the ravine had been, but she was remarkably free of such injuries, her skin pale and perfect. However, Dani couldn't see her wrists or the insides of her arms the way she was clutching herself, and Stephanie definitely wasn't all right, Dani realized when Stephanie raised a sweating, too pale face to peer blearily at her.

"Dan—?" The name was cut off at once, and Dani knew Leonius had slipped into the girl's head to take control of her and shut her up. In the shape she was in, it apparently wasn't a pleasant experience for him, because his face contorted with pain. She didn't know what he did, but after a moment, Stephanie's head drooped and his expression began to ease. Sighing with what sounded like relief, he glanced to Dani.

"I had just given her my blood and was about to tie her down when I heard the shots from next door," he said in a hushed voice, and then commented, "Those silencers don't work nearly as well in reality as they appear to on television, do they?"

Dani flinched at this news, worry for her sister immediately rising within her. There was no time for that now, however, and she forced it down, concentrating on how she could make more noise and, she hoped, attract the attention of the men in the room next door . . . If they were still there. She'd heard Justin and Decker talking as they walked past the room moments before the thud had made Leonius move her out of the hall. They had been talking about her, and the fact that she was missing and she'd wanted to scream, but hadn't been able to with Leonius holding her as he had.

"I know you want to make noise to draw your friends, but I'm afraid I can't allow that," Leonius said by her ear. "It's all terribly exciting to be hiding just feet away from where Lucian and his men are standing, but also fraught with danger. If you make a sound, I shall have to silence you."

He moved her closer to the bed so that they stood in front of Stephanie, and then shifted Dani, turning her toward the bedside table so that he could look the girl over. The teenager was rocking where she sat, her hands clutching at her stomach, but she wasn't making a sound, and Dani didn't know if it was because he was still controlling her or not.

"Twenty-one hadn't yet turned her when I got here an hour ago," Leonius muttered quietly. "Oddly enough he argued with me about doing it. He seemed to want to keep her as some kind of mortal pet. He hadn't even fed on her." He paused and then added, "I did before I gave her my blood . . . as I did you."

Dani glared at him over his hand, and he smiled widely. "The two of you share a common temperament. She tried to fight me off just like you did." The smile faded as he added with displeasure, "And Twenty-one was moved to try to stop me. He made such a nuisance of himself that I had to send him into the next room and lock the doors to get it done without interference. A fortuitous occurrence for me as it turns out, but not so fortuitous for Twenty-one."

He turned to glance at Stephanie again, and then said, "Of course, I have bigger plans for Stephanie than keeping her as a mortal pet; for both of you actually." He smiled cruelly and added, "Someone has to bear me more sons to replace the ones I've lost this week."

That was too much for Dani. Rage roared up through her like a tidal wave at the prospect of either her or Stephanie being broodmares for this animal. Leonius had moved her close enough to the table that she could reach the bedside lamp, and before Dani quite knew what she was doing, she'd grabbed it and was swinging it up over her head and back. There was a sickening crunch as it slammed into Leonius's head, and then he released her to stumble back.

Suddenly free, Dani staggered a step forward, banging into the bedside table, and then caught herself and turned to grab Stephanie by the arm and yank her to her feet. The confusion on the girl's face and the way she was shaking her head suggested to Dani that the blow to Leonius's head had sufficiently set him aback enough that he'd lost control of Stephanie. She knew that wouldn't last long, though, and pushed Stephanie ahead of her toward the small hall leading to the door, desperate to get her out of the room.

They had to pass Leonius to get there. He was upright, but looking dazed and clutching his head, and Stephanie stumbled past him all right, but as Dani followed, one of his hands shot out to seize her by the arm.

"Run," Dani screamed at her sister, struggling to break the hold Leonius had on her. Much to her relief, Stephanie staggered the few steps up the hall and managed to grasp the doorknob. She turned it and started to pull it open, only to stumble back as it was suddenly thrust open from the other side.

Dani could have sobbed with relief when she saw Decker appear. He took in the situation at a glance, and started to raise the gun in his hand, but then suddenly grabbed Stephanie and turned his back to the room, sheltering her as an explosion went off beside Dani's ear. She didn't recognize it as a gunshot until she saw the blood blossoming on the back of Decker's shirt.

A scream of horror was ripped from her throat as Dani noted the position of the wound. She knew at once that if it hadn't lodged in his spine, that it had probably hit his heart, and watched in horror as he crumpled forward, taking Stephanie with him to the floor in the doorway. Once on the ground, neither of them moved.

"Time to go," Leonius said, or she thought that's what he said. There was a ringing in her ears from the loud gunshot that made hearing difficult. He then began to force her forward and Dani lurched toward the hall, aware that someone was pounding on the connecting door.

"We shall have to leave Stephanie for now, but I'll fetch her later," Leonius assured her as he forced her around Decker's legs and up the hall.

Dani stared down at Decker as they moved past him. He lay on his stomach, his head next to Stephanie's feet, and was so motionless that, were he mortal, she'd fear he was dead. Then they were past him and moving into the hall.

Leonius had just turned her to force her up the hall toward the elevators when a series of pops sounded. When he suddenly released her and fell into the opposite wall, Dani whirled to find Lucian standing in the hall outside room 1413, arm raised, weapon in hand. In the next moment, she realized the weapon Lucian held was the crossbow, with an arrow notched, but not released. She whirled to peer at Decker as he lowered his gun and laid his head on the floor.

Chapter Nineteen

Decker!" Dani rushed back into the room, her gaze sliding over her sister on her way past. Stephanie's eyes were open and she was panting heavily. Having been through the turn herself, and knowing she couldn't do a damned thing for her, Dani continued on to Decker and knelt beside him as he groaned and began to move.

She helped him roll over, gasping with horror when she saw that the hole in the front of his chest was much larger than that in the back. Leonius had hit him with a much more powerful weapon than his sons had shot Decker with that first night in the clearing. Worry clouding her eyes, she pressed on the wound trying to stanch the flow of blood.

"I'm all right," he muttered. "Look after Stephanie."

Dani shook her head, pressing both hands down on him now, but he winced and then caught her hands and moved them away. Forcing himself upright to lean against the wall, he said, "The nanos will fix me up.

Look, the bleeding is slowing. The bullet missed my heart by a mile."

"More like a millimeter," she said with a frown as she noticed the bleeding was indeed slowing.

"I'm fine," he insisted. "Go see to Stephanie."

She hesitated, her gaze sliding to her sister, but when the teenager moaned and started to shift, Dani straightened and moved to kneel next to Stephanie as she rolled onto her side in the doorway.

"Stephi?" she said, pressing her hand to the girl's cheek. "Are you all right?"

Stephanie blinked her eyes open. Dani saw the confusion and pain there and felt her heart ache for the girl. She knew exactly how she was suffering right now.

Movement in the corner of her eye brought her distracted gaze to the hall. Lucian had moved to stand over Leonius's slumped figure. He peered at the rogue for a moment, crossbow hanging at his side, and then swung it forward and shot the notched arrow into Leo's chest.

Definitely a heart shot, Dani thought with satisfaction as Lucian then bent to grab him by the collar to drag him toward the open door to the room. She started to turn back to her sister, intending to try to move Stephanie and Decker out of the way, but cried out as the girl suddenly lunged upward, catching Dani's hand and stuffing the fingers into her mouth. Stephanie sucked at them desperately as she knocked her backward.

It happened so fast and took her so by surprise Dani didn't even struggle at first. By the time she did, Stephanie was on top of her, her earlier weakness replaced by an incredible strength as she licked and gnawed at Dani's hand. Seeing the flecks of blood on the bit of hand sticking out of the girl's mouth, Dani realized what a stupid thing she'd done. She'd tried to stanch the flow of blood from Decker's wound and then had gone to her sister and as good as waved the bloody hand under her nose.

Dani heard a curse and glanced around to see that Decker was trying to get to her, and then a thump drew her attention to the hall as Lucian dropped Leonius and came to her aid. He lifted Stephanie as if she were weightless and then turned her in the air to peer at her.

"She's turning," he said grimly, and stepped over her to carry Stephanie into the room.

Dani scrambled to her feet to follow, telling Decker, "I'll be right back. Stay put."

"Unlock and open the door," Lucian ordered, heading for the connecting doors as the earlier knocking resumed in a much calmer fashion.

"Why doesn't he just use the hall and come around?" Dani muttered with exasperation.

"Because I ordered him and Justin to stay in the room," Lucian answered dryly as she moved to do as he asked. "Justin has to keep an eye on Leonius's son to be sure he doesn't come around and slip away, and Mortimer has to keep an eye on the mortals."

"Oh." Dani sighed as she unlocked the door and opened it.

"Everything all—?" Mortimer broke off as Lucian suddenly thrust Stephanie at him. Dani watched long enough to see he had ahold of her and then turned away as Lucian announced, "Decker's been shot and this one's turning. She needs to be taken to the house."

"And Leonius?" Mortimer asked.

Dani didn't catch Lucian's answer. She'd crossed to the entry hall, and on spotting Decker now on his feet, moving slowly up the hall, scowled and rushed to his side.

"I told you to stay put," she muttered, and started to shift under his arm, but paused as she glanced out into the hotel hallway. A woman with long blond hair was picking up Leonius as if he were a small child rather than a full-grown man. When she straightened with him in her arms, Dani opened her mouth to shout a warning to the men, but the woman's head shot around. Fangs and silver-blue eyes flashed, and Dani found herself closing her mouth and simply standing there unable to say a thing as the woman glared at her, concentration on her face.

"Dani?" Decker frowned down at what was probably her blank face, and then it was as if a switch had been thrown in her head. She felt herself falling, and the last thing she saw before darkness claimed her was the woman moving away toward the stairwell at the end of the hall.

"Dani!" Decker managed to catch her with one hand as she started to faint. He then pulled her against his chest as he slumped against the wall. The wound he'd taken to the chest was much worse than those he'd gotten from the peashooter Leonius's son's had been using in the clearing. This one was going to take a lot of blood to heal. Until he got it, Decker was going to be weak and suffering.

"What's wrong with her?" Lucian asked, crossing the room toward them.

"I don't know," he admitted. "She just stopped, looked out in the hall, and . . ." Decker paused as he glanced over his shoulder and saw that the hallway was empty. Leonius's body was missing.

Decker heard Lucian curse and then his uncle moved past him, rushing out of the room, heading in the direction of the elevators.

"What is it?" Mortimer asked from the connecting door when Decker cursed.

"Dani has fainted and Leonius is gone," he said grimly, and leaned heavily on the wall as he moved the last couple of steps to the end of the entry hall so that he could see the other man.

"How the hell could Leonius be gone?" Mortimer asked with dismay, seeming oblivious to the moaning and restless girl in his arms. "Lucian just finished telling me that he shot an arrow into his heart. That's as good as a stake through the heart. He shouldn't be up and about."

Decker just shook his head and glanced to the door as Lucian hurried past, headed for the door to the stairwell. When he glanced back to Mortimer the other man was holding Stephanie with one arm around her waist as he pulled out his phone to call and warn the men to keep an eye out for Leonius.

Decker was considering setting Dani down and going over to take Stephanie from Mortimer so that the other man could help Lucian search, but a sound behind him made him peer around to see Lucian reentering the room.

"Anything?" Decker asked, already reading the answer in the disgust on his face.

"No," Lucian said as he joined him and then glanced to Mortimer. "Call the—" The order died on his lips as he saw that Mortimer was already on the phone.

"How the hell did he get away?" Decker asked with frustration.

Lucian shook his head, his gaze sliding to Dani. "She might be able to tell us . . . or not," he added dryly after concentrating on her for a moment. "She has a blank spot in her memory."

Decker frowned and glanced down to Dani, wondering what she'd seen that someone would want to erase, then her eyes flickered.

"Dani?" he said softly.

Her eyes opened, awareness slowly sliding into them, and then she frowned as she realized she was slumped against him, her head on his chest beside his wound.

"I'm sorry," she mumbled, straightening to take her own weight. "Are you all right?"

"Yes, of course," he assured her, running his hand soothingly down her arm.

"What happened?" she asked with confusion. "The last thing I remember is coming over to give you hell for getting up and moving around on your own."

"You looked past me, appeared alarmed, and then fainted."

She looked past him now, her eyes landing on the empty hall. "Leonius is gone."

"Yes. Did you see him go?"

Dani glanced to him with surprise, but shook her head. "No . . . At least, I don't think so."

Decker squeezed her arm as she frowned, searching her mind for a memory that just wasn't there. He said softly, "It's all right. It doesn't matter."

Dani lifted her eyes back to him and opened her mouth to speak, but then paused and glanced toward her sister when Stephanie moaned. Decker followed her gaze to see that Mortimer was off the phone, but the girl was more than restless, she was starting to thrash and the enforcer was having trouble holding her even with both hands. Decker forced himself away from the wall, relieved to find that while his legs felt a bit weak, they were no longer trembling under his weight. Placing his arm around Dani, he glanced to his uncle and said, "We need to get Stephanie back to the house and get her tied down."

Lucian nodded and glanced toward Mortimer. He raised his eyebrows. "You're in charge."

Decker smiled faintly when Mortimer rolled his eyes at that. The only one in charge when Lucian was around was Lucian. He took control in most situations, or allowed others to take control until they made a decision he didn't agree with, then he took that control back.

"Justin," Mortimer said suddenly.

"Yeah?" the younger immortal asked from the bowels of the next room.

"You're driving these four back to the house."

Justin moved to the doorway and glanced to Lucian, Stephanie, Decker, and Dani, and then back into the room, before glancing to Mortimer to ask, "What about Leonius's son?"

"I'll take care of him and the mortals," Mortimer answered, passing the girl over to Justin.

"What if someone calls hotel security or the police about the noise up here?" Decker asked as the thought suddenly occurred to him.

"I've already taken care of them," Mortimer said calmly. "I called the boys downstairs while I was waiting for the connecting door to be opened. They were going to take care of hotel security and handle the police if they showed up."

Decker nodded, thinking that Lucian had obviously made the right decision putting Mortimer in charge. He was going to make a good chief for them.

"Here." Lucian took off his long coat and crossed to hand it to Decker. "It's hot, but will hide the mess on your chest."

Decker glanced down at his bloody shirt and the hole revealing the ugly wound beneath and released Dani to accept the coat. She immediately moved to help him don it, but it still caused him a good deal of pain.

"Are you all right?" she asked worriedly, eyeing his sweating face as she did up the top four buttons for him.

Despite the pain he was suffering, Decker smiled faintly and nodded. Bullet wound or not, he was all right now that she was safely at his side . . . and he was going to make damned sure she stayed there.

"Let's go." Lucian headed for the door, saying, "We'll take the stairs to avoid attracting too much attention."

"The stairs?" Justin complained, scooping up Stephanie to follow. "That's fourteen floors."

"Thirteen," Dani corrected as Decker urged her to follow. "This is really the thirteenth floor. They just call it fourteen because too many superstitious people refuse to stay on the thirteenth floor."

Justin grunted as he maneuvered his way out the door, turning sideways to carry Stephanie through. "I can see why. That means Leonius's son was really in room 1313, and that wasn't really lucky for him."

Decker saw Dani smile faintly. But the smile faded as they stepped out into the hall and she asked, "What will Mortimer do with Twenty-one and his victims?"

Decker urged her up the hallway after the others. "He'll have Twenty-one removed to be taken for judgment, and then probably make an anonymous call reporting screams heard from 1413 so that the mortal authorities can find and help his victims."

Dani was silent as they reached the door to the stairwell and passed through it. Justin and Lucian were already out of sight, but they could hear their footsteps echoing from the next flight down.

"Stephanie can never go home now, can she?" Dani said as they started down the stairs. Her words were laced with sadness.

Decker considered whether he should remind her that Stephanie had only a one in three chance of surviving the turn with her mind intact, but then decided not to add to her worries. She would remember that soon enough herself. "No, she can't. There would be no way to hide what she was from your parents. She's a teenager and a new turn and will be constantly feeding for a while . . . and then there's the need for her to stay out of the sun, the fact that if she's injured, she'll heal more quickly than she would were she mortal . . ." He shook his head. "No, she can't go home."

"I hadn't thought of that," Dani admitted unhappily. "I was just thinking of Leonius."

"Leonius?" Decker asked.

"He said he wanted Stephanie and me to bear him sons to replace the ones who died this week," she told him. "And when he was forcing me into the hall he said we'd have to leave her for now, but he'd come back for Stephanie." Her mouth tightened. "My parents could never protect her from him."

"We will."

Decker paused and glanced down to see Lucian and Justin waiting on the next landing. Justin was holding a struggling Stephanie in front of him now, frowning as he tried to control her, but Decker's attention was on his uncle; Lucian had obviously heard Dani's words. His face was grim as he added, "We'll arrange security at the enforcer house. She can stay there. Sam can help look after her, and Mortimer and the boys can train her on how to survive as one of us. The two of you are welcome to stay there as well." He glanced to Justin as he grunted and cursed as Stephanie kicked him in the groin in an effort to get away, and then turned back, his mouth twitching with amusement. "Now you two kiss and tell each other you love each other so we can get moving before your sister hurts Justin."

"*Before* she does? If it weren't for nanos I'd be a eunuch by now," Justin muttered, scooping up Stephanie to follow the ancient immortal as he started down the next flight of stairs.

Decker smiled faintly, but then glanced to Dani when she touched his cheek.

"There's a lot to sort out yet," she said solemnly. "And I'm not sure what the future holds, but he's right. I do love you Decker."

Smiling, he caught her hand and pressed a kiss to it. "I know."

"You *know*?" she asked dryly. "I tell you I love you and you say *I know*?"

"Well, I've already told you I love you," he pointed out. "And of course I knew you would come to love me. The nanos are never wrong."

"The nanos are never wrong," Dani echoed with disbelief, then whirled on her heel and started down the stairs, muttering, "Of course he knew I'd love him. The nanos are never wrong. Why even bother telling him?"

Decker smiled as he started to follow. He loved it when she got all huffy. She was so cute when she got like that, he hadn't been able to resist teasing her.

"So much for romance," Dani continued as she reached the next landing. "Here I am giving up my practice to become some vamp ho and I get *nanos are never wrong*. I should just— Ack!" she cried out, grabbing for his shoulders as he suddenly scooped her up.

"What are you doing?" she asked with dismay.

"Giving you romance," he said solemnly, stepping closer to the wall to lean against it.

"You're wounded, Decker," she cried with exasperation. "Put me down before you hurt yourself. Dear God, you—"

Decker kissed her into silence, not stopping until she stopped struggling in his arms. Then he lifted his head and said, "I love you, Dani McGill, soon to be Maybe-Argeneau-Maybe-Pimms."

The anger melted out of Dani, her eyes softened, and she sighed. "I love you too, Decker."

"You are not a vamp ho, and while you might have to give up your practice, you can still practice your profession. There are many situations where your medical degree would come in handy and our boys can always use your skills."

"I somehow don't think so," she said with amusement.

"You're wrong," he assured her.

"Decker, I'm a gynecologist."

"Did you say gynecologist?" Justin asked, drawing their attention to the fact that he, Stephanie, and Lucian were waiting on the lower landing again. A big grin was stretching his face as he said, "What an awesome job! You get to spend the entire day looking at—"

"Justin!" Dani, Decker, and Lucian snapped at once.

"We'll wait for you in the van," Lucian growled, pushing Justin toward the next flight of stairs.

Decker watched them go and then turned to find Dani peering up at him. He cleared his throat and said, "Immortals have babies too."

She nodded, but said, "Stephanie's going to be upset about not being able to go home."

"We'll have to help her through it," he said quietly, and saw her eyes mist before she leaned her head against his shoulder.

"What about our parents?"

He sighed and set her down, trying not to look too relieved as he did. She wasn't heavy, but he wasn't as strong as normal, and holding her had hurt his chest though he'd never have admitted it.

Once on her own feet, she continued, "Will they think we're just missing, or—?"

"That's up to you," he said solemnly. "They can be left to wonder what happened to the two of you, or we can arrange for them to believe your bodies have been found with those in the ravine up north along with the others."

She glanced at him sharply. "The authorities haven't been sent to find the women yet?"

"No. Lucian thought it would be better if we waited to see what happened with you and Stephanie first."

"In case we had to be added to the bodies?" she realized grimly.

He didn't answer, but suspected that's what his uncle had been thinking.

"Our parents will be upset," she added.

"We can arrange to help them through it, make it less painful for them," he said, and then added carefully, "Or we might be able to arrange it so that they think everything's all right. They could continue to believe that you and Stephanie were just enjoying a couple of days in the city."

"But she can't live with them," Dani said with a frown.

"No, but we could put it into their minds that Stephanie's at a boarding school and that you've just taken a job elsewhere. That way the two of you could occasionally visit with your family."

"For another ten years only, though, right?" she asked quietly.

Decker nodded. "I'm sorry, Dani. I wish I could make this easier for you."

"You do, just by being here. I can't imagine facing all this alone." She slipped her hand into his, squeezing it. "I guess that's what love is, sharing the good and the bad, the happy and the sad."

"Yes," he murmured. As they started down the stairs again, he was wishing he could take all the bad and sad away for her.

"And family."

"Family?" he asked uncertainly.

"Well, I'll still have family with you."

Decker was worrying that she meant babies and was imagining her heartache should they have a stillborn or a child who was born mad like Leonius when she added, "Your mother and father and brothers and sisters and that aunt you are so fond of."

"Marguerite," he murmured with relief.

"Yes. Your aunt Marguerite. We'll have them, and each other. We'll be okay." She raised a smile to his face and said, "We will."

"Yes." He bent to kiss her gently and then assured her, "We will."

As they broke apart to continue down the stairs, Decker started making plans; ways to keep Dani and Stephanie safe, ways she could still see her family for now, even visits to his aunt and cousins . . . Anything he could think of to help her through this. He knew it wasn't always going to be easy, but he was going to work very, very hard to do his best to make Dani happy. She hadn't chosen to be turned, but she was his life mate, and the woman who had brought peace and passion to his life. He was going to make sure they were more than okay. He was going to make her—

"I'm going to be happy," she said suddenly. "And make sure you're happy too."

Decker smiled as he realized her own thoughts must have been traveling along the same lines as his. Squeezing her hand, he assured her, "I already am."

Who rescued Leonius?
Will Stephanie ever be able to go home again?
What is Nicholas Argeneau up to?
For answers to these questions and more
Don't miss
THE RENEGADE HUNTER
By Lynsay Sands
Coming to you October 2009
From Avon Books

At Avon Books, we know your passion for romance—once you finish one of our novels, you find yourself wanting more.

May we tempt you with . . .

- **Excerpts** from our upcoming releases.

- Entertaining **extras**, including authors' personal photo albums and book lists.

- Behind-the-scenes **scoop** on your favorite characters and series.

- **Sweepstakes** for the chance to win free books, romantic getaways, and other fun prizes.

- Writing **tips** from our authors and editors.

- **Blog** with our authors and find out why they love to write romance.

- **Exclusive content** that's not contained within the pages of our novels.

Join us at
www.avonbooks.com